Haunted Ground

By
Irina Shapiro

Contents

Prologue

England, 1650

Blood-red rays of the setting sun just barely touched the tips of the trees, illuminating the blazing colors of fall with a rosy tint that gave the forest an almost magical quality which would last for only a few moments, before the sun sank behind the tree line, and the gathering darkness claimed its nightly victory over daylight. The faint outline of the Hunter's Moon was already visible, but still transparent in the darkening sky. The lengthening shadows began to stretch across the ground as an unnatural hush fell over the meadow.

A man melted out of the darkening forest and gazed toward the stone house still bathed in the rosy glow of the sunset. The peaked roof barely reached the lowest limb of the stout oak that grew in the yard; its limbs black against the setting sun. The man broke into a run, breathing hard as he finally reached the house, his eyes never leaving the tree as he sank to his knees, oblivious to the spongy ground caused by last night's rain. He stared up, his face contorted by an expression of unbearable pain, and wrapped his arms around his torso, bending over until his head almost touched the ground. He stayed in that position for some moments, his shoulders heaving as he wept. As the sun finally sank and darkness descended on the meadow, he forced himself to look up and confront his worst nightmare. His eyes never left the tree as he reached into his boot and pulled out a dagger.

The full moon rose above the trees and began its ascent into the autumn sky, but the man was oblivious to the beauty of the evening. He was oblivious to everything except what he had to do.

The Present

Chapter 1

Be careful what you wish for, at least that's what my mother always said, for life has a way of granting wishes in the strangest way possible, sometimes taking what you love most as payment for a dream fulfilled. I never really knew what she meant, and she always clammed up as soon as I asked, a veil of sadness descending over her eyes as she smiled brightly and changed the subject. I learned not to ask, but the lesson stayed with me, making me wary of wishing for things too fervently.

There was one dream, however, that I just couldn't ignore. It had been with me since I was a little girl, always there at the back of my mind, beckoning to me, and calling me in that way that dreams do, like a pot of gold at the end of the rainbow. I have no idea where it came from or why it was so special to me, but it was always there. I'd learned not to talk about it to my parents since they got upset, telling me that I was too fanciful for my own good, and that I needed to concentrate on making a life for myself here and now, but the pull was always there. England. It was always England. I'd never even been there, and when I asked my father for a trip for graduation he balked, telling me it was no place for a young girl to be traipsing around on her own. He never liked the place, he said, having been there on business. Cold, dreary, full of people he couldn't understand, but I still wanted to go, wanted to make my home there despite his objections. To me, it was a place like no other; a place steeped in centuries of political turmoil and bloodshed, a place of romance and history.

As Mom predicted, the dream became possible in a most unexpected and terrible way, on an ordinary day that started out with burnt toast and nearly being late to work due to a sick passenger on the subway. I'd only been behind my desk at the Marriott Marquis Hotel in Times Square for over an hour when the call came. I hadn't even bothered to pick it up since I was in the midst of checking in a group of Italian tourists, who were so exuberant and loud that I hardly even heard the phone ring above the cacophony of their voices. It was only when the manager came rushing out of her office and brought another concierge with her to take over my duties that I realized that something was dreadfully wrong. My father had suffered a heart attack in his office and was currently en route to Lenox Hill Hospital uptown. My mother was already on her way, so I grabbed my purse and dashed outside to grab a cab and pray that the morning traffic wouldn't turn a ten-minute ride into an hour.

I was nearly hyperventilating with anxiety by the time the cabbie finally dropped me off in front of the hospital nearly forty-five minutes later, and I exploded through the Emergency Room entrance, running straight for the admissions desk. The woman behind the desk gave me a sympathetic look as she told me where to go. I found my mom sitting alone in a curtained-off partition, her eyes dazed as she looked up at me. She was holding a Ziploc bag with my father's belongings: his watch, wedding ring, and wallet clearly visible through the plastic.

"Mom, is he in surgery?" I asked as I kissed her soft cheek. "What are the doctors saying?"

My mother reached out and took my hand, her voice barely audible over the sounds of the Emergency Room. "He's gone, Lexi. He died on the way to surgery fifteen minutes ago. They tried to save him, they really did, but there was nothing they could do."

My mother wasn't crying, but the expression on her face was of someone who could at any moment go to pieces in such a spectacular fashion that it would be like watching a train wreck. My parents had been high school sweethearts and married at the age of nineteen. They'd been married for nearly forty years, and now my mom would have to learn to live without her Jack. It'd be like relearning to walk — or breathe. I just held her in my arms,

9

feeling her stiff back and shuddering breath. She wouldn't allow herself to come undone now. She'd do it in private when no one was watching.

My mom held it together until the funeral, but I made all the arrangements and took care of my father's business affairs until the reading of the Will. My father's wishes came as no surprise to either of us. My mom was well provided for, but I was the one he bequeathed his paper goods company and all its assets to; suddenly making me a wealthy woman in my own right. My father had always made it clear that he wanted me to follow in his footsteps, scoffing at my decision to earn a degree in Hospitality and Tourism Management. He said it was just a passing phase, and I would get tired of dealing with overexcited tourists and complaining hotel guests, and eventually see the joy and sense of accomplishment in running my own company; a company that was successful and profitable and just waiting for me to step up to the helm.

It was with a heavy heart that I sold Maxwell Paper Products as soon as I got an attractive offer from one of my father's competitors and golf partners. I knew he'd be heartbroken if he knew, but I couldn't face a life of selling packing boxes and file folders to bored buyers, haggling over every penny and wishing I were anywhere but there. I was now independently wealthy, and the money offered a glimpse of freedom I'd hitherto never imagined. I was free to follow my dream.

Chapter 2

The house loomed in front of me, tall and gray; the stone walls bleached by decades of sunshine and rain and buffeted by wind, the south side dressed in a thick coat of ivy that crept almost as far as the gabled roof. The half-lowered blinds in the upstairs windows gave the impression of hooded eyes, wearily watching me as I stood there on the lawn, my whole being flooded with joy and a sudden sense of déjà vu. This was it; this was the house I'd been looking for. I didn't know where I would find it, but I knew exactly what it would be like, and how I would feel when I finally saw it. It had taken me nearly four months of searching; visiting town after town, and rejecting house after house until I stumbled onto this village in Lincolnshire. It wasn't even on the map, but I needed to stop for gas and get something to eat before I continued back to my hotel in Lincoln.

I'd always been geographically challenged, even with a GPS, so I promptly took a wrong turn off the motorway and wound up not in the village, as expected, but somewhere on the outskirts; driving down a country lane flanked by ancient trees that formed a green tunnel around my rented car, with the GPS announcing over and over that it was recalculating.

I saw the house in the distance, hidden behind a scrim of trees that did little to obscure its charm. It was nestled in a verdant valley dissected by a gurgling stream; its elegant shape offset by the palest blue sky dotted with wispy clouds tinged with rosy pink and golden peach; the type of sky only England could boast after a drenching rain. I turned off the lane, and drove through a pair of stately stone pillars topped by giant urns from which wildflowers spilled in profusion. A faded sign hung on one of the pillars, announcing that the house was available to buy or let. I whipped out my cell phone and dialed the number on the sign, hoping that it was still available and there was someone in the office this late in the afternoon willing to show me around. I was more than ready to whip out my checkbook and pay for it right then and there, but I had to go through the motions before throwing caution to the wind.

The woman who picked up the phone sounded incredulous for a moment, asking me to repeat where I was and which house I was referring to, but then I heard a sharp intake of breath and the scraping of a chair.

"Don't move from that spot, you hear? I'll be there in five minutes at most." I could hear the slamming of a door as she must have dashed to her car, the cell phone still pressed to her ear. Evidently, I wasn't the only eager beaver in town.

I leaned against my car and just gazed up at the house. Some empty houses had a tendency to look forbidding, but this one just seemed kind of sad and neglected. It would need much work, but the potential was definitely there in its elegant architecture and solid stonework. As long as the house was structurally sound it would suit my purposes, and judging by the number of windows, there were plenty of bedrooms on the second and third floors to accommodate a fair amount of guests. My mind was already buzzing with possibilities, doing calculations, and mentally decorating rooms which would be a replica of what bedrooms might have looked like when the house was occupied by its original owners.

The screeching of tires announced the imminent arrival of the estate agent, who took a quick look in the mirror before getting out of the car, her hand outstretched, and her eyes taking my measure. She was around thirty, with a blonde pixie cut and slanted green eyes that gave her a somewhat catlike appearance. Her wide mouth was stretched into an impish smile, and her gray pantsuit was offset by a scarf in a mixture of vibrant colors that instantly drew the eye. She was young, stylish, and modern, which was a contrast to most of the agents I'd dealt with over the past few months who appeared tired and bored. This woman was vibrating with an excitement that matched my own.

"Paula Dees," she announced as we shook hands. "Well, I must say you took me by surprise. Can't remember the last time someone asked to see this place. For a moment there, I couldn't remember where I'd stashed the keys. Total panic attack," she confided in me as she fished the keys out of her designer bag. "Shall we?"

Paula hung back and let me look at each room. She wasn't pushy, but filled me in on the background of the house and gave me some more practical information regarding the heating, plumbing, foundation, and all the other technical stuff I might need to know before making any kind of decision. I had to admit that I wasn't even really looking at the rooms. I was interested in layout and proportions, picturing the bedrooms as guestrooms and downstairs rooms as dining room, sitting rooms, and breakfast nook. I would take a closer look later, when I was alone and could really take it all in.

"So, what's the asking price?" I asked casually, hoping it wasn't more than I was able to afford. My jaw nearly dropped as Paula named a figure. It was a little more than half of what I expected, an absolute steal. I had been willing to pay more than the asking price, if that's what was required, but I had to keep the excitement out of my voice and the look of ecstasy out of my eyes as I cautiously told Paula that I would like to make an offer on the house.

"Don't you want to see the rest of the property, love?" the estate agent asked, watching me with a carefully bland expression, afraid to believe that she was about to unload this monstrosity after more than two years.

"Of course," I replied, having already made up my mind anyway. Paula led the way, and we walked behind the house where Paula pointed out several outbuildings which at one time had been the stables, storage sheds, and dairy. Some of the old outbuildings had been torn down over the years, but the remaining ones appeared in good order. It was a sizeable estate, consisting not only of the manor house, but several acres of arable land. I glanced to the opposite shore of the creek, studying the tumbling ruin on the other side.

"What about that?" I asked, pointing to the site.

"Oh, that's part of the property, I'm afraid. I don't know why the old owners never did anything with it, but that's been there for hundreds of years, since the seventeenth century. Mrs. Hughes was rather attached to it, said it wasn't to be touched. It's even mentioned in her Will, but I think you can do as you wish once you've settled in, assuming you buy the place that is. The clause in the Will doesn't apply to you, only to her family." Paula Dees looked at me, hoping I would confirm that I was indeed making an offer.

"Why didn't she want it touched? Does it have historical significance?" I asked.

"Oh, I don't know. She was a strange old bird, especially after…" Paula's voice trailed off, her eyes sliding away from mine as she made a production of looking at her watch and then searching for something in her purse.

"After what?" I asked, my curiosity piqued.

"It's nothing really. She suffered a personal tragedy some years ago, but it had nothing to do with the ruin. Are you sure you don't want to see the inside of the outbuildings?" she asked, eager to change the subject.

"No, I've seen all I need to see. I'd like to make an offer," I repeated, hoping that Paula couldn't hear the thudding of my heart. I prayed that they would accept, but if they didn't, I'd offer more and more until the house was mine. I'd finally found it, and I wasn't walking away. Not ever.

"Why don't we go back to my office and contact the seller? You can follow me in your car." Paula was practically skipping to her car, eager to get the process started. "What do you plan to do with the place? Will you live here alone?" she asked, eager for a chat now that her end of the business was almost complete.

"I want to turn it into a hotel. The house dates back to the late seventeenth century, so I intend to recreate what it might have looked like in its heyday, which I guess would have been the eighteenth century. It would be like stepping back in time." I was full of ideas, and desperate to share them with someone since my mother didn't want to hear anything about it. She was still hurt that I'd chosen to sell the company and leave, but I knew she would get over it in time and come see my little place. My friends had been supportive, but I knew they were baffled by my desire to move across the pond and leave everything and everyone behind.

Paula shook her head in wonder, looking back at the house with new eyes. "Yes, I suppose it will make a nice hotel, but it will take such an awful lot of work. I don't mean to put you off, but everything inside is an antique, and not the valuable kind. I don't think the appliances have been changed in at least four decades, and the plumbing would have to be modernized to accommodate additional baths. Of course, the lack of modernity is reflected in the price," she added hastily, realizing that she might be talking me out of buying the place. "It is a lovely old house though, isn't it?"

I threw one last longing look at the house as Paula walked me to my car.

"Would you like to join me for a drink at the pub tonight? I might even have an answer for you by then. Doctor Hughes lives in Bath. He's a cardiologist of some renown, but he won't keep me waiting. We go back a long way, Roger and I, and he's eager to get rid of the place. He's been trying to sell it ever since Mrs. Hughes died."

"Why is he so eager to sell?" I asked, praying that he wouldn't change his mind at the last minute and decide that he hated to part with this part of his family history.

"His life is in Bath, and frankly, I don't think he feels any attachment to the house. He never actually lived here. Mrs. Hughes was his aunt, and she lived there with her daughters. Roger lived on the other side of the village with his family."

"Why didn't she leave the house to the daughters?" I asked, eager to know as much as possible about the history of the place. Strange that such a charming house and vast property would be left vacant.

"Mrs. Hughes's youngest died a long time ago, and there was some bad blood between her and Myra. I think she left the house to Doctor Hughes just to spite her. Not that Myra has been here for more than a day or two in two decades. She lives in London now. Has her own staffing agency." I noticed that Paula seemed very tense as she divulged this information, but whatever was bothering her had nothing to do with me. I'd found my perfect house, and I meant to have it. Decades-old family feuds would not change my plans, especially if this Myra had no interest in her family home.

I followed Paula through the gates, eager to get to her office and start the ball rolling. The car was stuffy, so I rolled down the window taking in the beautiful scenery that raced past the car. It was early June and everything around me was in bloom, bursting with life, fragrant and lush. The sky seemed bigger here somehow, vast and endless, the sun hurting my eyes until I fished my sunglasses out of my bag and put them on. I don't know if my imagination was working overtime, but this place seemed almost magical to me, unlike anywhere I'd ever been before. It was modern and ancient at the same time; the old ways still alive and well despite the relentless march of time and progress. I hoped I would fit in, knowing how difficult it was for outsiders to assimilate in a place where people's families had lived for hundreds of years, their blood and sweat permeating the soil, and their histories intertwined with each other in ways Americans could never understand.

September 1650

England

Chapter 3

Brendan Carr pulled his hat lower over his face in a futile attempt to keep the moisture out of his eyes. The sheets of rain that came down almost horizontally soaked him to the bone hours ago and rivulets of rainwater ran down every surface, including the flanks of his horse and straight into his well-worn boots. Brendan wiped his eyes with the back of his hand, trying to get his bearings, but the fog was so thick he could barely make out the outline of the hills in the distance, especially since they looked as if they'd been wrapped in gray wool by the thick clouds that hung so low you could almost reach out and touch them.

Brendan looked around in desperation, his eyes searching for anything that could pass for shelter. He was way past feeling wet and cold, but the gnawing hunger in his belly reminded him that it was time to stop. He didn't have much food, but he desperately needed rest, or he would just fall asleep astride and slide off his sodden horse, most likely without even noticing. Falling off his horse was the least of his problems, he thought grimly as he listened to the windswept landscape around him. There was no sign of pursuit, but that could change at any moment, leaving him helpless and clearly visible; well, maybe not clearly, but still visible, in this barren valley. He'd been traveling for nearly a week now, but it had been slow going with him lying low whenever soldiers were in the area. It couldn't be far now, but the landscape didn't look familiar and the weather was slowing his progress to a crawl.

Brendan sighed and dug his heels into the horse's skinny ribs but got no response from the poor animal. Iver was just as tired and hungry as he was himself, ambling along at a glacial pace despite Brendan's urging to move faster. Just a little while longer, he told himself as he closed his eyes for just a few moments, feeling as if he might never open them again. But as soon as he closed his eyes, he saw images of carnage; bodies bloodied and mangled, their limbs at odd angles as they lay dead or dying in the field. Several horses wandered around, their eyes wild in their heads and their nostrils flaring at the smell of fresh blood and churned earth.

Countless Roundheads walked through the field, driving their steel into anyone they thought might still be alive, and robbing the corpses, grabbing anything of value that they might use or sell. Brendan wasn't sure how many were dead, but it was thousands, the field strewn with corpses of Scots and Englishmen alike. The Battle of Dunbar had been a resounding victory for Oliver Cromwell, the rebellion squashed and Scottish forces decimated. In the distance, Brendan could see the columns of prisoners who were heckled and beaten by the soldiers before they were led away to God knew where. Some of them wouldn't make it through the night, but many would be sold on to be shipped to the Colonies as indentured servants and worked to death before they died of disease and hardship. That was their lot for being Papists and proclaiming their support for King Charles II.

Brendan had joined the New Model Army four years ago, going from a simple cavalry soldier to captain within two years. The Self-Denying Ordinance of 1645 by which lords and members of the House of Commons could no longer hold military positions, had served him well, making moving up through the ranks easier, especially for someone who came from landed gentry. Had Brendan been a peasant, he'd still be a nobody, making two shillings a day to risk his life and live like vermin, but he was an officer, respected and better paid, if not better fed. Which made his desertion that much more visible. He hadn't meant to desert, hadn't planned to flee, but something inside him broke as he looked at that battlefield. He simply couldn't take another moment of this senseless slaughter; couldn't take another life without believing that what he was doing was just and ordained by God. He turned his horse southward and just kept going, hoping that his absence would not be noticed amid the chaos and smoke.

The thought of homecoming wasn't particularly pleasant either as Brendan would have to eat crow once his father heard of the desertion of his post. Wilfred Carr had forbidden his son to go when he proclaimed his support for Oliver Cromwell and the Commonwealth. Wilfred threatened and bullied him, but Brendan had been adamant and even recruited a few men from the estate to join him. They were all gone now, killed in various battles over the last few years. He wasn't ashamed of his desire to fight, but of his failure to bring the men home and keep them safe.

"Stay out of it, boy," his father had said, wagging a calloused finger in Brendan's face. "Kings come and go, but 'tis the common man who pays the price, aye? Your place is here. As my heir, you owe me your obedience and respect, and I forbid you to go. England has been decimated by Civil War and Oliver Cromwell has no intention of stopping the slaughter. He's executed the king, for heaven's sake. Do you think he won't massacre anyone who stands in the way of his Commonwealth? Let Charles II raise his army and fight his battles, but you don't need to be the one to fight against him. And the Papists… What bearing do poor Irish farmers or wealthy Scots barons have on our lives? Let them practice their papistry to their heart's content. I won't lose a son to the likes of them. "

"My conscience demands it, Father." Brendan had tried to explain, but his father bid him to be silent.

"Damn your conscience. You'll die for naught on some battlefield and crows will peck out your eyes. We are isolated enough here that it doesn't matter who's in power, be it Cromwell or King Charlie. We will survive as long as we keep our heads down. Now go about your chores and mind your sire." He patted Brendan on the shoulder signaling forgiveness. His father often said that he admired his fire, but thought little of his desire to fight.

Wilfred was pragmatic to the bone, his first priority keeping his family and holdings safe.

Brendan sighed, his shoulders dropping even lower with fatigue and defeat. Maybe his father had been right all along. Cromwell had crossed into Scotland with 16,000 troops and the backing of the fleet, ready to squash the rebellion and possibly annex Scotland to the Commonwealth in the process. The killing Brendan witnessed was like nothing he'd ever seen before. Principle was all well and good, but now thousands of families had lost their menfolk, left to fend for themselves and face the coming winter. How would they survive, all those wives and fatherless children? Who would care for them? They were the true price of war. These families would be left to starve, and worse, left at the mercy of the Roundheads who would roam the countryside.

Brendan turned the horse in the direction of an outcropping of rock that rose high into the ominous clouds; the surface slick with rain, and gnarled roots and branches protruding from the cracks, dripping and limp. It took him a while to find it, but he finally spotted it among the brambles — a fissure in the rock, a crevice really, but enough for him to enter and bring the horse. The cave smelled damp and earthy, the interior dark as a moonless night, but it was shelter and a place to lie down for a while and sleep. Some roots were poking through the rock, hanging overhead and pulling at his clothes as he lowered his head to advance further into the cave. The roots were dry, so at least he could make a little fire and warm himself for a bit before settling in for the night.

The fire sent shifting shadows dancing on the walls of the cave, filling the small space with the smell of smoke and burning wood and making Brendan's coat steam as it began to dry. He pulled off his boots, emptying them of water, and set them by the fire before turning to his meager meal: a stale heel of bread, a hunk of cheese, and a half-empty skin of ale was all he had left, but it would tide him over until he got home, hopefully tomorrow. Brendan bit into the bread, cursing eloquently as he nearly broke a tooth on the hard crust. He dipped the bread into the ale, letting it soak for a few seconds before trying again. He chewed very slowly, making the food last for as long as he could in the hope that his stomach would be fooled into thinking that it was full, but it growled in protest, wanting more. He'd been on starvation rations for the past few weeks and his body was crying out in protest, asking for enough food to sustain Brendan's powerful frame and lean muscle. Brendan curled up as close to the fire as he dared and allowed himself to sink into a deep sleep, praying that he wouldn't dream of the battle or of violent death.

The Present

Chapter 4

My hand shook with anticipation as I took the key out of my pocket and inserted it into the old-fashioned lock. It was only a week since I'd made the offer, but the whole process took much less time than I expected. Doctor Hughes was only too happy to unload the place, accepting my offer immediately right over the phone. He didn't seem interested in how much I was offering, only in the fact that he was finally going to be rid of the responsibility of fulfilling a promise to his aunt and discharging his duty. Paula said that he planned to share the money with Myra, but it didn't matter to me. What he did with it was none of my business. All I cared about was getting the deed of sale and racing over to the house to inspect my little kingdom.

I pushed open the door, inhaling the musty smell of the dim foyer. Several doors opened off the cavernous space which was bigger than some apartments I'd seen in New York, and a sweeping wooden staircase rose to the second floor. The house seemed guarded and silent around me, almost holding its breath until it knew if the interloper was friend or foe. I walked in and opened a window in the front room. It needed to be aired out, among other things, but that would come later. When I had toured the house with Paula, I hardly noticed the details, focusing on the number of rooms, baths, and general layout, but today, I could walk around at my leisure and take it all in.

The rooms were well-proportioned, with high ceilings and tall mullioned windows flanked by moth-eaten curtains of heavy velvet. They were threadbare in places, as were the rugs on the scarred wooden floors. I was surprised to see dusty doilies, yellowed with age, covering the end tables next to the chintz sofa, and a ceramic vase full of plastic flowers in the hearth of the living room fireplace. A television set that dated back to the '80s was in pride of place against the opposite wall, its wooden paneling covered by a thick layer of dust. Several lamps with faded shades dotted the room, and a few copies of The Sun and The Mirror were scattered on the wooden coffee table.

I crossed the hall and entered the other front room, this one probably a sitting room at some point. There were several old photographs clustered on the piano, depicting men in uniform who stood behind seated women and gazed earnestly into the camera. I wondered if they'd survived the war and came back to their sweethearts, but there was no one to ask. I looked to see if any of the photos were recent, but there seemed to be nothing of the last owners. A scratched mirror in a gilded frame hung above the mantel, and the once flowery wallpaper was so faded I could barely make out the pattern, strips hanging here and there as if someone tore them on purpose in a fit of rage. I didn't even bother to inspect the kitchen, as I had a fairly good idea of what awaited me there.

Instead, I made my way to the second floor, eager to inspect the bedrooms. Maybe there was something I could salvage for future use, but nothing seemed of any value. The beds were saggy and dusty; the headboards scratched and wobbly. There was only one bathroom with a rusty chain for flushing and a deep, claw-footed tub that needed a very vigorous cleaning.

I sat on the edge of the tub and sighed. The charming façade the house presented to the world was just a mask of genteel respectability that hid years of neglect and decay. A house like this required a lot of upkeep, and the Hughes family clearly didn't have the funds or the desire to modernize and maintain. The house would need a lot of work before it would be ready for habitation, but I didn't care. My plan was to open by next spring, so I had at least nine months to renovate and scour the countryside for antiques to fill the rooms. My mom had always loved antiquing, so I knew how to spot a gem at an estate sale or shop and buy it for a song, returning it to its former glory with a bit of varnish. I would have plenty of time to kill while the renovations were being done, and I looked forward to exploring the surrounding area and learning its history. The proximity to Lincoln was a bonus since there was much to see, especially the famed Lincoln Cathedral.

I left the bathroom and pushed open the door to the corner bedroom. I felt like an intruder despite the fact that no one had slept there in years. The house seemed to resent my presence, sighing with disapproval. The room was large and pleasant, the furniture slightly newer and more comfortable. This must have been a girl's room at some point since there were several dolls seated on top of the flowery bedspread, and empty bottles of perfume on the dresser. The perfume must have evaporated over time, but a barely distinguishable scent lingered in the air, suddenly making me feel weepy. It smelled familiar somehow, but I knew I'd never smelled it before. I held the bottle to my nose, trying to place where I might have been exposed to the fragrance, but nothing came to mind. It wasn't a brand I'd ever heard of. I was just being fanciful, I told myself, affected by the melancholy atmosphere of the house.

I pushed aside the curtain, releasing a cloud of dust in the process, opened the window and looked out. I could see the unkempt garden behind the house and the stream that cut the land in two. The current looked surprisingly strong, the brownish water rushing loudly past the house and under a stone bridge that looked much older than the house. The ruin was directly across from the window, the stones glowing in the slanting rays of the afternoon sun. It must have been a house once, but all that was left were the crumbling walls. The roof had rotted away years ago, and except for a few shards of broken glass in the window frames, there was nothing there but emptiness, now brilliantly filled with the rosy shafts of the setting sun. The place looked kind of romantic actually and would look great in my brochure. I'd take the pictures myself, choosing the best time of the day to capture the forlorn beauty of the spot.

I shielded my eyes against the light as I spotted something by what would have been the door, had it still been there. A solitary figure emerged from the ruin, walking slowly to the tree that grew a few feet away. It was an old tree, tall and stout, with thick limbs that hung relatively low to the ground. The tree looked as if it were holding out its arms in welcome, offering shelter from the rain and shade from the sun. The man, for that's who he was, reached the tree, stopping briefly before sinking to his knees and holding his hands in front of him, as if in prayer. There was something odd about him, but he was too far away for me to see clearly. I could see that he had dark hair that fell to his shoulders and was strangely dressed, as if wearing a theater costume for a performance of a historical play. I could just make out a coat that came to mid-thigh, and narrow pants tucked into high boots with the tops folded over to form a wide cuff. I felt like a voyeur watching this man praying, but I just couldn't look away, wondering what he had been doing in the ruin.

The man finally rose to his feet, his shoulders slumped and his head bent, as if in shame, and walked back, disappearing inside. Maybe he was just a tourist out for a walk. Many people were drawn by historic ruins, so he'd look around and go back to his hotel, or wherever he was staying. I turned from the window and sat down on the bed. The mattress was surprisingly firm, and the frame was made of dark wood which was intricately carved with some whimsical pattern. It was surprisingly out of sync with the rest of the house and more as I would picture the original furnishings to look. There was a dresser to match, and an escritoire, which was dusty and full of old papers, but would be perfect to use as my base of operations once I cleared it out. I would take this room for myself, I decided, and use it as a bedroom/office while the renovations were under way. Now all I needed to do was find a contractor who shared my vision of this place and then the work could commence. I couldn't wait.

September 1650

England

Chapter 5

Brendan was dead tired by the time he rode through the gates of his father's house about ten miles north of Lincoln. He hadn't allowed himself to dwell on his homesickness, putting home firmly out of his mind as he followed the army from place to place and battle to battle, but now that he saw the house, he felt an overwhelming surge of affection for the place and the people in it. Everything seemed unusually quiet, but then it was almost suppertime, so maybe they were all inside. Brendan saw a face at the window, but couldn't make out whose it was. The weather hadn't improved much, wisps of fog swirling around his feet and wrapping the house in its gauzy embrace.

He was so tired, he wished he could just let someone else stable Iver, but there was no one about, leaving him to do it himself. The poor horse deserved that much, having carried him all this way with little rest and not enough food. Iver was happily munching on oats as Brendan finally set off for the main house, trying in vain to ignore the butterflies in his stomach. His father would have much to say, none of it good, before he was welcomed home and given a meal and a chance to wash and change the clothes he'd been living in for nearly two weeks.

"Brendan!" Meg flew into his arms, letting him go just as quickly and wrinkling her nose at the smell that came off him in waves. "Thank the good Lord you're home at last. We heard about the victory at Dunbar. You must be pleased." She gave Brendan a curious look as he failed to show appropriate enthusiasm, but she took it for fatigue and went on talking as she slid her arm through his. "There've been changes since you left — big changes." Meg didn't get a chance to tell him what she meant as the door flew open and Jasper appeared on the threshold, a mug in hand.

"Well, well, look who's home," he said, stepping aside to let Brendan enter the front room which his father always used for seeing visitors and tenants. The room was the heart of the house, since that's where the family met as well and all the important decisions were made.

"Where's father?" Brendan asked, suddenly even more nervous about facing the old man. He hadn't come out to greet him, so he was still angry, probably waiting for Brendan to come to him and make his case. Their mother wasn't there either, but Brendan could smell the aroma of roasting meat and boiled vegetables wafting from the direction of the kitchen and assumed his mother was busy preparing supper. He'd go see her in a moment.

Jasper flung himself into a seat by the hearth and gestured for Brendan to sit across from him. They were never allowed to sit in their father's chair, but Jasper made himself comfortable, taking a swallow of his beer and silently toasting to Brendan as Meg handed Brendan a cup of cool beer, which was very welcome.

"Meg, get Brendan some food, will you?" Jasper called out to their retreating sister as he turned his attention to Brendan. "Father's dead, Brendan. Died of apoplexy, not long after you left. I've been running the estate since."

Brendan gripped the armrests of the chair, not knowing what to do with the terrible pain that coursed through him at the news. They'd never made up their argument, and now he'd never get a chance to tell his father that he was sorry, and that Wilfred had been right all along. His father had seen where this was all going long before it even happened. Brendan thought his father unenlightened and resistant to new ideas and change, but his father had a much greater understanding of the world and man's hunger for power. At least his father died without other men's blood on his hands, something that Brendan could no longer aspire to.

"And mother?" Brenda asked, suddenly afraid.

"She's sleeping upstairs. She's been poorly since Father died. I'm surprised she's lasted this long, truth be told. I think she was waiting for you." A look of annoyance crossed Jasper's face at that revelation. He'd always maintained that their mother loved Brendan more, and although she'd denied it vehemently, everyone knew it to be true.

"You look like hell, by the way," Jasper said with a sour chuckle, "and a bath wouldn't come amiss."

Jasper, on the other hand, looked the picture of health. He was about the same height as Brendan, but he'd always been stockier with a barrel chest and bulging muscles that strained the fabric of his shirt while he worked. He looked well-fed and pleased with life, his face ruddy from spending so much time outdoors. They were different in looks as well. Whereas Brendan took after their mother with dark hair, hazel eyes and a bronzed skin, Jasper was fair like their father, his eyes more brown than green and light skin that quickly turned red from sun or wind.

"I know. I'm dead on my feet." He wanted to ask Jasper about their father's final days, if he might have forgiven Brendan for leaving, but he couldn't form the words, didn't want to cry in front of his younger brother. He'd ask Meg later. She'd let him cry and hold him like she used to when he was little and she was his big sister. He gave her a grateful look as she handed him a plate of mutton and some fresh bread. Despite his sour mood he was starved, his body crying out for nourishment after months of living mostly on biscuit and cheese.

"We heard about Dunbar, of course," Jasper continued. "Four thousand dead and ten thousand taken prisoner. What a victory," he exclaimed, taking stock of Brendan. "Have you killed many?"

"Enough."

"Enough for what?" Jasper asked, eager to hear more about the battle.

"Enough not to want to do it anymore." Brendan didn't elaborate, but Jasper caught on fairly quick.

"So, you've deserted, have you?" he asked, eyes bulging with shock.

"I have. I don't have the stomach for it anymore. Father was right about all of it."

"And our men?" Jasper asked, his eyes full of scorn. "All dead, I presume, just as Father predicted?"

"They are." Meg made excellent mutton, but at the moment it tasted like ashes in Brendan's mouth, seasoned with bitterness, guilt, and the knowledge that nothing could undo the wrong he'd done to the families of the fallen. They'd only gone out of loyalty to him, not to the cause, and now they were all dead, their families about to be disabused of the hope that their men were coming back.

"Brendan, do you know what they do to deserters?" Jasper asked, his eyes surprisingly merry. "You can't stay here. You can rest tonight, but must leave first thing in the morning. They'll come looking for you, and if they do, we're all in danger. Your allegiance to Cromwell has kept us out of harm's way these past few years, but now that you've done a runner, there's nothing to protect us from the Roundheads. You need to lie low for a time — a long time." Jasper gave Brendan a searching look, his mouth stretching into a sly smile. "Besides, I'm now lord and master here, and you need to leave."

"What do you mean, you are lord and master?" Brendan asked, shocked. He was the eldest son, their father's heir. It's only natural that Jasper would take over with father dead and Brendan gone, but now that he was home, Jasper would need to step down.

"Oh, have I forgotten to mention it?" Jasper paused for dramatic effect, his eyes dancing with joy, "Father disinherited you after you left and signed over the estate to me in the event of his death." Jasper's face was a joker's mask of triumph and undisguised glee. He'd been saving that particular morsel for the right moment, and this was it.

Brendan felt as if he'd just been kicked in the stomach by a horse. Would his father have really gone that far to punish him? He'd grown up knowing that he was going to take over when his father died. The family had extensive holdings and Brendan would be a wealthy man, but if what Jasper was saying were true, he'd be left with nothing, especially if he couldn't stay and share in the profits of the estate. He'd saved most of his soldiering pay and had a purse full of coin, but that was about it. It wouldn't last him more than a year, even if he lived frugally.

"Where am I to go, brother?" Brendan asked, bitterness filling his soul. He'd always known Jasper was one to look to his own interests, but he never thought his own brother would boot him out for fear of harboring a deserter. Or maybe this was just a handy excuse for getting him out of the way so that he couldn't challenge Jasper's claim to the estate. This was the only home Brendan had ever known, and now he was being banished, possibly forever. Jasper wouldn't relinquish hold on the estate after getting a taste of power. He wanted to be the undisputed master, and the best way to accomplish that was to get rid of his older brother once and for all.

Jasper shrugged, turning his face to the fire. "Go to mother's kin. They'll take you in, if only for mother's sake. Uncle Caleb's always had a soft spot for you on account of having no sons of his own." He turned as Meg entered the room once again, quiet as a mouse. "Meg, draw a bath for Brendan," he called out, signaling that the conversation was over. Brendan rose to his feet and silently left the room. He needed to think before he acted, and not do anything rash. Jasper was his brother after all — his blood.

***

The water was steaming hot as Brendan shed his clothes and got in. He'd talk to Jasper in the morning and get him to see sense. He could just stay out of sight for a while and hide out on the estate. There was no need to leave. Jasper was just surprised

30

by Brendan's arrival and fearful for his position within the family. If their father had truly signed over the estate to him, then there was nothing Brendan could do but accept Jasper as the heir. They could both live off the estate. God knew there was enough for a dozen men. Brendan sank deeper into the water, enjoying a few moments of bliss before scrubbing the grime of the past few weeks away.

"Brendan." Meg slipped into the room, quietly closing the door behind her and kneeling by the tub. "I tried to tell you before, but didn't get the chance."

"It's all right, Meg. We'll work it out." Brendan tried to reassure her, but deep down, he wasn't feeling very confident that Jasper would be willing to work anything out. In this instance, he held all the cards. "Why aren't you at home with your children?" Brendan asked, surprised that Meg was still there. At this time of the evening women were at home seeing to supper and preparing their children for bed.

"Brendan, I have to talk to you," she whispered, watching the door with a look of naked fear in her eyes.

"What is it, Meg? What's happened?" Brendan touched her face, needing to see her smile, but her lips were pursed and her eyes darted hither and thither as she began to soap his back. "I have no proof, mind, but I believe father didn't die of natural causes. He was in robust health just days before he collapsed," Meg whispered urgently. "Jasper had father make out a deed naming him heir. Father wouldn't have done it, but he was so angry after you left, he was ripe for the picking, and Jasper was relentless in his campaign to become the heir. Father died only a few days after the deed was signed. I think Jasper had a hand in it," she murmured. "I wouldn't put anything past him these days."

Brendan turned to face his sister, his mouth opening in a silent O of shock as her words sank in and took hold, painting his homecoming in a different light. "Are you suggesting that Jasper killed him?"

31

"Was there anything to suggest that he had?" Brendan asked, his mind reeling.

"About a week after Father died, I'd gone to see Old Bertha. Remember her?" Old Bertha had been called 'Old' for as long as anyone could remember, although she likely wasn't older than fifty. She was a wisewoman, skilled in the ways of healing and midwifery. Everyone in the surrounding area came to Old Bertha for medicinal potions, love charms, and just good old advice.

"The boys were running a fever and I went to fetch some willow bark. We fell to talking and Bertha happened to mention that Jasper had been to see her recently. Now, why would Jasper, who's not been ill a day in his life, go to see Bertha? Hmm?"

"What are you suggesting?" Brendan hissed as he heard footsteps in the other room.

"I am suggesting that Jasper might have purchased some poison. A death from poison could easily be mistaken for apoplexy. It's not as if there was a physician to attend father. He died and was buried, so no one would be the wiser."

"Meg, Old Bertha is a shrewd woman, one well-versed in the ways of human nature. Do you think that if Jasper came and bought poison and a few days later his father died of apoplexy, she might not have been suspicious?" Brendan was surprised by the stubborn look on Meg's face. She'd always been so calm and practical, and now she sounded nearly hysterical, her fears getting the better of her. He wished he could reassure her somehow, but at this point, he had no idea what to believe.

"Perhaps, but as you pointed out, she's wise enough to know when to keep her mouth shut. With Father gone, Jasper is now the landlord, and Bertha lives on his land. What good would it do her to start trumpeting her suspicions? He could have her evicted, or worse… Maybe telling me was enough to soothe her conscience."

"Meg, even if that were true, you don't have a shred of proof. So Jasper went to see Bertha. He could have been suffering from constricted bowels, for all you know. Or maybe his humors were out of balance from all that drinking. He wouldn't be the first or the last to seek some tonic from the wisewoman. Had she actually said that he bought poison?" Brendan asked patiently.

"Well, no," Meg conceded. "Maybe you're right. I just haven't been myself lately. It's all been too much to bear. I didn't get a chance to tell you about Rob."

"Rob?"

Meg nodded miserably, nearly jumping out of her skin as the door flew open, a tipsy Jasper leaning against the doorjamb as he took in the scene.

"I know you've been lonely since your husband died Meg, but try to keep your hands off your own brother," he sniggered, obviously pleased with his tasteless joke. "Just say the word and I'll find you a new man, although they're thin on the ground these days, thanks to Brendan. How many men did you take with you when you left?" he asked, not waiting for an answer before stumbling off to bed.

"Rob's dead?" Brendan choked out, as he took in his sister's gaunt face and unusual pallor. That explained much. "When?"

"A few months now. A fever. I'm completely at Jasper's mercy now, and I've never known him to be this cruel," Meg mumbled as she handed Brendan a towel. "I fear for you, Brendan. Go to mother's people. You'll be safe there for the time being, and once this war is over you can come back and claim what's yours with no fear of being betrayed by Jasper."

"Meg, I know Jasper has never been particularly softhearted or generous of spirit, but you're suggesting that he killed our father and would gladly betray me — knowing that I would be executed — just to retain control of the estate. I just can't believe that. I won't." Brendan looked at Meg in the hope

33

that she would agree with him, but she shook her head at his naiveté.

"Brendan, have you not seen what men will do for power? Jasper has always resented you and now that he's gotten what he's always wanted, he's not about to just voluntarily step aside and let you reclaim your rightful place."

"I can appreciate that, but murder??? This is our brother we're speaking of."

"He's changed, Brendan. He's no longer the Jasper we knew as children. Promise me you'll go. I need to know that you're safe."

"Will Mother be all right?" Brendan asked, his mind spinning with shock at Meg's insinuations.

"She'll be fine. I'll look after her as I always have. The children have been staying with Rob's family these past few weeks so that I can devote myself to caring for Mother. Besides, Jasper's got his hands full these days. He's getting married next month. Mary has finally accepted him now that he's lord and master."

"My Mary?" Brendan cried out in outrage.

Meg turned her back to Brendan as he got dressed, his hair still dripping bathwater onto his clean shirt.

"She's your Mary no longer. Did you think she'd just wait patiently until you came back? She's had Jasper wrapped around her little finger since the day you left; knowing that he would inherit should anything happen to you." Meg sighed with frustration as she turned to face Brendan again. Men were so incredibly naïve when it came to women. They thought of women as commodities, ones that could be put by until they were in need of them. Meg supposed some women were like that, but not Mary. Mary was as clever and calculating as any man, her intellect conveniently disguised by a comely face and a fine figure.

"Lucky Jasper. I see things are going well for him at last," Brendan quipped as he pulled on his breeches. He still thought that Meg was being overly dramatic, but he would be sleeping fully dressed tonight, in case he needed to make a quick getaway.

"Good night, Meg," Brendan said as he gave his sister a warm hug. "I'll leave at first light, and I promise I won't do anything foolish, if only for your sake. I wish I'd had time to see your boys."

Meg just nodded into his shoulder as she wrapped her arms around him.

"God keep you, Brendan," she mumbled, then turned on her heel and ran from the room. Brendan made his way to his old room and stretched out on the bed. He hadn't slept in a real bed in longer than he could recall, but he couldn't rest, his mind going over and over what Meg said.

Would Jasper really betray him that way? He'd always been somewhat morally ambiguous, more concerned with what he could get away with rather than with what was right, but they were brothers, flesh and blood. And could he have had anything to do with their father's death? Even thinking these thoughts seemed disloyal, but was it possible? Jasper most certainly profited from his death, but would he actually stoop to murder? Brendan shook his head, unable to accept that his little brother could have become so vicious, but Meg was the oldest and she'd known them since they were children. If Meg believed that Jasper was capable of murder, he'd better take heed.

And Mary… He could hardly blame Jasper for lusting after Mary. She'd always been the loveliest girl in the village, but Mary had been promised to Brendan these past six years, a contract arranged by their fathers when Mary turned twelve. The contract was still binding since Brendan was alive, but as far as Jasper and Mary were concerned, he might as well be dead since neither one of them saw fit to honor it. What would Mary's father have to say had he known of Brendan's return? Would he want his daughter to marry the penniless, disinherited son? It hardly mattered now.

Brendan reached for his dagger and slid it beneath his pillow. *Welcome home*, Brendan, he told himself before drifting off into an uneasy sleep.

Chapter 6

The day dawned clear and bright, the sky a brilliant blue after days of drizzle punctuated by severe downpours; fluffy clouds lazily drifted across the face of the sun and cast shadows onto the muddy yard. The beauty of the September day was a stark contrast to Brendan's mood as he packed a few belongings and chose a fresh horse from the stable. Poor Iver wasn't ready for another journey. Brendan turned on his heel and walked back into the house, his mind made up. Jasper had asked him to leave quietly, but he would see his mother and say goodbye. Lord knew when he'd see her again, if ever, considering her ill health.

Nan Carr looked small and still in her bed, her skin ashen against the white linen of the embroidered pillowcase. His mother was not yet fifty, but she looked like an old woman, having aged decades since his departure and the death of her husband. Several small pots containing evil-smelling potions sat on a stool by the bed, but they seemed to be doing little to heal his mother. If not for the barely perceptible rise and fall of her chest, she might have appeared dead. Brendan bent down and kissed her brow, making a sign of the cross over her in silent blessing. She never opened her eyes, but grabbed his hand with her bony fingers, holding his palm to her shriveled cheek, which was cold to the touch despite the blankets heaped on the bed. "I love you too, Mam," he whispered in her ear before taking his leave.

"Brendan, wait," Meg called out as he came down the stairs. "I packed you some food for the journey." She handed him a small bundle and a skin of ale, which he accepted gratefully.

"Meg, take care of yourself. You are a young woman still; you must see to your own life." Meg shook her head in dismay.

"Brendan, men see to their own lives; women take care of others. I can't leave Mother in her condition, and I have two little ones to raise. 'Myself' is not a word that often comes to mind these days." She kissed Brendan's cheek and smiled up at him in that way that often hides a desire to cry. "I wish you didn't have to go, Brendan. You're the only one I trust these days."

"I will come back," he promised.

"Do."

Jasper was outside, leaning against the stable wall, his lips stretched into a smile that was brimming with smugness. Brendan stopped a few feet away, surveying his brother. He knew Jasper wouldn't tell him the truth, but he had to ask all the same. He knew his brother well enough to spot a lie. "Did father really die of an apoplexy, Jasper?" he asked conversationally, studying Jasper's face closely, his head cocked to the side like a watchful hound ready to pounce on its prey.

"Aye, but I can't say as I'm sorry. Chose a very opportune moment, he did," Jasper replied, the smile never leaving his face. "I'm as strong, as smart, and as ambitious as you are, but being the younger son that'd never have mattered, would it? You sealed your fate when you rode out of this yard bent on your heroic quest to fight for liberty and equality. Fortune doesn't always favor the brave, does it? Sometimes it favors the ones who are there at the right time."

"Thank you for your honesty, Jasper," Brendan replied caustically. He couldn't tell if Jasper had anything to do with their father's death, but he could hear the threat in Jasper's words. Jasper would see Brendan dead before he gave up what he perceived to be rightfully his, and whether he got it by an act of violence or by sheer cunning, he was here to stay.

Brendan vaulted onto his horse, ready to depart. The way things stood, he wasn't coming back home anytime soon, so he took a last longing look at the house where he was born and lived most of his life. It was solid and gray, its twin-peaked roof a stark contrast to the brightening sky, the windows alight with the rosy glow of the morning sun. The morning was filled with birdsong and the sound of restless animals in the barn; cows and goats needing to be milked and horses eager for their oats. A few chickens pecked in the dirt in search of juicy worms and a gray cat snuggled against the wall, its fur indistinguishable from the color of the stone until the cat opened its green eyes and gave Brendan a hard stare. He'd miss this place, now even more than when he was away fighting, for now he knew there was no going back.

"Go with God, Brendan," Jasper called out, waving a half-hearted goodbye as he stood in the center of the yard, the master of his domain.

Brendan cantered out of the yard. He never looked back, having no desire to see the self-satisfied expression on Jasper's face. He didn't believe that Jasper killed their father, but he'd seized the opportunity life presented him with, taking the reins of the estate, betrothing himself to a girl Brendan had once hoped to marry, and getting rid of Brendan under the pretense of worrying for the safety of the family. *Well done, brother*, Brendan thought as he spurred the horse to a gallop, *well done*.

Chapter 7

Brendan looked around in an effort to distract himself from the lump of bitterness firmly lodged in his throat. The gentle breeze caressed his face while the sun warmed his shoulders and thighs, making him feel sluggish as he cantered along. The air smelled of damp earth, grass, and burning peat coming from some crofter's cottage downwind. Unseen birds were singing their little hearts out, glad that the rain had finally given way to sunshine and warmth.

At any other time, Brendan would have been happy just to be alive on a glorious morning such as this, but his stomach burned with anger as his mind kept returning to Jasper. He tried to calm himself by counting his blessings. At the moment, he was dry, clean, and well fed, so that was something. He'd always liked Uncle Caleb's family, although he hadn't seen them often. The last time had been Maisie's wedding over five years ago. She was the youngest, so Uncle Caleb and Aunt Joan might be on their own and glad of some company and an extra pair of hands around the farm. Where some families lived ten to a room, Uncle Caleb had a fine cottage with lots of outbuildings and plenty of land. There'd be work for Brendan to do to repay his uncle for taking him in. There was peace to be found in hard work, and after what he'd seen, he was more than ready to step away from the fighting and devote himself to the life-affirming routine of daily living.

Brendan smiled grimly as he thought of Mary. He naively thought that he was coming back to her, but clearly, it was never him she was interested in, but the status he would offer her. She'd been pliant and eager the few times he cornered her in her father's barn, her kisses shy and intoxicating and her body soft and warm against his own. She'd been willing to let him go further, but he drew away from her as he murmured promises in her ear. He should have taken her when he had the chance, but he thought himself an honorable man and wanted to wait for their wedding night. It wouldn't do anyone any good to leave her pregnant as he went off to fight, and Mary didn't wish to be wed until he returned. Now he understood why. Had he still stood to inherit, she would have married him in a heartbeat, but had he been killed, she'd be a young widow who would have to mourn her husband and possibly miss out on the chance to marry his brother, who would now be the heir. *Clever girl, our Mary*, Brendan thought as he took a sip of ale. He supposed he should thank Jasper for saving him from a loveless marriage. *Let them have joy of each other*, Brendan thought, *they're a fine match.*

Brendan stowed the empty leather skin in his saddlebag, his body tensing as he heard the sound of hoof beats coming from somewhere behind him. Three men appeared on the horizon a few minutes later, a cloud of dust churning under the hooves of their galloping horses. Soldiers could be easily identified by their short hair and garb, especially if they wore armor, but these men were civilians, farmers by the looks of them, and likely not a threat unless they were bent on thieving. He didn't have much to take. Brendan drew to the side of the road prepared to let the men pass, but they seemed to slow down as they approached him from behind. Brendan glanced back to gauge the men's intentions when his breath caught in his throat. He recognized them; they were friends of Jasper's, and they were heavily armed. There was only one reason why three farmers would be out on the road this early armed to the teeth — this was no coincidental meeting.

Brendan's mind did a quick assessment of the situation. He couldn't possibly outrun them, so he had to stay and fight. They were farmers, not warriors, and his only advantage was that he, at least, was better trained and blooded in real battle. But the odds weren't in his favor. He looked from man to man, hoping that once they were face to face they might be dissuaded from their course, but all he saw in their eyes was sheer determination to carry out whatever their mission was. Brendan put his hand on the hilt of his sword, but he wouldn't strike the first blow.

The men reined in their horses as they finally reached him. Brendan's assumption that this was prearranged was reaffirmed by their lack of surprise at seeing him, and their hands on the hilt of their swords. Jasper must have left as soon as Brendan was out of sight, summoning his minions to do his dirty work.

"I have no quarrel with you," Brendan said, in a futile attempt to avoid a confrontation.

"Nor we with you," replied Gareth Carr, a distant cousin and a thug through and through. Gareth had always been built like an ox; his sheer size enough to intimidate any man. Gareth would have made an excellent soldier, but he only fought when the odds were in his favor and the outcome a foregone conclusion; he wasn't one to risk his life in vain. The other two were Donald and Bob Haskell. Brendan hadn't seen them in years, but they hadn't changed much; still thin and wiry, with shifty eyes that betrayed their greedy nature. They'd kill their own mother for a few gold pieces if they could get away with it.

"Then be on your way," Brendan replied calmly, although he felt his chest constricting with foreboding. No one was going anywhere.

"Oh, we will be, as soon as we've delivered compliments from your brother," Gareth replied with a twisted smile. Brendan had already surmised that the men were here at Jasper's behest, but hearing it from Gareth still had the power to shock him. He'd been a fool not to listen to Meg, and now he was alone, exposed, and outnumbered. *Bloody fool*, Brendan thought viciously, annoyed with himself for leaving himself open to an attack.

He'd seen bloodlust often enough to recognize the signs and tightened his hand on the hilt of his sword. He'd known these men for most of his life, but that obviously held no sway over them as they reached for their steel. What had Jasper promised them to inspire such loyalty? Was it just coin, or was something more on offer? Gareth clearly had the lead, while the other two hung back a little, waiting for him to strike the first blow.

Brendan flexed his hand around the hilt, tensed like a cat that was about to pounce, and cleared his mind of all thought except that of survival. He'd learned fighting techniques on the battlefield, and the tiniest distraction could be the difference between life and death. Being on horseback was a disadvantage, since he couldn't turn fast enough to ward off a blow from the back, but if he dismounted and they didn't, they'd hack him to pieces from above, wielding their swords like axes. He wished he was riding Iver. Iver had seen fighting many times and wasn't as easily frightened as this horse that was nervously snorting and panting with fear as it sensed danger.

The men surrounded Brendan, their smiles leering as they enjoyed their advantage. They were in no rush to charge him, using the anticipation of the blow to come to unnerve him and provoke him into making a mistake. Brendan's gaze was fixed on Gareth, since Brendan was sure that he would be the first to strike. Gareth finally lunged at him and Brendan twisted out of the way of the sword, forcing Gareth to lose his balance for a moment. Brendan thrust forward, but Gareth managed to evade just as Bob Haskell came at him from the side and slashed his sword through Brendan's thigh.

Brendan roared in fury as pain ripped through him and blood soaked his breeches within moments. There was no chance of this being a fair fight, so he had to use whatever advantage he had before they chopped him to pieces. That blow was meant to wound, not to kill, so they wanted to play with him awhile, until he was weak and unable to fight. Well, he wouldn't give them that pleasure. Gareth was laughing, his guard momentarily down as he turned to Bob with a grin on his ugly face. This was his moment. Brendan bent down as if in shock from the pain, then quickly raised his sword and brought it down with both hands on Gareth's collarbone, nearly cleaving him in half. Gareth slid off his horse like a sack of turnips and fell to the side, his blood mixing with the dust as it flowed freely from the wound. Gareth still had a grin on his face, except there was also a look of surprise in his dead eyes that made his expression grotesque.

Somewhere at the back of his mind Brendan was amazed that Gareth left himself open to the blow, but he didn't dwell on his good fortune and focused on the other two, who were gaping at him with a mixture of fear and determination. With Gareth gone, Brendan thought they might flee, but whatever Jasper held over them was stronger than the fear of Brendan's sword.

There were still two against one, and the odds were in their favor, even if they weren't born warriors, especially since he was already wounded and losing blood. He could feel his heart hammering against his ribs, his senses alert to every movement of his enemies. Soon he would start to feel lightheaded from loss of blood and his vision might start to blur, but for now, he was ready to fight — if not ready to die.

Gareth had been about brute strength, but these two were more clever and agile. They exchanged a quick glance before starting to circle Brendan in an attempt to disorient him while they waited for the perfect moment to strike. He had to make the first move before they distracted him too much, so Brendan lunged at Donald just as his brother's sword came down on his back, white-hot pain engulfing him in its grasp, but he couldn't afford to lose focus. Brendan spun around, driving his sword into Bob's stomach as another blow from Donald caught him on the arm. He could barely lift his sword, but he managed to swing it with both hands, catching Donald across the face.

Donald yelped, holding his hand against his bleeding face as if to hold it together, but the blood oozed between his fingers, soaking his sleeve and dripping on his thigh. Brendan didn't wait for him to recover as he drove his sword between Donald's ribs, watching in fascination as the man's mouth opened in astonishment before he fell into the dust, his lifeblood draining out of him and mingling with the dirt. Rob was still alive, moaning and begging Brendan for mercy, but there was nothing to be done, even had he been of a mind to help the man who'd been sent to kill him. The only thing he could do for him was put him out of his misery, which he would have done had he been able to get off his horse.

Brendan felt faint as the bloodlust began to ebb and the reality of his situation sank in. He was bleeding profusely and feeling weaker by the minute as blinding pain held him in its grip from all sides. He hugged the horse's neck, resting his head against its warm flesh, the silky mane comforting against his burning cheek. If he didn't get to his uncle, he would die here in the middle of nowhere, and no one except for Meg and his mother would know or care.

Chapter 8

Thick clouds obscured the sun and the sky turned nearly black as another storm threatened to break at any moment. An ominous silence descended after a flock of crows rose into the sky like black omens of doom, cawing madly and flapping their wings against the gathering wind. Brendan's horse ambled into the yard just as the first crack of lightning split the sky and the rain began to pelt his back, marginally cooling the burning wound. Within moments he was soaked, blood-tinged rainwater running down his legs and over the flanks of the horse. Brendan would have fallen into the mud had his uncle not caught him under the arms, barely managing to keep his own balance. He had no recollection of the ride to his uncle's house, slipping in and out of consciousness as he held on to the horse's mane for dear life to keep him from sliding off.

"I got you, lad, I got you. What in God's name happened?" Uncle Caleb panted as he half carried Brendan into the house, calling to his wife for water and bandages. Brendan tried to reply, but his tongue wouldn't work and an all-encompassing blackness descended on him as he gratefully embraced it.

The room was shrouded in darkness as Brendan came to, rain lashing against the shutters with a ferocity that filled the house with the sound of the downpour. Thunder rumbled somewhere in the distance, but the brunt of the storm seemed to have passed. Brendan nearly cried out with pain, but bit his tongue at the sight of the girl. Her profile was illuminated by the single candle burning only inches away from her face; the flame flickering in the wind seeping through the crack in the shutters. She was grinding something in a mortar as she gripped the pestle with both hands, using all her strength. Brendan tried to get a better look at the girl, but his vision was blurred and the room was too dim to see her features clearly. She wasn't one of his cousins, of that he was sure. Maybe she was a servant. His mind refused to focus as wave after wave of pain radiated from his wounds making him feel as if he'd been flayed. He must have moaned because the girl's head shot up, her frightened eyes glued to the bed.

"Hello," he croaked, hoping he hadn't scared her.

She gave an almost imperceptible nod before adding a dollop of something to the mortar and coming to sit by him on the side of the cot. Her eyes found his, but still she said nothing, only laid her cool hand across his forehead more as a sign of benediction than a healer's need to check for a fever. She gently took him by the shoulder and indicated that he should lie on his stomach. The agony that sliced through Brendan as he tried to move nearly took his breath away, but he carefully rolled over, giving her access to the wound in his back. His arm and leg were already bandaged, so he must have been out for quite some time.

The girl used a rag soaked with warm water to wet the dried blood, and carefully peeled the tatters of his shirt from his back before applying the poultice. Brendan wanted to howl as her fingers touched the raw flesh, but he clamped his teeth, refusing to shame himself in front of this girl who was only trying to help him. He gave her a weak smile of gratitude, but she averted her eyes from his, almost as if she were afraid of him.

"What's your name?" he asked through gritted teeth, needing something to distract him. She seemed to be flustered by his question and continued to apply the medicine without replying. Brendan could feel a tremor in her hand as she finished and busied herself with the bandage which needed to be rolled under his chest. She touched his shoulder in a silent command for him to lift his body, finished bandaging, and left the room without so much as by-your-leave. *Had he done something to offend her?* Brendan wondered as he tried to find a comfortable position. The pain was more of a dull ache than a scorching heat if he didn't move, and he finally drifted off to sleep, still thinking about the strange girl.

***

It was still dark by the time Brendan woke up. The rain had abated and was now more of a melodic patter that soothed his troubled mind; the wind moving through the trees outside with a loud murmur like an afterthought to the howling of a few hours ago. Despite the pain, Brendan was hungry and thirsty. He carefully shifted his weight in an attempt to rise from the cot, but the pain was like a bear awoken from hibernation, ferocious and relentless. He sank back down, relieved to hear someone coming.

The girl walked in carrying a wooden tray laden with a bowl, a cup of something, and a hunk of bread and set it on the trunk by the window. Aunt Joan was right behind her, her face creased with worry in the light of the candle she was carrying, her hand cupped around it to protect the flame from the draught.

"Go find your bed, Rowan," she said quietly as she pulled back the blanket to check the bandages. "I'll help him." Rowan threw a furtive glance at Brendan before she left the room, closing the door softly behind her.

Brendan was relieved that the girl had left. It was absurd to feel embarrassment in his situation, but she'd seen enough of him to last her a lifetime, since his clothes were in shreds and he was naked under the blanket. Joan was a married woman, so she wouldn't be shocked. She sat down on a stool next to the cot and set the tray on her lap, prepared to feed him like a child. Joan tore up the bread and mixed the chunks into the stew to absorb the gravy before spooning the food into his mouth and giving him an occasional sip of ale.

"No matter how much pain you're in, food always makes everything better," she observed as she set the empty bowl back down on the tray and lowered it to the floor. "Is there anything you need before I go? Don't try to get up; you'll only injure yourself further."

Brendan nodded in acquiescence, his mind on the young woman who tended to him so tenderly. "Who's the girl?"

"That's Rowan, my niece. She's my sister's child come to live with us." Joan looked uncomfortable all of a sudden, but Brendan wasn't ready to drop the subject.

"Have I done something to offend her? She wouldn't answer me."

"She doesn't answer anyone, lad; not anymore." Joan looked away for a moment, her face waxy in the feeble light of the candle.

"Why?" Brendan asked. He knew he was being overly inquisitive, but he wanted to know and Rowan herself wouldn't tell him.

"She was such a sweet, happy girl, just like my sister, before her father left to go and fight. Delwyn begged him not to take up soldiering, but he wouldn't listen. Died during the war. Fought on the side of the king, he did. Loyal through and through." Joan gave Brendan a defiant look knowing he, himself, had been a supporter of Cromwell, and went on with her story. "Rowan showed up here, about four years ago. She just stumbled into the yard, much as you did today, half-starved and frightened to death. We asked her over and over what happened, even had the reverend come and talk to her, but she just wouldn't answer. She'd lost her ability to speak. Whatever she'd seen had terrified her so badly, she just went to some place inside her head where everything was safe. All we got out of her with looks and nods was that my sister was dead and their house gone. Caleb offered to go and see if anything could be salvaged, but Rowan got into such a state that he just abandoned the idea. It seemed to comfort her, so we just let her be in the hope that someday she would come back to us."

"But she hasn't?" Brendan asked, feeling overwhelming pity for the girl. What had happened to her to cause such a breakdown?

Joan shrugged her shoulders, rising to her feet and picking up the tray. "Don't ask her any questions, Brendan. She's a good, kind girl, who needs our pity and understanding. There's nothing you can do for her other than offer her kindness."

"Please thank her for tending to my wounds," Brendan called out to Joan as she left the room.

"Thank her yourself," Joan replied. "She's mute, not deaf."

***

Brendan didn't have too long to wait to thank Rowan. She came back just as the impenetrable blackness of a stormy night was broken by the grayness of an overcast morning. The room was still lost in shadow, but he could now make out the outline of the trunk and stool and the wooden rectangle of the door. He'd tried to sleep, but the relentless pain and his even more relentless thoughts kept sleep at bay.

Rowan walked so quietly, Brendan barely realized she was there until she sat down on the stool and pulled down the blanket to check on his wounds. The cut in the arm thankfully wasn't that deep, but his thigh and his back were badly damaged and would need time to heal. Rowan nodded as if satisfied with what she saw and rose to her feet to throw open the shutters. The room filled with the milky light of predawn, the draught from the open window dispelling the smell of blood and sweat that permeated the room. Rowan sat back down and looked Brendan full in the face. That was the first time she really looked at him and there was something in her gaze he didn't understand. It's as if she was willing him to see something, to acknowledge something. Now that he was finally seeing her in the light he realized how fair she was. He couldn't quite make out the color of her hair beneath the cap, but he could see her eyes; a blue-gray, clear and wide, fringed with sooty lashes that matched her arched eyebrows, which happened to be furrowed at his lack of understanding.

"What is it, lass? What are you trying to tell me?" he asked gently, hoping he wasn't upsetting her further.

Rowan just shook her head, as if annoyed by a pesky mosquito and rose to her feet. Whatever it was, she was willing to

50

let it go for the time being. She was just about to leave when Uncle Caleb entered the room, his face grim as he took in Brendan's condition. "Run along now, Rowan, I've a mind to speak to my nephew alone." He gave the girl a warm smile to soften the dismissal and she fled from the room, leaving the two men alone.

Uncle Caleb listened carefully as Brendan described everything that happened, his face thoughtful as he stroked his beard. "Are you sure you knew the men?" he asked, doubt written across his face.

"Yes, Uncle, besides, no one except Jasper, Meg, and mother knew I'd come back or where I was headed. He sent them; they admitted as much."

"So, you're sure it wasn't your purse they were after?" Caleb asked thoughtfully.

"They were sent by Jasper," Brendan repeated.

"I just can't believe Jasper would do such a thing. He has much to gain by your death, and men have killed for less, but I just can't accept it. He was always a good lad, maybe a little too calculating for his own good, but hardly a murderer. These strange times bring out the worst in people."

"I suppose they do," agreed Brendan. All he wanted was to close his eyes and go to sleep. He was so tired; his head was swimming with fatigue and little bursts of color kept exploding behind his eyelids. He must have lost a lot of blood to feel so weakened. He fought to stay awake as Uncle Caleb put a hand on his wrist. "Brendan, if what you say is true, then you can't stay here. Jasper will find out soon enough that you got away and killed his men, and you now know that he's tried to do away with you. He'd be a fool not to try again, and next time he'll make sure he gets it right. You must leave tonight."

Brendan believed himself to be a strong man, but at that moment he wanted to cry like a babe. He'd been told to leave twice within the last twenty-four hours — a man without a home or family. He might as well have died in battle, for there was nothing left for him in this life. He had little money and no place to go. He turned his head to the wall to hide his misery from his uncle, but Uncle Caleb patted him on the shoulder to get his attention. "I know of a place you can stay. You'll be safe there until you heal. I'll take you tonight. We'll wait until midnight to leave to make sure no one is about. You just get some rest and don't fret. You'll be all right; I promise." With that, he left Brendan to rest.

The Present

Chapter 9

I trudged up the stairs and returned to what I now thought of as my room, feeling tired and annoyed. I'd seen several contractors who came out from Lincoln that afternoon, and my hopes of finding someone who understood my ideas quickly faded. The solid, middle-aged men who came by were all obsessed with modernizing the place and bringing it into the twenty-first century. They spoke of mosaic tiles, modern kitchen appliances, and jet steam showers with whirlpools. All those ideas would have been wonderful had I not wanted to actually bring the house back in time and not forward.

I reclined on the bed, allowing my mind to tour the hotel as I saw it in my dreams. The bedrooms on the second floor would be more luxurious, more expensive, but the smaller rooms on the third floor would be economy, good for single travelers or people on a budget. The first floor would have a breakfast room, a dining room for those who chose to eat at the hotel, and two lounges with fireplaces and comfortable sofas and chairs, perfect for reading or having a glass of wine before dinner. They would be elegant and inviting, filled with fresh flowers and lovely paintings.

I got so carried away with my daydream that I didn't notice the knocking right away. It was only when the knocking turned into banging that I flew off the bed and ran down the stairs to see who my first visitor might be. The man on my doorstep was young and attractive, his longish sandy hair ruffled by the breeze and falling into cornflower-blue eyes as he surveyed me, smiling at my disheveled state.

"Can I help you?" I asked, trying to regain my composure in the face of his scrutiny, but only succeeded in blushing to the roots of my hair.

"Hello there. My name is Aidan Mackay. Paula Dees sent me. She said you're looking for a contractor."

"Ah, yes," I stammered. "I am, actually. I'm Alexandra Maxwell."

"A pleasure to make your acquaintance, Miss Maxwell." I wasn't sure what surprised me more, the old-fashioned phrase coming from this young man or the Scottish burr with which it was delivered.

"Are you a Scot?" I asked unnecessarily.

"Aye, well spotted," he replied, the smile never leaving his face. "May I come in then?" I hastily backed away from the door, inviting him inside. I wasn't normally this flustered, but he unnerved me, gazing at me as if he'd never seen anyone so fascinating. It was probably a great way of getting new clients. Charm them from the get-go.

"I've always wondered what this place was like inside," he mused as he looked around, taking in the faded wallpaper and ancient furniture. "And now I know," he said, rolling his eyes in mock horror at the plastic flowers in the hearth. "So, what did you have in mind?"

"For what?" I asked stupidly.

"For the house. What would you like done? I can't give you an estimate if you don't tell me what it is you're wanting done," he explained patiently, watching me with those laughing eyes.

"Right. Did Paula tell you that I'd like to turn this place into a hotel?"

"She did, and I think it's a grand idea. The only place to stay 'round here is the pub. They let rooms on the second floor, but this area is a magnet for tourists, being so close to Lincoln, so something a bit more upscale should do very nicely. What did you have in mind?"

I liked the way he said 'very'. It sounded like 'verra' and for some reason I found that verra appealing. Most of the people I'd met in England had either a clipped, precise way of pronouncing things or a cockney-like accent that I found difficult to understand. Aidan Mackay's rounded vowels sounded more warm and natural, and surprisingly easier to comprehend.

I filled him in on my plan as we walked through the house, Aidan taking notes and measurements as we went. He seemed to understand exactly what I wanted, making helpful suggestions and shaking his head when I mentioned that I wasn't about to put TV's in the guest rooms.

"I understand that you want to recreate an eighteenth-century atmosphere, but there's not much to do here in the evenings. Your guests might get a bit bored, unless you're planning on holding poetry readings by candlelight, musical soirees, or card games that go into the wee hours as they would have during that period," he said, smiling sheepishly. "People are very attached to their gadgets these days."

"I know, but that's a risk I'm willing to take. I want this place to look and feel as authentic as possible. Some people might enjoy being disconnected for a few days."

Aidan gave me an understanding smile, but wouldn't concede his point entirely. "Well, I hope you'll at least have Wi-Fi," he suggested, moving on to the next room. "I can give up the telly for a few days, but not my phone and computer. If you force people to go cold turkey, they might just retaliate by giving you bad reviews, and bad reviews are bad for business." He had me there.

"Yes, I think I will," I replied with a grin and followed him down the stairs and out the front door. I liked the fact that he wasn't afraid to argue with me to make his point. Many people would just agree with whatever I said to get the contract, but Aidan wasn't just talking to me as a prospective contractor, he was giving me his insight into the running of a business, and that was something I appreciated. Despite my education and work experience in a major hotel, I'd never actually owned one, or made decisions that might make or break my business. It was nice to have someone to bounce ideas off.

I was surprised when instead of heading for his truck, Aidan walked around the south side of the building toward the overgrown back garden. The path was nearly impassable with weeds and brambles, and the trellis choked with ivy that had grown unchecked for years and intertwined with climbing roses which were fighting for their place in the sun. Flowers bloomed among the weeds, their brilliant colors adding a festive touch to the unkempt garden that was crying out for the loving hand of an enthusiastic gardener.

"It would be nice to put out some tables in the garden once it's been set to rights. You can serve breakfast there in the summer or tea in the afternoon. The view is wonderful, especially at sunset. You have the advantage of having this unspoiled landscape," he mused, looking out over the lush meadow that stretched toward the line of trees behind the ruin. "I bet that hill looks much as it had hundreds of years ago — no cell towers, no factories, and no council flats. Just a meadow, stream, and trees as nature intended."

"And the ruin," I added.

"The ruin is an added benefit. To some it's a tumbledown eyesore; to others, a passage to the past steeped in romance and history. Would be good if you had a story to go with it. Do you know anything of who lived there or why it went to pot?"

"No, but I intend to find out."

"Better yet, make up a tale of yer own if there's nae historical import to yon old croft. Might add a wee bit air o' mystery. Might be ye've seen a restless ghost or some fairy folk?" He said this in a thick Scottish accent that made me laugh. I had a feeling he turned on the Scots brogue for the ladies, as it was irresistible.

I nodded, pleased with the idea. I almost told him about the man I'd seen in the ruins the other day, but decided not to. He was probably long gone, having found nothing to interest him. If he were a history enthusiast, he could find far more interesting things elsewhere. I turned away from the ruin and gazed over the garden, imagining the possibilities.

Actually, Aidan was right. The slanting rays of the afternoon sun bathed the garden in a mellow, golden light, the arrow-like shafts of light piercing the canopy of ivy and striping the walk in bands of sun and shade. The mullioned windows of the upper floors were alight with the sun's reflection, making the gloomy façade appear gloriously vivid and welcoming. A lazy butterfly flitted from one rose bush to another, the exquisite fragrance filling the air with a delicate perfume. I suddenly wanted nothing more than to sit among all that overgrown profusion and have a cup of tea myself, but there was nothing to sit on, so tea would have to be in the antiquated kitchen tonight, all by my lonesome.

I followed Aidan to his truck, noticing how he scrutinized the stone path and cracked flower urns sitting atop pillars at the end of the drive. He didn't miss a thing, which was good since I hadn't given either the path or the urns another thought until that moment.

"May I call you in a few days with an estimate?" he asked as he opened the door to get in.

"Yes, definitely. I will, of course, need to get a few other estimates as well," I replied, trying to hide the eagerness in my voice. I liked this guy, and I could already see him taking on the project.

"Do you work alone?" I asked, suddenly realizing how much work would need to be done.

"I have a couple of lads who come in to do the heavy work, but I like to do the more decorative bits myself. I enjoy it," he replied, suddenly looking shy.

"I enjoy the decorative bits as well," I replied. "They are the fun part."

With that, we shook hands and I watched as Aidan Mackay drove away, leaving me in much better spirits than I was before he came. I was buzzing with ideas, and I couldn't wait to inform him that he got the job.

Chapter 10

"How're you fixed for dinner tonight?" Aidan asked once we were done with the formalities. He'd called after lunch to ask for my email address so that he could send me a detailed estimate which itemized everything that would need to be done, complete with the cost of labor and supplies. Of course, there would be many unpredictable expenses, ones he couldn't figure into the total until the men actually went to work and began to discover dry rot, termites, leaky pipes, and all the other surprises that could lead to a minefield of expenditure. I was prepared for that. "Let me take you out tonight and we can talk further about your plans. I actually have some photos I'd like to show you. I've been doing research to get some ideas. What do you say?"

What I had to say was that I was delighted. After spending a few days alone in the rambling old house I felt more than ready to spend a few hours in someone's company. The deafening silence was weighing on me and I felt lonelier than I'd ever been in my life. I'd lived alone in New York, but I was surrounded by family and friends whom I could always call if I felt like a bit of company. Here, I was completely alone; new to the village and this way of life. Of course, it would take time to meet people and make new friends, but I hadn't realized how quickly I would start to feel isolated and paranoid. I wasn't familiar with the sounds of the house, and there were several times when I'd actually crept downstairs armed with a stout stick, my heart pounding with the certain knowledge that someone was in the house. Thankfully, it was just the house sighing and creaking around me, but my sleep had become disrupted, and I kept wandering over to the window and staring at the ruins, half expecting someone to materialize out of the darkness.

I'd expected Aidan to pick me up in his truck, but he came driving up the lane in a slick red two-seater with the top down. It was the perfect night for it, and I suddenly felt young and carefree as we whizzed down the twilit road toward the village. I hadn't been into the village since signing the contract at Paula's office, so I looked around like a tourist, my head swiveling from side to side as we drove up the winding main street flanked by shops and restaurants. I had to admit that I was thrilled by the picturesque charm of my new home. I couldn't wait to explore further on my own, especially since I was running dangerously low on supplies and needed to visit the grocery store.

Aidan pulled up in front of an ancient-looking pub and switched off the engine. The ground floor was constructed of solid gray stone, crowned by a half-timbered upper story of white plaster intersected by dark wooden beams, proclaiming the pub to either be a Tudor original or a clever replica. The diamond-paned windows glowed with warm light, and the heavy wooden door swung open periodically to either admit or disgorge patrons who all seemed to be in very good spirits. The brightly painted sign swayed gently in the evening breeze and pronounced this fine establishment to be *The Queen's Head*. The sign depicted the crowned head of a rather unattractive woman with an axe buried in her blood-spurting neck. I made a face and turned to Aidan. "What a charming image. Would this be any particular queen, or just a demonstration of the local attitude toward the Monarchy?"

"That would be Anne Boleyn," he explained. "The people in these parts were staunch supporters of Katherine of Aragon, so when Anne Boleyn lost her head, it was cause for celebration, and as the sign attests, commemoration of the happy event. The Brits love their monarchs," he added in an undertone which made it clear that he didn't necessarily share the sentiment being a Scot.

"I see," I murmured as Aidan took me by the elbow and steered me through the low doorway into the dimly lit dining room of the tavern. It was exactly as I expected it to be. The dark beams crisscrossed the low ceiling which made the interior close and intimate. There was a bar area and a dining room with tables that were awfully close to each other. I couldn't help noticing that most patrons seemed to know each other, and people at neighboring tables participated in each other's conversations as if it were the most natural thing in the world. The pub was buzzing, people drinking at the bar and waiters weaving between tables with food-laden trays. A few people gaped at us as we came in, but I assumed it was because they saw a new face in a place filled mostly with locals. Well, I'd be a local soon enough, so I might as well try to fit in.

Aidan returned a few greetings and claps on the shoulder before steering me toward an unoccupied table in the corner and holding out a chair for me before taking a seat himself. An older man passed by the table and stopped for a chat, eyeing me with undisguised curiosity.

"Abe, this is Alexandra Maxwell, the new owner of the Hughes house," Aidan said by way of introduction. "Abe's the owner of the pub."

"And a pleasure it is to meet you, Alexandra," Abe said, his face split by a wide smile as he shook my hand. "About time that place came back to life. Welcome to the village."

"Please, call me Lexi," I asked, returning Abe's smile. "You too, Aidan. Alexandra is so formal."

"I hope to see you here often, Lexi," Abe said as he winked at me, "perhaps even with our Aidan."

"Stop playing matchmaker, Abe. It doesn't suit you," Aidan replied with a grin, suggesting this wasn't the first time.

"Oh, you'd be surprised at how many people I've gotten together," Abe said. "I'm a regular Fairy Godmother of Upper Whitford."

"What you are is a meddlesome old woman," Aidan replied with a chuckle. I could see that they both enjoyed this friendly banter and this was probably a running joke between them.

With that, he wished us a pleasant evening and headed for the bar. I suddenly wondered if he thought we were on a date, but dismissed the thought as I spotted Paula having a glass of wine with a group of people. She waved as if she'd just seen her best friends in the world and left her group to come and say hello.

"So, I see you've met. I'm so glad. I knew Aidan was your man as soon as you described what you had in mind. He has that flair," she said and made a gesture with her hand like the queen acknowledging her subjects on a royal parade. Paula had clearly had a few before we got there, and her business persona of a few days ago had been replaced by a good-time girl who'd be dancing on the bar in about an hour if someone didn't cut her off.

"I look forward to seeing you around," she said, slurring her words slightly. "Just stop into the office anytime you're in the village. I love a chat, especially on slow days. Well, I'll be off now. Cheers." She nearly lost her balance, but regained her foothold with a graceful pirouette and headed back toward the bar where someone must have told a joke since the crowd erupted in good-natured laughter.

"Good friends, are you?" I asked, my eyes still on Paula as she slumped against a tall man who gently took the glass out of her hand and pulled up a bar stool for her to sit on despite her protests.

"She's a good sort. Throws some work my way from time to time. I met her through my fiancée." Aidan suddenly stiffened and buried his face in the menu as if the meaning of life were printed on the laminated page. I shrugged and picked up my menu. Aidan's domestic situation was none of my business, I told myself, but a tiny worm of disappointment began to gnaw at my gut. Just like at home, the good ones were always taken.

I forgot all about Aidan's fiancée as he spread the numerous prints on the table in front of me while we waited for our food. I never thought that wainscoting or crown moldings would be so fascinating, but I was reluctant to put the pictures away as the food arrived. It smelled divine, and I suddenly realized that I hadn't had a proper meal since I left my B&B in Lincoln. I'd been living on tuna fish sandwiches and canned soup since I took up residence at the *Maxwell Arms,* as I began to refer to my future establishment.

I took a last sip of my wine and pushed away the empty plate. I was feeling mellow, pleasantly full, and bursting with anticipation. The work was about to begin, and I would truly be on my way. Luckily, Aidan had been in between jobs, so his crew would be at my house by Monday morning ready to tear the old place apart.

"So, where do we start?" I asked, eager to make some definite plans.

"We start with a Midsummer bonfire."

"Seriously? Do you do that with all your clients?" I blushed as I realized how it came out. I didn't mean to be flirtatious, but I'd had two glasses of wine and the effects were beginning to show. Next I'd be asking him what his astrological sign was. I was normally shy around men, but for some reason, tonight I felt almost giddy, and strangely comfortable in the company of this man I just met. There was something easy and unassuming about him, which made me feel as if I could be myself. Besides, this wasn't a date, so I didn't have to impress him or worry about how he would take my remarks or whether I was sending the wrong signals. We were two people discussing business. Thankfully, Aidan didn't seem to notice my playful mood and answered seriously.

"Absolutely. Normally, the village council might take issue with us burning rubbish out in the open, but on Midsummer, no one will give it a second thought." He pulled out a roll of red-dot stickers from his backpack and handed it to me. "Your first assignment. Go through the house and put a red sticker on everything you're getting rid of. I expect that will be almost everything. I'll have my lads take it out and stack on the hill behind the ruin. All that rubbish will make a fire big enough to be seen from outer space," he chuckled. "Should burn all night. Would you like to come and watch? It will be your first Midsummer celebration."

"Sure," I replied happily. It sounded like fun.

"Great. I'll bring the beer and you supply some nibbles," Aidan suggested. "We'll make a night of it." I was about to blurt out something about his fiancée joining us and making it a threesome, but bit my tongue just in time and resolved never to drink around Aidan again. He had a strange effect on me. I honestly couldn't remember the last time such suggestive comments formed in my brain, much less tumbled unbidden from my lips.

Chapter 11

It took me a moment to figure out what woke me up. The house was peaceful and silent all around me, the rumbling of thunder clearly audible over the gentle pitter-patter of rain and the rushing of the stream outside. Normally, I found these sounds soothing, but for some reason my heart was pounding as my ears strained for sounds of an intruder. I finally burrowed deeper into the covers, berating myself for being such a scaredy cat, and willing myself to go back to sleep. The room was cool, the curtains billowing like sails of a ship, and the air fragrant with the smell of rain and damp earth. I tried breathing exercises, counting sheep, and focusing on a pleasant memory, but nothing helped. I was wide awake. I peered at my watch, hoping that it was close to dawn and I could just get up and start working on Aidan's project. The roll of stickers was downstairs in the kitchen, ready to be put to good use. It would take the whole day to go through every room and mark every item. But, the clock showed 1:15, making me turn over in frustration and resort to taking a roll call of yet another herd of sheep.

By 2:00 a.m. I gave up on the sheep and rose from bed, pulling on a warm robe. In New York, I would be sweltering without air conditioning in the middle of June, but here I actually shivered with cold as my feet hit the chilly floor. I'd just go downstairs and make myself a cup of tea, and then call my mother. It'd be around 9:00 p.m. in New York, the perfect time to catch her at home. I just turned to leave the room when something caught my eye. I pulled the robe tighter around myself and walked over to the window, pulling aside the curtain to get a better look at the sodden meadow.

The landscape outside my window was completely dark, the half-moon obscured by thick clouds, and the outline of the hills just slightly darker and more solid than the murky hue of the stormy sky. But there was one pinprick of light. It flickered and nearly gutted out in the wind, but the flame came back, small and bright, dancing merrily in the inky darkness of the night. It seemed to be coming from the ruins, but I could barely see through the gathering mist. Perhaps it was my imagination playing tricks on me. I'd seen a pair of binoculars in the mud room, sitting on a shelf above the rows of Wellingtons that had belonged to the Hughes family. Maybe someone had been a birdwatcher and took the binoculars out into the woods, spending hours in wait for a rare bird, but I would use them for a vastly different purpose. I needed to either put my mind to rest, or prove to myself beyond a shadow of a doubt that someone was indeed camping out in the old ruin. I raced to the first floor and came back, bringing the binoculars up to my face.

The hair on the back of my neck seemed to stand on end as a shiver of fear ran down my spine, my hands quaking as they held the heavy binoculars. The light was coming from a second-floor window of the old ruin, the room glowing warm from what appeared to be a single candle atop a low three-legged stool. The man I'd seen earlier was sitting on a narrow cot, his back against the wall as he held a book close to his face, straining to read by the feeble light of the candle. He wasn't wearing his coat, just an old-fashioned white shirt and dark pants, his feet bare. I could just make out his boots, carelessly tossed under the bed, and a plate and cup on the small chest beneath the window. I tried to focus on his face, but his dark hair obscured his profile as he bent his head over the book, making it impossible to make out his features.

I lowered the binoculars to the windowsill, my breath coming fast and hard as I tried to understand what I had just seen. I hadn't explored the ruin, but it looked uninhabitable; what used to be the living space open to the elements and the windows just empty holes devoid of any glass or shutters. What was the man doing there, and how did he manage to stay dry? Maybe there was a piece of the roof left intact and this man, who was obviously homeless, took shelter there and made it his home.

Was he a tramp? He didn't look dirty or disheveled, and from what I could make out, he looked able-bodied and healthy.

Why didn't he have a job and a home of his own? What was his attachment to the ruin and why did he pray beneath the tree? I wasn't sure why, but I was terribly scared, alone in the middle of nowhere with just some strange man less than a hundred feet away. What if he was deranged, or violent? I suppose I would have been less intimidated had I spotted some teenagers drinking beers and telling ghost stories, but seeing a grown man calmly reading in the ruin by candlelight left me trembling with fright. I sprang into action, checking all the locks and windows to make sure he couldn't get in if he tried. I'd report him tomorrow and see what the local constable had to say.

I found that I no longer wanted tea. I climbed back into bed with my robe still on and pulled the blanket over my head, cocooning myself inside my hiding place. My heart was beating wildly as I curled into a fetal position, trying to calm myself. The man didn't look as if he were dangerous, I told myself. He was simply reading a book in the middle of the night, sitting in a tumbledown ruin, and wearing what looked like period clothes. I hadn't seen any weapons, not even a knife and fork next to the dirty dish, so maybe he wasn't armed. God, he better not be armed, I thought, squeezing my eyes shut and drawing up my knees closer to my chest.

Chapter 12

I must have dozed off eventually because when I woke up, bright sunshine was streaming through the open window, the cold wind of last night replaced by a gentle breeze that caressed my face as gently as my mother's hand. I might have stayed in bed a little longer if it wasn't for the sound of cars in the driveway, low voices of men, and the slamming of car doors. So, Aidan was here with his crew. I forced myself to get up, running a hand through my hair and tying my robe to hide my pajamas before going downstairs to open the door.

"Had a nice lie-in, love?" a burly man asked, squeezing past me into the narrow hallway. "I'll be happy to join you, you only need to ask," he quipped, winking at me as he took in my attire.

"That's enough from you, George," Aidan called out as he walked into the house followed by three other men. A warm smile lit up his face as he greeted me, discreetly taking in my disheveled appearance. "Are you all right, Lexi? Did we wake you?"

I was about to answer him when the fear from last night took hold of me once again, my eyes filling with tears and my voice shaking as I tried to tell Aidan what I saw. I thought I'd feel braver in the sobering light of day, but the bone-chilling terror I felt last night had gone deeper than I'd expected, leaving me quaking like Jell-O as I described my experience. I couldn't help but feel embarrassed as I heard my words tumbling from my mouth and saw Aidan's eyes open wider in disbelief, but there was no one else I could turn to at the moment, so I plowed on, telling him everything I'd seen until I took refuge under the covers.

Aidan didn't reply immediately, but took me by the arm and led me into the kitchen away from the curious stares of the men who weren't even pretending not to listen, their lips quaking with amusement. He pushed me into a chair, put the kettle on the stove, and set two mugs down on the table in front of me before rummaging through the nearly empty cabinets for some tea bags. He finally found some and calmly poured us some tea before taking a seat across from me and pushing the mug toward me.

"Now, have a cup of tea, calm down, and tell me again exactly what you saw last night." I was glad to see that there wasn't a glimmer of derision in his eyes; instead, he looked more concerned than amused. I couldn't have borne it if I thought he was laughing at me. I took a sip of tea as I tried to organize my thoughts, not wanting to appear foolish or frightened. Aidan listened carefully, his eyes opening a little wider once or twice during my narrative, but he remained silent, allowing me to finish my story.

"Lexi, that ruin is not fit for habitation, not even for a vagrant," he explained patiently. "There's nothing there but jagged rocks and rotted timber, and there's no second floor. There is no floor, or even stairs for that matter." He took a sip of tea, watching me intently. He must have thought I'd gone off the rails just rattling around this big, old house all by myself.

"I know what I saw," I repeated stubbornly, sticking to my guns.

"All right, I'll show you. Why don't you get dressed and we'll take a walk over there?"

I shook my head. I didn't want to go there, didn't want to see the place where the man had been. What if he were still there, lying in wait for someone to disturb him? "I don't want to go. I'll just call the police."

"All right, I'll go on my own then."

"Take one of the men with you," I suggested, but he shook his head.

"There's no one there, Lexi."

"I'm coming with you then." I wouldn't be responsible for something happening to him. I was scared, but I would go.

A quarter of an hour later we approached the ruin, the sun at our backs and our feet damp from the rain-soaked earth and morning dew. I was a little nervous about crossing the stone bridge, but despite its ancient appearance it was sturdy under our feet, built to last centuries by people who had nothing more than chisels and axes. I strained my ears for any sound that might be coming from the ruin, but all I heard was the joyous singing of birds, and the droning of bees as they went about their business of pollinating flowers and collecting nectar from the clover that grew in such profusion in the meadow.

I hung back as we stepped into the shadow of the great oak in front of the house allowing Aidan to go first. He lowered his head as he stepped through the narrow doorway, treading carefully over broken stones that littered the ground. The floor must have been made of wood once since I could still see a few rotted planks beneath the stones, but now it was mostly earth, grass and roots poking through the spaces created by fallen stones. I followed, half expecting someone to jump out at us, wielding a club, but all was silent and peaceful; the breeze moving through the open space. We could see the entire ruin as we stood by the doorway. There was nowhere to hide and as Aidan predicted, there was no one there.

I looked up at the patch of sky visible through the nonexistent roof and surveyed the walls. There was no second floor. There was nothing; just a husk of a house that must have been comfortable and spacious for its time. It had been a two-story structure with a fireplace at both ends, the blackened symmetrical chimneys poking into the summer sky. There must have been at least one room upstairs, but now there was nothing but open space and a few broken beams sticking out of the crumbling walls.

I placed my palm against the wall closest to me in the hope that I would sense something of the people who'd lived in this house, but all I felt was cold, unyielding stone. I turned and looked around. Today, a structure of this size might be used for storage or as a single-car garage, but in its heyday this house probably housed an entire family; a family whose living space consisted of one room downstairs, possibly divided by a curtain to partition off the sleeping quarters, and the loft where the children would sleep, all in the same bed. I could see remnants of a wooden table and a broken bench, but not much else. There was nothing to tell me more. There were no broken dishes or pewter candlesticks, no bits of fabric or leather, or corroded metal from tools. A few rotted beams in the corner might have been a bedstead, but it was hard to tell after centuries of wind and rain eating away at the exposed wood. The ruin was barren and desolate with no traces of habitation, ancient or modern.

"You see?" Aidan asked. "There's nothing here, no remains of a fire, no table, and certainly no bed. You must have been dreaming." He put his hand on my shoulder in a gesture of reassurance.

I just nodded in acquiescence, but I knew what I had seen. I hadn't been dreaming, and I was certainly wide awake when I saw the man kneeling by the tree a few days ago. He'd been as real as Aidan and I, so I stepped through the narrow doorway to look beneath the leafy branches in the hope that he might have dropped something or left an imprint of his knees, which was, of course, ridiculous to expect after last night's downpour. The ground beneath the tree was undisturbed. I turned back to Aidan, desperate to try one last idea.

"Is there anyone in town who matches his description?" No one could accuse me of giving up easily. Maybe he was some naturalist or bird watcher who'd spotted something in the great oak.

"Not that I know of." Aidan shrugged, turning to leave. "I haven't seen any long-haired men dressed in period clothes wandering about; I would have remembered. Maybe you've seen a ghost," he suggested with a twinkle in his eye. "I proposed that you make up a story, not actually believe it."

"I don't believe in ghosts," I answered, sounding angrier than I intended to. He must think me some hysterical female, afraid of spending a night on her own.

"Nae one does till they clap their eyes on one," Aidan countered with a smile. "The wilds of England are nae place for the faint o' heart," he said with a broad Scots accent, making me laugh. "Come now lassie, let's get yer house sorted, aye?"

I followed him meekly back to the house, but I knew what I had seen. I'd find the answers on my own, and the most likely place to start was the town, but my inquiries would have to wait. I had furniture to mark and closets to empty.

September 1650

England

Chapter 13

The storm had passed, leaving in its wake a lung-seizing freshness that made Brendan shiver under the thin blanket as he lay in the bottom of the straw-lined wagon driven by his uncle. The moon was out tonight, the clouds lit up from behind like something out of a biblical apocalypse every time they floated over its bright surface. The wind rustled in the leaves, the treetops swaying darkly against the moonlit sky, the leaves dripping as if the whole world was quietly weeping.

Rowan was sitting in the wagon next to him; her arms wrapped around her knees as she hummed softly, the tune barely audible above the cacophony of creaking wheels and the hooting of owls. *So, she isn't completely silent*, Brendan thought as he watched her in the darkness. Rowan's face was shrouded in shadows, but when the clouds momentarily parted, her face was pale as the moon itself, her eyes dark and unreadable, and her full lips tightly pressed together even as the mournful tune carried on the wind. There was something so unbearably sad about this girl, something that tugged at his heartstrings in a way no one had. Even the young women Brendan had seen in Ireland and Scotland, women who were terrified and defiant, were full of life and passion, bursting with a desire to live and love, but Rowan seemed strangely removed and as distant as the moon her face resembled.

Brendan barely registered Reverend Pole's house as his uncle helped him out of the wagon and supported him as he led him inside. Brendan's clothes had been torn and bloodied, so he wore his uncle's cast-offs, which were somewhat too short and

73

way too wide as his uncle was of middling stature with a rotund belly that bespoke of a comfortable middle age, but Brendan barely noticed. The room shifted in front of his eyes, and his knees buckled as his uncle maneuvered him to a bench. A merry fire burned in the grate, and the large room smelled of bread and stewed vegetables with a slight overtone of melting wax coming from the guttering candle on the table next to an open text and an empty plate. Reverend Pole must have been reading late into the night, too engrossed to even clean up after his evening meal. He was tall and cadaverously thin, his fine gray hair sparse and barely covering his egg-like head. A pair of intelligent eyes peered at Brendan, quickly replaced by a look of astonishment as he noticed Rowan. Reverend Pole took out three wooden cups and filled them with mead, setting one in front of Brendan and the other two before Caleb and himself. He didn't pour one for Rowan.

"I make it myself," he said proudly, nodding toward the cups. "Do try it." The mead slid easily down Brendan's throat, the potency disguised by the honeyed taste. He normally preferred wine or ale, finding mead to be sickeningly sweet, but at the moment any kind of relief was more than welcome. It didn't take long for the alcohol to enter his bloodstream, taking the edge off the pain that seemed to be devouring him from the inside. He nodded his thanks as Reverend Pole refilled his cup while listening to Uncle Caleb's account of what had happened. The reverend nodded in understanding, glancing at the ladder that led to the darkened loft.

"Aye, I think he'll be safe here," Reverend Pole muttered. "Most of my parishioners seek me out at church. I do get the occasional summons to attend the dying, but those callers hardly ever come in, not having any time to spare under the circumstances. Brendan should be comfortable in the loft, and no one will question Rowan coming more often. Everyone knows I'm getting on in years and need a bit of help around the house. It's very kind of you to help, child," he added, smiling at Rowan, an odd look on his face. She just nodded and stared at her folded hands, her face pale.

Brendan eyed the ladder leading to the loft. He balked at the thought of having to climb it with his injuries, but he had no choice, so he gulped down the last of his mead and rose to his feet unsteadily. Uncle Caleb gave him a gimlet eye, putting a hand on his shoulder to steady him. "Will you make it up there?"

Brendan just nodded, gritting his teeth as he lifted his uninjured leg to the first rung and gripped the ladder with his good arm. He had to try to put as little strain on his injuries as possible or he might not make it to the top. He gritted his teeth and climbed the ladder, acutely aware of Rowan's eyes on him as he ascended. He was in agony, but he wouldn't shame himself in front of the girl by showing weakness. He wasn't sure why that was important to him at the moment, but he chose to focus on her rather than on his pain and it helped.

The loft was fairly spacious, furnished with a narrow cot, a wooden trunk, and a three-legged stool, but it showed signs of neglect. The floor was covered with a thick layer of dust, and the straw mattress was made up with dirty linen and a stained blanket that was likely crawling with vermin. The air in the loft was close, smelling of dust motes and mouse droppings. An intricate spider web filled one corner, the spider still very much in residence as it went about its task undisturbed by humans. Rowan gestured to the stool as she disappeared down the ladder again, returning a moment later with clean bedclothes, a fresh blanket and a broom. Brendan didn't sit, but leaned against the wall with his good shoulder, and closed his eyes as a wave of vertigo nearly made him lose his balance. He was so weakened he could barely stand, but he had to wait while Rowan changed the sheets, swept away the cobwebs and quickly ran the broom over the dirty floor. Caleb helped Brendan to the cot while Rowan opened up the tiny window and threw open the shutters to let in some air.

A fresh breeze filled the loft, bringing with it the sickly sweet smell of clover and the scent of rain and damp earth. Brendan inhaled deeply and allowed his eyes to close. He felt as if something was dragging him under and he could no longer fight its power. He was sinking, the dark waters closing over his head as he fought to stay conscious, but he lost the battle, his body going slack as he succumbed to the enveloping blackness. He had no recollection of Uncle Caleb and Rowan removing his clothes, or of Rowan tenderly tucking the blanket around him and brushing the hair out of his face, before making the sign of the cross over him in silent benediction and following her uncle from the loft to collect the items she'd brought with her.

Rowan would stay at Reverend Pole's this night to keep an eye on Brendan. She was surprised that he could even walk or climb the ladder given the amount of blood he must have lost, but he was young and strong; a weaker man would have succumbed to his injuries by now. Rowan drew in a ragged breath at the very thought of it. She would do everything in her power to heal Brendan. She wouldn't let him die.

Chapter 14

Rowan dipped her fingers into the salve, her eyes never leaving Brendan's wound. Thankfully, the gash in his back wasn't as deep as the ones in his thigh and upper arm, but it was long and dissected his back nearly in half, making it appear flayed. She would bind it tomorrow, but for now, she would just put the ointment on it and leave it open to the fresh air, just as her mam had taught her. One good thing about a sword wound is that at least it was a clean cut as opposed to the torn and jagged flesh as might be left by a boar tusk.

Rowan gently applied the salve, relieved to see that she wasn't causing Brendan any pain. He was off his head with the mead Reverend Pole had given him, his eyes closed and his lashes fanned against the lean cheek. Good, he needed to rest after what he'd been through, and she would add some tincture of the poppy to his next drink to help him sleep some more. Her mam always said that sleep helped to regenerate blood. Pain from one wound was enough to addle a man's brain, but Brendan was badly hurt in three places, so he must be in unbearable agony when awake.

The skin around the wound felt hot to the touch and slightly puckered, but the salve should soothe and heal, and hopefully prevent any festering. Rowan wiped her fingers on her apron and set down the bowl before gently covering Brendan with the blanket up to the waist. If she pulled it up higher, the fabric would stick to the salve and have to be ripped off come morning. He'd be cold tonight, but that couldn't be helped.

Rowan reached out and touched his cheek. Thankfully, it was cool to the touch, so no fever then — not yet. She watched for a moment as Brendan's eyes moved rapidly behind the eyelids, his hands curling into fists, his body tense. No doubt his mind was replaying whatever happened to him, as her mind still did whenever she was at rest. She'd never made the decision to stop speaking, but when she finally stumbled into her uncle's arms on that day four years ago, she simply couldn't bring herself to tell him what happened. The words had stuck in her throat, threatening to choke her unless she forced them back down, into some dark corner where they couldn't hurt her anymore. After all, words had the power to kill, to rob you of those you loved, to destroy. For weeks after she'd come, her aunt and uncle, and even Reverend Pole kept asking her what happened, needed her to explain, but every time she opened her mouth to speak, nothing would come out except hot, bitter tears that flowed down her cheeks and onto her hands as she covered her face in a useless attempt to try to block the memories. Only Reverend Pole had been able to guess at part of the truth, but he kept it to himself, realizing that to speak of it to others would cause Rowan more pain. She wouldn't be able to bear the questions or the pitying looks that would come, followed by suspicion and malicious remarks which might cause history to repeat itself.

Eventually, everyone gave up and left her alone. They addressed her less and less frequently, and after some time she became a shadow who lived in Caleb and Joan Frain's house, someone who wasn't quite there, not in the way other people were. The people in the village went from giving her curious stares to just shaking their heads in dismay, wondering how a perfectly normal girl could have gone soft in the head, as they thought of her. After a time, they stopped seeing her as well, treating her as a piece of furniture or a tree on the side of the road. She thought she'd mind, but she didn't. It made her feel safe. If people didn't truly see you, they wouldn't hurt you.

But Rowan wanted Brendan to see her. There'd been no spark of recognition when he saw her at the house, but he had been so weak from loss of blood that he likely wouldn't have recognized his own mother. Would he remember her? She remembered him. He was one of the few good memories she kept in her heart, one of the memories from the past she allowed herself to relive whenever she felt despair threaten to engulf her; a memory of a time when everything in her life was happy and safe, and tragedy was something that happened to others.

It'd be about six years now since she'd seen him. He was a lad of seventeen then, but she'd been only twelve, excited beyond words to travel to her uncle's village for the wedding of her cousin. How she'd envied Maisie then. Was there anything more wonderful and romantic than to stand before the reverend with your loved one and pledge eternal love as you were joined in matrimony, to live in God's blessed sight for the rest of your lives? Rowan had been breathless with wonder as she watched Maisie get ready for the wedding; Maisie's cheeks stained with a rosy blush as her mother explained what was expected of her on her wedding night.

They hadn't known Rowan was there, hiding behind the chest, or her aunt wouldn't have spoken so plainly, but Rowan had been shocked to the core to learn the secrets of the marriage bed. No wonder no one ever spoke of such things. It would be terribly wicked, if it wasn't sanctioned by God and the Church. She'd thought about it long after the wedding as she lay in her bed at night, wondering what it must be like to allow a man to do those things to you. It had seemed utterly disgusting to her until she saw Brendan at the church. His family had been late getting to the service due to the muddy roads caused by the endless rain of the past few days. Luckily for Maisie, the sun had come out on her special day, painting the sky in bands of pink and gold, and making everyone suddenly much less sullen and angry, eager to enjoy the lovely day and the party to follow.

Brendan had come with his parents, younger brother, and sister, Meg. Meg was so pretty, with her raven hair flowing down her back and that wide smile that had all the lads asking her for a dance back at the house, but Meg was already betrothed to a man named Rob Garrow, who'd come with the family. He was stocky and tall, his jaw covered by a golden stubble that matched the fair hair on his head, and Meg had eyes only for him. They'd be wed after the harvest, but Rowan's mam said they would not attend the wedding. It was too far to travel for someone who wasn't even kin. Rowan would have loved to see Meg get married, if only for another glimpse of her handsome brother. She didn't like Jasper though. He was a good-looking boy of around fourteen, but he had a cruel set to his mouth and looked around with derision, as if searching for something to mock.

Jasper's eyes swept over the congregation before they settled on her and narrowed in speculation. He didn't smile or give her a polite bow; instead, he just watched her with his head cocked to the side, his eyes boring into her in a way that bordered on insolence. Rowan looked away, feeling suddenly self-conscious and uncomfortable. She inched closer to her mother whose attention was wholly on the couple in front of the altar. Her mother always cried at weddings, but not at funerals, something that Rowan found rather odd, but then her mam wasn't much like the other women she knew. Her mam was beautiful and special, a woman who had secret knowledge that she shared with only those she loved.

After the service was finally over, everyone walked back to Uncle Caleb's farm for the wedding party. Long tables were set up outside, and several women from the village were already hard at work, bringing out pies, platters of roasted meat, vegetables, and loaves of freshly baked bread. There were several barrels of beer, and even a keg of whiskey. The adults were talking loudly as they took their seats, hungry after church and eager to enjoy such a feast.

Rowan licked the grease from the pie from her fingers, enjoying the smoky flavor of the meat filling that clung to her hands. She'd like to have eaten more, but she was full to the bursting and tired of sitting for such a long time. The adults were all talking and laughing, the men making veiled suggestions about the coming wedding night. Rowan didn't understand what they meant, but judging by the sly looks at the bride, and the merriment the comments caused, it must have been something shameful. She slid off the bench and headed for the outbuildings. It would be nice to have a few moments to rest before the bonfire was lit and the dancing began in earnest. The party would go well into the night, and she meant to enjoy it. Normally, she went to bed once it got dark, but today she was allowed to stay up as long as she wanted, and she planned to take full advantage of such a promise.

Rowan walked into the barn and sat down on a bale of hay, leaning her head against the rough wooden planks of the wall. It was nice and quiet, the animals chewing their cud and shifting restlessly in the stalls, as if somehow aware of all the gaiety going on not too far away. She supposed they could sense that today was different, or maybe they couldn't. She always attributed human emotions to animals, something her mother found to be endearing.

She must have dozed off because she woke up with a start, a shadow looming over her in the dim light of the barn. Jasper Carr stood in the doorway, his large frame blocking out most of the light. He was big for a boy his age, tall and broad. He gave her a charming smile as he advanced slowly toward her.

"Rowan, is it?" he asked. Rowan nodded, suddenly feeling trapped. He wasn't doing anything to frighten her, but she felt an overwhelming need to get out of the barn and into the summer sunshine. She got to her feet and brushed the straw off her skirt as she took a tentative step toward the door, but Jasper blocked her exit. He moved quicker than she expected, and she felt the first twinges of fear as she tried to get around him.

"Wait! Where are you running off to in such a hurry? I only wanted to sit with you awhile." He was smiling, but the smile didn't reach his eyes, which frightened Rowan all the more. Her mother always said that the eyes were a window to the soul, and Jasper's gaze was hard and threatening.

"My mam will be looking for me," Rowan mumbled as she tried again to get around Jasper's bulky frame. He reached out and caught her, dragging her against him like a sack of flour. He smelled of beer and Rowan wondered how much he'd drunk.

"Your mam is too busy having a good time to be looking for you," he breathed, his face moving closer to hers. "How about I teach you a game? Would you like that?"

Rowan shook her head vehemently. "No, I don't want to play a game. I just want to go back to the party."

"What a silly little girl you are," Jasper said, pulling her closer until she felt his breath on her face. She instinctively tried to back away, but Jasper's arms were like bands of steel around her. "If you don't learn how to make a man happy, no one will ever want you. You'll be an old, dried-up spinster." He laughed without humor and suddenly cupped her breast. It was too small to fill his hand, but he didn't seem to mind, squeezing it and rubbing his thumb over her nipple through the fabric. Rowan tried to pull away, but Jasper just laughed, pushing her against the wall and sliding a hand under her skirt. "Shall I show you what else men like?"

Terrified, she struggled against him, but he was too big for her to even budge. He was enjoying the game, releasing her for a moment and then grabbing her even harder. Most likely he hadn't come upon her by accident, but followed her from the main house. He'd had this in mind all along, ever since he spotted her in the church. Hot, angry tears began to flow down Rowan's cheeks. She was still too innocent to understand what Jasper could do to her, but the feeling of helplessness that engulfed her was frightening, making her realize that someone could exercise power over her against her will and she could do nothing to stop it.

"Let me go," she begged, but Jasper just chuckled and tried to pull down her bodice. Rowan was about to scream when Jasper beat her to it. He let out an angry bellow as he was practically lifted off his feet and tossed against the wall by his brother.

"Get out!" Brendan roared. Rowan expected Jasper to put up a fight, but he just looked at his brother with contempt.

"I was only having a bit of fun. I wouldn't have hurt her," he said, clearly trying to appease Brendan. It seemed that Jasper actually looked up to him and wanted his forgiveness, but it wasn't to be given.

"Get out," Brendan repeated, quieter this time.

"She's ugly anyway," Jasper sniggered as he got to his feet. "Ugly, and flat as a wooden plank. No man will ever want her, unless he's blind." Jasper spit at Rowan's feet and stumbled from the barn, but not before he gave his brother a mighty shove. Brendan didn't budge or spare Jasper a glance.

"Are you all right?" He'd taken her by the shoulders and looked into her eyes, his gaze so different from his brother's. His eyes were kind, and an understanding smile played about his lips as he watched her dissolve in tears. She was so ashamed and stung by what Jasper had said about her.

"Did he hurt you?" Brendan gazed into her eyes, his face full of kindness and sympathy, which made her feel even worse.

Rowan just shook her head. She'd already forgotten about Jasper's clumsy advances, but the words rankled. Was she really ugly? What if he was right and no man would want her when the time came? There were two women in their village who never married, and everyone always felt sorry for them, saying they'd been unlucky in life and a burden to their families. Was that to be her fate?

Rowan was distracted by the sound of the violin as old Mr. Graham tuned his fiddle in preparation for the dancing. She loved to dance, but at the moment she wanted to just go off somewhere and be alone. Who'd want to dance with her? She was so preoccupied with her thoughts that she barely noticed Brendan studying her, a slow smile spreading across his face.

"You know, I have a mind to dance. Would you do me the honor? I wager dancing with the prettiest girl will make all the other lasses take notice of me." He was grinning at her, and Rowan thought that all the girls at the party already took notice of him and were probably scheming to get his attention and an invitation to dance, and here he was, asking her. Brendan held out his hand to her and Rowan took it, enjoying the feel of his large hand closing around hers and making her feel safe and wanted. She followed him back to the yard, her heart thumping in time to the music. Maybe he was just feeling sorry for her, but she didn't care. She certainly wasn't the prettiest girl, but he was the handsomest lad, and right now she was the happiest girl in the world.

The Present

Chapter 15

The last hint of fuchsia faded from the summer sky as darkness finally settled on the meadow, thousands of stars shimmering in the clear velvety sky. A half-moon that looked like a slice of a juicy apple hung just above the treetops as it slowly began to ascend into the starlit expanse above us.

I stared into the leaping flames, mesmerized by the orange and crimson tongues that darted between the bits of wood, licking, caressing, and ultimately devouring everything in its path. The wood crackled, sending a shower of sparks into the night and making my face feel suddenly hot. Only a half hour ago, I could still make out the shape of tables and dressers that Aidan's men had dragged to the hill, but now the individual pieces were indistinguishable from one another in the pyre. I'd spent the better part of the day administering red stickers, and now the house looked strangely empty after room after room had been cleaned out entirely. I did come across a few nice pieces which I decided to keep, but most of the late Mrs. Hughes's possessions were consigned to the flames.

I could see the dark outline of the house against the navy-blue sky, the twin peaks of the pitched roof solid and symmetrical in their beauty; the numerous windows currently dark, the square panes of glass reflecting nothing but the nighttime sky. I'd run out to the shops while the furniture was being removed to get something for our bonfire picnic. It was my first solo foray into the village, and I walked up the street, looking at storefronts which were already closed for the night. Thankfully, the grocery store was still open, so I ducked in, grabbed a shopping basket and quickly tossed in some bread, cheese, ham, fruit, and some breakfast essentials. My next project was to clean the old stove and start cooking for myself. I couldn't live on canned food for long.

The woman at the counter cast curious looks my way as I made my way down the narrow isle and finally arrived at the cash register with my shopping, tossing in a couple of bags of chips that were prominently displayed by the counter. How could I have forgotten chips?

"Will that be all, dear?" she asked in sugary tones. "Always a pleasure to see a new face hereabouts. I always tell my husband, "There's not a single person I don't know for miles around. I never forget a name or a face. Never."

The woman was close to sixty, with wiry gray hair and a spherical shape that was displayed in all its rotund fullness by a sweater set in an unfortunate shade of canary yellow, paired up with a skirt of brown and beige plaid. Her dark eyes were lively as a young girl's and nearly devoured me with undisguised curiosity. Her gaze travelled from my pony-tailed hair, over my face, down to my lime-green V-neck top and my jeans and flats, snapping back up to my face as I answered.

"Yes, for now." I normally enjoyed talking to people, but this woman was appraising me as if I were a brood mare, no doubt collecting vital details to be shared with other patrons about the newcomer to their village. She was likely the village's premier gossip, so being rude was not a good idea. It would just feed into the notion that all Americans were ill-mannered. I smiled brightly and introduced myself.

"I'm Lexi Maxwell," I ventured. "I just bought the old Hughes place."

"Don't I know it?!" she exclaimed. "Such a shame that no one wanted the house after Eleanor died. But, it couldn't have turned out better, could it?" she said cryptically.

"In what way?" I asked, confused.

"Well, it's been in the family for generations." She made this statement as if she were telling me something obvious, but I had no idea what she meant.

"And you have Aidan MacKay doing the work, I hear? Recommended by Paula Dees?" she asked with a look of naked disapproval. "Thick as thieves, they are, but he does good work, or so I'm told. Frankly, I have my doubts about him. He's a Scot, a Highlander, and you know how they are." She gave me a meaningful look, but I really had no idea how Scots were. Did she expect him to charge down the hill wild and barefoot, waving a sword and shrieking, his face painted blue with woad? Or were those Picts? Clearly I had my barbarians confused, but I wasn't about to share that fact with the erstwhile shopkeeper. I could only imagine what she'd make of Aidan and I having a Midsummer Bonfire, but I wasn't about to enlighten her.

"Ah, thank you," I mumbled as I grabbed my shopping and stowed it in the canvas bag I'd brought along. I had to dash if I were to make sandwiches before sunset.

"It's Mildred Higgins, dear," the woman called after me as I left the store. *Mildred Higgins*, I thought, *a perfect name for a busybody.*

***

I handed Aidan another sandwich and watched him swallow it in two bites. He'd been quiet for the past few minutes, just staring into the flames clearly as mesmerized as I was, the pyre reflected in his clear blue eyes. *No sign of the wild Highlander*, I thought, as I took in his pensive expression.

"Are many people lighting bonfires tonight?" I asked, less because I wanted to know and more because I wanted to draw him into conversation.

"There are some. Mostly young people. They don't really care about tradition, just like the romance of a roaring fire on a summer's night. It's still celebrated in Cornwall and Wales, and of course, Scotland where they also light fires on Beltane to celebrate the beginning of summer."

"So, it's a Pagan tradition then?"

"It used to be a celebration of the summer solstice, but the Church decided to appropriate it, as it did the winter solstice and turned it into Christmas. They made June 23rd St. John's Eve, since supposedly John the Baptist was born on June 24th. It used to be a time of merriment and feasting, but the Church wasn't pleased with the pagan elements of the celebrations and demanded that June 23rd should be a day of fasting instead. They sure know how to ruin a good time, don't they?" he said with a grin.

"So, not a churchgoer then?" I quipped, hoping he'd tell me more about himself.

"Well, I come from a long line of sour-faced Scottish Presbyterians, but I like the old ways when people were less concerned with religious dogma and more in tune with the world around them. I guess I'm a Pagan at heart. What about you?"

"Lapsed Catholic. I haven't been to church since my confirmation."

To be honest, the last thing I wanted to do was discuss religion. I was curious about his fiancée and why he hadn't brought her to the bonfire, but it seemed too forward to ask. Our relationship, technically speaking, was a business one, and although sitting here with him felt more like spending time with a friend, I was loathe to be the one to cross the line, but I hoped he would.

"So, why England?" Aidan asked as he took a sip of his beer and reached for another sandwich.

"I wish I could explain it, but it's something I've wanted since I was little. I used to draw all these pictures of a house that looked much like this one with a river behind it, telling my parents that's where I wanted to live. In my imagination, it was always in England. It used to drive my father mad. He didn't like England for some reason. One year for Father's Day, I gave him a drawing of him, Mom, and myself in front of a house flying a Union Jack. Let's just say he didn't put it up on the fridge."

"Do you have British ancestry?"

"No. My father's family settled in New York in 1842. They'd survived the Potato Famine in Ireland, and left as soon as they could manage to pay for their passage, only to lose two of their children during the crossing. Their name was McCormack, but they changed it to Maxwell, thinking it would help them avoid prejudice directed at the Irish in those days. But the name change hadn't really helped. You can take a man out of Ireland, but you can't take Ireland out of the man just by changing a name. They struggled for many years, living in some tenement on the Lower East Side. I believe it was called Five Points then. It was a brutal place, run by brutal people. Few families survived intact. If it wasn't the disease that got them, it was the crime."

My father liked to tell the story of his family, painting a vivid picture of life in Five Points and the hardships the McCormacks endured. It took two generations for them to finally leave and move to Queens where they lived still.

"My father often spoke of the plight of my ancestors, which made him all the more proud that his own father, having come back from fighting in Europe after WWII, pulled himself up by his bootstraps and started Maxwell Paper Products, which he bequeathed to my father, who hoped, despite all my protests, that I would take over the company when he retired."

"Does he still think you will?" Aidan asked, his eyes straying to the dark outline of the house down the hill.

"My father died of a heart attack nearly a year ago, and I sold the company soon after. He would have been heartbroken, but I just couldn't bring myself to devote my life to selling boxes and file folders. I felt a crushing guilt, but that just wasn't my dream."

"Well, we all have our dreams, don't we? My own father is actually a doctor, but my granddad had been a carpenter, so I probably take more after him. I like to work with my hands. There's nothing like the feeling of satisfaction when you see the direct result of your work," he said, as if feeling the need to explain why he chose to forsake his university education and do something else.

"I know a few famous carpenters who left a mark on the world," I replied with a smile.

"Are you comparing me to Jesus?" he asked in mock horror.

"I wouldn't dare," I giggled. "I was simply making a point."

"And what of your mother?" Aidan asked. It pleased me that he wanted to hear about my family. It wasn't often that people took a real interest, and I could tell that he genuinely wanted to know and wasn't asking simply to pass the time.

"My mother's family is originally from Italy. They came over after the war. My grandfather had been a Communist for about five minutes, but my grandmother knocked that out of him pretty quick, or so the story goes. She said he had to turn in his party membership if he expected her to marry him, since she wasn't about to marry some penniless upstart. They opened a salumeria in Brooklyn, selling the finest sausage and cheese anyone had ever tasted, or so my grandfather claimed. He loved telling tall tales. My grandmother took to the new country like a fish to water, but my grandpa always pined for the old world."

"And do you pine for home?" Aidan asked. "Was it easy to leave?"

I assumed he was asking whether I left someone special behind, but the answer to that was a resounding no. I had been single for some time, my last relationship having ended when after three years of dating, Greg informed me that he wasn't sure he loved me and needed to sow his wild oats before he could even consider settling down and starting a family. Truthfully, once I got over the hurt of the rejection, I realized that maybe I hadn't loved him either, and just talked myself into staying because of the comfort and security the relationship provided. In retrospect, I'd never felt any great passion for Greg or the few men I dated before him. Sex was something that was expected and given, but it never made me feel as my friends seemed to feel. My best friend Sarah always seemed to be in a state of slow burn, something which men responded to like moths to a flame, but although I felt a degree of passion during the lovemaking, I never felt the all-consuming desire that seemed to rule Sarah's life. There was no urgency and no overwhelming need to feel Greg's touch or feel his lips on my own. I secretly worried that there was something wrong with me, but Sarah said that I just hadn't met the right man.

"Sex is not cerebral, Lexi. It's pure animal instinct between two people, fanned by attraction and affection. Greg is a nice guy, but deep down, you were indifferent to him and ultimately, that's what drove him away. You didn't hunger for him the way he did for you, and on some primal level, he knew that." I nearly burst into tears as Sarah laid it out for me like that. What if I never felt that way about anyone? Sarah seemed to feel animal attraction with just about every guy she met, and there I was, Miss Prim and Proper, talking myself into liking someone and ordering my body to comply. I could never admit it to Sarah, but I'd never experienced an orgasm, and once Greg even called me 'frigid' in a fit of frustration.

Sarah said that love was like an insatiable hunger. You were never sated for long, always wanting more, needing more. It made you feel alive and rejuvenated the colors brighter and the perceptions more acute — the lifeblood that kept you from becoming old and hard. I had yet to feel anything like that, and I secretly prayed that I had the emotional capacity to experience even a fraction of what Sarah seemed to take so for granted.

"Lexi?" Aidan was watching me, clearly perplexed by the emotions that flitted across my face as I considered his question. No, it wasn't easy to leave, but not because I left a love behind. It was hard because I tore myself up by the roots, but sadly, my roots didn't grow very deep because my soul was always searching for a place to call home.

"It wasn't easy to leave. I miss my mom and my friend Sarah, but we talk on the phone daily, and email and text, so I don't feel as lonely. I wish they were here though, but I'm a big girl and it's time I followed my star. "Be the leading lady in the story of your life," that's what Sarah always says."

Aidan leaned back on his elbows and gave an approving nod. "I like that philosophy. I think too many people just kind of muddle through, never taking charge of their lives and simply reacting to whatever comes their way. Well, I'd say that selling your father's company and moving halfway around the world to pursue your dream certainly puts you center-stage. Is there anyone else in your play or is this a one-woman show?"

"That remains to be seen," I replied, hoping that wasn't the case. "And what about you, Aidan? What brought you here?" I felt a little shy about asking, but he didn't seem put off by the question.

"This is where my fiancée's family is from. I met her at St. Andrew's University where she was working toward her degree in Finance and I was doing a course in Art History. She wanted to return home after graduation, so I followed. My parents weren't too pleased with me leaving Scotland since I'm their only child. Our family has lived on Skye for roughly two hundred years, and before that, they lived in the north, but were driven out by the clearances that took place in the nineteenth century. As a matter of fact, some of my ancestors fought in the Jacobite Uprising of '45. My parents regarded my move to England as the act of an unpatriotic traitor, but I was in love, and Scottish independence didn't figure into that."

Aidan stared into the flames, a closed expression on his face. I knew I shouldn't pry, but I couldn't contain my curiosity. Wouldn't his fiancée have something to say about him spending the night with me by a bonfire, or was she so secure in his love that she didn't see me as a threat? I don't suppose many women would. I'd never thought of myself as anything special, although there'd been a few boyfriends who told me I was beautiful. I never really believed them though.

"So, why didn't you invite her tonight? Or doesn't she like Pagan rituals?"

Aidan never looked away from the fire, but I could see that he resented the question by the tensing of his shoulders and the way his jaw worked beneath the day-old stubble. "We're no longer together, her and I. She lives in London now, or so I heard from her mother the last time I ran into her in the village. She also informed me that Noelle is happily seeing someone who not only has family money, but a title that can be found in Burke's Peerage."

I would have liked to ask why he chose to stay on in Upper Whitford, but this wasn't the right time. Clearly he was still upset about the breakup. Either way, it was none of my affair. Aidan had retreated into silence, so I just stared into the flames, suddenly feeling lonely again.

Chapter 16

Aidan stared into the leaping flames, suddenly ashamed of himself for his little outburst of self-pity. He'd sounded so bitter and resentful. And now Lexi was sitting there, enveloped in silence, the shifting shadows cast by the fire playing over her lovely face and reflecting in her eyes, which were averted from him. She'd been full of good humor only a few minutes ago, but now she seemed pensive, lost in her own thoughts and maybe recalling her own bad breakup that might have led to her desire to flee New York and start a new life in England. He hadn't meant to let his resentment show, but his response to Lexi's question took him by surprise. He thought he was doing well, but the bitterness that crept into his voice as he spoke of Noelle reminded him that somewhere deep inside he was still hurting.

Aidan wanted to recapture the easy camaraderie of a few moments ago, but suddenly had no idea what to say. He felt foolish in the extreme, and Lexi seemed put off by his change in mood. He didn't want to think of Noelle; didn't want to remember. He'd spent enough time agonizing and second-guessing, wondering if he'd missed any of the signs or sent the wrong signals, but the end result was still the same, and it was time to move on. He thought he was.

If Aidan were honest, the whole idea of the bonfire was a bit of a ploy to get to know Lexi better. Naturally, he would not have suggested it had his clients been a middle-aged couple or an elderly woman, but Lexi was young and beautiful, and spending a few hours with her in front of a roaring fire under a blanket of stars seemed like a good idea. In truth, he'd been awfully lonely of late, and there was something about this girl that made a tiny crack in the armor he'd worn since ending his engagement. She had a warmth and an openness that appealed to him, and that American way of just saying what she meant without coating it in layers of hidden meaning. He'd had a hard time keeping a straight face at the pub when she blurted out a few suggestive comments without intending to, then watched her blush in embarrassment as she realized how they must have sounded. It would be fun to get her into that kind of mood again.

"Would you like another beer?" he asked, but Lexi just shook her head, her eyes never leaving the pyre. She didn't seem inclined to talk, so he just sat there, silently cursing himself for the fool that he was and an opportunity missed.

Aidan barely noticed when Lexi's eyes seemed to grow heavy and she curled up on her side, still watching the flames as she drifted off to sleep beside him. He pulled a blanket out of his backpack and wrapped it around Lexi, tenderly brushing away a lock of hair that fell into her face. She looked so childlike in sleep, her lips stretched into an enigmatic smile brought on by a pleasant dream.

He couldn't help but be curious about her. Why would a young woman leave her family and friends to come to a small village in England? Surely there were plenty of places in the U.S. where one could open up a Bed and Breakfast. Why here? Aidan had lived in these kinds of rural settings all his life, but he couldn't imagine going from the thrumming pulse of New York to a sleepy little village, where the most exciting thing was watching cricket at the pub with a few mates or finding out through the extensive gossip network that someone was having an affair. Would she get bored once the work was complete? Maybe she'd get restless and leave this place to return to a life she was accustomed to.

The thought of Lexi leaving made Aidan suddenly sad. She was a breath of fresh air who'd reminded him that what he'd been doing for the past year wasn't living, but just going through the motions in the hope that his emotions wouldn't get the better of him and stay safely buried where he'd stashed them. But tonight's conversation showed that they weren't buried at all, and that Lexi had the power to unsettle him. And that maybe it was time he put Noelle firmly behind him and allow himself to rejoin the living.

Chapter 17

Aidan wasn't sure if it was the trilling of birds, the sun in his eyes, or the dampness on his cheek that woke him up, but he held up his hand to block the sun before opening his eyes and was instantly aware of Lexi curled up against him, her back pressed against his chest and the curve of her lovely butt right up against his pelvis. Aidan's arm had been protectively curled around Lexi's waist, and the smell of her hair was still in his nostrils as he carefully sat up so as not to wake her.

He'd meant to wake her last night, but she was sleeping so peacefully that he snuggled under the blanket next to her and went to sleep, not wanting to leave her alone on the hillside. Aidan was still tired, especially after having drunk at least three beers last night, but he needed to get home, shower, change, and get to the bank where he had an appointment in exactly one hour.

He glanced over at Lexi's relaxed face. The bonfire had burnt itself out, tiny spirals of smoke still curling and dissipating in the morning air which was tinged with the acrid smell of ash. A few charred sticks and pieces of metal remained in the circle of blackened grass — all that remained of furniture, rugs and moth-eaten velvet drapes. Things took so long to make, but were so quickly destroyed, just as in life. Thinking of destruction brought him back to Noelle. Speaking of her after all this time was almost cathartic, the floodgates of memory and emotion sweeping over Aidan as he pressed his palms against his eyes in an effort to block her out.

It'd been almost a year since she left, but the pain was still there, a dull ache that kept reminding him that he wasn't quite over what happened. Had it been another man, he might have been able to move on. Hurt would have turned to anger, and anger would eventually become acceptance and indifference. But there'd been no other man, at least as far as he knew. What Noelle had done haunted him, especially since he'd had warning. Funny that his father should have seen it long before he had. Angus Mackay had Noelle pegged years ago when they visited Skye the spring before graduation. Aidan had been besotted; a ring already picked out and a romantic proposal in the works, but Angus had reservations, which angered Aidan. Why couldn't his father see how special she was, how smart, beautiful, and loving? But Angus Mackay wasn't one to mince words, especially not with his only son.

"It's not love I see in her eyes, son," Angus said as they sat in his father's boat with their fishing poles one chilly morning. Noelle had decided to have a lie-in and then help his mother with lunch, which would center around the catch of the day.

"No? So what do you see, Da?" Aidan had asked, rankled by his father's comment. He felt himself stiffen, his eyes gazing out over the still waters sparkling with the blood-red reflection of the rising sun. The water lapped at the sides of the boat, the gentle rolling leaving father and son in a state of peaceful drowsiness. Aidan wanted to enjoy this time with his father and not engage in a discussion that would leave him feeling defensive and angry, but his father wanted to have his say, and when Angus made up his mind to something he wouldn't be deterred.

"I see ambition. You will never be her priority, Aidan; not in the way she's yours."

"You're wrong, Da. She loves me. As a matter of fact, I'm going to marry her," Aidan added, sounding like a petulant little boy who wanted to spite his father. Had he been twenty years younger he probably would have stuck out his tongue, a fact that wasn't lost on him. He wanted to be treated as an adult and not a child, but his father made him feel even worse by looking at him as if he were about to commit the biggest mistake of his life.

"Well, son, I can't stop you, but I can warn you," his father had replied, and warn him he had. How right Angus Mackay had been in his assessment of Noelle. Aidan had known that Noelle had aspirations beyond living in a small village and working in a bank in Lincoln, but he'd had no idea how her ambition would destroy his life.

He hadn't meant to turn gruff when Lexi asked, but he'd managed to keep the reason for their breakup a secret, which was no easy thing to do in a small village. What happened had been so deeply personal that he didn't tell a soul, not even his parents. He simply told them that they'd grown apart and decided they wanted different things. Well, that was true on some level, but no one ever knew the depth of Noelle's betrayal.

Aidan sighed, disgusted with himself for being so maudlin so early in the morning. It was time to get going if he was to make it to the bank on time. He gently traced the curve of Lexi's cheek with his finger and watched her eyelids flutter open, her expression going from one of confusion to surprise and then to embarrassment. She instantly scooted away from Aidan, quickly realizing that she'd been sleeping in his arms for the past few hours.

"I have to get going," Aidan said, rising to his feet and giving Lexi his hand to help her up. "I have an appointment at the bank this morning regarding my business loan." He wasn't sure why he was telling her that, but it seemed rude to just run off without a good reason.

"Oh, of course. Thank you for the bonfire. That was fun. My first Midsummer celebration," she said, shielding her eyes from the brightness of the sun. "Well, I'll see you later then."

"Yes, you will. The lads will be there at nine to start stripping the wallpaper," he added as he began walking down the hill. He felt a bit foolish, but a sudden smile spread across his face. This was the closest he'd come in over a year to sleeping with a woman — it was a start.

Chapter 18

I ambled down the hill, eager for a hot shower and a cup of coffee with some toast. My eyes felt as if they were dusted with sand and my mind was in a fog, as if I'd taken too much cold medicine. I must admit that I was a little confused by Aidan's behavior. There were moments when he was friendly and flirtatious, but those moments were usually followed by a swift withdrawal and forced formality. He'd been the one to invite me to dinner and to the bonfire, but he seemed uncomfortable when the conversation became too personal. I suppose I took his actions for overtures of friendship, but maybe he was just being polite; although, I found it hard to believe that he would be making Midsummer bonfires with all his clients or sleeping with them on the hillside snuggled under one blanket. Maybe we just had our signals crossed, and the best thing under the circumstances would be to tread carefully until I got to know him better.

I was just about to put Aidan firmly from my mind when I saw a woman sitting on the steps of the house and anxiously glancing at her watch. I was sure I hadn't made any appointments with anyone, but I began walking faster all the same, loathe to keep her waiting. The woman sprang to her feet as I approached, dusting off her tweed skirt and smiling brightly. She was dressed conservatively, but her modern shoulder-length bob and a colorful scarf gave her a stylish appearance, which made me wonder all the more what she was doing on my doorstep.

"Good morning," she called out as I approached.

"Good morning." I smiled at her, waiting for her to state the purpose of her visit. She seemed suddenly embarrassed, looking somewhere behind my shoulder.

"Eh, my name is Dorothea Martin. I used to do for old Mrs. Hughes." She looked at me expectantly, but I didn't quite understand what she meant.

"Do what, Mrs. Martin?"

"Cooking, cleaning, weekly marketing, and the like." She became even more flustered as I finally understood what she was asking me.

"Are you looking for a job?" I asked, the surprise evident in my voice.

"I heard that you were opening a hotel, so I thought…" her voice trailed off as she stared down at her feet. I felt sorry for the woman. She was old enough to be my mother, and clearly in need of work despite her smart suit and tidy appearance.

"Oh, clever you," I said, "I hadn't even thought that far. I suppose I will need someone once I'm fully operational. Look, I'm dying for a cup of coffee. Would you care to join me and we can talk more about it?"

"Oh, yes. I'd love a cuppa," she said. "Why don't you let me fix you some breakfast? That cooker is a bit tricky if you don't know how to use it, and I've been battling with it these past twenty years. Mrs. Hughes always liked a soft-boiled egg in the mornings, with toast, butter, marmalade, and hot tea."

"That sounds wonderful, but I would prefer coffee. I just picked some up yesterday. Instant, I'm afraid."

Mrs. Martin was already through the door and on her way to the kitchen.

"I'll just be a moment," I said as I walked up the stairs. I'd have a shower later, but I had to at least brush my teeth and splash some cold water on my face.

The kitchen smelled pleasantly of toasted bread as I returned and took a seat at the old Formica table. Mrs. Martin had hung her bag over a chair, put on an apron and was pouring milk into a creamer that she found in the cabinet. She clearly knew her way around, so I let her serve me. She put a plate in front of me, with an egg in an egg holder in pride of place and poured me and herself some strong coffee.

"Aren't you going to have some?" I felt awkward eating while she just sat there.

"Oh no, I've already had my breakfast, but thank you. And please, call me Dot. That's what Eleanor always called me."

"So, you knew her well?" I was curious to learn something of the occupants of the house. I suppose it was natural since their presence could still be felt all around me, even with most of the furniture gone.

"I'd known Eleanor since I was a girl. I was friends with Kelly all throughout school." She suddenly looked nervous, her hands going to smooth down her skirt.

"Who's Kelly?"

"Kelly was Eleanor's youngest," she replied quietly. "I still miss her so, even after all these years."

"Oh? Did she move away?" I asked as I sliced the top off the egg and dipped my spoon into the runny yolk. Dot looked momentarily horrified, but I could see that she was dying to talk, so I remained quiet, knowing she'd be unable to resist and fill the silence.

"I wasn't going to tell you if you didn't already know, but I suppose you should be aware, since it might scare off some potential guests. Kelly was murdered — in this very house," she said, looking pointedly toward the front room. I turned and stared at the room, now empty and full of sunlight since the curtains had joined the rubbish heap along with the rug and the furniture.

"Was she killed by an intruder?"

Dot just shook her head, her coffee forgotten. "Killed by her husband. While their daughter played by the hearth." She shook her head and wiped away a tear that slid down her supple cheek. "Eleanor never recovered from Kelly's death. She suffered a breakdown and hardly left this house for the past twenty-odd years."

"What happened to the husband, and the child?" I wasn't yet thinking about the effect this might have on my business, but the tragedy that happened in this house made me lose my appetite.

"Neil is enjoying Her Majesty's hospitality," she replied tartly, "and Sandra was taken away by Myra. We never saw her again, but Myra came to visit her mother from time to time. She took her sister's death very badly as well."

It took me a moment to understand what she meant about Neil, but I concluded that he was serving a sentence for the murder of his wife.

"Why did he kill her? Was she having an affair?" I asked, curious despite my better judgment.

"Seems he thought the child might not have been his. Utter nonsense that was, too. Kelly never had eyes for anyone but him. We were all at school together and the two of them were a pair since they were fifteen. His parents had to move away after it happened. Couldn't face their friends and neighbors after what their son had done."

"Is that why the house was on the market for so long?" I asked, mentally raging at Paula Dees for not telling me all this before. Her explanation had been that with the downward economic spiral, people tended to stay away from large properties that required a hefty monetary infusion, and that the owners were crippled by paying the death duties on the place and only wanted to break even at this point.

"Oh, I reckon so. People don't care to live in a place where a murder took place, if you don't mind my saying." She suddenly realized that she'd said too much and busied herself with pouring me a fresh cup of coffee. "But don't you worry. You're American, so that should be all right."

I wasn't sure what she meant by that comment, but decided not to ask. Was it that as an American I wasn't as sensitive to other people's tragedies, or that I wasn't as sentimental and would proceed with my plans regardless?

"Strange that you resemble her so," Dot suddenly said as if struck by something.

"Resemble whom?"

"Nobody. I'm just being a silly old bag. Anyway, I must be getting on. Do think about that job, won't you?"

"Yes, I will," I replied, feeling bemused by what I'd just learned.

September 1650

England

Chapter 19

Rowan pulled a blanket over Brendan, tenderly brushing a strand of hair out of his face. The morning sun was shining brightly through the small window, a golden shaft of light filled with twirling dust motes casting a square of light onto the wooden floor, but the cot where Brendan lay was still lost in shadow. Rowan collected the blood-soaked bandages that she'd removed from Brendan to wash out at the creek. They'd be dry by the time she needed to change bandages again tomorrow. He gritted his teeth as she carefully peeled the bandages off to administer more salve and check for putrefaction. The torn flesh looked raw and swollen, but thankfully, not hot to the touch. She hated to leave him, but Uncle Caleb had come to collect her bright and early, so no one would suspect that she hadn't spent the night at home.

"She'll be back tomorrow," Uncle Caleb said as he turned to leave. "Rowan is good with potions and such, and will see to your injuries. It would look odd if Joan or I kept coming by to see the reverend, so if you need anything, you just tell Reverend Pole and he'll pass the request along. For now, just rest, and then we'll put our heads together and come up with a plan." Caleb patted Brendan on the shoulder in an attempt at a fatherly gesture, before disappearing down the ladder followed by Rowan, who threw one last look at Brendan before leaving.

The large quantity of mead had dulled the pain somewhat last night, but now rest would not come easily. Brendan would have liked nothing more than to surrender to the oblivion of slumber, but thoughts were racing through his mind, stumbling over each other and colliding in unwelcome conclusions. He tried to accept what happened and make some sense of it, but his heart wouldn't listen, wouldn't be reasoned with. His mind kept replaying images of himself and Jasper as children, playing hide and seek in the woods, fishing, splashing in the stream on a hot summer's day. Sure, Jasper had squealed to his father when Brendan had sat on the pig at the age of six and broke its back, and let him take the blame for the broken pitcher that his mother left on the kitchen table and the pie that he'd pilfered from the windowsill and ate all by himself in the barn. Brendan had taken the punishment in silence, feeling a certain sense of pride at being able to protect his little brother and set an example, but these were all childish things, things that had nothing to do with the man Jasper had grown into. What would drive Jasper to murder?

Brendan supposed that as the eldest he never really pondered the laws of primogeniture, but Jasper must have given his "younger son" standing a great deal of thought. Brendan would inherit the whole estate, while Jasper would be allowed to live there with his family, but never be master, only tenant. He would have shared in the profits and anything that Brendan had, but clearly it wasn't enough for him; he wanted it all. Brendan sighed, closing his eyes in resignation. He supposed if he had been killed on the battlefield Jasper would have played the grieving brother, but Brendan ruined all his plans by returning home to claim his inheritance.

And Father… Had he really died at Jasper's hand, as Meg claimed? He hadn't believed it, but now he had cause to think otherwise. He was only alive by God's grace, but his position was precarious. Brendan broke out in a cold sweat as a wave of panic washed over him. What was he to do now? Where was he to go once he was back on his feet? If he went home, he'd have to confront Jasper and possibly do him an injury; besides, Father had signed the estate over to him, so there was no real reason to return. He had nothing except his wits and his ability to fight. He supposed he could try soldiering or maybe join the court of Charles II, but what could he offer His Majesty, especially after years of supporting Cromwell and his crusade against the monarchy?

Brendan carefully reached for the cup of mead Rowan had thoughtfully left by the bed and gulped it down, desperate for rest. His worried mind finally surrendered and allowed him to float peacefully on a cloud of intoxication; magnified by the tincture of poppy Rowan had added to the brew. Brendan closed his eyes and took deep breaths, the smell of clover no longer cloying but soothing as he began to drift off, grateful for a respite from his troubled thoughts.

***

The sun was still streaming through the open window as Brendan woke from his stupor, but it was no longer the bright light of morning, but the slanting rays of early afternoon. His head felt as if it was stuffed with cotton wool, flashing lights behind the eyes, and a merciless pounding in his ears completing his miserable state above the neck. Below the neck, things were no better. His arm was swollen and hot to the touch; his thigh felt as if someone was holding a hot poker to the torn flesh, and his back was throbbing with agony if he so much as moved an inch. He nearly cried with relief as Rowan appeared above the opening, raising her skirts above shapely ankles as she climbed into the loft, a cup of something with a thick slice of bread on top balanced in one hand. He hoped it was more mead.

She gave Brendan a shy smile as she set his meal down and sat on the low stool.

"Good morrow," Brendan said, gratified to see her smile at him. He hadn't seen her properly the day before, but she was bathed in sunlight now, a golden halo around her pale face. Brendan nearly forgot to breathe as he looked into her eyes, luminous pools of blue-gray, the color of the sea on a cloudy day. They were fringed with thick lashes, the same color as her hair, which tried to escape from the confines of her cap. The curls were a very dark red, almost like the pelt of a fox, strands of gold and cinnamon shimmering among the copper as sunlight caressed her. Rowan blushed at his scrutiny, averting her eyes and lowering her head.

"Forgive me," he stammered, "I didn't mean to stare." He needed to use the pot, but had no idea how to ask her without humiliating himself completely. She must have read his mind because she reached under the cot, pulled out the pot and helped him to stand up. Brendan nearly fainted as blood rushed to his head, and he sat back down heavily like a sack of turnips dumped from a cart. Rowan just placed the pot between his feet and turned away; letting him do his business in private while she returned downstairs for something she'd forgotten.

Brendan carefully reclined on the pillow, stars exploding before his eyes as he tried to catch his breath. He'd never felt this weak or helpless in his life, and it left him frightened and embarrassed. He'd been blooded several times in battle, but it was nothing compared to this. There had been a field surgeon who tended to the men, his preferred method of healing simply sawing off limbs and leaving men crippled and barely able to fend for themselves. Most of them died from loss of blood or infection, but Brendan had been lucky enough to escape the physician's notice since his wounds never festered. Hopefully, his luck would hold out, and Rowan's salves would prevent putrefaction and allow him to get on his feet sooner rather than later.

Rowan returned with a basin of warm water and began to silently sponge his face and hands before holding a cup of milk to his lips and feeding him the buttered bread. He tried not to stare at her as he chewed, confused by her expression. She tried not to make eye contact, but when she did, she looked confused — no, scared. Was she repulsed by his wounds? Caleb said she had knowledge of herbs, but maybe she'd never seen such carnage before, tending only to occasional fevers and cuts.

"How do you know about medicines?" he asked conversationally, not really expecting an answer. Rowan seemed to stiffen, her cheeks going a bright red before she finally looked back at him. She folded her arms as if rocking a baby and then pointed to herself.

"Your mother?" Brendan asked. She nodded, glad that he understood. People so rarely asked her anything that she'd forgotten how to communicate, mostly nodding or shaking her head when a response was expected.

"I see. Are you an only child, then?" he asked. It was unusual to have only one child, unless the others died, of course. She wouldn't be here if she had other family to care for her. Oh, dear God, why did he bring that up? He probably upset her even more. But Rowan just sighed and nodded, then pointed to him while she busied herself with checking his bandages and applying more salve as he answered her question.

"I have a sister, Megan. She's a widow with three lads under the age of six. I'd like to have seen them before I left," he said, thinking of his nephews. "I haven't seen them in four years. The youngest was just a babe then."

When he imagined having children of his own, he always pictured them something like Meg's boys, but he'd like to have a little girl as well. Brendan sighed. The way things were going, he wasn't in any position to think of marriage or children. All that fell by the wayside when Jasper decided that he no longer deserved to live.

"And then there's Jasper." Brendan was surprised to see a cloud pass over Rowan's face. He supposed she knew what happened from Uncle Caleb. "We were the best of friends once, but that was a very long time ago. I suppose now we're enemies — not a path I'd have chosen, but one I must travel all the same."

He was surprised when Rowan sat on the edge of the cot and slid her thumb over his brow, as if to smooth away the lines of worry. It was such an intimate gesture, and one that brought much comfort. Almost without thinking Brendan turned his face toward her hand, holding it against his cheek as he closed his eyes for a moment. He felt her soft lips against his forehead as she kissed him before pulling her hand away.

Rowan gave him a shy smile before picking up the empty cup and leaving him to his own thoughts once more. He heard her clattering about downstairs, and Reverend Pole's soft voice before the door slammed shut and the house sank into silence. Any other time, Brendan would have felt restless, but his body needed time to heal and he sank into a broken sleep, haunted by images of war, and the more recent recollections of the attack. He surfaced from time to time, and then was dragged back down into sleep, unable to keep his eyes open for more than a few minutes.

It wasn't until dusk began to settle over the meadow outside the window that Brendan was finally able to shake off the drowsiness. The pleasant smell of hay and wildflowers filled the loft, carried on the fresh breeze, and the appetizing smell of cooking meat wafted from downstairs. It was warmer in the afternoon, but now there was a bite of chill to the air reminding Brendan that winter was on its way. He was hungry and thirsty, but in marginally better spirits. The mead had done its job.

Brendan was glad to see Reverend Pole laboriously climbing the ladder. The old man finally stepped into the loft, wheezing and gulping lungfuls of air until he was finally able to catch his breath.

"It's cold up here," he said as he closed the window and shutters and set about lighting the candle. The darkness was dispelled by a flickering light, which left most of the space in shadows, illuminating only a small circle created by the glow of the candle. Reverend Pole set the candle on the trunk next to the cot to give them some light.

"You must be hungry," he stated, pushing the stool next to the cot. "Rowan will bring you some supper directly. She's making rabbit stew. I suppose you need meat to get your strength back. I used to enjoy roast pork and venison, but lately I have no stomach for it. Porridge with milk is a good enough supper for me." He sat down and placed his hand over Brendan's. "How are you, my boy? Rowan added juice of the poppy to your milk to help you sleep. I hope you were able to rest." So, that explained his addled brain. Brendan had to admit that he was grateful. Sleep was the great healer, and Rowan had given him that gift.

"Shall we pray together?" Reverend Pole asked, grinning at Brendan's shocked expression.

"Of course," Brendan replied. How could he tell the reverend that it'd been a while since he set foot inside a church? A battlefield did much to tear down a man's faith, and although he still prayed, it wasn't in a house of God, but rather at night, when a great silence descended and countless stars sprinkled the heavens, reminding Brendan that maybe there was something above them after all. He still believed in God, but it wasn't the God that was portrayed by the Church or its teachings. It was a benevolent being who was dismayed and shocked by the actions of his children; one who tried without success to stop the madness and bring peace and order to the world. He couldn't imagine this Heavenly Father wishing the Papists dead or burned, or bestowing a blessing on the execution of a king and his supporters. Were they not also his children?

Brendan obediently repeated the words after the reverend without giving them much thought. They were second nature, but they held little meaning. Brendan wondered if the old reverend ever had doubts or a crisis of faith, or was he able to fit everything that happened into a biblical context and still find peace and absolution? In any case, the old man was doing him a great kindness, so the least he could do was pray with him for a few minutes and show respect. Reverend Pole genuflected as he finished the prayer and suddenly gave Brendan a mischievous smile.

"I have something for you. I thought you might need something to read to divert your mind from your troubles, so I took the liberty of bringing you a book. I think you'll like it."
Reverend Pole pulled a well-worn volume from inside his coat and handed it to Brendan. The worn leather was soft under his fingers, but he needed to hold the book closer to the candle to make out the title which was nearly rubbed off. Brendan looked at the reverend with mock shock as he read the words.

"I know, I know," Reverend Pole said with a chuckle. "Not the kind of book you'd expect a reverend to have, much less to pass on, but some merchant surrendered it to me when he claimed to find faith again, thinking this would somehow buy him the Lord's forgiveness. I told him I'd throw it on the fire, but I could never destroy a book, any book. Besides, Mr. Chaucer is rather witty, wouldn't you say? I must confess, I read a few pages."

The Canterbury Tales were known for their bawdy wit and wry observations, but Brendan was still shocked that a man of the cloth would enjoy them. He was grateful, however, for something to read, especially something that would lighten his mood. It was nice to know that the reverend had a sense of humor as well as a mischievous side — it made him more human.

"Thank you, Reverend. I will treasure it."

"Maybe you could read some of the tales to Rowan. That girl could use a little humor in her life. Just leave out some of the more wicked parts for propriety's sake. They might be too shocking for an innocent maid like her."

The reverend rose to his feet as Rowan's head appeared at the top of the ladder.

"I'll bid you good night then," he said to Brendan before turning to Rowan. "Will Caleb be coming to collect you?"

Rowan shook her head, indicating that she would walk home on her own.

"Better not stay too late then. It's not safe for a young woman to walk alone after dark."

Brendan wished Rowan would stay for a while, but he wouldn't dare detain her. He wanted her to get home safe, so he thanked her for the meal and wished her a good night. She seemed reluctant to go, but finally nodded and sank into a brief half-curtsy before disappearing down the stairs.

Chapter 20

Over the course of the next week, Rowan came by regularly under the pretense of helping Reverend Pole. She checked on Brendan's injuries to make sure they were healing cleanly, and made him food and drink. She also helped him wash, which left Brendan torn between embarrassment and pleasure. He liked the way she dipped the cloth in warm water and gently moved it over his body, her fingers brushing his bare flesh like the wings of a butterfly. Sometimes she hummed while performing this task to diffuse some of the awkwardness caused by such intimacy. Her voice was low and melodious, the song one of longing and lost love, or so it seemed to Brendan.

Rowan handed him the cloth after she was finished and turned away while he washed areas that a young girl had no business seeing. He was thankful for that, as she might have gotten more of an eyeful than she bargained for. Her ministrations did not go unnoticed by his body, especially since it had been a long time since he'd been with a woman. There were whores aplenty to be had if a man had coin or even food to pay with, especially since so many women were reduced to begging and whoring to support their children after losing their men in the wars. Brendan tried not to succumb to his needs, but sometimes, especially after a battle, he could no longer ignore his throbbing cockstand and had to take care of it in the only way that was available to him. The couplings were quick and frenzied, and provided some release, but there were no kisses or caresses, and definitely no love. There'd been nothing even resembling affection since he left Mary, and now he knew what that'd been worth. Mary's affections had been transferred to Jasper, or to be more precise, to the sizeable estate Jasper had inherited.

Rowan was the first woman, besides Brendan's mother and sister, to show him any kindness without expecting payment. She didn't just go through the motions of caring for a wounded man, she put her heart into it, her eyes lighting up with joy when she saw progress, and her brow furrowing with concern when Brendan felt warm to the touch or seemed in more pain than before. She was a sweet and kind girl, and Brendan spent more time than not wondering what had happened to her to make her lose the ability or the desire to speak. He longed to help her and care for her the way she cared for him.

They seemed to have developed a unique relationship of their own, one he could never have envisioned when he first met her. Strange, how a person who didn't utter a word, still spoke volumes. Every glance, gesture, and silence held its own meaning. A cocking of the head, a raised eyebrow, a small smile or a pursing of the lips could all convey that which she didn't actually say. Brendan learned to watch for every movement, every look, so as not to miss anything that she might want to share with him. She seemed to like it when he talked, so little by little he told her everything that had been on his mind for the past few years. He'd been constantly surrounded by men, but putting aside the camaraderie of soldiers, or the company of like-minded individuals who supported a cause, there was no one to really talk to about what was in his heart.

Brendan hadn't spoken to anyone of his desertion from Cromwell's army. He wasn't sure what she knew of politics, but anyone who'd lived in England for the past few decades knew of the carnage of the Civil War and Cromwell's ever-evolving agenda. Like so many others, Rowan had lost her father in the war. She must have been very young when he died, but one never quite got over losing a parent, especially as a child. Brendan had a clear recollection of Rowan's mother from Maisie's wedding. She was a beautiful woman, still in her twenties, and many a goodwife at that wedding would have scratched her eyes out for attracting the attentions of her husband. Delwyn had been surrounded by men asking her to dance; especially the widowers who could only hope to win the affections of such a lovely woman.

Once Brendan remembered the mother, he remembered Rowan as well. She'd been a coltish girl of twelve who'd had the misfortune to be bullied by Jasper in a barn. The poor girl had been so distraught, especially by Jasper's cruel words, that Brendan took it upon himself to put a smile back on her face. He'd danced with her around the bonfire, and he remembered the blush on her lean cheeks and the glow of those amazing eyes, as he twirled Rowan around while pretty young maids watched and wondered what possessed him to dance with a child. Brendan tried to recall the sound of her voice, but couldn't. They'd spoken so little, and after, she went off with a smile as he bowed to her and thanked her for the dance. He'd made her night, or so he thought, being the cocky young buck he was then. Brendan wondered if he should bring up that night to Rowan, but decided against it. Whatever happened, happened shortly after, and he didn't want to remind her of something that robbed her of her speech and trust. Some things were best left unsaid, so he spoke to her of other things, things that had no power to hurt her.

Rowan liked to sit on the low stool, facing Brendan as he talked. He wasn't sure if she realized how the sunlight from the window illuminated her lovely face and set her hair ablaze, stealing his breath away whenever he looked at her. Her eyes were full of understanding, and at times she laid her hand over his forearm to stop him and ask a question. At first, he found it odd the way she found a way to ask something without saying a word, but by now he found it amusing, admiring the clever ways she came up with to mimic what she wanted to know. Just now, she'd put her hand behind her head with four fingers showing behind the cap and then drew a finger across her throat before pointing at him.

"You want to know if I was there when the king was executed?" Brendan asked, hoping that he'd understood her correctly. She nodded eagerly, so he continued. "Yes, I was there. I think that was truly when I felt the first seeds of doubt in my heart. I was blinded by Cromwell's vision, by his single-minded desire to change the government of this country, but I never really expected him to go as far as regicide. The trial of the king was a farce, a witch-hunt for the benefit of the bloodthirsty crowd. It had already been decided that the king would die, regardless of any promises he made. I've been vehemently opposed to the way he abused his power to the detriment of the people, but to execute the man was sheer barbarism.

Of course, Cromwell's logic was that as long as the king remained alive, there'd always be Royalists who would try to put him back on the throne even had he been exiled."

Rowan rocked an imaginary child in her arms, and Brendan continued. "You're right; nothing's changed. There are those who want to put his son on the throne and will stop at nothing to achieve their goal. This country is used to having a king, and with all the powers Cromwell has been granting himself, he might as well be one. There are those who believe that before long he will crown himself king and then all this bloodshed would've been for naught."

Brendan stopped as a shadow passed over Rowan's face. She was watching him intently, staring at his chest.

"What is it? I don't understand," he said, suddenly worried about what she was thinking. Rowan just pointed to him and then pointed two fingers at his chest as if firing a gun.

"You think they might execute me for deserting? Aye, I suppose that's always a possibility, although I think Cromwell has his hands full with the Irish and Scots at the moment. I don't think finding one disillusioned follower is a priority for him, although I must admit that he has a long memory and is merciless to anyone he perceives to be opposed to him." Brendan smiled at her grim face. "Cromwell has bigger fish to fry. Have you heard of John Lilburne?" he asked, noting no sign of recognition in her eyes.

"You might have heard of him as "Freeborn John." Some people call him a Leveller, but he doesn't like that title since what he's advocating is not so much leveling the rights of land ownership, but the rights of all men. He believes that all men have "freeborn rights," which are not the same as the rights granted by a government or a monarch. He preaches that all men are equal in the eyes of God, and should be before the law. An odd notion for some, especially the nobility, but makes perfect sense if you think about it. Of course, John Lilburne's ideas are downright conservative compared to the Ranters."

Brendan smiled at her perplexed expression. He was probably filling her head with a lot of nonsense, but he didn't believe that a woman should live in ignorance, and Rowan seemed eager to know. He'd tried to explain to her about the various groups that had formed over the past few decades: the Levellers, the Diggers, the Ranters, and some others which he hadn't even bothered to mention.

Rowan touched his arm, eager for him to continue. He hadn't even realized that he'd grown quiet, suddenly acutely aware of how absurd all this sounded, even to him who'd experienced these things firsthand.

"The Ranters are a group of people who believe that God is in everything: every tree, flower, and creature. They reject the authority of the Church as a representative of God. The Church has labeled them as heretics. In truth, they're a dangerous element as they don't believe in the laws of men and claim that sin is a product of the imagination. What do you think of that?" he asked, not wanting to delve deeper into the doctrine of the Ranters. He'd met a prominent member named Laurence Clarkson last year in London and had a discourse with him over a pint of ale, walking away more confused and opposed to the group than he had been before the conversation.

"I can accept the idea of equal land ownership and God-given rights of men, but I can't agree with the notion that sin is just an illusion. If you do away with right and wrong, what's left to keep people from killing, raping, and shirking their responsibilities?"

He almost laughed at the raised eyebrows and pursed lips that this comment met with. Then Rowan just rolled her eyes in exasperation at his obtuseness as she tried to mimic what she wanted to say.

"You're right, of course; people have been doing that since the beginning of time. Cromwell is certainly not a Ranter, but the amount of killing and pillaging that took place in Ireland, and lately in Scotland, is enough to sicken even those who have no heart or compassion left in them. Did anyone ever tell you that you're a skilled opponent in a political debate?" he asked, making her giggle. She was so pretty when she smiled, and her face was softened by happiness. Brendan reached out and grabbed her wrist, but she deftly pulled it away, giving him a look of reproach. She nodded toward the ladder to indicate it was time for her to go, but Brendan wasn't ready to part with her yet.

"Will you sing to me?" he asked in a desperate attempt to keep her from leaving, but Rowan just shook her head and gave him one last smile before disappearing down the ladder. She had to return home, especially since her chores at Reverend Pole's were complete, and she was needed around the house to help Aunt Joan. Brendan could smell the stew she'd made for their supper and his mouth watered at the thought. He was always hungry these days. Maybe it was because his body was slowly recovering, or because he had too much time to think.

The Present

Chapter 21

After nearly two hours of being shooed out of the way by the workers, I decided that I might as well get out of their hair and make better use of my time. I would take a walk into town and stop in at the bookstore that had been closed when I came in for supplies yesterday. I'd find some literature to bone up on local history, and maybe find an interesting tidbit or two to include on my future website and brochure. I would also see if I might find something at the library about the history of the ruin behind my house.

I walked at a brisk pace down the lane, feeling as if I were on an adventure. The sky was a brilliant blue, dotted by puffy white clouds that looked as if they were painted on by a clever artist. They floated lazily across the sky, their shadows scuttling across the lush landscape and the verdant hills in the distance. I wished I'd brought my camera so that I could take a few pictures for the website, but there was plenty of time. The summer had just begun and there would be many gorgeous, sunny days in the months to come.

It was nearly noon on a Tuesday, so all the shops were open; several vans making deliveries, and village women strolling down the street with their shopping baskets and small children. A few teenage boys raced past me on bikes, nearly splattering me with dirty water from a nearby puddle. Laughter and shrieks could be heard from a daycare across the street where the children were out, enjoying the playground and the glorious weather. A few passersby cast curious glances my way, but I simply smiled in greeting and continued to my destination. I was just passing the estate agent's office when I was waylaid by Paula, who was immaculately dressed in a wraparound print dress with matching pumps.

"Lexi, pleasure to see you. How're you getting on?" She was totally sober this morning, but still perky and gregarious. I supposed this was all part of her salesperson persona, but today I wasn't in the mood to be engaged.

"I'm well, thank you," I replied, but didn't stop.

"Lexi, wait. It's almost noon. Would you like to join me for a quick bite?" she asked as she checked her watch.

I didn't mean to lash out, but her breezy attitude suddenly made me angry. "Why didn't you tell me about Kelly?" I demanded as I turned to face Paula. She took a step back, surprised by my outburst, but instantly regained her composure and smiled in a conciliatory way.

"Come inside and we'll have a chat, Lexi." Several women had already stopped on the opposite side of the sidewalk, craning their necks to see what the fuss was about, so I followed Paula into the office and allowed her to shut the door. Paula took her seat behind the desk and gestured for me to sit across from her.

"Why didn't you tell me?" I repeated, annoyed by her cool-as-a-cucumber demeanor.

"And why would I?" Paula asked. I'd expected excuses, or a half-baked apology, but I didn't expect that.

"A woman was murdered in my house, and you didn't see fit to warn me? Isn't there some kind of "full disclosure" clause in your line of work?"

Paula just shrugged and spoke in an even, no-nonsense tone. "Lexi, you fell in love with that house long before you even dialed my number, so would it really have made any difference?"

She stared me down and I suddenly felt a little foolish. She was right; it wouldn't have made a difference. I knew that house was meant for me from the moment I saw it through the trees, and unless there happened to be a bloody corpse lying on the doorstep when I came to look at it, nothing would have stood in the way of my desire to own it.

"No," I conceded, "but I still would have liked to know."

"And now you know," Paula answered triumphantly. "Friends?"

I had to give it to her; she sure knew how to diffuse an argument. I nodded, but refused to return her smile. I wasn't finished.

"Paula, who did that house in the meadow belong to?"

"What, the old ruin?" She was still smiling, but the smile didn't reach her eyes, and she suddenly seemed to take on an air of extreme busyness. She pulled out a few files and began leafing through them as she looked up and finally answered me. "If you are so determined to find out, I can search the database and check that lot." She was probably hoping that I would just tell her to forget it and leave, but I really was curious and not about to pass up an opportunity to see what Paula's records might reveal.

"Please do," I replied, refusing to take a hint and leave her in peace.

She turned to her computer and punched a few keys before turning back to me with an expression of false cordiality. "That parcel of land originally belonged to the Church until it was sold to Bartholomew Hughes in 1677. It's been in the Hughes family since. Why are you so interested anyhow?"

"I've heard of the Church buying up land, but I haven't heard of them selling it. Why would the Church sell?"

Paula shrugged and turned away from her computer. "God, Lexi, you're like a dog with a bone, aren't you?" she replied with a forced laugh. "How would I know why they sold off the land back in the seventeenth century? They just did. Now, are you coming to lunch or not?"

"Not," I replied, but gave Paula a grudging smile. "Maybe some other time, but thank you for the info."

"Anytime," Paula replied as I made to leave the office. She was still smiling, but I was sure she hadn't told me the whole truth.

I was still thinking about what Paula said as I made my way up the street toward the book shop, hoping it was open this time. It was one of those little places where shelves and shelves of books were visible through the front window, the storefront reminiscent of something straight out of Dickens. That was one of the things I found so charming about the village. A store that was probably built sometime in the eighteenth century and still looked much as it had then, was displaying The Inferno by Dan Brown, and a certain erotic trilogy that had captured the hearts of housewives around the world. The seamless blending of old and new was something the British really had a talent for, and I hoped to be able to pull it off once I'd opened my doors for business.

The bell above the door jingled as I entered, disturbing the somnolent atmosphere of the place and bringing an elderly gentleman from the back room. He smiled broadly as he approached, the smile freezing on his thin lips as he saw my face. I glanced behind me to see what he was staring at, but there was nothing there except the door.

"Good afternoon," I said, feeling exposed under the man's curious gaze.

"Ah, yes, good afternoon," he mumbled, still staring at me as if he'd seen a ghost. "How may I be of assistance?"

I told him what I wanted, but he didn't move right away. He just stood there studying me with that odd expression. "So, you found your way back, have you?" he suddenly asked, looking instantly embarrassed. He turned away before I could reply, shuffling to a shelf toward the back, his shoulders tense underneath his cardigan.

121

"I stopped by yesterday, but you were closed," I offered as he handed me a few books on the history of Lincolnshire. The man looked momentarily confused by my answer, but then regained his composure and gave me an apologetic smile.

"That's not really what I meant, but I must have mistaken you for someone else. It's just that the resemblance is uncanny, you understand. My mistake," he mumbled, avoiding my eyes.

"Resemblance to whom?"

"Kelly, Kelly Hughes." He averted his eyes as if he'd said too much and concentrated on giving me my change from an old-fashioned till and placing the books into a plastic bag.

"I bought the Hughes house," I mumbled, suddenly upset. Yesterday I'd never even heard of Kelly Hughes, and suddenly, she was on everyone's lips.

"Yes, I'd heard. Well, much luck to you then." The man bowed his head slightly and walked toward the back without so much as a backward glance. I shrugged and took my purchase, stepping back out into the street.

My next stop was the library. It was a small, low building, boasting a number of scarred bookshelves and a few round tables with chairs for readers. I noticed several teenage girls poring over the latest fashion magazines, and a woman with two small children who were fighting over a picture book as their mother tried to shush them. The librarian threw the woman a look of annoyance before turning her attention to me. Strangely, she had a similar reaction to the owner of the shop, but she didn't stare as openly.

"How can I help, dear?" she asked, her fingers twisting a ring on her finger, round and round.

"I was wondering if you might have some information on the ruin behind the Hughes house. I've just bought it and wanted to learn something about the history of the estate." The librarian gave me a sad smile, her eyes full of sympathy.

"Of course you do," she said, patting my hand. "Perfectly understandable. Now, let me see what I can find for you."

She walked off, leaving me somewhat confused. My initial reaction had been to think that people were wary of strangers, especially American ones, but why did they look at me with pity? Was there something I should know about the house? Did they think it was haunted?

The librarian returned to her desk, carrying a yellowed scroll. "I'm afraid I don't have much, just an old map showing the village as it had been during the seventeenth century when the house was built. The map dates back to the late 1600s." She unrolled the scroll, showing me the crude drawing. "Here's the house, the stream, and some outbuildings. I'm not sure if this is what you were hoping to find." I gazed at the map, disappointed by the lack of information. This didn't tell me anything about who lived in the house or what happened to them.

"Do you know anything about the ruin or who lived there?" I persisted.

The woman shrugged. "It has no historical significance, if that's what you mean. Just an old house that fell into disrepair. I suppose once the big house was built, no one wanted to live in that hovel."

I thanked her and left, leaving the scroll behind. It wouldn't do me any good to study the location of the outbuildings. I had to admit that I was perplexed by her reaction. I didn't know much of the ways of these people, but I knew that families tended to stay on the same land for generations. Even if the family had died, there would have been some relations in or around town, someone who might have ties to those long-ago people who inhabited the house. If I could at least get a name. I stepped back into the street, feeling discouraged and aimless.

Chapter 22

It was close to 5 p.m. by the time I arrived back at the house. The men were packing up and loading their tools into the back of the truck, their good-natured banter washing over me as I walked up the stone path. Aidan called out a greeting, but I gave a wave and kept walking, my mind swirling with questions and doubts. I walked into the kitchen, set down my bag of books and sat down at the table, the only place in the house besides my room that still had something to sit on. I propped up my head on my hands and stared into space as Aidan came in.

"Lexi, are you all right?" he asked, cocking his head to the side and giving me a searching look. "You look distinctly down in the mouth."

The funny expression made me smile a little, which is what he no doubt intended, but hot tears sprang into my eyes and I rummaged in my bag for a tissue, wiping away the moisture angrily with my hand when I failed to find one.

"Go on without me," Aidan called out to George, who came in to tell Aidan they were ready to go. "I'll see you at the pub later."

George was about to make some comment about the two of us being left on our own, but noticed my tear-stained face and just retreated silently, while Aidan popped some bread into the toaster and began to open and close cabinets as if searching for something. I was grateful that his back was turned to me so I could have my little cry.

A short time later, Aidan presented me with a mug of milky tea and something on a plate that was brown and oozing.

"What in the world is that?" I asked, blowing my nose and giving Aidan a watery smile.

"That, my dear, is the meal of champions — beans on toast. Now, eat up."

"You seriously expect me to eat this?" I asked as I gently moved the plate away from me. I'd never been a huge fan of beans, but to have them presented this way, on what was now soggy toast accompanied by tea was just revolting. And since I hadn't actually bought any canned beans, the logical conclusion would be that they'd been sitting in the cabinet since poor Mrs. Hughes was alive.

"Some Englishmen consider this to be a rare delicacy," Aidan informed me as he took a seat across from me and took a sip of his own tea.

"Then you can have it." I moved the plate toward him and took a sip of tea. I'd never really taken it with milk, but this was strangely comforting.

"So, what happened?" Aidan asked. It made me feel a little better to see that he was genuinely interested, and not just being polite and discreetly looking at his watch to see how soon he could decently leave and join his mates at the pub. He had a look of single-minded concentration, which made me feel as if at that moment I was the most important person in the world, but still I hesitated. I wasn't sure that I should be dumping my problems on my contractor, but at the moment he was the only one willing to listen, and the closest thing I had to a friend in this new life I had chosen for myself. I took a deep breath and plunged in. He might not be able to do anything about my predicament, but it was nice just to be able to share with someone. Sometimes just saying things out loud made them appear different than when kept inside, where they always managed to fester and take on a greater significance than they deserved.

"One: A murder took place in this very house and no one thought to tell me about it." I folded down one finger and continued. "Two: people keep staring at me and implying that I look like the woman who was killed." I folded down a second finger. "And three: I keep seeing a man in those ruins, but the physical evidence suggests that he's not there." I was about to start crying again when Aidan gave me a brilliant smile.

"What are you smiling at?" I asked petulantly.

"You. And there I thought you had some serious problem," he replied, still smiling in a way that suddenly made me feel silly.

"Did you know about Kelly?" I asked, my feelings ruffled.

"Of course I did. A violent death of a young woman might not be news for long in New York, but in a place like this, the story will live on in infamy for generations. There's not a person in this village who hasn't heard of Kelly Gregson."

"Well, why didn't you tell me?" I asked, my tone full of accusation. Why the conspiracy of silence?

Aidan gave a non-committal shrug as he held my gaze. "To what purpose? This occurred nearly a quarter of a century ago, and as it happens, you'd be hard-pressed to find any place in Europe where someone wasn't killed at some point in history. If people refused to live where others had died, we'd have had to colonize the moon by now."

I couldn't help smiling at his logic. He did have a point. Aidan took my hand in his large one, making me feel strangely comforted as he went on, "As far as the other things go, you are simply feeling a little out of your element and your nerves are on edge. There's no man in the ruins, and people often notice resemblances that aren't necessarily there. You bought a house in a small English village, and they want to believe that something special brought you here, like family history. They like to find meaning in what people do and find connections to the past. Get used to it, Yank!" he said with a grin.

"Well, since you put it that way, I feel kind of silly now," I grudgingly admitted. I was reading too much into things and seeing things that weren't there. I'd always had an overly romantic imagination, so it stood to reason that I was allowing my fantasies to cloud my judgment. I still had my doubts about the man in the ruins, but there had to be a logical explanation for what I'd seen. The most likely explanation was that I'd seen an actual person who just happened to come upon the ruins and stopped to explore. He was long gone, so I had nothing to worry about.

"Good, now eat your beans."

"That, I refuse to do." I was laughing now, my misery of a few moments ago forgotten. It was nice having someone to talk things over with.

"I think the last thing you need is to spend an evening alone in this empty house. Why don't you come back to mine? We'll watch a movie and get a pizza, since you refuse to taste my culinary masterpiece."

"Thank you, Aidan, but I think I'll just have a bath and read a little. I'm actually kind of tired. Didn't get much sleep last night," I added sheepishly.

"Like that, is it?" He got to his feet and put his mug in the sink. "Well, ring me if you change your mind. I can come and collect you, so you don't have to walk."

"I won't change my mind," I said, "but thank you all the same."

Chapter 23

"Drinks in the garden?" Alastair Dees called out as his wife slammed the door shut behind her and kicked off her expensive pumps. Paula didn't bother to reply as she let herself out the back door and into the garden, which at the moment was a riot of blooms, lovingly tended by Alastair in his every spare moment. Normally, Paula loved to sit out there in the evening, enjoying the blissful tranquility that was her sweet little cottage, but tonight she was positively livid.

A promising deal had fallen through, and then she had the encounter with Lexi Maxwell — all before noon. The rest of the day wasn't any better, with Paula staring resentfully at the telephone which rang only once in the afternoon — an inquiry that amounted to nothing. Business usually picked up a little at the end of the school year, with parents opting to move while the children were off for the summer holidays, but there weren't many properties for sale anywhere in the village or thereabouts, and the third quarter promised to be much slower than the second, which at least yielded the sale of the Hughes place.

Paula gratefully accepted a glass of Merlot from Alastair and gave him a wan smile. It wasn't his fault she had a bloody awful day. The sight of Alastair always lifted her spirits though. Not every woman was lucky enough to have such a wonderful husband, a fact on which she congratulated herself daily. Alastair carelessly brushed a stray lock from his forehead and settled across from Paula, his expression one of concern. Paula was so rarely in a bad mood that when she was, Alastair feared something catastrophic had occurred.

"What is it, love?" he asked gently. "You look positively draconian." It always made her laugh when he used words like that, being a linguistics professor, but today it failed to amuse.

"It's that bloody Maxwell woman," Paula hissed, taking a healthy sip of her wine. As much as Paula was upset about the business side of things, it was the confrontation with Lexi that had thrown her off balance. That was personal.

"The one who bought the Hughes pile? I thought you were happy about that. You were positively giddy last week." The amount of the commission check did make Paula giddy, especially since linguistics experts didn't rate much these days, at least not in any financial sense. If only Alastair could secure a position at Oxford or Cambridge — something that would not only boost their finances considerably, but also give them the kind of social standing that Paula always craved. Being married to an Oxford don was almost as prestigious as having a minor title, in her opinion, but Alastair was perfectly happy puttering in his garden and working on his book. He'd chosen some obscure theory which delved into the origins of "ye olde English," as Paula called it, that likely no one would ever care to read, much less actually publish.

"She came in this morning accusing me of withholding information about Kelly Hughes," Paula mumbled, pouting like a small child who'd been told off by her mum.

"I suppose she has a right to know," Alastair offered in his most conciliatory tone. He was never afraid to tell Paula the truth, but presentation made all the difference to how she took it.

"I took a calculated risk. I knew she'd find out soon enough, but by then I'd have the money for that lovely holiday in Ibiza, and no one would be the wiser. That's not what really upset me though." Paula gave Alastair a sad puppy look that made him get up, walk over to her side of the table and plant a kiss on top of her head.

"Out with it, love," he said as he settled back into his seat and raised the glass of wine to his lips.

"She keeps asking questions about the ruin."

Alastair shrugged, failing to see the cataclysmic implications of Paula's statement. "So what? There's absolutely

129

nothing to find. Nothing. All that happened nearly four hundred years ago, and there's not a soul in this village who even knows about it."

"I know, and so did old Mrs. Hughes. She might have told Kelly and Myra. I won't have this stain on my family name exposed." Paula's normally pale face was stained red with indignation and worry.

"Sweetheart, countless men from this village died in the last hundred years alone. Between the two world wars, this village was left nearly without men. What difference does some four-hundred-year-old murder make in the face of that?" Alastair tried to sound reasonable, but Paula's color rose and her eyes flashed daggers at him.

"You just don't understand. There's a difference between dying on a battlefield, and being betrayed and murdered in cold blood. There's divine retribution." With that, Paula drained her glass and marched off in the direction of the bedroom, where she slammed the door with enough force to make the windows rattle in their panes.

Alastair leaned back in his chair and took a deep breath of the sweet June air. It was fragrant with the smell of flowers blooming all around him, freshly cut grass, and a whiff of resin from the lawn chairs. Life was wonderful, and Alastair was damned if he would allow himself to worry about something that happened centuries ago. His wife really was too dramatic sometimes, but that's what made her so fun. Her theatrics extended to the bedroom, so were well worth putting up with. Alastair smiled happily and took another sip of wine. When Paula's passion was aroused, he was the beneficiary, so he had better not drink too much. He'd need his strength tonight.

September 1650

England

Chapter 24

The house was quiet as a chapel when Brendan woke up on Sunday morning. A gentle rain fell outside, the leaden sky making the gloom in the loft nearly impenetrable as Brendan gritted his teeth and forced himself to get up. He took a few tentative steps around the loft before sitting back down again, his muscles shaking with tension from disuse and his head light from the loss of blood he suffered. Pain was his constant companion these days, dulled only by cups of mead before bedtime. Brendan reached for the glass of milk and slice of bread so thoughtfully provided by Rowan before she left last night. The milk was pleasantly cool, but the bread, which Rowan had wrapped in a piece of muslin to keep from getting stale, was a bit hard, so Brendan dipped it in the milk to make chewing easier. A tooth on the right side had been bothering him for months, the pain shooting into his jaw as he thoughtlessly bit on something hard. At this point, the only part of his body that felt intact was his feet, but he was too weak to use them.

He'd been at Reverend Pole's for nearly a week now, but neither his aunt nor uncle had come to visit him. He understood their reasons, but perhaps they felt relieved to be rid of him, although he didn't really believe that. Uncle Caleb was the type of man you could trust implicitly; the type of man you wanted next to you in battle, and in life. Brendan always relied on first impressions, and Uncle Caleb was the type of man who on first impression appeared to be a man of sound judgment and stout principle. He could not be bought or cowered, and would do the right thing, if only to appease his conscience. Brendan trusted Caleb with his life.

Aunt Joan was also a kind woman, much like his mother when it came to those she loved, and she'd always treated him like a son. If they hadn't come, it was for his own safety, he reasoned, needing to feel that someone in this world besides Meg and his mother still cared for him.

Brendan perked up as he heard movement downstairs. Reverend Pole was back from church, so it must be around noon. Brendan stilled in an effort to hear any sounds made by Rowan, but it seemed Reverend Pole was alone. It would make sense for Rowan to go home after the service and have Sunday dinner with the family. She likely wouldn't come at all today. The thought depressed Brendan, but he resolutely put it out of his mind, cursing himself for a fool.

The creaking of the ladder announced the imminent arrival of the reverend. It took him a long while to make it up to the loft, especially if he were carrying something in one hand. The poor man was a mere shadow of the man he'd been only a few years ago at Maisie's wedding. He was gaunt and frail, his rheumy eyes faded with age. They must have been blue once, but now they were more of a washed-out gray, almost colorless, as was his face. Brendan suddenly wondered if he would ever get to grow old, and if there would be anyone by his side when he did.

He hadn't had much time to dwell on the future in the past few years, especially since it was assured, as long as he came back alive. He'd marry Mary, inherit the estate, and go on much as his father had, content in the knowledge that he'd done his bit to try to bring about change and improve the political process of this country. Brendan cursed himself for a fool once again, smiling humorlessly at his own naiveté. Young girls didn't wait patiently while men pursued their own ends; fathers had the power to alter the line of succession, and a fight for freedom was sometimes nothing more than a struggle to further one man's ambitions. Fool!

The reverend finally made it up and placed a plate of cold roast pork, pickle and bread on the wooden trunk as he took a moment to catch his breath. There was a wheezing noise coming from deep inside his chest as he sucked in air, almost in vain since he was still out of breath. It took a few minutes for the reverend to finally recover from his ordeal, making Brendan feel terribly guilty for putting the old man into this position.

"How are you, my boy? On the mend, I hope. I know I'm a poor substitute for Rowan, but she's with her family today. They'll be joined for Sunday dinner by Stephen Aldrich and his children. It's become their custom of late."

Brendan took a bite of pork and chewed thoughtfully, making sure not to bite down too hard with his aching tooth. The pork was a welcome relief to the bread, which despite the milk felt as if it'd lodged in his throat. Was there some significance to Reverend Pole mentioning this bit of information about Stephen Aldrich?

"I don't recall meeting him in the past. Is he a friend of my uncle?" Brendan could see from the reverend's expression that he had been anticipating the question and he took a moment to answer, thinking how to phrase it best.

"I suppose they're friends, but he's Rowan's intended. They are to wed in the spring once Stephen's year of mourning for his wife is at an end." Brendan's look of misery wasn't lost on the reverend, who told him of Rowan's engagement on purpose to subtly discourage any affection he might harbor for the girl.

"I'm sorry, Brendan, but I thought it best you knew. She's not likely to tell you herself, so I took it upon myself to be the bearer of sad tidings. I might be an old man, but I see the look on her face after she's been up here with you, and I have every reason to suspect the feeling is not one-sided."

"Thank you, Reverend, but no apology is needed. Rowan is a lovely girl who's been very kind to me, but I have no claim on her, and nothing to offer any woman at the moment; not until I reclaim the estate from Jasper." Brendan continued to chew, but the pork suddenly tasted bland and chewy in his mouth, as did the fresh bread which now felt like dust on his tongue. He didn't know why he was so upset; as he told the reverend, he had no right to be, but his stomach was in knots and he suddenly felt sorry for himself, not a quality he admired. Brendan carefully set the plate aside and took a sip of ale, grateful for the cool liquid which washed the bitterness from his mouth.

The old man smiled apologetically as he reached for Brendan's hand. "That's not all, I'm afraid. I have some bad news that has nothing to do with Rowan. I spoke with your uncle after church today. He can't come to see you for fear of giving away your hiding place." Reverend Pole looked toward the little window, his face a mask of misery. "It seems that some men came looking for you yesterday, informing your uncle that you've been accused of murder. They mean to bring you to justice."

Brendan just stared at the reverend. Of course he had committed murder, but it was in self-defense. It was kill or be killed, so how could anyone prosecute him for that? In fact, how could anyone know it was him anyway, since there were no witnesses and the only person who might know was Jasper? Brendan voiced his argument to Reverend Pole, who shook his head sadly, a look of pity in his colorless eyes.

"It seems some items belonging to you were found by the bodies."

"What items?" Had he dropped something as he fled? He barely had anything on him other than his sword, a purse with a few coins in it, and the bundle of food Meg had given him for the journey.

"There was a prayer book with your name in it and a ring your father had given you on your eighteenth birthday." Brendan nearly gagged at the injustice of it all. It was ludicrous. He had not had a prayer book on him, and the ring his father had given him was still on his finger. He hadn't taken it off since the day he proudly put it on, so whatever ring was found at the scene of the

134

attack was not the one. Jasper had obviously planted these things when he found his men dead in an effort to tie Brendan to the crime without having to explain his own part in it. A venomous snake in the grass, his brother was.

"Brendan, the penalty for murder is hanging, and as a reverend, I wouldn't be treated kindly for aiding and abetting a criminal."

Brendan felt as if icy fingers closed around his heart, making it difficult to breathe. "Are you asking me to leave, Reverend, or telling me politely that you are going to turn me in?" Brendan asked through clenched teeth, his hands balled into fists. The reverend laid a hand on his arm in a conciliatory gesture, suddenly realizing the way he must have sounded.

"Neither, my boy. I know that you are innocent in the eyes of God, and that's good enough for me. I will hide you for as long as it takes, but I simply wanted to alert you to the situation and explain why your uncle hasn't come to see you. We must be very careful, for Rowan's sake as well. She has her own reasons to fear the law, so let's not do anything that might endanger her."

Brendan opened his mouth to ask, but Reverend Pole put a gnarled finger to his lips, shaking his head. Whatever Rowan had done, was between him, her, and God, and he wouldn't speak a word against her. Brendan nodded in understanding, respecting the man that much more. If Rowan wanted to share with him, she would, but he wouldn't pry. She was risking her own safety to care for him, and he was eternally grateful, regardless of what secrets she carried in her heart.

Chapter 25

Stephen Aldrich helped his children into the wagon and waved a last goodbye to Rowan. She waved back, but her gaze seemed to focus somewhere just behind his head, her shoulders hunched as she wrapped her shawl tighter around herself against the early evening chill. Rowan usually waited until they were well on their way before going back inside, but today she spun on her heel and disappeared through the low doorway before the wagon even left the confines of the yard. Stephen had been looking forward to seeing her all week, but something seemed different today, something he couldn't put his finger on. Caleb mentioned that Rowan had been helping Reverend Pole with some housekeeping since the old man could barely manage for himself these days, but Stephen saw no reason why that would so alter his future bride.

It wasn't that anything was outwardly different in Rowan's actions. She set the table and served him as she always had before taking care of the children, but she barely looked at him, and when she had, it wasn't a look of tenderness, but one of apprehension. Had he done something to offend her? When could he have? They hadn't seen each other since last Sunday, and everything seemed right as rain then. He hoped she wasn't having second thoughts about marrying him. He'd only asked her a month ago, so it was possible that she still wasn't sure. Perhaps it'd been too soon, but few men waited more than a few months after their bereavement before casting a net for a new bride. They didn't have the luxury of mourning, not when there was a house to run and children to be minded. At least Stephen's children were old enough to fend for themselves, but there were many in the village who were left with babes, and had to marry as soon as possible to provide their children with a caretaker while they were out working to put food on the table.

There were those in the village, he knew, who thought him a fool for courting Rowan. They believed her to be soft in the head, and not fit to be the wife of any man, but Stephen thought differently. Rowan was beautiful, kind, and smart. He'd felt awfully sorry for her when she first showed up a few years ago, frightened and silent, and hoped that in time she would recover, but it was not to be. He didn't mind the silence though. His first wife, Agnes, talked nonstop, always complaining or berating him for something he had or hadn't done. He'd loved her when they first married, but as the years wore on, he often wished that she would just leave him be. The pregnancy had been a surprise; he thought they were past all that, and was more than happy with the two children that they already had.

Agnes had been even more difficult during the final months, but Stephen did everything in his power to keep her happy and comfortable. She wasn't a young woman anymore, and her condition was taking a toll, making her tired and cranky. She couldn't stand for long periods of time and her ankles and feet swelled to twice their normal size, forcing her to go barefoot on the cold earthen floor of their house in the dead of winter. Poor Agnes was constantly shivering with cold, no matter how much wood she threw on the fire to drive out the chill. Her back ached incessantly and it took her hours to finally settle down and go to sleep, her tossing and turning keeping Stephen awake when his body was exhausted from the day's work and begging for a well-deserved rest.

The babe was very late, according to the midwife, and kept growing inside the womb, getting larger by the day.
By the time the pains finally came, Stephen prayed for them both, but it did no good. The child was too big, and after four days of labor, both Agnes and the babe were called to the Lord. In a way, it was a blessing that the child was never actually born, as it wouldn't be buried in hallowed ground without the sacrament of baptism; instead relegated to a quiet corner of the yard where dogs would come sniffing at the grave or hogs would root for acorns. Agnes was buried in the cemetery by the church, the fully-formed baby still inside her — together in life and death. Stephen took

Lizzie and Tim to visit their mother's grave every Sunday after church. Agnes had been a good and loving mother to them, and deserved their sorrow and respect. But after they paid their respects, Stephen took them to Caleb's house for Sunday dinner. It would do them good to get used to Rowan and her ways before they married, so the adjustment would be an easier one.

Stephen tried not to think of what married life with Rowan would be like. It wasn't proper to think of her in that way, but sometimes late at night, he pictured her warm, naked body beneath his and he nearly burst with longing, wishing the spring would come soon and he could finally make Rowan his. He'd give her a child if she wanted one, but he'd asked the midwife for ways to avoid pregnancy, and he would do it if he could, to keep her safe; to keep her alive.

Chapter 26

Jasper hurled a chicken leg into the fire and watched with satisfaction as it sent a shower of sparks into the chimney, the fire burning brighter for just a moment before resuming its merry crackle. He hadn't bothered to light the candles, and the shifting shadows cast by the flames were the only light in the room, the gloom a fine reflection of his mood. It'd been over a two weeks since his accursed brother had come back, and everything had gone awry from the moment he set foot on the estate. Even Meg had changed toward him, her once affectionate gaze chastising him and judging him every time she walked into the room. She'd become a right venomous shrew, she had, especially since the death of their father, her eyes always full of accusation and scorn.

He'd told Brendan the truth; Wilfred Carr had died of apoplexy, but he hadn't quite signed the legal document Jasper had then made public to the rest of the family. Father had raged at Brendan for leaving and threatened to cut him off, but his bark had always been worse than his bite. In time, he would have forgiven his son, and everything would have gone on as before had Jasper not tried to add fuel to the fire by riling his father up and skillfully maneuvering the conversation to Brendan's disobedience and desertion. But, no matter how angry his father had been, he'd never have disinherited his firstborn. Wilfred Carr was a man of tradition, and it was the eldest son who inherited the lot, not the spare one who hardly merited any notice unless something happened to his older brother. Jasper had idolized Brendan until he realized one day that although they were equally reared, they were destined for entirely different lives. It wasn't Brendan's fault that he came first, but Jasper needed a target for his resentment, and it was easier to hate Brendan, especially after he left, than to take issue with their father who wouldn't countenance any breach of tradition.

Forging the signature had been easy enough since few people had ever seen Wilfred Carr sign his name. He wasn't a man of letters and could barely read, finding education to be an unnecessary burden for a farmer. He had a good head on his shoulders though, and a talent for making profit; taking their estate from near poverty to prosperity since he'd taken over on the death of his own father, who found a lot more solace in the bottle and a pair of dice than in hard work. It would have all been so easy and natural had Brendan just got himself killed on some battlefield, but he'd come back, expecting to claim what was rightfully his, and Jasper panicked. Brendan would have challenged the document, and Jasper would be exposed for the fraud that he was.

Sending the men after Brendan had been a form of insurance. They were meant to make it look like a robbery, taking Brendan's purse and horse and leaving his body on the side of the road for some passerby to find, but things didn't quite go as planned. Instead, Brendan was gone and the men were dead, their families now Jasper's responsibility. He'd gone after the men when they failed to come back, and was nearly sick to his stomach when he came upon the mangled corpses strewn on the ground, the earth soaked with blood and flies already buzzing over the bodies as the crows began to gather sensing a fresh kill. The horses were grazing nearby, oblivious to what had happened and enjoying the lush grass that grew at the side of the road.

Jasper gulped lungfuls of air, his guts twisting and writhing with fear and shame. What if Brendan had recognized the men and figured out Jasper's part in this ambush? He might accuse him of attempted murder and have him sent to gaol, or worse. No, that would never do. Jasper jumped off his horse and paced in agitation, his brain working feverishly until inspiration struck. He rummaged in his saddlebag looking for the prayer book. It had been Brendan's, but he left it behind when he took his leave and Jasper sometimes took it to church when he couldn't find his own. Brendan's name was carefully scrawled inside the front cover, written years ago by a ten-year-old boy who was just learning his letters. Wilfred Carr hadn't bothered with learning, but he made sure his son got an education from the village reverend, an education that would serve him well once he became master of the estate. Jasper threw the book on the ground and pulled off his ring. It wasn't the ring his father had given Brendan, but it would do in a pinch. No one would know the difference. All he had to do now was raise the alarm and make sure that the items were found by the bodies, incriminating his brother and sending him to the gibbet.

Jasper rubbed his stubbly jaw as he stared into the dancing flames, his fingers making a rasping sound against his skin. At least he still had Mary. He'd better move up the wedding just in case. He meant to have her, and have her soon, and the quicker he got a child on her, the better. He'd mark her as his own, physically and legally, and no man would be able to take her away.

Jasper rose from his chair with a grunt and drained the remainder of his ale. It was time for bed, and tomorrow would be a better day, especially if Brendan was found and dragged off to prison to await his murder trial and subsequent execution. In the meantime, Jasper would spend a few pleasant moments fantasizing about his wedding night as he pleasured himself in the darkness of his bedchamber to relieve the mighty cockstand he was suddenly sporting. Soon it would be a reality, and he would finally be able to slake his lust on his willing bride. *Yes, things were bound to get better*, he thought as he climbed the stairs.

The Present

Chapter 27

I allowed the curtain to drop back into place, having watched my strange tenant retreat back into the ruin as the sun dropped below the horizon, and the purpling sky began to twinkle with the first stars of the evening. No amount of rationalizing on my part made the man disappear or offered any logical explanation for his presence — save one. It'd become my daily routine to watch him kneel under the tree at sunset before disappearing from view. I was no longer afraid, just curious. He clearly meant me no harm, and whatever kept his spirit tethered to this world, for I knew now that he wasn't real, had nothing to do with me or the house. What was he praying for? Was it for his restless soul to finally be set free or was there something more to this nightly routine?

The strange thing was that none of my enquiries over the past few weeks turned up anything of value. No one seemed to know anything about the ruin behind my house. I always thought that in villages like this one, where families had lived for generations, stories never really died, but no one seemed to remember this one. I'd carefully asked around, but got nothing but blank stares and shrugs, so my ghost was still nameless. There must have been someone who'd known him and loved him during his time on Earth, but there seemed to be no one left who'd remember, or if there were, they might be in another part of the country. Perhaps the man had been passing through when he died. Or he might have been killed by highwaymen, or even by friends or business associates who turned on him during an argument over money. My imagination was running rampant, but I still didn't have a shred of information about the mysterious young man who knelt under the tree.

"Who are you?" I whispered into the gathering darkness, "and what happened to you? Am I the only one who can see you?"

I was taken aback when the man suddenly turned and looked toward my window. I was sure he wasn't looking at me, but at something from his past, but it was the first time I'd seen his face. I grabbed the binoculars and trained them on his face. He was younger than I'd expected, in his mid-twenties perhaps, with a straight nose and full, unsmiling lips. I couldn't make out the color of his eyes, but they were fairly large and long-lashed, his eyebrows knitted in concentration as he continued to gaze toward the house.

"What's your name?" I asked aloud, but the only answer I got was the movement of the wind through the trees and the sound of a car horn somewhere in the distance. I watched the man disappear and lowered the binoculars, my hand shaking slightly because suddenly he seemed that much more real.

Chapter 28

After several weeks of construction, I was forced to purchase a patio set for my newly cleared back garden. It was the only place where I could get any peace during the day and avoid the constant banging and clouds of dust that seemed to permeate the entire house. I busied myself with researching eighteenth-century furniture, artwork, wall and bed hangings, and cuisine. It was too soon for me to start scouring the countryside for antiques since I had nowhere to store them, but it wasn't too soon to be prepared. I had to make a list of what I needed, create a budget, come up with a business plan, and start gathering material for my future website. I would add pictures and prices later, but for the moment, I could start working on the basics. I'd never built a website before, so it was frustrating, slow-going work.

Being away from the noise wasn't the only reason I wanted to get out of the house. I needed to keep a safe distance from Aidan as well. Being around him made me feel like a teenage girl with a crush. I found myself sneaking peeks at him as he worked, blushing when he caught me looking and averting my eyes when he smiled back. An accidental brush of the hand or a meeting in a narrow hallway left me breathless and full of longing. The air between us seemed to crackle with unseen electricity, something I'd never experienced before, not even when I fancied myself in love. I could see from his gaze that he felt it too, but although I was probably sending a lot of mixed signals, I wasn't sure how I wanted to proceed. He hadn't asked me out since he invited me to his place for a movie and a pizza, and I hadn't invited him either, partly afraid of rejection, and partly unsure of my own reaction to him. In truth, he scared me and made me feel things that I didn't know I could, and for someone like me who'd always relished being in control, that was the scariest thing of all.

And then there was Colin… At first I thought the young man was simply shy, but over the past few weeks, I sensed something in him that put me on my guard. He was always watching me; his eyes gliding over my body as I passed by or came in to say good morning or good night. He never replied or smiled back, just stared at me with an intensity that I found vaguely alarming. As I passed by the room where the men worked I heard the other workers teasing him and chatting between themselves, but Colin stayed mostly quiet; intent on his work and oblivious to the loaded looks the men gave him every time I was in the vicinity.

Colin had never done or said anything to offend me, but I found being around him uncomfortable. The other two men were fun and easygoing, so I chatted with them often as I offered them numerous cups of tea and biscuits that I brought from the village, but Colin took his tea by himself, sitting on the steps and taking drags of his cigarette between gulps of the tea. He refused the biscuits with a curt shake of the head, and seemed to prefer that I put the cup down before he picked it up rather than taking it from my hands.

I tried to be as nice and friendly as I could, smiling at Colin and attempting to include him in the conversation in the hope of drawing him out. Perhaps he had some kind of social disorder which made it difficult for him to relate to people or socialize. *He wouldn't be the first*, I thought sadly as I reflected on the rising number of cases, both at home and abroad, of people whose symptoms ranged from mild to severe on the autistic spectrum, often impairing them to the point where they couldn't lead normal lives or forge intimate relationships. All I could do was try to treat him as I treated the others and avoid showing him my unease.

I took a sip of my iced coffee and turned back to my laptop. It was a beautiful day outside, the sun gentle on my face; the buzzing of bees as they circled over the clover in the meadow and gurgling of the stream soothing as I settled to my work. The ruin looked tranquil in the bright light of the summer morning and I felt at peace, knowing that my ghost wouldn't be showing up for many hours yet. I was just poring over some photos of canopy beds with damask hangings when Aidan came strolling across the lawn. He was wearing his work overalls and his hair was covered with dust and something that might be cobwebs, but he still managed to look attractive, his stride full of purpose and his eyes crinkling at the corners as he gave me a beatific smile before grabbing a seat across from me and gazing at my screen.

"Those look expensive," he pronounced as he looked at the beds.

"I'm just getting some ideas. I'm not going to buy actual antiques. I'm going to find affordable replicas, and I can actually make some of these bed hangings and drapes myself. All I need is to buy the fabric and some fringed trim. Piece of cake."

"Hmm, sounds like you have it all figured out. I look forward to seeing the finished product. In the meantime, there's something I wanted to ask you. George and Colin were just in the basement with the plumber. Since you want to add several baths, we'll have to break the walls and install additional plumbing. Anyhow, I was wondering if you might have a large, brass key lying around somewhere."

"Is this a riddle?" I asked, puzzled by the question.

"No. When Paula gave you the keys to the house, was it just the keys for the front door?"

"There was also a key for the back door, but it's not large or made of brass. What are you going on about?" Aidan had a strange expression on his face, one of childish curiosity and suppressed excitement. "What did you find? Is it a large chest of money and jewels, like something from Aladdin's cave?"

"No, it's not quite as exciting as that, but the boys did find a hidden door with a huge padlock that looks to be a few hundred years old. Maybe it's a secret passage, or perhaps there is something of value. Why put a lock on something for no reason?" he asked, cocking one eyebrow in a way that made me laugh.

He was vibrating with excitement and I caught the bug, eager to see what was behind the secret door. "I don't know of any key, but do you think we can break the lock down?"

"I thought you'd never ask," he exclaimed as he jumped to his feet. "Let's go." I closed my laptop and followed Aidan back to the house. I couldn't imagine that the previous owners would leave something of great value, but who knew? They'd left the house full of furniture, personal papers, and even photo albums. I would have thought that to be valuable, but I guess they didn't want any part of their history.

The steps to the basement were made of stone and well-worn by numerous feet over the centuries. The rough-hewn walls and low ceiling made me feel a little claustrophobic, and I was glad of Aidan's comforting presence and industrial-sized flashlight, which he referred to as a torch. A torch would actually be very appropriate right about now, since I felt as if we'd stepped back in time. The vaulted ceiling and flagged floors reminded me of a crypt in a church, but there was nothing in the cavernous space save a few wooden wine racks which were mostly empty. A few dusty bottles could be seen here and there, but otherwise, everything had been cleaned out years ago, judging by the layer of dust and the cobwebs that seemed to fill every corner of the ceiling, hanging down like some gothic bridal veils from a horror film.

We took several turns until I had no idea what part of the house we were beneath. There had been a light bulb in the main part of the basement, but as we turned off into smaller tunnels, it was pitch dark except for the beam of Aidan's flashlight. He pointed it straight ahead, and I finally saw the door built into the stone wall. It was made of dark wood, arched, with rusted iron hinges and studs, and a huge padlock that looked as if it hadn't been touched in centuries.

"Maybe it was a torture chamber or a dungeon." I was going for a lighthearted tone, but my voice sounded tense and full of apprehension. I was suddenly very uneasy and wanted to turn back.

"I doubt it," Aidan replied, having taken my comment at face value. "It could be a secret chapel, if they were Catholics, or a reverend hole."

The idea of having to come down into the bowels of the earth to pray or hide didn't hold much appeal, but then that was the whole idea of clandestine worship. I tried to imagine what life must have been like in a time when practicing one's religion could lead to an accusation of heresy or worse and shuddered. It seemed wrong somehow to violate this sanctum, one that was hidden and locked by someone who needed or wanted to keep others out, but Aidan didn't seem to share my sentiments. He lifted the padlock with his hand to get a closer look, the beam of his flashlight hitting the section of wall to the right of the door and the corner.

"Wouldn't a reverend hole have a second exit so the reverend could escape in case of trouble?" I asked, my voice trembling. I didn't want to be here. I wanted to go back outside into the sunshine where things were safe and bright, at least until sunset.

"Normally, yes, and maybe there is a second exit. We'll find out once we get this door opened."

"Shine some light over here," I asked as I stepped off to the side. There, in a small alcove built into the stone was the key. It was so heavy, I almost needed both hands to lift it, and I nearly dropped it in disgust as a swath of cobwebs came off into my hand, the spider still very much in residence.

"Give it here, love," Aidan requested as he reached for the key. "And hold the torch for me just so."

I pointed the light at the padlock and watched as Aidan struggled to turn the key in the rusted keyhole. It took a few tries, but I finally heard a scrape as Aidan carefully removed the lock and put it back in the alcove with the key. He tried the door, but it didn't open right away since the wood of the door had become warped over time, and probably swollen with the damp that seemed to seep through the walls and right into my bones. Or was that fear?

Aidan put a shoulder to the door and it finally gave, opening with a shudder of protest to reveal a small chamber beyond. He reached for the flashlight and shone it on the walls of the little room. Sadly, it didn't contain anything that might have been a hidden treasure; instead, it boasted a wooden bench, two brackets for torches and a stone slab on a plinth. I couldn't see any evidence of another way out; the walls were solid stone, so probably not a reverend hole, unless the way out wasn't immediately visible.

I followed Aidan into the room and looked around. It was about ten by ten, with a low ceiling and thick stone walls decorated only with cobwebs and rusty brackets. It was, in essence, a stone box deep beneath the earth that made me feel claustrophobic and short of breath. At first, I took the chamber to be a secret chapel of some kind, with the slab serving as an altar and the bench used as a pew, but the altar seemed too high for a reverend to stand behind, the top not smooth, but carved with something that might have been an effigy.

"Is that what I think it is?" I whispered, as if the occupant could hear me and object to the disturbance. I shivered with apprehension as Aidan drew closer while I hung back, feeling safer by the door.

"I think so. It looks like a tomb." Aidan walked slowly around the coffin, running his hand over the stone as if looking for something.

"What are you doing?" I whispered again.

"I'm looking for an inscription of some kind. I want to know who it belongs to."

"Do you really think there's someone inside?" I asked as I backed even further toward the safety of the doorway.

"There's only one way to find out." Before I could protest, Aidan handed me the flashlight and pushed the lid of the sarcophagus with all his might. The stone made a loud scraping noise that filled the small space and set my teeth on edge. It was like something out of *Indiana Jones*, and I almost expected Aidan to release some ancient curse, but nothing happened as he reached for the light and shone it inside, his face alight with curiosity, like a little boy's.

"Well?" I asked, too afraid to see for myself.

"Occupied," he replied as he shone the light beneath the lid toward where the feet would be. "Very strange," he mumbled as he continued to gaze into the coffin, mesmerized.

"We shouldn't be disturbing someone's resting place," I hissed as Aidan moved the heavy slab back in place before continuing his search for an inscription. It took him a few minutes, but he finally found it and asked me to shine the light on it.

The writing was worn off, but we could still make out the name. "Brendan Carr. Born 1626. Died 16—."

"I can't make out the date he died," Aidan said as he peered at the number. "It could be 1650 or 1690, or neither. The number is illegible."

"It can't be 1650," I pointed out. "This house was completed in 1681, so it'd have to be after that for him to be interred here."

"Yes, I think you're right." Aidan was looking around, but I was starting to feel anxious in this small, dark space containing the remains of an unknown man, who had for some unfathomable reason been entombed in this chamber.

"Aidan, please, can we go now?" I pleaded, my voice shaking.

"Of course," he replied, sensing my unease.

I felt better as we got closer to the steps leading to the ground floor. The damp darkness of the basement was oppressive and creepy, and I breathed a sigh of relief as we finally stepped into the sunlit hallway off the kitchen. Aidan followed me to my haven out back and took a seat across from me, absentmindedly brushing the cobwebs from his face. I noted that his expression went from one of excitement to one of confusion as he stared off into space, lost in thought.

"What is it?" I asked. I was still terribly uneasy, and Aidan's silence scared me even more.

"It doesn't make any sense," Aidan finally said, his brow furrowed as he continued to puzzle things out. "People in the seventeenth-century were deeply religious and took burials very seriously. It was of paramount importance to be buried in hallowed ground, and I've even heard of instances where women who'd given birth to a stillborn or whose babies died before the sacrament of baptism, secretly buried their children on the outskirts of church graveyards just to have them lie in consecrated ground. Why would someone forego a church burial and hide a casket in the cellar of their home?"

"I have no idea, but it creeps me out." The idea of sharing a house with someone's remains made me feel very uncomfortable.

"There's something else," Aidan continued as his eyes met mine. "The skeleton in the sarcophagus seems to have been buried naked."

"How could you know that after all this time?" I asked, staring at him in shock.

"When I looked inside, there were no bits of cloth, metal, or leather. Something would have remained, such as buttons, shoe or belt buckles, or a sword, had he been buried with one. There was nothing at all except for some loose dirt at the bottom."

"Maybe he'd been buried in a shroud and the fabric had decomposed after all this time," I suggested, shivering at the gruesome thought.

151

"Maybe, but did you notice that there was no smell when I opened the lid? Had he been buried right after he died, the smell of decomposition would have been trapped inside the coffin and been released. All I smelled was dust and stale air. And where did the dirt come from?"

"So, what are you suggesting?" I asked, suddenly realizing that I would have to come to some kind of a decision about the tomb. I could hardly just leave a sarcophagus in the basement while paying guests were upstairs unaware of the sinister room just below their feet.

"I don't know. It's just all terribly strange, don't you think?" Aidan asked, his face aglow with curiosity. He didn't seem to be disturbed by our find — just intrigued.

"I think that's the understatement of the year," I replied as I glanced uneasily toward the sunlit ruin.

Chapter 29

I knew it was silly, but I left the light on as I prepared for bed that night. Knowing that there was an occupied tomb two floors beneath my room made me feel as if I'd just watched a scary movie and expected something to jump out at me at any moment, despite knowing that it had all been a product of someone's imagination. I wasn't frightened, exactly, but I shivered at the thought of sharing my house with someone who'd been dead for hundreds of years. I jumped out of bed and locked the bedroom door; as if the skeleton would suddenly rise, slide open the lid of his stone casket and come wandering through the house in search of the American usurper who now owned his resting place. I let out a nervous giggle at the thought, still amazed at our discovery. Had the last owners known of the secret room, or had they never ventured that far into the subterranean space? It didn't seem as if any work had been done on the house in decades, so it was possible that no one actually went down there.

I finally turned out the light, but sleep wouldn't come. My mind kept spinning, imagining all the possible scenarios that could have played out on this very spot in the seventeenth century. It'd been a bloody time in English history, and there were any number of ways my new housemate could have died. I must have eventually fallen asleep, but my mind still wouldn't rest. I was haunted by images of battlefields running crimson with blood as riderless horses wandered between the fallen, and soldiers of the victorious army walked from body to body, stabbing them with their swords to make sure they were really and truly dead. The air was filled with an acrid smell of smoke, which mixed with spindly fingers of fog to cover up the horror beneath.

Then the scene changed and I was in the village, watching from somewhere up above as a rickety cart filled with corpses rolled down the narrow street, stopping periodically to accept more

dead from the terrified families hiding behind doors. The doors
did precious little to protect them from the plague which killed so
rampantly in those days, claiming the lives of young and old alike,
with no consideration for social status or wealth. The corpses in
the cart were covered with sores and their own filth, already
decomposing as they made their final journey to a mass grave dug
on the outskirts of the village, where a young reverend muttered
words of prayer as several men whose faces were covered by
handkerchiefs tossed bodies into the yawning hole, and quickly
covered them with a thick layer of earth to keep the disease from
spreading. A plague doctor in a hideous birdlike mask stood in the
shadow of a tree, his eyes peering through the holes in the mask as
he watched the proceedings dispassionately, resigned to the futility
of his task.

I woke up screaming, my face covered with cold sweat and
my hands frantically searching my body for plague sores. It took
me a few minutes to finally calm down and banish the dream from
my mind as I lay back panting, terrified to fall back asleep for fear
of reliving the nightmare from which I'd just awoken. Thankfully,
dawn wasn't far away.

***

Cranky and tired after a restless night, I made myself a cup
of strong coffee and some breakfast as I considered my plans for
the day. The men would be here in about an hour, so I would be
wise to get out of their way. They would be breaking walls in
order to start laying plumbing for several bathrooms that would be
installed in the guestrooms of the second and third floors. In other
words, I had to make myself scarce. Aidan had mentioned talking
to the vicar, and there was no time like the present. Maybe he
could shed some light on the Carrs of this area. The manor house
had been built by the Hughes family, but there had to be some
connection to the man entombed in the cellar, and I meant to find
it, one way or another.

I put on a strapless sundress and a pair of sandals, then,
after a look in the mirror, grabbed a denim jacket from the closet.
It didn't seem proper to go into a church in a strapless dress. A

little decorum might go a long way in obtaining information, especially if the vicar was an elderly man. I hadn't set foot inside a church in years, but if my past experience was anything to go on, modesty was always the right answer.

"Where are you off to looking so pretty?" George called out as I walked past him in the front yard. Colin was by the truck, watching me as usual with that hooded look that made me feel uneasy. I included him in my greeting, but my instinct screamed to give the young man a wide berth, so I walked the other way which led me past Declan. I wouldn't care to be alone with Colin in the house or anywhere else for that matter. Declan just gave me a warm smile as I passed. He was engaged in a spirited discussion with the plumber, debating the merits of copper pipes. The plumber, who was a tubby little man with a balding pate, was vehemently advising against copper, saying that they corroded faster in a rural environment. I made a mental note to research pipes once I got back to the house. It was just another thing to add to my list of things I knew nothing about.

"I'm just going to pop into the village. Need anything?" I called out.

"A kiss would do," George replied, blowing me a kiss which I pretended to catch and slip into my pocket. I liked George. He reminded me of construction workers back home who considered it their duty to whistle at every pretty girl and call out something suggestive. Some of my friends bristled at the insult, but I found it kind of sweet as long as the comments weren't degrading or mean. I never took being admired for granted, and George's comments were always more good-natured than lewd.

I passed through the gates and set out down the lane that led to the village. It was a bit of a hike, and I suddenly wished that I had accepted Aidan's offer of cleaning and oiling the bicycle he'd found in one of the sheds. It would be useful in getting around until I bought a car. The bicycle had an old-fashioned basket which looked childish, but was probably most useful when bringing home shopping bags. I couldn't help wondering who the bike belonged to. Mrs. Hughes had been too elderly to be whizzing around on a bicycle, but it might have belonged to one of her daughters — possibly Kelly. I was probably better off walking after all, I thought. I wasn't ready to ride a dead woman's bike.

It took me a moment to realize how negative my thoughts had become, so I forced my brain to put all my worries on hold and concentrate on the beauty around me. The morning was brisk, but full of promise, as the sun gradually began to warm the air. Dew glistened on emerald-colored grass like shards of crystal, and the air was filled with glorious birdsong, uninterrupted by the sounds of traffic or passersby. I stopped and looked over the lush landscape, breathing deeply as I felt the stress drain away and a feeling of serenity take hold of my troubled mind. Whatever happened, happened, and nothing could or should mar my joy at living my dream. I was exactly where I wanted to be, doing what I'd fantasized about for years. How many people were as lucky? I suddenly felt dizzying happiness flow through my veins like mercury. I was the luckiest girl in the world and no skeletons in the closet could ruin that.

I began to walk faster, driven by my newfound exhilaration. All this was just research into the past and an interesting story to regale my guests with. It had nothing whatsoever to do with my real life, and I'd be wise to remember that.

Chapter 30

The old Norman church occupied pride of place in the village, its gray façade overlooking the village green and presiding over all the happenings like a silent sentinel who'd been on duty for centuries. I walked through the gate and down the stone path that ran through the graveyard, dotted with headstones old and new. Some were so ancient they leaned drunkenly to the side, the inscriptions almost completely erased by time and the elements. The newer stones appeared to be farther away from the church since the cemetery must have grown and expanded over the years, but the stone wall that encircled the graveyard seemed to be as old as the church itself, the church's territory marked in a distinct and unyielding way.

I suddenly imagined desperate young women sneaking into the churchyard at night, and burying their unbaptized babies close to the wall or under the yew trees that grew throughout the cemetery, praying that no one would notice the freshly dug earth and evict their beloved children from consecrated ground. How heartbreaking it must have been to think that an innocent baby would be consigned to Limbo for eternity. Luckily, most people didn't believe that anymore, but centuries ago the prospect was very real, and considering the amount of children who died before, during, or after birth, Limbo must have been teeming with tiny souls, crying for their mothers.

I forced myself to put my morbid thoughts aside and entered the church porch which was shaded and almost entirely covered in ivy. I pushed open the door and walked into the cool interior of the church. It wasn't large, but very pretty, in that way that old churches tended to be. I'd never liked the modern churches that were so bright and devoid of ornament. This old church, although Anglican, instantly made me feel peaceful and calm. The colorful rays of sunlight filtered through the stained glass windows and cast a kaleidoscope of color onto the wooden pews and stone nave. The church smelled of polish and flowers, which were at the moment being arranged by some old biddy from the village.

"Oh, hello, dear," she called out as I walked toward the altar, the heels of my sandals clicking on the stone floor like hammers on an anvil.

"Good morning. I was looking for the vicar," I replied, feeling suddenly very awkward. I hadn't spoken to a member of the clergy since my confirmation half a lifetime ago, and I didn't remember that as a particularly pleasant experience. I'd been nervous and apprehensive as the priest explained to me the Sacrament of Confirmation as outlined by the Catechism of the Catholic Church. I thought he'd be the one performing the confirmation, but it had been performed by the bishop, which was even more intimidating. To make matters worse, my father had insisted that I go to confession a week before the ceremony, which left me nearly paralyzed with fear. I had nothing to confess other than having some uncharitable thoughts about a girl in my class who'd been mean to me, and more embarrassingly, some impure thoughts about Brad Pitt after watching *Legends of the Fall* with my mom.

I mumbled my confession after being prodded several times by the priest, and exploded out of the confession box like a circus performer who'd been fired out of a cannon. That had been my first and last confession, and I had resolutely refused to go to church with my parents after that. My obstinacy resulted in many fights, especially with my father, but I stuck to my guns and eventually proclaimed myself an atheist which made my father hit the ceiling. He never did forgive me my rebellion, but he learned to live with it.

The elderly woman finished her flower arrangement and disappeared through a door in the apse, which I assumed to be the sacristy or an office of the vicar. She reappeared about a minute later, followed by another woman who beamed at me as if she'd been waiting for me all her life. It took me a moment to realize that I was looking at the vicar of Upper Whitford.

"Good morning, and welcome," she said as she offered me her hand. "I'm Vicar Veronica Sumner." She was no older than forty, with thick dark hair worn in a ponytail, blue eyes that sparkled with good humor, and a smile that lit up her face. She was a little chubby, her cassock stretching across her ample breasts in a way that seemed incongruous on a member of the clergy. I felt instantly drawn to her, and all my nervousness evaporated as she invited me to sit with her in the first pew.

"I'm Lexi Maxwell. I bought the Hughes place," I began by way of introduction.

"Yes, I heard. Lovely old pile, isn't it? Shame for the family to let it go after all these years, but sometimes change is good. I hear you want to open an inn." She seemed genuinely interested, so I gave her a quick rundown of what I had in mind.

"Splendid. Absolutely splendid. This village can use a little new blood, not to mention some income from tourists. An eighteenth-century manor house hotel is just what we need to put us on the map. Have you got a name picked out?"

"I thought of calling it *The Maxwell Arms*. Too pompous?" I asked, watching her face closely.

"Not at all. In fact, I quite like it; has a nice ring to it. As long as you don't call it the Queen's Head and have an image of a severed, blood-squirting neck. Every time I pass that sign I cringe. You'd think they'd have come up with something a little less gory by now, but the villagers seem to love it. It's their bit of Tudor history."

I was glad to see that Vicar Sumner was more amused than dismayed by the ways of her parishioners. Fire and brimstone were clearly not part of her repertoire. I was curious what her sermons were like, but I hadn't come to church for spiritual guidance.

159

"Vicar, speaking of history, I was wondering how far back the parish records go? There was someone from the seventeenth century I wanted to look up and thought I might find some information here."

"The records actually go back to the sixteenth-century, and would have gone further back had there not been a fire in 1562. And," she added triumphantly, "they're all on my computer." She smiled at my expression of surprise and leaned forward a little, her voice conspiratorial as she explained. "My son is a bit of a rascal, to say the least. He gets into trouble routinely, so I devised a punishment for him a few years ago that would benefit the community. I had him transcribe all the records into a database which the villagers could use when putting together their family trees and searching for lost relatives. Who did you say you wanted to look for?"

It took me a moment to recover from this bit of information. Of course, I had forgotten that Anglican clergy were allowed to marry and often lived with their families in the vicarages attached to the church. They were not required to take a vow of celibacy, and I had the briefest image of Vicar Sumner in a compromising position with a faceless man before I gave myself a mental slap and turned my attention back to the purpose of my visit.

"Carr is the family name," I replied as I rose to my feet to follow her to her office. "Actually, Brendan Carr is the person I wish to find."

"Ancestor of yours?" the vicar asked breezily as she plopped into a well-worn leather chair.

"Not exactly."

"Well, no matter. We can look him up in a tic." The vicar sat in front of her computer and brought up the database, entering "Carr" into the search field. Nothing came up. She tried "Brendan Carr" with the same result.

"Are you sure you've got the correct spelling?" she asked as she looked up at me.

"Fairly sure. Can I ask you something, Vicar?"

"Of course. That's what I'm here for. Fire away."

"Why would someone in the seventeenth century choose not to bury a corpse in a churchyard?" I expected her to be shocked by the question, but Vicar Sumner just shrugged her shoulders as if she had no clue and turned away from the screen.

"My best guess would be that the person who died was of a different religion. There were many secret Catholics in England during that period, so the person might have received last rites from a Catholic priest and was interred somewhere where the family thought their resting place was safe. They likely wouldn't want to bury a Catholic in an Anglican churchyard. Does that help?"

"Yes, I think it does. Would there be any other possible reasons?

"Had it been a suicide, the person would have been buried at a crossroads, as was the custom back then. Other than that, I can't think of any other reason why someone would forgo being buried in hallowed ground."

"What if the person in question was a traitor and the family didn't want their grave desecrated?" I wanted to explore all the possibilities, although I could think of no others beyond that one.

Vicar Sumner leaned back in her chair and folded her hands in her lap, her eyes clouded with thought. "The seventeenth century was a very volatile time in English history, so one man's traitor might have been another man's hero. Perceptions changed so quickly in those days."

"Where did this village stand, politically I mean?" I asked.

"I can't answer that with any certainty. Good or bad, Catholic or Protestant, England had always had a monarch until the execution of Charles I. The common people had never thought to question the rights of a king, seeing him as God's representative on Earth; nor had they thought to question the rights of man. These were radically new concepts in those days. Of course, some people supported the new order, but others were terribly frightened and longed for the old ways. In general, I would have to say that most of the common people tried to keep their heads down and survive as best they could."

Vicar Sumner sighed before she continued, obviously warming up to the subject. "After Oliver Cromwell had himself declared Lord Protectorate, more people began to question his motives, now seeing him as someone who, for all intents and purposes, crowned himself king. Maybe the Protectorate would have endured had Cromwell's son been a stronger leader, but the Protectorate was followed by the Restoration, when Charles II was invited to come home from exile and retake his father's throne. It was a period of considerable joy." The vicar looked at me to see if I was following the history lesson. I'd read some of this in the past, but it was interesting to hear it from a person rather than a book.

"Were people that happy to have their king back?" I asked, trying to envision that period in history.

"Many saw it as a return to the divinely ordained way of things, and others were just happy to see Puritanism wane. The theaters reopened, music and dancing were once again permitted, and there was a period of general joie de vivre," the vicar said, making a wholly Gallic gesture with her right hand. "And of course, none of this answers your question."

"No, but it helps. Thank you for explaining it to me," I said, reluctant to leave. I had really enjoyed talking to this fascinating woman.

"Oh, anytime. I'm forbidden to speak about history at home. My husband and children just roll their eyes and suddenly remember important things they have to do like taking out the rubbish bins and cleaning their rooms. I'm always eager for an audience."

"Well, you can have an audience of one. I love history, but it comes truly alive when someone knowledgeable tells you about it."

"Just pick a subject and I'll gladly tell you more," the vicar promised, glancing at her watch. "I'm afraid it won't be today though."

"I'd love to hear about what happened after Charles II died and his brother was exiled due to his religion, but I can wait."

"That's a story that can take several hours," the vicar replied as she rose to her feet and adjusted her cassock. I still had a hard time believing that this approachable woman, who was also a wife and a mother, was the religious leader of this community. I'd never thought I would think it, but I suddenly longed to go to church, if only to hear her sermon.

"I hope to see you on Sunday," the vicar said as we shook hands in front of the altar.

"You just might, Vicar. You just might."

Chapter 31

I walked out of the church, suddenly unsure of where I wanted to go next. It was too early to go back home, so I wandered through the cemetery, looking at the headstones. I've always had a morbid fascination with death and its aftermath. There were always gravestones that had fresh flowers, a sure sign that someone still cared and missed that person deeply, but the majority looked neglected, the deceased forgotten in the whirlwind of daily life. Those are the ones that always made me feel sad, especially when the dates indicated that the person who died had been young. I walked around staring at names that meant nothing to me until I came across the graves of Kelly Gregson and Eleanor Hughes.

Mother and daughter were buried side by side, their graves surprisingly well tended with remnants of flowers that had wilted no more than a day or two ago. I couldn't help wondering who came to visit them since Myra was gone, and Neil Gregson was still in prison as far as I knew. Kelly and Eleanor had lived in this village their whole lives, so someone must have loved and cared about them besides their family.

"Came to pay your respects, have you?" a voice behind me asked, nearly making me jump out of my skin.

"Oh, I'm sorry. I didn't mean to startle you," Dorothea Martin said as she appeared next to me. "I come every week."

"Were you very close with Mrs. Hughes?" I asked, glad that someone visited the graves.

"More so in later years," Dot said as she went about picking up the wilted flowers and dead leaves. "I used to come 'round quite often when the girls were still at school and we were all friends, but it wasn't until after Kelly's death that I began to work for Mrs. Hughes. Myra hired me to look after her mother, so I saw her every day. She was a good woman, very motherly, and she reminded me of my own mum when she was still alive. Sometimes Eleanor forgot herself and called me Myra or Kelly. There were days when she was lucid, but then there were other days when she just retreated into the past, forgetting that her daughters were gone. And on those days, she kept asking for Sandy, her granddaughter. She kept worrying that Sandy had gotten lost and wouldn't find her way back. Those were the days that broke my heart."

Dot placed fresh flowers on both graves and rose to her feet, brushing invisible dirt off her skirt. She touched her fingers to her lips and then pressed them to each gravestone before turning to leave. "I hope you'll come by for a cup of tea one of these days. I'm just down the road. It does get lonely when you're on your own, doesn't it? My husband passed a few years ago, but sometimes I still think that I hear him on the stairs, or that he's just gone out to the pub for a drink. And then I remember that he's gone, and it's like losing him all over again."

"Thank you, Mrs. Martin. I would love to come for tea, and you're right, it does get lonely. This is the first time I've truly been on my own, and I'm finding it rather hard."

Dot noticeably perked up, a smile lighting up her face. "Why don't you come by around four? I'll make us a nice shepherd's pie. That was my Brian's favorite. I don't cook much these days. Usually just make a sandwich for my tea, but I do enjoy cooking for a guest."

"That sounds wonderful," I replied, glad to have made someone happy. Talking to Dot made me miss my own mother terribly. I'd asked her to come to England with me, but she refused. Maybe she'd come once the inn was open and she could stay as my guest. My mother had never been much of a cook, but she did enjoy eating out, and we spent many a Sunday morning enjoying brunch in the city. I'd taken those outings for granted, but now I'd give anything to spend a few hours with my mother; just talking things over and asking for her advice. I knew that she missed me dreadfully as well, but for some strange reason, she was stubbornly refusing all my invitations to come and stay.

Chapter 32

I showed up at Dot's cottage at precisely 4 p.m. bearing a store-bought cake and a bottle of wine, just in case. I wasn't sure if wine was proper for tea, but I didn't want to come empty-handed. Dot was overjoyed to see me and gratefully accepted my gifts, setting the cake on the sideboard and rummaging in a drawer for a corkscrew, which she finally unearthed and handed to me triumphantly before disappearing into the kitchen. She set the steaming shepherd's pie on the table and took off her flowery apron before inviting me to sit down. The pie looked delicious; the potato crust perfectly browned and sprinkled with shredded cheese. There was also a salad and some freshly baked rolls.

"Dot, that smells amazing. I've never had shepherd's pie, but it seems like the ultimate comfort food," I said as I took my first bite and rolled my eyes in ecstasy. It was heaven.

"Oh, it is. Nothing satisfies like meat and potatoes, does it? But I'm glad you like it. It's too much of a bother to make for one person, but I do enjoy cooking for company. I'll be sure to give you some to take home. Do you cook?" she asked, her interest not altogether innocent. I was beginning to guess that there was more to Dot's invitation than mere hospitality. She was auditioning for a job, and at this rate, I was very likely to give it to her. My role would be to manage, but I'd still need someone to clean and cook for the guests, and although I might have to hire a chef to prepare exquisite dinners, Dot would be perfect for making good, local fare that would be available to those who didn't care to spend hundreds of pounds on a meal.

I had to admit that I had ulterior motives of my own, other than getting a home-cooked meal that didn't involve beans. Dot was clearly fond of talking, and I wanted to find out more about the Hughes family and the murder. My father always used to say that information was the most valuable commodity, and I tended to agree with him. I had to be prepared for any eventuality, and frankly, I was also morbidly curious which made me feel slightly ashamed, but undeterred.

"So, was Neil Gregson a violent man?" I asked innocently, hoping to steer Dot toward the subject of Kelly's death. That question was all it took. From that point on, all I had to do was listen.

"Oh no, not that anyone could say. Neil was a gentle soul, the type of man you'd never suspect of an act of violence. He loved Kelly since he was a lad, always trailing after her and carrying her satchel after school. She went with him, but I don't think her heart was ever truly in it. She just liked the idea of having someone love her that much. I suppose she was curious too, as we all were. We weren't as open back then about our sexual experiences, not like today. Girls and boys were experimenting, but they kept it to themselves until someone got in the family way and there was a quickie wedding. There were plenty of children born out of wedlock in the big cities, but in a village like this, the old ways linger. I think Kelly was sleeping with Neil, but I suspect it was more out of curiosity than true passion. I asked her about it a few times, but she was a coy one, giving very little away. The trip to America changed her."

I poured Dot another glass of wine, but didn't interrupt the soliloquy. I wanted to keep her talking.

"See, Kelly was the type of girl who wanted to be a big fish in a small pond, but Myra wasn't satisfied with village life. That one was always chomping at the bit, as you Americans say. She wanted to see something of the world, and be a part of something bigger. She did a secretarial course in Lincoln, and fled to America as soon as she could afford it. Said she had some friend there who would put her up until she found a job. She invited Kelly to come and visit her, and that seemed to have been the catalyst for everything that happened later. Kelly came back a changed girl, and suddenly all the things she loved made her feel stifled, including Neil."

"Did you go to the trial?" I asked as I accepted another piece of the pie. I was stuffed, but I had to admit, it was irresistible.

"Oh, yes. I went for Eleanor's sake, and of course, Kelly had been my friend. The whole trial lasted less than an hour, mind you; it was over before it began." Dot took a sip of wine, her eyes shining with the pleasure of being able to enlighten someone who was so clearly in the dark. These were the kind of moments she'd probably relished. I could almost picture her prattling on about all the village gossip, as her husband silently chewed his food and made occasional sounds to let her know that he was actually still listening. Or maybe he loved hearing about all the people in the village. My own father had encouraged my mother to share all the gossip with him. He particularly enjoyed all the romantic "shenanigans" as he called them.

"How could a murder trial last less than an hour?" That didn't make sense at all. Just the opening arguments would probably take that long.

"Neil had refused counsel and asked to represent himself. He pleaded guilty, and naturally, got the maximum sentence. He didn't say a single thing in his own defense. I heard some people talking outside the courthouse, and they said the charge could have easily been reduced to manslaughter had he allowed legal representation. You see, it wasn't as if he shot Kelly point blank, or stabbed her. They had a row, and he hit her so hard she fell and hit her temple on the edge of a table; so for all intents and purposes, it might not have been his intention to kill her at all. It wasn't premeditated, you see, but a crime of passion."

"So you think he wanted to go to prison?" I asked, shocked. What kind of person would want to spend decades in prison if he didn't have to?

"I think he was just so broken up over what he'd done that at that point, he simply didn't care what happened to him. He appeared dazed in court. Half dazed and half dead."

"You felt sorry for him, didn't you?" I asked, seeing the look of sympathy in Dot's eyes.

"I did, rather. Neil was a nice lad, the kind of lad any girl would have been happy to have on her arm. He really loved Kelly; we all knew it. Something dreadful must have happened to drive him to such a fit of rage, and if anyone was capable of provoking him, it was Kelly. I certainly don't condone physical abuse, but had Kelly fallen the other way, she'd probably still be alive now, and Neil would be a free man, although one with a record for domestic violence. It was just bad luck for all involved, especially poor Sandy."

"Are there any pictures of the family?" I asked as Dot cut the cake and poured me a cup of strong tea, to which she added a splash of milk.

"There was a box of family albums in the house, but Eleanor took it up to the attic after Sandy was taken away. She couldn't bear to look at them. I reckon the box is still there, unless you consigned it to your bonfire."

"No, I would never do that. Had I seen it, I would have offered to return it to either Myra or Roger Hughes. I'm actually very surprised that neither one had bothered to go through the house and clear it out."

Dot took a sip of tea and a dainty bite of cake, which seemed to meet with her satisfaction. "That house holds too many painful memories for Myra, and as for Roger, he was never the sentimental type. He had very little to do with Eleanor in later years, so I wouldn't expect him to take the time to bother with her belongings."

I couldn't help feeling sad for Eleanor Hughes. Not only had she lost a daughter, but her granddaughter had been taken away, her eldest daughter moved to London, and no one cared enough to even try to salvage something of Eleanor's belongings. How sad to think that the possessions she acquired over a lifetime, valued and preserved, meant so little to other people that they couldn't be bothered to sift through them and keep even a memento of the woman who was no longer there. I wouldn't expect Myra or Roger to hang on to the outdated furniture or old-fashioned appliances, but to leave a box of family pictures for a stranger to find? That just seemed awfully callous.

"… and Aidan Mackay?" Dot's voice interrupted my thoughts, her eyes shining with curiosity over the rim of the cup as she continued to sip her tea.

"I'm sorry, Dot, did you ask me something?"

"Oh, I was just asking if there might be something brewing between you and Aidan. He's another dark horse, so beware. Broke off his engagement to a lovely young woman just days before the wedding. Young men these days are so terrified of commitment. The poor thing was so heartbroken she left the village. Of course, that's not much of a deterrent for women these days, is it? There's not a girl in this village who hasn't set her cap for him since Noelle left. He is good-looking, I'll give you that, with those dreamy blue eyes and that sexy smile. Oh, don't look at me like that!" Dot laughed. "I might be old enough to be your mother, but I can still appreciate an attractive man, and Aidan is an attractive man. Had I been about thirty years younger, I'd try for him myself."

"No, there's nothing going on. He's doing a job for me; that's all." I felt myself blushing, and hoped Dot wouldn't notice my discomfort.

"Oh, come now. You must have noticed how attractive he is."

"He is, but our relationship is strictly professional." I suddenly remembered waking up next to Aidan on the hillside by the embers of our fire, my butt pressed against his pelvis. I could feel his arousal through my jeans, and the memory turned my cheeks from flushed to full-blown crimson. Dot just smiled serenely and poured me another cup of tea. I had a feeling that

171

there was very little she missed, and that made her a great ally and a dangerous enemy.

As I walked home, I couldn't help thinking of everything I'd learned from Dot. She was right about one thing: it was really all about luck. Had Kelly and Neil fought someplace else, or had she fallen onto the sofa or to the other side of the coffee table, she'd still be alive now and Neil wouldn't be serving a sentence for murder. Their daughter would still be in Upper Whitford, not somewhere out in the world, torn apart from the only family she had known, and Myra would probably not have run away for fear that she was somehow responsible for what happened to Kelly while she was away. Eleanor Hughes wouldn't have died a broken and lonely old woman. Funny how life worked out sometimes. One terrible argument led to so many broken lives.

I hadn't wanted to gossip about Aidan, but the things Dot said gave me pause. Did I get him all wrong? I unwittingly put my trust in him and allowed him to become more than just a contractor. He had become my friend, and I would be lying if I said I didn't find him attractive, but Dot painted a very different picture of him. Was he the type of person to break off an engagement a few days before the wedding because of cold feet, or was there another reason? He'd mentioned that his fiancée had left, but had it been her decision or had he driven her away from her home with his callous behavior? Had he been seeing someone else behind her back?

Stop jumping to conclusions, I admonished myself as I slid the key in the lock, *you have absolutely no basis for your speculation*. Whatever happened between Aidan and his fiancée was none of my business, and he owed me no explanations. If there ever came a time when we got closer, he might tell me, but for now, I would put it out of my mind.

October 1650

England

Chapter 33

Rowan huddled deeper into the bedclothes, pulling her legs up to her chest, more for comfort than for warmth. The October days were still deliciously mild, smelling of sun-warmed earth and hay, but the nights were cold, the chilly air nipping at her bare skin when the thin blanket slid off in her sleep. Her aunt smoored the fire at bedtime, allowing the house to become cold as a tomb overnight, but Rowan slept close to the hearth and could still feel some warmth from the chimney stones. They radiated heat like the warm brick that her mother used to put at her feet during the coldest months of the winter.

She hoped Brendan was warm enough. Reverend Pole rarely lit a fire unless it was bitterly cold. The old reverend was oblivious to bodily discomfort, eating only when there was something to eat, and sleeping only when he could no longer stay upright. He'd become forgetful, but miraculously could still recite the scripture from memory, and write sermons that left everyone's behinds numb after hours of sitting in the hard pews. Going to Reverend Pole's house daily to care for him was not a ruse. He'd probably forget to eat and starve if someone didn't come in, light the fire, and prepare something warm to put in his belly. Rowan also made sure to wash his shirts and underthings since he wasn't likely to do it himself.

Only a few years ago, the old man had been in robust health, walking for miles to see a parishioner or to clear his mind with vigorous exercise. Reverend Pole was deteriorating, and Rowan felt a pang of sadness at the certain knowledge that he wasn't going to last much longer. That was the strange thing about life; it gave you people to care for and then took them away, sometimes suddenly, leaving you bereft and grieving, unable to do anything to alleviate the hurt that was burning a hole in your heart.

And Brendan… He was up there in that loft with nothing to keep him warm but his fury. He'd been beside himself when he found out about the accusation of murder. If he were caught, he was as good as dead. No one would believe that his own brother had sent men to kill him, or that he had planted Brendan's belongings by the bodies to incriminate him. Whatever his reasons, Jasper wanted his brother dead. How could people who were supposedly made in the image of God and who claimed to be decent, God-fearing folk be so unbearably cruel? This train of thought led her down a dark passage to a door she tried to keep locked at all times. Even a slight peek left her shaking violently, her heart hammering against her ribs until she thought it might break with the strain. She knew that sooner or later she'd have to face the truth and find a way to move forward, but the memories were still fresh and heartbreakingly real, and the dreams that haunted her nights a merciless reenactment of the horrible day which changed her life forever.

Rowan wrapped her arms around her knees, bringing them even closer to her chest until she was in a fetal position. It made her feel safe, although as she learned the day her mother died, there was no such thing as safety. She had begun to feel somewhat removed from the nightmare, living with Uncle Caleb and Aunt Joan, until Brendan appeared out of the blue, tearing her peace apart at the seams, and reminding her that destiny had come knocking, just as her mother said it would. Rowan had tried to keep her distance, averting her eyes when she could, especially when applying the salve to his wounds, her hands touching his warm flesh as he gazed up at her, trying to catch her eye. He wasn't just angry; he was lonely and lost, and he needed her as much as she needed him. His hazel eyes were so warm and melancholy when he looked at her, silently asking her not to leave so soon and spend a little more time with him. She wanted to, oh dear God, she wanted to, but every conversation, every shared smile, every touch would lead her further down the path of destruction.

The wise thing to do would be to marry Stephen as planned. His period of mourning would be over very soon, and once she took her vows in the sight of God, there'd be no going back. Stephen was kind, sweet, and devoted to her, but her heart didn't skip a beat when she looked into his eyes, and she involuntarily pulled her hand away whenever he intertwined his fingers with hers as they walked down the lane. She might have grown to love him in time if it wasn't for the unexpected arrival of the one man who'd haunted her dreams since she was a girl — Brendan Carr.

Rowan hadn't even realized that she was smiling as she mouthed his name into the darkness. How was it possible to feel so much for someone she barely knew; to crave his smile and long for his touch when no words of love had been spoken? But she knew in her heart that they would be, and she would be there to hear them, because as God was her witness, she wasn't leaving him to marry Stephen.

Chapter 34

Brendan gingerly turned onto his stomach to take some pressure off the wound on his back. After a few hours, it felt as if it were being roasted over an open flame, no matter how much salve Rowan put on it. It needed time to heal, and no amount of medicine would make it better. Brendan gritted his teeth as he settled into the new position. The loft was cold as a grave, the fire in the hearth downstairs long since burnt out. He could hear Reverend Pole snoring loudly, the sound alternating between rumbling and wheezing, punctuated by a wet cough that seemed to come straight from the old man's chest.

Brendan had no idea what time it was, but it had to be past midnight. The tiny square of sky outside the window was pitch black, and even the forest creatures were silent, sleeping in their burrows and nests. He fancied he could hear the sound of waves lapping at the shore, but that was only his imagination playing tricks on him since the sea was too far away to hear anything, even in a great storm. Brendan wished he could just fall asleep and find temporary oblivion from the thoughts that had been racing through his brain since Reverend Pole told him of the latest development. Every time he thought of his belongings being found on the bodies, his chest burned as if he couldn't get enough air into his lungs.

It wasn't bad enough that his own brother, his flesh and blood, tried to have him murdered, but now he'd gone as far as to try to incriminate him and take away the only thing he had left — his good name. Brendan had turned the matter over in his mind countless times, but he couldn't find any way to prove his innocence or reclaim the estate. Jasper had stitched him up pretty good. Maybe that's why Brendan was hearing the sound of waves. His mind was telling him to turn to the sea. He could sail to the Colonies and start a new life, away from the political turmoil of England, and away from his treacherous brother. Let him have his victory, and may it taste bitter in his mouth. Brendan would be happy enough to leave if only he could be sure that Meg wouldn't be harmed and that her boys would be looked after. He hoped his sister might find another husband, one who would care for her and her children. She was still a young woman, and could give a man children of his own, if that's what he desired. Jasper would probably be only too happy to see the back of her, especially once he was married to Mary. Unless Mary fancied keeping Meg at the house, treating her as a servant instead of a good-sister. Was Meg even safe, considering that she believed Jasper had a hand in their father's death?

Brendan sighed and closed his eyes. He was mentally exhausted; the same thoughts spinning in his brain for the past two days, the questions torturing him with their futility. What could he do? He couldn't even decamp to the New World until his wounds healed, by which time it would be too late in the year to sail. He'd have to wait till spring, trapped in this loft unless he wanted to be arrested for murder and hanged. He suddenly wished he could talk to his father and ask for his guidance. He hadn't appreciated his father's wisdom when he tried to impart it, and now it was too late to make amends, too late to ask for help.

The only bright spot in all this was Rowan. He counted the minutes each morning until he heard her light footstep on the wooden floor below, and almost held his breath in anticipation until the top of her head appeared above the opening into the loft, her eyes fixed on him as if he were the only person she wanted to see. She'd avert her eyes after a moment, but Brendan would smile inwardly, certain that he'd seen her look of longing, and allowed himself a moment of happiness before remembering his predicament, his thoughts chasing each other like rats in a maze until his head ached.

Brendan smiled in the darkness as he thought of Rowan. She gave him hope, and as long as there was hope, there was life. Giving up wasn't an option, and he would come up with a way out of this situation. He must allow himself time to heal, and then he would come up with a solution, one that would put everything to rights.

October 1650

Scotland

Chapter 35

Oliver Cromwell closed his eyes and gently massaged the bridge of his nose in the futile hope that the vicious headache encircling his skull like a metal vise would ease up, but the pounding continued, bright spots appearing before his eyes when he dared open them again. *Damn the Scots*, he thought vengefully, as well as the Irish. Why did God, his God, tolerate these Papist vermin? At the moment, they were the bane of his existence, but the Irish and Scottish campaigns were just stepping stones to bigger issues that were brewing back home in England. It'd been less than a year since the execution of Charles I and already there were some who were clamoring for a new king. These narrow-minded fools could not grasp the idea of a republic. All they knew was a monarchy; the king being God's representative on Earth. Without a king they were lost, frightened like little children who got separated from their mother, or father in this case.

Cromwell wasn't ready to address the issue just yet, but at some point a new figurehead would have to take the place of the king and occupy the throne. Cromwell smiled despite his headache. Who was he kidding? A new figurehead indeed. He would sit the throne of England and no one else. Not after everything he'd sacrificed and done for the country. Of course, calling himself a king would only bring fresh outrage and debate from the accursed Parliament, so he might have to give himself a different title, one that granted him all the powers of a monarch, but still allowed the common people to believe that he was serving the Republic. That was a pleasant thought which was interrupted by a knock at the door. Cromwell filed away his precious fantasy to be examined more closely later and called out for the visitor to enter.

"Captain Mortimer, what can I do for you?" Cromwell asked, watching the captain from under hooded eyes. Captain Mortimer was a good man, a man to trust and a man to reward. He had unshakeable faith in God, and in Oliver Cromwell, both to his credit. "May I offer you a cup of barley water, Robert?" Cromwell asked as he poured some for himself and gestured to an empty chair by the hearth. The fire wasn't lit, but it was better to sit side by side, rather than have Mortimer on the other side of the large mahogany desk, feeling more like an underling than an equal. Well, almost an equal.

Robert Mortimer accepted the cup of barley water, but made no move to take a drink. He'd rather go thirsty than drink this swill Cromwell favored. Cromwell never partook of strong spirits and had prohibited drinking throughout the land, which in Captain Mortimer's opinion was like prohibiting breathing or procreation. He followed and obeyed, like the good soldier that he was, but he was no Puritan and took his pleasures where he found them. Mortimer lowered himself into the chair, thankful for a few moments of rest. He dreaded the coming conversation, but his loyalty to the Republic was greater than his loyalty to a friend, and may God forgive him for what he was about to do since he'd likely never forgive himself.

Cromwell steepled his fingers beneath his chin, as if in deep contemplation, and waited for the captain to begin. In truth, he would have much rather retired to bed, having been up for more than twenty-four hours, but Captain Mortimer was a loyal and sensible man, so whatever was causing him anxiety must be something urgent and needful of consideration. "What's troubling you, Robert?"

Captain Mortimer scratched his head and stared into the empty hearth for a moment before turning to face Cromwell at last. He was looking for encouragement, but Cromwell remained silent, watching the myriad emotions chasing each other across Mortimer's rugged features before he finally spoke, his voice low and raspy.

"It's Captain Carr, sir. All the dead and wounded have now been accounted for and Carr appears to be neither. Seems he fled after the battle, using the chaos of the aftermath to mask his escape. Several of his men have come forward attesting to this. They'd seen him riding away. His desertion has caused unrest among the men."

Captain Mortimer looked pained, but continued when Cromwell failed to comment. "Carr was a highly respected officer, a leader the men looked up to. His departure has sown seeds of doubt about the righteousness of our cause, here and in Ireland. I told the men that Brendan had a crisis of conscience since his grandfather was a Scot, although a Presbyterian, but that's done very little to comfort them. Three more men have stolen away during the past week."

Mortimer gulped down the barley water without thinking and nearly gagged before setting the cup on the floor with a bang, angry at the current situation and Brendan's part in it. They'd been friends for years, and fought side by side in Ireland before coming with Cromwell to Scotland. Brendan did occasionally dissent, but Captain Mortimer never expected him to just turn tail and run. Yes, his granddad on his mother's side had been a Scot, but what of it? That didn't change the fact that those infernal Scots had declared Charles II their king and threatened the Republic they've fought so hard for. Scotland and Ireland were the back door to England, and needed to be dealt with in the severest manner, so as not to be a threat again. Yes, he was doing the right thing, he told himself for the hundredth time, but although his mind agreed, his treacherous heart condemned him, just as he'd condemned Brendan to death.

Cromwell rubbed the bridge of his nose again. His headache had abated somewhat, but now it came back full-force, leaving him blinded with pain. He was fully aware of Carr's desertion and personally, he wanted to drag the man to the gallows and put a noose around his neck, but if he gave chase to every single man who disagreed with his politics and deserted the army, he'd have no army left. Carr wasn't worth the effort. He was a competent soldier, and a one-time friend, but not enough of a threat to expend manpower on.

"What do you propose, Robert?" he asked, more out of politeness and desire to be done with this topic than because he really wanted to know. It must have taken Mortimer much soul-searching to come to him, so the least Cromwell could do was talk it over with him and make him feel respected and appreciated. He smiled inwardly, reflecting on Mortimer's loyalty to him. If only all his men were so steadfast.

"Permitting high-ranking officers to decamp without consequences is a sign of weakness, and allows the men to think that they have a choice. What's to stop them from deciding that they've had enough and want to go home? The battle of Dunbar was a resounding success, and the men are buoyant and content for the moment, but we might not be victorious in the next battle or the one after that, and more discontent will lead to more desertion. There must be retribution." Captain Mortimer banged the armrest of the chair for emphasis, his mouth set into a thin line, and his eyes blazing with purpose.

"I couldn't agree more, Robert, but I can't spare good men to pursue every ruffian who doesn't agree with my policies. I'm doing God's work. If Captain Carr, or whoever else, can't see that, then let God punish them, as I'm certain he will. I have bigger battles to fight, but I would like to hear your suggestion. Seems you've given this a lot of thought." Morale among the men was always of paramount importance, so rumbles of discontent were not to be ignored. Captain Mortimer would not be here if he didn't believe action was required.

"I have a few men who are feeling restless, sir. They are the type who only come alive when fighting and killing. Let me send them to arrest Carr. They'll bring him back to stand trial. It will be good for the men to see that you're in control and won't be undermined by dissent," Captain Mortimer suggested.

"I was under the impression that Carr was your friend. Was I mistaken?" Cromwell inquired, watching Mortimer intently. He needed to be sure there were no ulterior motive here, like a woman.

"Friendship has no place in politics, sir." Mortimer sat up straighter, supported by his moral superiority and zeal.

Cromwell studied Captain Mortimer's profile as he turned back toward the hearth. He looked older than twenty-eight, the years of fighting having taken a toll on the man's body and soul. Mortimer cared deeply about the cause, and his loyalty needed to be rewarded, especially since Carr had been his particular friend. A public trial of a deserter, and his subsequent execution, would reassure those still loyal and discourage those who were wavering in their conviction — a satisfactory outcome all around.

"You're right, of course, Robert. I defer to your judgment in this case. Send your men, but make sure they bring Carr back to stand trial. Killing him in England will serve no purpose other than vengeance, and that's not my goal in this matter. We'll make an example of him. Now, please leave me. I have some work to do before I retire."

Captain Mortimer gave Cromwell a stiff bow, jammed his hat on his head and left the room, closing the door softly behind him. *Cromwell looked exhausted and ill*, Mortimer thought, *and needed his rest*. He sighed, knowing he'd get no sleep tonight, plagued by guilt over what he'd just done to a man he'd called a friend.

October 1650

England

Chapter 36

Rowan forced herself not to yank her hand away as Stephen shyly reached for it during their walk. On fine days, they took a walk after Sunday dinner, Stephen talking of his farm and the children, and of the life they would have once they were married, and Rowan enjoying a few hours away from the never-ending chores and the attention of a kind, loving man who was soon to be her husband. Stephen always made her feel cherished and safe, but today she felt a restlessness that was new to her. Rowan had to admit that she had never before minded Stephen's attentions. His hand was large and warm, swallowing her smaller one and making her feel like a child walking with a parent. She'd even allowed him to kiss her a few times. The kisses were just like Stephen himself; tender and loving, but not terribly exciting.

Rowan fully accepted that she would have to share her bed with this man once they were married, and the knowledge neither enticed nor repulsed her. It was a fact that she acknowledged and was willing to live with. She knew that Stephen would never hurt her and be careless of her feelings or health. He'd already lost one wife, and he would do everything in his power to prevent losing another. He already had a son, so there would be less pressure to produce a male heir to take over Stephen's farm once he was gone. Rowan was sure Stephen would want children with her, but he wasn't the kind of man who wanted to see his wife pregnant with a new babe every year. Some men thought it proved their virility, regardless of what it did to the poor women who barely had time to recover from one birth before they were with child again. Few of them survived into their forties, worn out by the demands of their children and hard work that never seemed to end.

Stephen smiled at Rowan as he squeezed her hand a little tighter and continued talking of the successful harvest. He did very well this year at the market and thought that the extra money he earned could go toward something Rowan might want for the house. It wasn't often that a woman of her station was presented with an opportunity to go shopping, but the suggestion left her flat. The idea of sharing a house with Stephen for the rest of her life suddenly seemed frightening and made her feel short of breath, as if she couldn't get enough air into her lungs.

"Are you ill, Rowan?" Stephen asked, his eyes full of concern. "You must be tired after such a long walk. Would you like to go back?"

Rowan smiled in gratitude and allowed herself to be turned in the direction of the village, eager to get home. It was too late to go check on Brendan, but at least she would have a few extra hours to work on the shirt she was sewing for him.

***

A merry fire crackled in the hearth as Rowan bent over her work. She'd have the shirt finished by the end of the week. She could have finished it sooner, but she took extra care with the stitches, making sure her work was perfect and the shirt didn't look like something made for a farmer, but a piece of fine clothing for a gentleman. She smiled to herself, picturing Brendan wearing her handiwork. She was sure he'd be pleased. She blushed slightly as she caught Uncle Caleb's look. He was standing by the hearth as he filled his pipe with tobacco from a small leather pouch at his waist, his eyes reflecting the light of the fire. Rowan knew Uncle Caleb felt awkward around her, not knowing what to say to the girl who'd suddenly gone mute, but he did his best to let her know that he cared about her and her wellbeing. Caleb patted her on the shoulder before stepping outside to smoke his pipe, followed by Aunt Joan, who frequently joined him on the bench for a few minutes of fresh air and conversation. It was a fine evening, if a little chilly, and their soft voices carried on the wind, washing over Rowan as she went about her work.

She had to admit that she felt different these last few weeks. She'd built a wall around herself after what happened to her mother, and the wall had served her well. Her heart had begun to heal, albeit very slowly, and the fear came only at night when she couldn't sleep, or worse, when she could, and she dreamed of that horrible night, the flames leaping into the darkening sky and the screams that would tear at her heart for the rest of her days.

Rowan had made herself nearly invisible in her need to recover, to heal. She just wanted to feel safe without drawing attention to herself, but suddenly that was changing. It'd been a long time since she felt the desire to speak, but these past few days the words suddenly came alive again, building up and colliding with each other in a desperate attempt to break the dam that she'd so carefully constructed. They threatened to tumble over the top, cascading in a fierce torrent that would wash away the last remnants of the barrier, finally allowing her to feel free and move forward. She wasn't ready quite yet, but she felt things beginning to thaw, like ice on a lake after a long winter. The cracks were starting to appear, and eventually the ice would start to melt, releasing her heart.

Chapter 37

Edward Sexby pulled his hat lower over his eyes to shield them from the brightness of the afternoon sun. He loved these rare days when everything seemed just a little brighter and more intense; the senses in tune with nature. It was a feeling second only to being in battle, when one felt unbearably alive knowing that any moment could bring death. Those were the moments he lived for, the moments when he felt as if he was exactly where he was meant to be. Many men took up arms, but few really enjoyed the clash of steel, the screaming of frightened horses, and the exquisite feeling of driving a blade into a man, his eyes full of shock and disbelief as he realized that he'd just been killed.

Sexby prayed every night that he would die in battle and not as an old man sitting by the hearth with a rug over his aching bones waiting to expire. Death on a battlefield was honorable; death of old age was feeble, especially if one died alone with no wife or children. Once in a while, Sexby regretted not having married or siring a son or two, but everything he'd seen in his thirty-four years led him to believe that surrounding yourself with love could only lead to unbearable loss. He wasn't a man given to pity, but even he could feel something shifting in his heart as they slaughtered the Catholics in Ireland; men, women, and children whose only crime was to worship in a way different from those of the invaders. Sexby, himself, didn't believe in God. What kind of God would tolerate the horrors that people inflicted on each other, but then again, who was he to question the ways of divinity? Maybe it was all part of a greater plan, and one day people would look back on this period of history and declare it a time of enlightenment and change — not slaughter and chaos.

Edward Sexby threw the reins of his horse to Will Barnett and unlaced his breeches to relieve himself. Barnett had picked a picturesque spot by a lively stream to set up camp for the night.

The lad had quite a romantic streak when he wasn't murdering people. There were still a few hours of daylight left, but Sexby didn't mind stopping early. He'd volunteered for his assignment for one reason and one reason only — to get a break from the fighting. No matter how much a man loved his wife, he still needed to fuck someone else's from time to time, and Sexby needed a change of scenery.

He'd chosen Will to accompany him for a reason as well. Besides having no conscience, the boy hero-worshipped him and was very eager to please, which was a rare convenience when traveling. Will took care of the horses, prepared food, and best of all, left Sexby in peace as they made their way south. At eighteen, Will had been a mercenary for several years, and a good man to have at your back in a fight. Sexby didn't think taking Brendan Carr prisoner would require much manpower, but it was good to have a natural-born killer like Will at his side. He'd met Carr several times over the past few years, and although the man was a competent fighter, he didn't enjoy the kill, so wasn't as dangerous of an opponent. Besides, Sexby had no intention of taking him openly and honorably. He was no fool. The best way to apprehend Carr would be to ambush him when he least expected it and wasn't armed. The hardest part would be to keep Will from using unnecessary force just for the sheer pleasure of it.

Sexby stretched out on a nice, lush patch of grass by the fire while Will set about preparing their meal. They'd purchased, and that's a term he used loosely since he paid a fraction of what the food was worth to the terrified goodwife, some pork sausages, cheese and bread in the last village they'd passed. The appetizing smell of sizzling sausage filled the autumn night and made Sexby's mouth water. He'd eat and get some much-needed rest before continuing on tomorrow. He sighed with contentment. This was practically a holiday.

The Present

Chapter 38

I woke up in the morning to rain lashing against the windows and a howling wind rattling the panes in a way that left me eager to stay in bed. I wouldn't be able to work outside today, so I would be pretty much confined to my room in order to stay out of the way of the men. At this point, the house was beginning to look like something out of a war zone with holes in the walls, toilets standing in the hallway waiting to be installed in the additional bathrooms, and pipes gleaming through gaps in insulation and drywall. My room was the only sanctuary at the moment, not counting the kitchen, which Aidan would work on last per my request.

I forced myself to get out of bed, got dressed, and went down to make some breakfast before the workers arrived. I had a mad craving for a cheese omelet and a strong cup of coffee. I might also have to borrow Aidan's truck and drive into the village to get some more supplies since I was running short. At some point, I would have to consider getting a car or truck of my own. Eventually, I would have to start scouring the countryside for furnishings and bits and pieces I could use for period detail, not to mention stock the kitchen with food once I had actual guests to feed. I supposed I could arrange for some kind of weekly delivery from the grocery store, but I hoped to be able to provide local produce and maybe some delicacies that were not to be found in Mrs. Higgins's shop.

I poured myself a second cup of coffee and stuck a piece of toast in my mouth as I prepared to make my way upstairs. The men were already outside, unloading their tools in the pouring rain.

I watched Aidan run up the steps, his hair dripping rainwater as he burst through the door and wished me a good morning.

"Want some coffee?" I asked as I tried not to stare at his sodden T-shirt which clung to his chest in a way reminiscent of Colin Firth in *Pride and Prejudice;* a scene I had watched many times and never grew tired of. Whereas another man might look like a drowned rat, Aidan managed to look sexy in the extreme, his hair spiky and his dark lashes tipped with drops of rainwater which he wiped away absentmindedly as he smiled at me.

"Thanks, but I just had breakfast." Aidan threw his wet jacket over the banister and brushed his hair off his face in a gesture of irritation, his eyes on Colin and George, who were arguing as they walked through the door. I wondered why he kept Colin on, since he clearly annoyed Aidan, but I wasn't about to ask. Instead, I wished the men a good morning and returned to my sanctuary determined to be productive.

After a while, I got bored with sitting in my room, my restlessness preventing me from working on my future website which just didn't look as I wanted it to, or bring me to the right place when I clicked on a particular tab. I actually had a strange desire to see the tomb in the basement again. I couldn't help thinking that maybe we'd missed something, some vital clue that could lead us to the identity of the man. The more I thought about it, the more I became convinced that the man in the basement and the ghost in the ruin were one and the same. They had to be. It made a convoluted sort of sense. They would have lived around the same time, and it was possible that whatever prevented him from being buried in the churchyard was what kept his soul tethered to this particular place, unable to move on for eternity.

I tried not to think too much about the man in the ruin, but I found him dominating my thoughts, especially at night when I couldn't sleep and watched for the pinprick of light that was his candle dancing amid the sinister darkness of tumbled stones. I lay in bed wondering about who he'd been and what happened to him to cause him such pain. I'd never believed in ghosts or put much stock into what people said about troubled souls not being able to pass on, but this man just broke my heart, and in some naïve way I wanted to help him in any way I could, if such a thing were possible. Now that there was some physical evidence of his existence, I had something to go on, but it wasn't enough to solve the puzzle.

I shut my laptop with a sigh of exasperation and made my way to the ground floor. No one seemed to be around; the men dispersed throughout the house as sounds of banging reverberated through the foyer. Everything was covered with a thick layer of dust, blanketing every surface like a coating of snow on a winter's day. I'd tried cleaning a little every evening after the men left, but it was futile, so I just gave up, leaving it all for later when the work was finally at an end; whenever that may be.

I grabbed a flashlight from the kitchen counter before opening the door to the basement. Aidan had replaced the burnt-out lights and several naked bulbs bloomed in the darkness, the path dimly illuminated, but still just as intimidating. *Don't be a coward*, I told myself as I descended down the stone steps, *there is nothing to fear*. After all, no one was in the basement besides a man who'd been dead for hundreds of years. He couldn't hurt me. Still, I walked as quietly as I could, loath to make any unnecessary noise and disturb the tomblike silence of the basement. I noticed that some of the cobwebs had been cleared away since the plumber and his men had been down there several times over the past week. Once the work was finished, I would have the cellar cleaned out and the wine racks restocked, but for now, I had to contend with it looking like something out of a low-budget Halloween special.

My footsteps echoed on the flagstone floor as I stealthily made my way toward the hidden room at the back. Aidan had left the key where we found it, and I pulled it out of the alcove and inserted it into the old iron lock, using both hands to turn it. I removed the lock and set it aside before picking up my flashlight and opening the door. The room was colder than the rest of the basement, the air trapped inside smelling of dust and something else that I couldn't identify. It wasn't unpleasant though; it was the type of smell one found in old churches — a little musty and woodsy. All that was missing was incense and some Gregorian chants.

I made sure to leave the door wide open so that the light from the lightbulb shone through the opening and painted an elongated replica of the door on the stone floor. It wasn't much, but it made me feel better. The sarcophagus was there just as before, sitting on its plinth as it had done for centuries. I held the flashlight in my left hand as I traced every inch of the surface with my right, looking for anything that might be an inscription of some kind or even a coat of arms, but there was nothing aside from what Aidan and I had found before — just the name and the dates.

Part of the pattern chiseled into the stone was worn away, the nose of the effigy chipped off, and the hollow eyes staring at the low ceiling as they had been for centuries, but when it had been new, the casket must have been magnificent — the work of a true artist. It must have taken considerable time and money to produce something so fine, so someone had cared enough to commission this tomb and try to recreate the likeness of the man within. Someone must have loved him. Someone in this village.

I hadn't heard anyone approaching, but I suddenly had the distinct feeling that I was no longer alone. The room grew darker as something filled the low doorway and blocked out the light from the bulb, sending shivers of dread down my spine. I knew I had no reason to be afraid, but logic didn't play into my reaction, my over-active imagination suddenly conjuring up the ghost who was displeased to find me trespassing in his burial place. I was terrified. I spun around on my heel, hoping to find Aidan, but was surprised to see Colin leaning against the stone wall, a small smile playing about his lips.

"Oh, Colin, you startled me," I said. "Were you working on something down here?"

Colin didn't bother to answer me as he shut the door behind him, throwing the room into near darkness. He advanced slowly into the room, his eyes never leaving mine as he closed the space between us. I couldn't really see his expression since my flashlight was lying atop the lid, the beam of light pointed at the ceiling, but I was certain it wasn't a friendly one.

"Colin? Can I help you?" I asked again, but he just cocked his head to the side and stopped about two feet away from me. "Well, I'll be going now," I said and made to get around him, but he suddenly stepped into my path, effectively blocking my way to the door.

"Colin, please move," I demanded in my best authoritative tone, but he continued to stare at me, unbudging. His silence scared me more than the fact that he was blocking the exit. It meant that whatever he meant to do wasn't negotiable. He didn't want to engage. I tried to get around him again, but he grabbed me with both hands and slammed me against the wall, scraping the back of my head and my hands on the rough stone. I tried to break free, but he held me tighter, his thighs pressing against mine in an effort to keep me pinned.

"What do you want?" I cried, now really scared. His face was inches from mine, but the pool of light on the ceiling did nothing to illuminate his features, so all I saw were the whites of his eyes and the gleam of his teeth in the darkness.

"It's not what I want; it's what you want. You wear those sexy summer frocks and tight jeans in order to entice me. I know you do. You watch me as I work, and you smile at me, hoping I'll notice." His breath was ragged, his voice low and laced with malicious intent as he pressed himself even closer.

"I smile at everyone," I countered as I struggled against him. I didn't bother to argue with him about my clothes. My summer dresses were relatively modest, as were my jeans. They were what any woman my age might wear, but Colin seemed to think differently. He was panting now, his erection pressing into my pelvis as his hips ground against mine.

"Your shirts are stretched so tightly across your tits, I can almost see your nipples, and it excites me. I know you want it; it's obvious." He raised my arms above my head and grabbed both my

193

wrists with his left hand as he slid his right hand up my bare leg, lifting the skirt of my dress. I gasped as I felt his finger slide into my underwear.

"Colin, please, you misunderstood. I wasn't trying to lead you on. I'll dress more modestly, I promise," I whimpered, but I could see from the look on his face that nothing I said would make any difference. He was in a grip of madness, one fueled by lust and delusion. He clearly believed that I had toyed with him and meant to play him for a fool. Had he planned this or had he followed me on the spur of the moment, eager to take advantage of the opportunity I unknowingly presented him with? My mind was spinning out of control as his fingers slid inside. I needed to say something that would make him doubt his purpose, but at the moment, I had no idea what that might be.

"Colin, please…"

"Shh," he said, his voice laced with irritation. "Stop fighting it. You know you want it. All you slags are the same. You protest, but deep down you want it so bad you can barely see straight."

My heart began to hammer against my ribs as his fingers slid even deeper, probing and violating. He was taking his time, enjoying the game and toying with me the way a cat toyed with a mouse before it killed it. He clearly wasn't expecting anyone to find us, and the thought made me physically ill. I was completely at his mercy, and mercy wasn't something he was about to dole out.

"Mm, isn't that nice?" he murmured. "You are so hot." Colin pulled his hand away and slowly licked his finger, his eyes never leaving mine. "Want to taste?" he asked playfully as he ran the finger over my lips.

"Colin, please, let me go," I begged, but he just gave me a vicious grin before shoving his hand between my legs again.

"Your knickers are in the way," Colin panted, and tore them off with a practiced motion. He continued sliding his fingers

194

in and out, then began to rub my clitoris with his thumb in an effort to arouse me. "I can tell you like that," he whispered in my ear. I was now trembling violently, knowing that he wasn't going to just stop at fondling me. He wanted more. Colin suddenly withdrew his hand and yanked down the front of my dress, exposing my breast as the fabric tore. He cupped it in his rough hand and brought my nipple to his mouth, licking it before taking it into his mouth and sucking hard. His touch repulsed me, and his hardness against my thigh terrified me. I tried to scream, but Colin clamped his hand over my mouth and nose, effectively preventing me from breathing. I continued to struggle, but it was pointless. He was grinding against me now, his mouth open and panting.

"Now, promise not to scream and I'll take the hand away." I nodded in acquiescence, simply because I needed oxygen in order to stay conscious. Colin finally took the hand away as I gulped air into my lungs, but my relief was short-lived as he unzipped his jeans, and I felt flesh against flesh as his cock rubbed against my pelvis.

Oh, dear God, I thought, *he's going to rape me down here and no one will know.* Suddenly, an even more horrible thought occurred to me. What if he locked me in this room and didn't tell anyone? By the time anyone thought to look down here I might be dead. A sob escaped from me as I tried to fight him again, but he swiftly turned me around and slammed me against the wall knocking the wind out of me. I tasted blood as the cut in my cheek began to bleed more profusely from being rubbed against the stone. Colin used his knee to push my legs apart, and I cried out as I felt him trying to enter me from the back.

He was breathing hard, his frustration mounting as I tried to swivel my hips to keep him from achieving his goal. He slammed my head against the wall to subdue me as he tried again, but I pressed myself against the wall, making it harder for him. I could feel his hard prick between my legs, his hand guiding it inside me when suddenly Colin let go, and I crumpled to the floor, sobbing and shaking.

I heard a sickening crunch as Aidan hit Colin in the face, making him stagger backwards, stunned as much by pain as by the interruption. He nearly lost his balance, but managed to right himself, his face twisted with fury. Blood was trickling from his nose into his mouth and staining his teeth like a vampire who'd just been feeding. Colin let out a bellow of rage and charged Aidan, knocking him into the wall and punching him in the stomach again and again with a demented viciousness that left Aidan gasping for breath and trying to ward off the blows. I looked around desperately for something to use as a weapon, but there was nothing besides the flashlight, which was on the other side of the room. My mind was screaming for me to go get it, but I felt paralyzed with inaction, my limbs trembling uncontrollably as I just lay there in a heap, sobbing.

I crawled into a corner, wrapped my arms around my legs and rested my forehead against my knees, eyes closed. I could hear sounds of struggle, the dull thud of fists finding their targets, and Colin's vicious curses, but I couldn't bear to look. I felt dizzy and nauseous, desperate for some fresh air and light, but I couldn't get up even if I had a mind to. My legs felt like Jell-O and my ears were ringing, probably from the blow to my head.

I finally opened my eyes and tried to focus on the scene before me, but in the dim light of the room, it was difficult to tell who had the upper hand. Colin was still bleeding, the front of his shirt stained red as he continued to pummel Aidan. Colin was crazed, his eyes rolling in his head, his mouth in a snarl as he tried to kick Aidan in the stomach. Aidan punched Colin hard; sending him crashing to the floor with a loud thunk before jumping on top in an effort to subdue him, but Colin was thrashing and trying to throw Aidan onto his back. I screamed in terror as I saw the glint of a blade in Colin's hand.

"I'll kill you, you bloody wanker!" Colin screeched. "I'll slash your face to ribbons."

He was stabbing at Aidan blindly, dazed by the fall. Aidan pinned Colin's hand to the floor and ground his wrist into the stone until Colin finally let go of the knife, panting and spitting in Aidan's face.

"You bloody bastard," Aidan spat out, breathing hard. "If you ever come near her again, I'll kill you with my bare hands, but first I'll geld you with your own knife, just to show you I'm serious." Aidan punched Colin hard in the face several times until the fight finally went out of him and his eyes rolled into the back of his head, his body going slack.

"Lexi, are you hurt?" Aidan asked gently as he crouched beside me and touched my bruised face. "Did he...?" I shook my head as Aidan pulled me close to him. I tried to remain strong, but the terror of the past few minutes washed over me. I began to sob uncontrollably, my whole body shaking as Aidan tried to hold me and soothe me, whispering words of comfort and kissing the top of my head. The front of my dress was torn and my underwear about a foot from Aidan's feet, thrown there by Colin after he tore it off. I tasted blood and the salt from my tears as I buried my face in Aidan's shoulder, holding on like a drowning person to a bit of flotsam.

"You're bleeding," Aidan said as he held his hand up to his face in the dim light of the room. "Did that filthy piece of shit hit you?" The back of my head was stinging where it scraped against the rock and my left cheek and my wrists were scratched and bleeding, as was my lip which split when Colin hit my face against the wall.

"I'll kill him," Aidan muttered viciously as he looked at Colin, who was lying in a heap on the floor.

"Aidan, I'm all right, really, I am," I lied, but he just helped me to my feet and held on to me as I nearly lost my balance. My legs wouldn't hold me up, so Aidan walked me out the door and propped me against the wall as he put the padlock back on.

"What are you doing?" I asked in horror. Was he planning to just leave him there?

"That should keep him on ice till the coppers get here. Now, let's get you upstairs." Aidan lifted me off my feet, and I gratefully rested my head against his chest as he carried me through the basement and back out into the light of the kitchen. It was still pouring outside, the room nearly as dark as it would be at dusk, but compared to the basement the light seemed brilliant.

"What in the bloody hell happened?" George asked, his mouth hanging open as he beheld my battered state and torn clothes and Aidan's bruised face.

"Call the police," Aidan said and walked right past him toward the stairs. "And bring me a basin of warm water and a towel."

"Bloody hell," George uttered again as Aidan brushed past him. "Where's Colin?"

"Locked up in the cellar," Aidan replied as he carried me up the stairs and set me down on the bed. I could tell from the look in his eyes that I looked way worse than I first thought. My head was throbbing, and my lip was beginning to swell. I tried to smile, but it turned into a grimace as the cuts on my face split further open and began to bleed.

Aidan accepted the basin of water and a towel from George, who was gaping at me in horror. "Colin did that?" he asked, obviously unable to wrap his brain around what he was seeing. "Bollocks."

"George, why don't you ring Doc Delaney and ask him to come over right away?" Aidan suggested as he gently sponged my face with warm water.

"I'm fine," I mumbled, but my legs were bouncing on the bed, and my teeth chattered as my body reacted to the shock of what I experienced.

"Nevertheless," Aidan said, gesturing for George to get going.

I sat up and wrapped my arms around Aidan's neck, needing to feel his strong arms around me. He made me feel secure, and that was what I needed at the moment. The physical scars would heal, but the sudden notion that something horrible could happen to me when I least expected it was just taking root in my mind. I hadn't liked Colin, but I never expected him to attack me. Had Aidan not come along when he had, Colin would have raped me, and possibly even killed me. I had no idea how far he'd been willing to go. I tried not to think of the knife he pulled on Aidan. He might have killed him had I not screamed when I did and the thought nearly made me sick. Aidan could have died because of me, because of my carelessness.

"How did you find me?" I finally asked as I pulled away and studied Aidan's worried face.

"I passed by your room and saw that you weren't there, so I thought you might have gone down to make a cup of tea. The big torch was missing off the counter, the door to the cellar was open, and Colin was nowhere to be seen. I got worried."

I pulled further away from Aidan and scrutinized his face. "Why would you be worried if Colin went after me? Has this happened before?"

"There was an incident a few years ago. Colin had assaulted a girl he'd been seeing and worked her over pretty badly. He was still a minor then, so he was sentenced to several months at a juvenile facility, which he served and was released early for good behavior. He seemed genuinely remorseful and went to apologize to the girl as soon as he was freed. She forgave him, but has given him a wide berth ever since. Colin had a hard time getting a job, so I hired him as a favor to Paula. I thought he deserved a chance, but I never would have let him in the house had I thought he might hurt anyone."

Aidan looked as if he were about to cry, clearly feeling responsible for what happened in the basement. I cupped his cheek as I tried to smile without making my lip bleed again. "Aidan, you couldn't have known he would do this."

"No. I thought it was a one-off and he'd learned his lesson, but I was wrong. So wrong."

"It wasn't your fault," I said firmly, but Aidan just looked away, his battered face contorted with guilt. He'd taken quite a beating and his sharp intake of breath didn't go unnoticed when I accidentally touched his stomach. "It wasn't your fault," I repeated. He nodded, but I knew he blamed himself anyway.

"Why did Paula want you to hire him?" I asked, suddenly realizing what he'd said earlier.

"He's her brother. She's actually thrown a lot of work my way by way of thank you. I'm so sorry, Lexi."

"He said that I purposely provoked him and led him on. Did I do something to cause this?"

"Of course not. It was all in his mind. He has trouble with women, and maybe he misread the signs, which is in no way an excuse for what he's done."

I heard the sound of a siren as a police car pulled up to the house. "I'll be right back," Aidan promised. I suspected he wanted to talk to the officers without forcing me to relive what'd happened. I closed my eyes and tried to block out the sound of the voices. The whole thing still felt unreal, like a terrible dream, but the stinging of my head and face was proof enough that I hadn't imagined it.

A young cop poked his face in the door and took a look at me before retreating into the hallway. I supposed I would have to make some kind of a statement, but thankfully, it didn't have to be right now. He'd seen enough to know that Aidan had been telling the truth. I put my hands over my ears as I heard Colin cursing at the officers and threatening to kill Aidan as he was escorted out of the house, and then I started crying again.

Chapter 39

I liked Dr. Delaney instantly. He looked exactly as I would expect a country GP to look: white-haired, bespectacled, and ruddy from the outdoors. He smiled at me warmly, which made me feel better. I've always been put off by pursed lips and expressions of concern, so I was glad that he didn't appear horrified by my appearance, although I was sure he was trying to hide his shock.

"A filthy day out there," he announced as he set down his doctor's bag and sat down on the side of the bed, taking my hand and checking my pulse without me even realizing it at first. "Fog as thick as pea soup. How are you enjoying our English weather, my dear?"

"It's been pretty good so far," I answered, surprised to be discussing the weather after what just happened downstairs. I supposed it was meant to distract me and make me feel more at ease, and it was working. Had I been feeling better, I might have noticed the way his eyes widened behind his horn-rimmed glasses when he saw me up close, or the way he tried to immediately rearrange his features to hide his surprise, but I was too miserable to care. I was getting used to people staring at me in this village.

"Do you like fishing?" he asked as he pulled a stethoscope from his bag.

"Not particularly. I don't have the patience to just sit there with a fishing pole, waiting for fish to bite. I prefer instant gratification," I replied.

"You young people," Dr. Delaney said with a chuckle. "Fishing is the closest thing I have to a religion, but don't mention that to the vicar. There's nothing like watching the sun come up as you stand knee-deep in the river, your soul at one with nature, the world just beginning to wake up all around you as you reel in your first catch of the day."

I obediently allowed the good doctor to take my pulse and blood pressure, shine a light into my pupils, listen to my heart and lungs, and run his gentle hands over my head to make sure that there was nothing more serious than scratches. He asked a few delicate questions about how far Colin actually got, while regaling me with tales of his fishing trip to Scotland the previous summer. Thankfully, there was no need for an internal exam. Had Colin actually succeeded, there'd be a rape kit and a lot of probing and swabbing, but it wasn't necessary. Dr. Delaney put away his instruments and shut his medical bag with a snap of finality before turning his smiling face toward me.

"My diagnosis is that you are bruised and mildly concussed as a result of hitting your head." He made it sound as if I banged my head on the wall for lack of anything better to do. "I daresay it could have been a lot worse. I'd like you to stay in bed today and tomorrow, and I'll prescribe something for the headache. I can also give you a mild sedative if you'd like one."

Normally, I would have said no to a sedative, but I was feeling somewhat hysterical, and something that would take the edge off probably wouldn't hurt too much. I knew that the worst wasn't over. I was putting on a brave face, but inside, I was going to pieces, my mind replaying every moment of what happened in that basement and adding different outcomes, ones in which Aidan didn't appear in time. I hadn't even realized that I began to shake again as tears slid down my cheeks. I didn't protest as Dr. Delaney pulled a syringe out of his bag and gave me a shot of something. I just wanted oblivion.

I felt a wonderful heaviness begin to descend as the shaking diminished and my limbs seemed to sink into the mattress. My mind stopped spinning, and I felt a pleasant drowsiness envelop me in its embrace. I could still hear the doctor's voice, talking to Aidan, but it came from somewhere far away, as if he were on Earth, and I was floating on some fluffy cloud high above the ground, a gentle sun shining on my face and a wonderful breeze caressing my cheek.

Chapter 40

By the time I awoke the house was silent. The storm seemed to have intensified, plunging the room into shadows as the clouds hung low over the horizon, the steady downpour creating the soothing symphony of flowing water. It was well past noon, so I'd been out for at least two hours.

My headache was still there, but now it was more of a dull ache and not nearly as intense as before, and my mouth felt as if someone had stuffed it full of cotton wool. I would have loved a glass of water, but I couldn't seem to find the will to move my limbs. Water would have to wait. I closed my eyes and waited for the drowsiness to pass, but my somnolence disappeared as I heard a noise from downstairs. Someone was in the house with me, and they were coming up the stairs. I knew I had no reason to suspect it was anyone who wished me harm, but after what happened that morning I wasn't thinking rationally.

I breathed a sigh of relief as Dot Martin poked her head through the door and gave me a warm smile. "Ah, you're awake. I thought you might like some tea and a sandwich. You've missed lunch and it's nearly teatime. How are you feeling, love?"

I must have been out longer than I thought. I didn't know if could manage a sandwich, but a cup of tea sounded heavenly. I sat up and accepted a cup from Dot, who sat down next to me companionably and bit into a biscuit. I was glad to see her. Her presence was comforting, and thankfully, she didn't ask any questions.

"I had no idea you were here," I said, hoping she'd fill me in on what happened since I fell asleep. The great thing about Dot is that all she needed was an opening sentence.

"Oh, yes. Aidan rang me and asked me to keep you company for a while. Said you weren't feeling well and needed looking after. Well, I'm always happy to help. Didn't have any grand plans, especially on a wet day like today. I did have a call from Mildred Higgins though. Seems Colin has been arrested this morning, but she didn't know the whole story yet. No doubt I'll have it from her tomorrow, gory details and all."

Dot's eyes were full of expectation that I might fill in the blanks, but I couldn't bear to talk of what happened. I knew that by tomorrow the whole village would probably know, and the thought made me sick to my stomach, but they wouldn't hear it from me. I was, however, curious as to what Dot had to say about Colin.

"Do you know Colin well?" I asked as I reached for a sandwich after all. I was suddenly hungry, which according to my mother was always a good sign.

"I've known him since the day he was born. Paula was none too happy, that I can tell you. Wanted a sister, she did. And Colin was such a dour little boy; nothing like his sister. One hardly noticed him except when he fixed you with that stare. Funny, their parents are the loveliest people. Makes you wonder about all that DNA business, doesn't it?"

"Has he ever been in any trouble before?"

"There were a few teenage hijinks, but nothing that I know of except for the incident with Lisa. Accused him of assault," Dot said confidentially, lowering her voice as if the walls had ears. "I never did buy into that whole story. She teased him mercilessly. Everyone knew he fancied her; all the boys did. A right slag she was, if you don't mind my saying. All those short skirts and tight little tops. Well, she drove him too far, most like, then accused him of rape."

"Didn't he hit her?" I asked, surprised at Dot's version of events.

"She had some bruises. No one ever knew how much of her story was true. The police had her examined at the hospital and said there were signs of intercourse, but she was shagging a few local boys. Who's to say it was Colin she'd been with? She claimed he forced her, but there was no physical proof. No semen. Now, how many rapists would put on a rubber before attacking someone?" Dot gave a meaningful look before reaching for another sandwich.

"The police released all that information?" I was aghast that the people in the village would know so much about a case.

"No, of course not," replied Dot, smiling at me indulgently. "Mildred's niece's daughter works at the hospital and was there when Lisa was brought in. She got it from one of the nurses."

"The rumor mill works around the clock around here, doesn't it?" I asked, disgusted that this poor girl had been afforded no privacy. No wonder she left. By tomorrow, everyone would know what happened, and I would be tried and judged by public opinion. Would people say that I provoked it and brought it on myself? Would they defend Colin because he was one of their own? Dot had seen my bruises and probably already knew exactly what happened, but she wasn't interrogating me, probably in the hope that I would confide in her and tell her the titillating details. The thought made me sick, and I suddenly wished that she would just leave. It was good of Aidan not to leave me alone, but I couldn't bear the thought that even while Dot appeared sympathetic, she was already preparing her report for Mildred and anyone else who'd listen.

I pricked up my ears as I heard the door opening downstairs. There were quick steps on the stairs and then Aidan appeared in the doorway. "Sorry I took so long. I stopped by my house to pick up a few things while the chemist prepared the prescription. I got some takeaway too. I thought you might be hungry." He set a bag of something that smelled really good on the nightstand and pulled out a bottle of pills from his pocket.

"Dot, I can give you a lift home if you like." I was amused to see Dot's face as she took in Aidan's duffle bag, but she made no comment and rose to her feet. Her mind was probably going a mile a minute, but I didn't care. I suddenly felt much better knowing that Aidan hadn't forgotten about me and wanted to spend the night. Colin was locked up for the moment, but having Aidan there was better than any medicine Doctor Delaney could have prescribed.

"Now, why don't you go back to sleep and I'll just run Dot home? Later, if you want, we can watch a movie. I brought a few of my favorites just in case. I can move the telly in here."

"Are they all action movies with car chases and lots of shooting?" I asked, wondering what type of movies Aidan liked.

"No, they are heartwarming romantic dramas with Colin Firth and Hugh Grant," he replied with a grin and made a face that almost made me laugh.

"All right, car chases it is then."

What we actually ended up watching was *Spamalot*. I'd never seen Monty Python, but I have to say that Aidan's choice was inspired. I wasn't in the mood for an action flick, and watching a romantic movie together might have felt too intimate. We had a few laughs and by the time the movie finished, I had my head on Aidan's shoulder and his arm was casually around me. As the DVD finished, the room was illuminated by the bluish light of the TV screen, and the rain outside continued to fall, adding to the intimate atmosphere. I was suddenly very aware of Aidan's body so close to mine, his masculine smell and stubbly cheek against my temple, and my feelings took me completely by surprise, especially after what happened that morning. Strangely, Colin's attack made me acutely aware of how alone I was, and although I'd never been the type of person to believe that a woman needed a man to feel complete, I wanted to be loved, and yes, protected. I wanted to feel cherished and secure, and somewhere deep inside, I believed that Aidan might be the one who could give me that.

I suddenly felt him tense up against me as he shifted his weight, and I looked up to find him watching me in the dim light of the bedroom. What I saw in his eyes was a reflection of my own feelings, and it was the most natural thing when his lips found mine, and his other arm went around me to pull me closer. Aidan's kiss was tender and sweet, but full of promise; a promise that would be fulfilled once the events of today were behind us. Now wasn't the time to explore our feelings for each other, and I certainly didn't want anything that happened to be tainted by the memory of Colin, so I snuggled closer to Aidan, feeling safe and cared for, and for the moment, that was better than anything.

Chapter 41

Aidan spread his sleeping bag on the floor and stretched out on top of it without getting inside. Good thing he had it in the back of the truck from the last time he'd gone camping with Declan. Sleeping in the same room as Lexi wasn't advisable under the circumstances, but he needed to be close enough in case she needed something during the night. He hadn't wanted to mention it, but he was actually pretty bruised himself. Colin was slighter than him, but he was strong and wiry, and he'd done his damage that morning when he pummeled Aidan with all his strength. Aidan could barely take a deep breath without feeling acute pain. He should have let Doctor Delaney take a look at him, just in case he had a fractured rib.

Aidan was actually glad to be on his own, since his head was spinning with all kinds of conflicting emotions that were fighting for domination inside his brain. Today had been an emotional roller coaster that began with the realization that Lexi was in the cellar with Colin. Aidan had to admit that his first emotion had been jealousy, the kind he hadn't felt in longer than he could remember. The idea that something might be going on between those two left him feeling as if someone had just punched him in the stomach. Little did he know that was still to come. He went down after Lexi not only to make sure she was all right, but to put his mind to rest. If Lexi was interested in Colin, he would just get his feelings under control and behave in a professional manner.

When Aidan first came upon Lexi and Colin in the room, it took him a moment to realize that what he was witnessing wasn't consensual. It was dark, and all he could see was Colin pressing Lexi against the wall, which could have been something other than what it was. It was only when he heard Lexi's cry of pain and saw her bloodied face that he realized what was happening, and then he was overcome with another emotion — one he'd never felt until that moment. He actually wanted to kill another human being, and had he been able to get away with it, he likely would have. The idea that he could have been too late was enough to inspire a blind rage that drove him to keep hitting Colin long after he had him on the floor, and to lock him inside the dark, dank room just to scare him. Aidan was glad when the coppers finally took him away to the precinct where Colin was safe from Aidan's bloodlust.

Seeing Lexi so scared and vulnerable was enough to break Aidan's heart. He felt for this girl, and for the first time since Noelle, he wanted to love and protect someone with all his being. Aidan thought that he might never find someone who was worthy of such devotion, but Lexi had unwittingly convinced him otherwise, and shown him that he needed to stop licking his wounds and allow himself the joy of caring for someone other than himself. She wasn't just lovely; she was warm and genuine, which was something Aidan responded to after the deceit of Noelle.

Aidan never made a conscious decision to be alone or taken a vow of celibacy, but after things with Noelle came to a head, he sort of retreated into himself, raising walls he didn't know he was building. He'd gone through the motions and went on with his life, but it wasn't until Lexi showed up that he suddenly realized how lonely he'd been, and how sexually frustrated. She was the first woman he'd found attractive in a long time, and he was terrified of doing the wrong thing and messing things up before they even began.

Aidan sighed and tried to find a more comfortable position, acutely aware of his aching middle. He thanked God that he'd been able to prevent the worst, but Lexi was still scarred physically and emotionally and would be for some time to come. He'd have to tread very carefully and not rush her into anything she wasn't ready for. He couldn't stop himself from kissing her earlier, and she had responded, but her response might have come from a different place than desire. She felt gratitude, a need for comfort, and a degree of loneliness since she had no one to turn to in time of need other than him.

He'd been reluctant to call Dot Martin that morning, but there was no one else he could ask to look after Lexi for an hour of two. Dot was a good woman, but her ability to ferret out information was secondary only to MI-5. By tomorrow, the whole village would know that something happened between Colin and Lexi that led to Lexi being banged up and Colin being locked up. Aidan fervently wished that Dot's desire for a job in Lexi's hotel would put the brakes on her inexhaustible tongue, but that was probably too much to hope for, especially since Mildred Higgins was her bosom buddy, and Mildred was the heart and soul of the Upper Whitford rumor mill. Well, that was village life for you. It hadn't been all that different on Skye when Aidan was a lad. Living in small places inspired people with small minds to rule the roost. Sometimes he wished that he could go to a big city like Edinburgh or London and just lose himself in the crowds, become invisible and inconsequential, and totally free.

Aidan stared at the ceiling, knowing that sleep wouldn't come quickly. Despite the open window, the room felt airless, so he finally gave up and decided to have a cigarette. He'd quit a long time ago, but in times of crisis, he permitted himself one just to settle his nerves. Aidan threw open the window, propped his hip against the sill and lit up, pulling the smoke into his lungs with a great sigh of satisfaction. Why did something so bad feel so good?

Aidan took another drag and stared out into the night, his hand stilling as he brought the fag to his lips. There it was, just as Lexi had said, the candlelight in the nonexistent second-floor window of the ruin. Aidan couldn't see the man clearly, but he knew he was there. The tiny pinprick of candlelight shone like a beacon in the night. He stared at the candle for nearly an hour, until the occupant of the ruin blew it out and presumably went to sleep. Not until that moment had Aidan truly believed Lexi had seen something. He thought she might have an overly active imagination, or had seen someone from the village wandering around, but now he had seen it for himself and had no choice but to believe.

"Well, I'll be damned," he muttered as he went back to his sleeping bag, knowing he wasn't sleeping tonight.

October 1650

England

Chapter 42

Rowan threw a shawl over her shoulders and slung a basket over her arm as she quietly let herself out of the house. It was just before dawn, and her aunt and uncle were still asleep, their snores resonating through the house and bouncing off stone walls. They used to get up earlier, but since Rowan came to live with them, she'd taken over some of the morning chores to give her aunt some respite. Aunt Joan was often in pain, especially when the weather was cold or damp, her joints swelling and stretching her reddened skin to the breaking point. Joan never complained, but Rowan saw the pained expression on her face, her mouth compressed into a thin line as she kneaded the dough for bread with her swollen hands and tried to ignore the pain. Rowan usually just put a gentle hand on her aunt's arm, letting her know that she would knead the dough and do the laundry, while her aunt wrapped a thick cloth around a hot brick and held it in her hands to relieve the worst of the pain.

Rowan had already milked the cows and left the milk on the table, away from the mischievous cat who tried to get into it at every opportunity. Aunt Joan called the cat Evelyn, but Rowan thought of it more as Evilene, although she never failed to admire the cat's determination to get at the cream or claim the warmest spot by the hearth. Rowan had lit the fire and moved the hook holding the porridge pot closer to the flame so the food would be hot by the time her aunt and uncle woke. Now she was free to go see Brendan.

Rowan made her way to the henhouse, slipping through the gate as quietly as she could, so as not to disturb the dozing hens. She'd collect some eggs and take them over to Reverend Pole's. Brendan's appetite had greatly improved over the past few days and he would enjoy having some eggs for breakfast, served with bread generously spread with fresh butter. She rarely came over at breakfast time, but today she'd make an exception. The poor man was probably tired of eating stale bread and drinking the ale she'd left for him the day before so as not to make the poor old reverend climb the ladder.

The shirt she'd sewn for Brendan was carefully folded and stored at the bottom of the basket, covered with a cloth just in case one of the eggs broke or some butter from the crock got onto the fabric. She smiled as she gently extracted the eggs, her soul filling with joy at the thought of seeing Brendan. She hoped Reverend Pole would go to the church, as he often did, to work on his sermon or prepare for a christening that was to be held later today for the Simmons baby. She wanted a few hours alone with Brendan, hours that filled her with a happiness that warmed her for the rest of the day as she went about her chores, humming quietly, her eyes smiling at the memory of being with him.

Rowan was surprised to find Brendan sitting on his cot fully dressed, reading a book. He'd read her a few snippets from the *Canterbury Tales,* and she was torn between blushing with embarrassment and giggling with mirth. How clever to write stories that could produce such emotions all at once. Maybe they could read some more today. Her mother had taught her to read when she was a child, but there were no books in Uncle Caleb's house, save a prayer book that he took to church. Come to think of it, there probably wasn't a book to be found in the whole village. These were hardworking, simple people; people who wouldn't spend their money on frivolous entertainment when the money could go to buy food or much-needed tools. She wondered where Brendan got the book, since he never mentioned it.

"I couldn't stand lying there in my nightshirt any longer," Brendan said by way of greeting. "I know I can't actually go anywhere, but getting dressed made me feel a bit more human." He smiled at Rowan's look of reproach. "The wounds are better. They're not seeping blood anymore, and some of the soreness is gone." Brendan grinned at Rowan. "I know, I know; I have to be careful or they'll open right up again."

Funny, how he always seemed to know what she was thinking. Rowan placed the plate of eggs on the stool in front of him, gratified to see his expression. "Thank you, Rowan," Brendan said as he tucked into his breakfast. "I don't know how Reverend Pole survives. He seems to live on bread, milk, and prayer. Not enough sustenance for me. Would you like to share?"

Rowan shook her head. She'd taken a bite to make sure the eggs were tasty before taking them up to Brendan. She'd cooked them in butter and added bits of pork and chives for flavor. She enjoyed watching him eat. She fancied that with every bite he got stronger and healthier, thanks to her, but that was a double-edged sword. Once he recovered, he would leave, and her life would go back to normal. The thought made her sick.

Brendan cleaned his plate and set it on the floor, inviting Rowan to come sit by him on the stool. He saw her looking at the book, but before he read to her, he wanted to talk, or more accurately, he wanted her to listen. He wished he could discuss his plans with someone, but Rowan was the only person who came to see him. Reverend Pole hardly ever came up, and getting up and down the ladder was out of the question for Brendan since the wound in his leg would open right up if he kept bending it. He needed a little more time.

"Rowan, I've written this note to Uncle Caleb. Will you deliver it for me? It's very important." Brendan handed the folded sheet of paper to Rowan and watched as she stuffed it in her pocket, her face full of questions. He'd thought long and hard, cooped up as he was in the airless loft day after day, and finally came up with a plan. All Hallows' Eve was in ten days' time, which would give him enough time to heal sufficiently to sit a horse. In this village where everyone knew each other, setting off in full view of the villagers, even at night, would result in his

215

arrest, but All Hallows' Eve would provide the diversion he so desperately needed. He'd consulted Reverend Pole, and it confirmed his belief that he was handed a unique opportunity.

Reverend Pole planned to go out that night and do what he could to put a stop to the abhorrent Pagan and Catholic rituals that still festered in this part of the country, even after the Reformation, but he knew that all his efforts would be in vain. Some beliefs held sway over the people, even if they had outwardly rejected them. In the mind of the villagers, All Hallows' Eve was the beginning of the darkest and most frightening part of the year, a time when people remembered their dead and faced their own fears. Even Christmas, which shone like a beacon of hope on the shortest and darkest day of the year, did little to lift the pervasive gloom that lasted till spring. On the night of October 31st, many farmers surrounded their fields with burning straw to ward off evil spirits, and people gathered around pitchforks crowned with a ball of straw set alight, and prayed for the souls of their dearly departed.

By November 1st, the appetizing smell of Soul-Mass cakes would be wafting from nearly every house, ready to be given to the poor who went from door to door singing Souling Songs. Each cake eaten would represent a soul rescued from Purgatory. Brendan hoped that someday someone would eat a cake for his soul, for surely he was going straight to Hell after all the men he'd killed in battle and during the occupation of Ireland.

At the time, he'd thought he was doing the right thing, but he'd had much time to think since coming to this village, and his conscience was not clear despite reassurance from the reverend. Reverend Pole assured him that, as a soldier, he killed in the line of duty and not out of any sense of personal vengeance or bloodlust. Killing in times of war was not considered murder, but a duty fulfilled, so Brendan shouldn't fear for his soul, but Brendan wasn't convinced. Maybe killing men on a battlefield wasn't a sin, but killing terrified women who were running for their lives, their children clutched to their breast as they stumbled, fell and were trampled by the hooves of the huge warhorses that bore down on them, was not an honorable endeavor.

Nor was it honorable to kill someone simply because they didn't worship in the same way. They all served the same God after all, unlike the Saracens who were slaughtered during the Crusades. The Church had proclaimed the killing to be God's will, just as Cromwell told his men that what they were doing was just and the will of God, but was it? Or was it just the justification powerful men and the Church used to achieve their own ends and keep the foot soldiers in line, like sheep?

Reverend Pole promised to pray for his soul, as well as help him with his plan. Few people would be surprised to see a reverend out on All Hallows' Eve, calling to the people to abandon their heathen ways. It was one of the few nights a year, along with Midsummer night, when people chose to turn to the old ways, going back to traditions that started long before the march of Christianity across England. Reverend Pole had reluctantly agreed to give Brendan his spare set of clerical robes, which would hide Brendan in open view. Few people looked past the robes to see the man underneath. They would simply think that the bishop had sent an extra man to assist the elderly reverend in trying to stamp out the Pagan rituals which were so repugnant to the Church. In other words, the perfect night to flee.

"I plan to leave on All Hallows' Eve," Brendan confided in Rowan. "I just need Uncle Caleb to provide me with a horse and provisions for a few days. Once I'm safely away from here, I will go to London. I have some friends who will see me through the winter, and then I've a mind to sail to America. I…"

Brendan opened his mouth to continue, but stopped mid-sentence, seeing the look of anguish on Rowan's face as silent tears slid down her cheeks. Her face was a grimace of such suffering that he dropped to his knees in front of her, heedless of his wound, and pulled her to him in an act of silent comfort. Her cap slid off her head, and her hair tumbled around her shoulders and over his arms. It was heavy, the strands silky and almost glowing in the morning sunlight pouring through the little window.

217

"What is it, lass? Have I said something to upset you?" he whispered into her hair, inhaling its scent. She must have used some kind of flower oil when washing her hair because it smelled of late-summer roses and possibly chamomile. Brendan pulled her closer as she shuddered against him, sobbing into his shoulder, her breasts heaving against his chest.

"Hush now. What upset you so?" Brendan held her away from him and lowered his head to gaze into her downturned eyes. "Rowan…"

"Don't leave. Please, don't leave me." Her voice was so low, Brendan thought he must have imagined it, but she finally looked directly into his eyes and said it again, a little louder this time. "Brendan, please don't leave."

Brendan wasn't sure what shocked him more, her speech or the fact that she was asking him to stay, but he tried not to show his surprise as he took Rowan's face in his hands. "Sweetheart, I have to go; you know that. I'm a fugitive accused of murder. Sooner or later, someone will find out I'm here, and then it will be the gallows for me. I must leave this place. And you must get married. I will call myself content if I know that you're well and happy." But Rowan just shook her head, fresh tears swimming in her eyes.

"I can't marry him. Not now. Not since you came," she choked out.

Brendan's mind screamed for him to stop and come to his senses, but he wasn't listening. His heart suddenly felt lighter than it had in years, his soul reaching for this beautiful girl who was telling him, in no uncertain terms, that she loved him. It was wrong of him to encourage her, cruel to give her any hope, but he wasn't thinking clearly as his lips brushed against hers, and felt them open to him, hungry and searching for something she thought only he could give her. She wrapped her arms around him, pressing her body against his in an act of surrender and trust, and he accepted it and kissed her with all the passion he'd been suppressing for the past few weeks. He'd never felt this way about

Mary. He wanted her, lusted after her, planned to make her his, but he never felt tenderness or the need to protect that he felt toward Rowan. He wanted to wrap her in his arms and keep her safe, and use his love to shield her from anything this life could throw at her that it already hadn't.

His mind reeled as she finally broke the kiss and took his face in her small hands. Her eyes were shining with love as she whispered his name, making it sound unbearably beautiful, tumbling from lips that hadn't spoken in years. Somewhere at the back of his mind, Brendan wondered if Rowan would continue to speak or grow silent again, but it didn't matter. She'd given him a tremendous gift, one that he had to keep secret until she was ready to share it with the rest of the world.

He finally began to come to his senses, something that was equivalent to plummeting to the earth from a great height and being smashed to pieces. What was he to do now? He had nothing to offer her, not unless he was able to prove his innocence and reclaim what was rightfully his, and he had no ammunition with which to fight. All the evidence was against him, with not a single witness to support his claim. Well, actually there was one, but he didn't dare ask. Meg had suffered enough, and Jasper would make her life unbearable if she spoke out against him. Besides, the magistrate would need tangible proof, not the suspicions of a grieving daughter and widow. Women were rarely taken seriously in a courtroom setting, especially ones believed to be in the grip of strong emotion.

Meg had her suspicions, but no solid proof. Brendan had to admit that he'd never seen his father's signature, or had any document that could be used to compare to the signature on the accursed piece of paper which disinherited him. He had no proof, just as he had no proof that he had been set upon by Jasper's thugs. There were no witnesses, no case. Most men wouldn't be mad enough to attack three armed horsemen, but it could be argued that they provoked him somehow or insulted his honor, causing him to charge them in a fit of insanity. The end result was still the same. They were dead, and his belongings were found close to their corpses. The best plan was still to flee to London before he was arrested and tried. But what about Rowan?

Chapter 43

Meg smoothed the coverlet around her mother's shoulders and lightly kissed her forehead so as not to disturb her sleep. She was fading fast, reduced to only a few moments of consciousness, which came on her mostly at night when she called for Brendan and begged Meg to put her out of her misery. Nan Carr was only forty-four, but she looked like a woman twice her age; her sallow skin stretched tightly over the bones of her face; eyes sunken into her skull and glazed over with pain. Meg had no idea what illness was devouring her mother from within since there was no physician within twenty miles of their village. The closest city was Lincoln, and there was sure to be a medical man there, but he wouldn't come so far for someone like her mother. Physicians were for the powerful and wealthy, not for the likes of them.

Meg covered the chamber pot with a cloth to keep the stench from making her nose burn and eyes water, and left the room, quietly closing the door behind her. At least Jasper wasn't in the house. Meg hated to be around him these days, although he didn't pay her much mind. He was too preoccupied with the running of the estate and his search for Brendan. He didn't tell her about it, but she knew he'd sent a man to Uncle Caleb's house to enquire about Brendan's whereabouts. Thankfully, Brendan wasn't there, and Uncle Caleb swore that Brendan never passed that way.

Meg sighed as she made her way carefully down the stairs so as not to disturb the contents of the pot. When had a selfish and mischievous boy become a conniving and ruthless man? Meg knew Jasper had planted the evidence on the bodies of the men; she'd seen him take the prayer book, and the ring had been on his finger when he left the house, but gone once he got back. She had to admit that Brendan had always been her favorite, but she loved

Jasper when he was a boy, and always defended him against their mother who called him "the spawn of the Devil," if only in jest.

They'd had a happy family once, but now everything was different. Their father was dead, possibly murdered; their mother wasting away, Brendan missing, possibly injured or dead, Meg's own husband gone, and Jasper now the head of the family. Next week, Jasper and Mary would be wed, and Meg's position would become even more untenable. Meg and Mary were friends once, but now Mary would be the lady of the house, and Meg's position would be precarious as the widowed sister of her husband. Meg depended on Jasper's generosity for her family's survival, and she needed to be on hand to care for their mother. Mary wouldn't do it, but she wouldn't like Meg constantly there, undermining her authority.

Meg sighed. Her mother would be gone soon; that was clear enough, and her only chance for any happiness lay in getting married again — and soon. She was barely twenty-six, and although she'd borne two children, she was still fairly comely with a good figure and a fine house. But, as head of the family, Jasper would have to approve her choice, which could complicate matters since he wanted full control of the estate. He'd want Meg to marry a man he could rely on, and dominate, not someone who would stand up to him and speak his own mind. A man to suit them both would be hard to find.

Meg was so preoccupied with her thoughts that she barely noticed the two men watching her from under a leafy oak at the bottom of the yard. She emptied the chamber pot into the privy out back and stepped back out into the crisp October morning, gulping air after the noxious interior of the outhouse as two men approached her on foot. Their faces were obscured by the brims of their hats, but she was sure they weren't local. Their clothes, although fine, were travel-stained, and swords hung at their hips, swinging as they walked toward her. Meg froze, unsure of what to do. They hadn't done anything to frighten her, but she felt a shiver of apprehension snake down her spine, pinning her feet to the ground and driving breath from her lungs. She prided herself on her good instincts, and her instincts were screaming bloody murder.

"Good morrow, mistress," the older of the two men said, giving her a brief nod and raising his hand to the brim of his hat in a casual greeting. "Fine day, is it not?" he asked, his eyes never leaving hers. He had a handsome face despite a faint scar that ran down the length of his cheek from temple to chin, but his eyes were strangely cold, light and narrowed as he cocked his head to the side, his mouth stretching into a humorless smile.

"Yes, it's pleasantly warm for October," Meg replied, praying that Jasper would come sauntering into the yard. If ever there was a time she'd be happy to see him, it would be now. "Is there something you wanted, gentlemen?"

"A cool drink would be most welcome," the older man said, still smiling. "Allow me to introduce myself. My name is Edward Sexby, and this is Will Barrett, an associate and brother-in-arms. We have some business with your brother. Would we find him at home, mistress?"

So, they were looking for Jasper. Meg allowed herself to exhale and wiped her sweating brow with the back of her hand. "I'm afraid you've missed him, sir."

She turned toward the house, dismayed to see them follow her.

"Perhaps we can wait for him?"

"I'm afraid he might be out all day. He has business on the estate. Maybe you can call around suppertime. I'd be happy to give Jasper a message," she offered, hoping they would just leave. The younger man hadn't said a word, but there was something in his expression that scared the wits out of her, and she didn't scare easily.

"Jasper?" Sexby asked.

"Yes, my brother Jasper. Mayhap you have the wrong house." Meg stopped before going into the house, reluctant to let them in, but Sexby was already pushing the door open and maneuvering his way inside. Meg was backed up against the table as the younger man positioned himself by the door, blocking her escape.

"It's your brother Brendan we are looking for. Brendan Carr." Sexby's eyes were narrowed as he watched Meg. She suspected that any lie she told would be recognized immediately.

"Brendan is not here, Mr. Sexby. He left weeks ago and we haven't seen him since." Meg inched backward, her hips pressing against the wooden table as Sexby advanced on her.

"And where would he have gone, mistress?"

"I don't know." Meg was taken completely by surprise when Sexby's gloved hand slapped her across her face with enough force to rattle her teeth.

"Shall we try this again? Where's Brendan Carr, mistress?"

"I d-d-don't know," Meg replied, stammering with fear. "I truly don't know. Jasper doesn't know either. He's been searching for him this whole while." Sexby hit her again and this time she fell, her head just missing the corner of the table. Meg rolled into a ball, covering her head with her hands, but Will Barrett dragged her to her feet and drove a fist into her stomach.

"Speak, woman," he growled.

Meg briefly thanked the good Lord that her boys were nowhere near the house. At least they would be spared. Whatever these men wanted, they meant to have it, and they would probably kill her to get it. She only hoped Jasper would take care of her children, being their nearest male relative.

"I don't know," she cried again. "I don't know. Please, don't hurt me," she begged as she covered her face in anticipation

224

of another blow. She instinctively felt Barrett get closer and raise his hand, but Sexby spoke before Barrett hit her again.

"She doesn't know, Will," he said, "leave her be. Perhaps we'll have better luck with Jasper."

Meg nearly jumped out of her skin as Sexby took off his glove and brushed a strand of hair from Meg's face, carefully tucking it back into her cap. He brushed his fingers across her bruised cheek, his eyes suddenly warm and full of humor. "How about that cool drink now? And something to eat as well. Bread and cheese will do, but if you have something heartier, it'd be most welcome."

The men settled themselves at the table, looking for all the world like welcome guests. Meg didn't even try to pour the ale since she knew she'd spill it all over the table with her shaking hands. She just set the pitcher on the table and pushed two cups toward the men, before getting a fresh loaf of bread and a hunk of cheese that she'd been saving for the midday meal for her and the boys. Sexby's eyes traveled to a sausage that was hanging above the hearth. "That too."

Meg reached for the sausage and wished she could use it to whack Sexby over the head, but a sausage was no weapon against two men with swords and fists. She just pushed it toward them and let them cut it up with their daggers. They ate slowly, enjoying their meal as if they were in a tavern and not in the home of a woman they'd just threatened and beaten.

Meg knew she should keep her mouth shut, but she didn't think they'd hit her again, and she needed to know. "What do you want with Brendan?" she asked carefully, taking a step back just in case. Sexby's amused expression wasn't lost on her. He enjoyed making people cower, that was clear, and he could sense her fear like a dog.

"Your brother is to be taken back to Scotland and tried for desertion. You do know he deserted, do you not?" Sexby asked conversationally, his hand playing with the dagger he'd used to cut the sausage. He drove it into the wooden table, gratified by Meg's shock. "Deserters are hanged."

Meg felt suddenly very cold despite the warmth of the hearth glowing behind her. She didn't know what to say or do, so she backed into a corner and sat on a low stool she'd used for nursing when her boys were small. She wanted to disappear into the stone walls and become invisible to these men, but all she could do was fold her hands in her lap and stare at the floor, praying that they would just leave.

Meg nearly jumped out of her skin as the door burst open, letting in a gust of cool air. The wind had picked up, and the house was momentarily filled with the smell of autumn which dispelled the revolting smell of the two men who likely hadn't bathed in weeks. Jasper stood in the doorway, surveying the scene. He had a dagger at his belt, but it would do little good against two armed men; a fact that he perceived very quickly.

Sexby and Barrett rose to their feet, the food forgotten. "You better step outside, mistress," Sexby said to Meg without turning around, "for your own safety." Meg bolted from her spot in the corner and darted outside. She wanted to run home as fast as her feet would carry her and make sure that her children were safe, but she had to stay close to make sure Jasper was all right after the men were done questioning him. She was sure that Jasper didn't know where Brendan was, but that didn't mean the men would believe him.

Meg slid to the ground beneath the oak tree and wrapped her arms around her knees, resting her forehead against them. She was shaking with fear — for herself, Jasper, but mostly Brendan. They wanted him dead. "Oh, Brendan," she whispered, "what have you done?"

It seemed like an hour, but it was no more than ten minutes later that Sexby and Barrett walked out of the house, their hats on their heads and their swords sheathed and on their belts. They tipped their hats to Meg and wished her a good day as if she were a lady at court and not a quivering mess with a tear-stained face and wild hair, crouching beneath a tree. Meg finally willed herself to get up once the sound of hoof beats died away, and shuffled on shaking legs toward the house. Jasper was calmly sitting at the table, a piece of sausage speared on his dagger and a cup of ale in his hand. He smiled indulgently at Meg and took a deep pull of his ale before pouring her a cup.

"You look like you need this," he said, studying her bruised face. "Did they hurt you?"

Meg just shook her head, amazed at Jasper's calm. He didn't have a scratch on him. "What did you tell them?"

"The truth. I have no idea where Brendan is." Jasper took a bite of the sausage and chewed thoughtfully, his eyes still on Meg.

"So, how is it that they didn't hurt you?" asked Meg suspiciously.

"Oh, I told them that I'm getting married next week and need to look my best." He chuckled at his own joke and tore off a chunk of bread. Meg suddenly felt her knees go weak. If the men simply left Jasper in peace that could mean only one of two things: he either told them where to find Brendan, or he made some kind of deal with them.

The Present

Chapter 44

I woke up to find the sky a pale blue, washed clean by yesterday's rain. The breeze blowing through the open window was fresh and cool, the sun just barely above the horizon, spreading a golden glow above the tree tops and tinting the walls of my bedroom a peachy pink. I expected to feel depressed, frightened, and angry after yesterday's ordeal, but what I actually felt was joy. I was almost giddy with it. I had gotten very lucky that Aidan came when he did, and I wasn't about to allow Colin to make me feel like a victim. What he actually made me feel was a hunger for life. Yesterday's incident reminded me how life could turn on a dime, and I didn't intend to spend another minute wallowing in self-pity. I wanted to live every day to the fullest, and I would start with today, but first, I wanted to take a nice, hot bath to wash away any trace of what happened from my body. I turned on the taps and rummaged around for my iPod.

The water was almost scalding, the delicious scent of lavender bath salts drifting up in soothing steam as I turned on my favorite playlist and closed my eyes. I felt as if I were floating, the water gently lapping at my breasts and the heat drawing out every bit of tension from my body. Images of Aidan floated in front of my eyes as my hand unwittingly strayed between my legs, my body suddenly no longer relaxed, but coursing with desire. Yesterday's kiss had awoken something which I had been suppressing for a long time, and I was suddenly vibrating with desire, desperate for it to be fulfilled.

My eyes flew open in alarm as something softly touched my arm. Aidan was standing above me, desperately trying not to let his eyes stray from my face. Oh, God, how long had he been

228

there? I thought I'd locked the door, but here he was, seeing me in all my soapy glory. I pulled the earbuds from my ears and smiled guiltily.

"You didn't answer, so I got worried," he explained, his gaze drifting over my body. "I'll just go now."

He sounded strangled, and I could see my own desire reflected in his eyes. I didn't say anything, just rose to my feet in the tub. My skin glowed from the heat and droplets of water slid between my breasts and down my thighs, but I didn't bother to reach for a towel. I smiled at Aidan as I stepped from the tub and stood a few inches away from him, my face flushed with heat. Aidan was transfixed, his eyes asking me for confirmation that this was what I wanted. I couldn't blame him after what happened yesterday. He needed to be sure, so I pressed my body against his and raised my face to receive his kiss. That was all the prompting he needed as he scooped me up and carried me back into the bedroom. Erotic scenes of slow seduction that played out in my mind before were pushed out by a need so strong, that I couldn't bear to wait another second. I grabbed for his belt buckle, but Aidan playfully pushed away my urgent hands. "Not yet," he whispered, "not yet," as he pushed me onto the bed and pulled off his shirt.

I was momentarily shocked by the bruises to his ribs and stomach, but Aidan didn't seem bothered. "It's nothing," he whispered as he kissed me, leaving me breathless with desire.

"Close your eyes and let me love you," he asked, and I did, giving myself up to him with total abandon. As Aidan's hands and lips explored every inch of me the words of an old-fashioned vow sprang to mind, "With my body I thee worship," and worship me he did. If I had any doubts about his feelings for me, all my uncertainty fled as he put his feelings into kisses and caresses. I hardly noticed as he pulled me to the edge of the bed and pushed my thighs apart, getting on his knees in front of me and paying homage to that most womanly part of me. Wave after wave of unbearable pleasure flowed over me, the orgasm leaving me shattered and utterly reborn in equal parts. I felt like molten gold, fluid and shimmering as I finally descended back to earth.

When I reached for him this time, Aidan didn't stop me, and I freely gave as much as I'd received, finally guiding him into my body and holding him there as the ancient rhythm of love overtook us, leaving us joined body and soul, and utterly fulfilled as Aidan gave me a kiss of unbearable tenderness and rested his head on my shoulder as his breathing finally returned to normal.

Now that the moment had passed, I was suddenly embarrassed by my wantonness. I'd never done anything like this before. All my previous sexual experiences had been initiated by the men, and I generally wanted to date for a while before letting things get that far. This was completely out of character for me, but Aidan didn't know that, and might think that I was some slut who threw herself at every guy she found attractive. I averted my gaze from him, but he gently turned my face back to meet his eyes.

"Don't turn away, mo gradh." I had no idea what that meant, but judging from his expression, I knew it was a declaration of love, or at least intense desire. He rolled onto his back and pulled me to him, his lips brushing my temple in a butterfly kiss. I was torn between unbearable joy and uncertainty, and had no idea how to express to Aidan what I was feeling, but he did it for me, putting my mind at rest.

"I can't remember the last time I've been this happy," he mused. "Funny how sometimes we don't even realize how miserable and lonely we are until someone reminds us what it feels like to love." Aidan lowered his head and kissed me again. He looked so peaceful and sated that I just wrapped my arms around him and pulled him down on top of me, kissing him with all my heart. I wasn't ready to say the words, but I wanted him to know how I felt. Aidan slid his tongue into my mouth as I felt his body responding to my advances, and I gasped with pleasure and surprise as he slid into me again, moving slowly and deliberately this time until I was floating on a cloud of sensation, my heart humming with the knowledge that it had found a home.

I was abruptly brought back to earth by the opening and closing of the front door, and the sound of footsteps on the tile floor of the kitchen. It was the equivalent of a bucketful of cold water being poured over me just as I got warm basking in the sun.

"Oh, God, it's Dot," Aidan said as he tried to suppress a giggle. "Can you just imagine her face if she finds us like this?"

I could, and I could also imagine how well-informed the entire village would be within a quarter of an hour. I wasn't ready to share my newfound happiness with anyone, least of all Mildred Higgins of the Gossip Shop, so I shoved Aidan out of bed and grabbed for my dressing gown.

"You certainly don't look like someone suffering from bruising and a concussion," he observed as he pulled on his T-shirt, covering up the ugly purple welts on his torso. What did I look like?

I sat up and studied my reflection in the mirror above the dresser. My hair was all mussed, my lips swollen from bruising and Aidan's kisses, and a few love bites bloomed on my neck. But what really gave me away was the blissed-out expression on my face. I looked like a woman who'd been properly… I couldn't even think the word to myself without wanting to giggle.

"Lexi, are you up?" Dot called as I heard her walking up the stairs. "I came to check up on you. I hope you don't mind; I let myself in with the spare key."

Aidan dashed out the door before Dot had a chance to see him in my bedroom, and I pulled the blanket up to my chin in the hope that Dot wouldn't realize that I was naked beneath the dressing gown. She poked her head in the door and gave me a bright smile.

"Are you feeling any better, dear? You certainly look much improved." She gave me a knowing look as Aidan appeared in the hallway, looking for all the world as if he had a peaceful night in his sleeping bag.

"She looks well," he announced with a wicked grin, "wouldn't you say, Dot? I took good care of her."

"No doubt you did, you scoundrel," she replied with a smile. "Away with you. I'll look after her."

"I don't need any looking after," I tried to interject, but no one was actually listening to me. "I'm perfectly well."

"Perfectly well, she says," Dot grumbled as she retreated. "Back into bed with you," she ordered as I made to sit up. "Dr. Delaney said a few days, did he not?"

I lay back on the pillows and allowed myself to enjoy the afterglow of my interlude with Aidan. Dot was here for now, so I might as well just let her take care of me. I had to admit that I felt a little lightheaded, whether from the concussion or from the treatment I just received at Aidan's hands. I tried to suppress a silly grin as Dot appeared again, carrying a breakfast tray.

"Where's Aidan?" I asked, wishing my contractor was still my nurse.

"Sent him packing, I have. You should have called me last night and I would have been here to look after you. This is no place for the likes of him." I didn't bother to ask what the likes of him were and just obediently accepted the cup of steaming tea.

"The whole village is buzzing," Dot informed me as I took a bite of toast. "To think that Colin would be capable of such a thing. And to pull a knife on Aiden… And he always seemed like such a quiet lad." She shook her head in confusion and disgust as she watched me. It reminded me of all those perplexed people who found out that their quiet next-door neighbor actually kept sex slaves in his basement for years and no one ever suspected a thing. Strange how people only saw what they wanted to see.

"Mildred was shocked that Aidan would volunteer to look after you," Dot continued, "it's not exactly appropriate under the circumstances. Is it?"

"Oh? What circumstances are those?" I asked, not really caring to know.

"Well, Colin works for Aidan; so for all intents and purposes, it was all Aidan's fault. Should have known better. I suppose he wants to get on your good side so his business doesn't suffer."

"It wasn't Aidan's fault," I retorted.

"And him staying with you last night... there'll be talk." Dot said that with such gravity that I nearly burst out laughing. She probably had the scarlet letter all ready to stitch to my bodice, although technically, I wasn't an adulteress. Maybe Dot had a 'T' handy for "Tart."

Aidan poked his head through the door, his smile full of apology.

"Away with you, I said," Dot commanded, sounding like a general about to engage in battle.

"I'm going, I'm going," Aidan replied with a laugh. "Sorry about the new regime, Lex," he quipped, giving Dot a pointed look. "It was a hostile takeover. I'll be back later to smooth any ruffled feathers."

"Looks like you surrendered without a fight," I countered, giving him a warm smile and already counting the moments until I would see him again.

"I know when I'm beaten." With that, he blew me a kiss, since Dot was manning the door like a fire-breathing dragon, and left. I had to admit that Dot's concern was kind of endearing. She appeared to be one of those women who wasn't happy unless she was taking care of someone, and at the moment, I was that someone. It was kind of nice to have someone fussing over me, especially since my mother was thousands of miles away and couldn't be there to baby me.

Spending the day with Dot reminded me of being sick as a child. I got the gold star treatment. Dot popped in every so often to make sure I was all right and bring numerous cups of tea, food, and the latest gossip from the village, but she didn't hover over me and left me to my own thoughts, which kept straying to the room in the cellar. Colin had interrupted my exploration, and I longed to go back and have another look at the coffin. I was fascinated by it, and desperate to find any clue that might help me figure out what happened to the mysterious Brendan Carr. The thing was that I didn't want to share my secret with Dot. I didn't want anyone in the village to know about the room, not because I wanted to keep the history of the place to myself, but because stories of skeletons in the proverbial closet could scare away future custom; although, on the other hand, they could also increase it. For every person who was put off by something spooky, there were ten more who'd welcome the opportunity to stay in my haunted mansion. In either case, I'd wait till Aidan came back. I didn't fancy going down there by myself, especially after what happened yesterday. At the very least, it would be nice to have someone hold the flashlight.

Chapter 45

By 6 p.m. Dot finally took her leave, after extracting numerous promises that I wouldn't do anything foolish such as engage in acrobatics, hang off the chandelier, or succumb to Aidan's advances. I wholeheartedly promised not to act like a circus performer, but as far as Aidan went, I kept mum. I couldn't make any promises when it came to him, since my heart actually did a somersault every time I thought of our lovemaking that morning.

But it wasn't just about sex. I wanted so much more than that. Aidan made me feel as no other man had before — safe. I had this odd feeling that no matter what happened, he would never do anything to hurt me, and would shield me from anyone and anything that meant me harm. I suppose that was a foolish assumption since according to Dot, he broke his fiancée's heart, but I'd never heard his side of the story, and I suspected it might be somewhat different than the village version.

I glanced out the window to make sure the coast was clear and got out of bed. I was sick and tired of just lounging about, and although I wasn't ready to walk, I could at least get dressed and sit. I still had a few hours before darkness fell, so I pulled on a pair of jeans and a top, applied a little make-up, brushed my hair, and grabbed my jacket before carefully making my way downstairs and out back to my little sanctuary. I loved the fact that summer in England wasn't as humid and stifling as it had been in New York. The air was fresh, cool, and fragrant with the smells of the country. Crickets filled the air with their song, and the rushing of the stream and gentle rustling of leaves made me feel wonderfully at peace.

I closed my eyes and filled my lungs with air, inhaling the scent of flowers, grass, and damp earth from yesterday's rain. I purposely sat with my back to the ruin to keep myself from watching for my ghost, but I literally felt the hair on the back of

235

my neck rise as the sun began to drop toward the horizon. I knew he was there without even turning around, and I saw it in Aidan's face as he rounded the house and froze, his mouth opening slightly at what he clearly saw behind me. He didn't say anything, just quietly pulled up a chair and watched in awe as the man went about his nightly routine. I wondered if he had been there last night when the rain came down in torrents, but then I didn't think a ghost would be much affected by the weather.

"So, you believe me now?" I asked quietly as the sun finally sank behind the horizon, and I knew that the man had retreated back into the ruin. Dusk was settling around us, the last remnants of pink leached from the sky as the first stars began to twinkle, and a crescent moon, thin and delicate as a sickle, appeared just over the tree line.

"I saw him last night," Aidan said. "Or more accurately, I saw his candle burning in the window of the room that's not there. Do you think he's the man entombed in the cellar?"

"I couldn't begin to guess," I replied, secretly gratified that Aidan didn't think I was mad, "but it's as if he dies all over again if no one knows what happened to him, don't you think?"

"I don't suppose it makes much of a difference to him what people know. Do you think he even knows we're here?"

"I'm not sure. There are moments when I think he's just an apparition, almost like a projection on a screen, and at other times, I think he's aware of his surroundings. It's very hard to tell without getting closer, but I must admit that I'm not brave enough to face him." The thought had crossed my mind to walk over to the ruin at sunset and see what would happen, but I quickly dismissed it. I didn't believe the man had any power to hurt me, but I was just coming to terms with the idea that ghosts did indeed exist; I wasn't ready to face one just yet.

"And maybe you shouldn't. Whatever happened to him left his soul in terrible turmoil, and whether he's aware of it or not, he has to continue his endless vigil over that tree for centuries to come. Maybe we'd better leave him to it."

"I don't think I can," I replied stubbornly. "I need to know what happened to him. Will you come down to the basement with me? I just want to have another look around."

I had to admit that I was gratified by Aidan's look of concern. "Are you sure you want to go down there after...?"

"Yes, and I want to clean up the blood. Colin desecrated this man's final resting place, and I want to put things right."

I was glad that Aidan didn't try to talk me out of it. I kept thinking about it throughout the day and felt strongly about respecting Brendan Carr's tomb. I owed him that much. I followed Aidan to the kitchen and grabbed a sponge, a basin of water, and a flashlight, and opened the door to the basement with a resolve I didn't really feel.

***

The room was much as it had been yesterday, except there was dried blood on the stone floor and smudges of what was probably my blood on the wall. Aidan took the basin and sponge out of my hands and went to work. I was grateful since the sight of the blood really upset me. Instead, I went back to exploring the tomb. I ran my fingers over every inch, but I didn't find anything new. If only there was something more to go on.

Aidan shone the light over the floor and walls to make sure he got all the blood when he seemed to fixate on something just below the stone coffin.

"What is it?" I asked.

"Can you hold the light?" Aidan asked as he sank to his knees in front of the tomb. "There's something in here, I think. Now that I saw what he was looking at I noticed it too. There was a niche close to the top of the plinth and right below the center of the coffin. When one looked quickly, it all appeared to be made of stone, but one rectangle appeared different from the others. Aidan ran his hand over the surface and then gently tried to work the stone to slide it out.

"Maybe there's something behind it," he said.

"Like what?"

"I don't know, but this is not made of stone. This is metal." Aidan ran his hand over it and wiped off a layer of dust. "Let's take it upstairs."

We laid our find on the kitchen table and carefully wiped away centuries of grime. The box must have been ornate at some point, decorated with carvings and possibly even stones, but now it was dark with rust and slightly corroded with age and moisture. It was locked, but it didn't take long for Aidan to break the lock with a screwdriver from his toolbox. I peered inside, surprised to see something flat and brown.

"What is that?" I asked.

"It's calfskin. I think it's a book." Aidan carefully lifted the package out of the box and laid it on the table next to the box. Whatever was inside was wrapped in leather to keep it safe from the elements. Aidan began to unwrap the package as I watched with a mixture of curiosity and apprehension. I'm not sure what I'd been expecting, but it wasn't pages, yellowed and curled with age. The ink must have been black at some point, but now it was faded to brown, the words written in what appeared to be old English. The letters were written in an old-fashioned hand, and there were a few splotches of ink as if it had slid from the tip of the quill as the author paused to think of an appropriate word or phrase. Aidan lifted the first page and read a few sentences to himself.

"This appears to be some kind of narrative, written in 1685 by one Anne Hughes. I'm guessing she was the first mistress of this house. Might make for fascinating reading. You just might find out who your mystery man was."

Aidan replaced the page and rewrapped the leather to keep the pages from being exposed to the light. I reached for the leather-wrapped package and held it against my chest, suddenly feeling possessive. I wanted to read it, but I wanted to be alone when I did, and I had to be emotionally prepared to find out what it contained. For now, I would hide it in my bedroom and return to it when I was ready.

It seemed Aidan had much the same idea, since he took the parcel out of my hands and laid it aside as he took me in his arms. My heart skipped a beat as he kissed me and whispered, "Let's go upstairs." He didn't need to ask twice.

October 1650

England

Chapter 46

Brendan could tell that the weather had changed without even setting foot outside. The wind howled in the trees and moved beneath the rafters of the roof, making the loft even colder than it already was. The temperature had dropped after nightfall, all the warmth soaked up by the stones from the glowing hearth during the day sucked out by the frigid night outside. Brendan pulled the thin blanket closer around himself, but he was still cold, and anxious. He prided himself on his ability to think a situation through and make the best decision, but for the first time in his life, he was torn in half; the fatal cut somewhere in the vicinity of his neck.

His head screamed for him to put Rowan out of his mind and keep to his plan. He was in danger, not only from Jasper and the law, but possibly from Cromwell's men. He had no indication that anyone was in pursuit, but he couldn't rule that possibility out. Staying in a small village where he would be visible the minute he set foot outside was paramount to suicide. He needed to get away, and all Hallows' Eve was the perfect time to slip away unnoticed. Besides, no matter how he yearned for Rowan, he had nothing to offer her at the present. She must have felt some affection for the man she was betrothed to, so maybe if he just made a clean break of it and left she would go on with her life and forget him. He had to admit that he would be heartbroken at the thought of leaving her and knowing that she would belong to another, but if he loved her, he had to do what was best for Rowan, and leaving was the only possible solution.

The problem with this logic was that although Brendan acknowledged that his reasoning was sound, his heart did not seem to agree. It howled with agony every time he thought of never seeing Rowan again, and the memory of their kiss seemed to overshadow all coherent thought, the feeling traveling through his body until it lodged itself firmly in his loins, which ached unbearably and caused him great discomfort. Brendan finally couldn't take it any longer and sat up, wrapping the threadbare blanket around his shoulders for warmth. He had to be a man about this and protect Rowan, if only from himself. He could bring her nothing but grief, and he had to be strong and just walk away from her. He could make it through ten days of agony until October 31st; he'd suffered worse. Brendan pulled the blanket tighter and put his head in his hands. He would tell Rowan tomorrow that he was leaving as planned, and she had to stay behind and marry Stephen Aldrich.

He should have felt better with the decision finally made, but he actually felt even worse than when he found out that his own brother meant to have him killed. He felt truly bereft and alone. *You should be used to it by now*, he thought to himself bitterly. *God doesn't seem to be on your side these days.* Brendan must have eventually fallen asleep because when he opened his eyes, a shaft of sunlight was moving across the floor, dust motes floating and twirling in the air, and the wind of the night before now calm and just a murmur outside the window. He supposed it was time to get up, but it's not as if he had anywhere to be. His escape plan had been put into action and now all he had to do was wait for the day and hope that nothing went wrong.

Brendan could hear the creaking of the bed as Reverend Pole awoke and went about his morning routine of using the chamber pot rather loudly, washing, and dressing. Once dressed, the old man stood at the bottom of the ladder and called out a greeting to Brendan before eating his meager breakfast and setting off for the day. Brendan hoped that Rowan wouldn't come today. He'd made his decision, but it'd be easier if she weren't there to test his resolve. He'd try to make it downstairs today and help himself to some bread and milk, as well as some water for washing. Brendan scratched his chin, annoyed with the thick growth of beard that now covered the lower half of his face. What he wouldn't give for a hot bath and a close shave, but he had to do with whatever he could find downstairs. Reverend Pole probably hadn't shaved in years. He had sparse, gray whiskers that matched the wispy hair on his head, but his chin was almost hairless and pink as a newborn babe's.

***

Brendan stared at his face in the tiny mirror hanging off a hook beside Reverend Pole's bed. The face that looked back was now clean-shaven and the hair was brushed and tied back with a leather thong, but the hazel eyes looked haunted and the skin was stretched more tightly over the bones of his face than he remembered, making him look world-weary. It felt good to be clean though.

Brendan nearly jumped out of his skin as someone knocked softly on the door. He'd locked it just in case, but he didn't think to close the shutters. Brendan stepped behind the bed curtain and watched as a shadow passed before the window. It was Rowan, and he was sorely tempted to let her leave, but good manners prevailed and he unlatched the door, letting her in. He was about to explain the locked door and his presence downstairs when Rowan simply walked toward him, wrapped her arms around his middle and pressed her cheek to his chest, listening to his heartbeat.

"I love you," she said simply, as if it was the most natural thing for a young girl to say to a man. Her lack of guile always left Brendan speechless with wonder. Most girls Rowan's age were coy and calculating, instinctively playing the mating game with a view to catching the best prospect possible, but Rowan was as innocent as a child, trusting him with her heart without any reservations, without any suspicion that he might use her for his own pleasure and discard her as so many men would.

"I love you, too," he whispered into her hair, "but I must leave you." Rowan just gazed up at him, her eyes full of pain and

242

confusion, telling him that people who loved each other didn't just walk away; they stayed and made things work. How could he explain to her the danger she'd be in with him?

"Rowan, I must leave. I'm a wanted man, do you not see that?" he asked gently. He didn't want to bring up the fact that he would swing if caught so as not to cause her any more pain. She'd probably witnessed a hanging at some point in her life, and the image of the victim kicking at empty air as they soiled themselves and clawing at the rope at their neck was not something one quickly forgot.

"I understand," she murmured. "Brendan, please take me with you. I won't be any trouble, I promise. I will come as your mistress if that's what you want. I will never ask you for anything you don't care to give, but please, don't leave me here. I've already lost someone I loved, and I can't live through that again. I won't live through that again. I want to be with you." She raised her face to his and shyly pressed her lips to his, letting him know that she was his for the taking. Brendan took her by the shoulders and gently pushed her away, cocking his head to catch her downcast eyes.

"Rowan, I want you more than you can possibly imagine, but I won't endanger your life. I want you to be safe and happy."

"I will never be happy," she cried, tearing out of his grasp and whirling away from him. "How can I be happy married to a man I don't love? How can I love his child when I wish it were yours? Yes, I would most likely be safe, but I would never be happy." She spun around, her eyes blazing in her small face, "I've loved you since I was twelve."

Rowan was hurt to see the look of confusion on Brendan's face. He didn't remember her; didn't remember twirling her to the music or giving her a kiss on the cheek before he went on to dance with someone else. And he would forget her now. Tears spilled down her cheeks, leaving Brendan feeling heartbroken and helpless. What was he to do? Her words tore through all his defenses and left him reeling. Did she really love him so much that she would risk everything just to be with him? He'd never known such love before. Mary only wanted him for what he could give her, although she pretended to care for him, and other women whom he'd met over the past few years were nothing but common whores, willing to do anything for a coin. This girl was so pure, it broke his heart. Was he a fool to walk away from such devotion?

"Rowan, do you understand the risk of being with me?" he asked softly, seeing a spark of hope in her eyes. "Are you willing to follow me anywhere and possibly live in poverty until I'm able to better our situation?"

Rowan just nodded, a rosy flush spreading across her cheeks as she looked up at him with shining eyes. "You'll take me with you?" she whispered. Brendan nearly laughed at the excitement in her face. She was practically bouncing on the balls of her feet as she clasped her hands before her. "We'll be together?"

"The only way you're coming with me is if we're properly wed. I won't make you my mistress. You deserve better than that, and I will do everything in my power to keep you happy and safe. May God help me," he added under his breath as Rowan threw her arms around his neck kissing his face, her lips finally finding his. He didn't push her away this time.

"We'll have Reverend Pole marry us," she gushed.

"He can marry us, but I'll ask him not to enter the marriage in the parish records book until after we've gone. If anyone sees the entry, they'll know I'm here."

Rowan just nodded happily. She looked as if she would burst with joy and although Brendan tried to keep a cool head, he suddenly felt swept up in her happiness. The thought of having her as his wife filled him with a quiet joy that he'd never known before. He'd give her a good life, a comfortable life, no matter what it took. Once they got to London, they'd stay with his friends, and he would find a way to earn some money before they sailed for the Colonies in the spring, so they would have something to start their new life with. Brendan sat on the cot and Rowan carefully perched on his uninjured leg, her arms around his neck. He wrapped his arms around her and rested his head against her breasts, enjoying a moment of contentment he hadn't felt in a long time. He'd come here half dead, and he'd be leaving with a new life.

Brendan stretched out on the cot with Rowan pressed against him. He wouldn't touch her until they were married, but it was nice to feel her body against his. She was so warm and soft, and willing, which made things that much harder. It was also difficult to ask her what he wanted to know, but he felt he needed to try. He knew so little about her, and it was important to know what had caused her such lasting harm.

"Rowan, you don't have to tell me if you don't wish to, but what happened to you before you came here?" Brendan tried to keep his voice low and non-threatening, but he felt her stiffen against him and wrapped his arms tighter around her in a silent promise of protection. "You don't have to talk about it," he repeated, sensing her alarm.

"No, I think it's time I spoke of it. It won't make it any easier to live with, but you have a right to know." Rowan lapsed into silence for so long, Brendan thought she'd changed her mind, but then she finally began to speak, her voice very low, as that of a small child who's afraid of the dark.

Chapter 47

Rowan closed her eyes, the images taking shape once again after years of being kept at bay, locked in a part of her mind where they couldn't hurt her. She'd woken up screaming for months after she came to Aunt Joan and Uncle Caleb, the horror seeping into her soul and leaving her shaking and helpless, thrashing in her bed until Aunt Joan finally managed to calm her down, usually with a cup of mead. The nightmares grew less frequent over the years, but the memory of that night was still there, as it always would be till the day she died.

"My mother was always knowledgeable about herbs and plants. She'd learned it from an old woman who lived in their village when she was a girl. She often went into the forest to forage for roots and leaves and make them into salves and potions." Rowan sighed and pressed closer to Brendan as she continued.

"My father forbade my mother to tell anyone of her skill. He was wary of the people in our village, but my mother said that he was just being overly cautious. These people were our friends and neighbors, and everyone knew her for the kind, God-fearing woman she was."

Rowan grew silent for a moment in an effort to get her shaking voice under control. It was still a little hoarse from years of disuse, and her throat ached from suddenly speaking so much at once as well as from the tears she was swallowing back.

"My mother begged my father not to leave, but he chose to take up arms and fight for his king. He died at Adwalton Moor in 1643. My mother tried her best to keep things going, but the two of us struggled to manage the farm. It was too much work for a woman and child. Some days we barely had enough to eat." Rowan grew silent, remembering the hardship of that awful winter.

Her mother had grown thin and silent, her lovely face suddenly lined and gray from lack of food and too much worry.

"A neighbor's child had gotten ill, so my mother went over with some willow bark tea to help bring the fever down. It helped, and the woman was very grateful. She gave my mother a few eggs and helped spread the word, which is exactly what my mother was hoping for. Within a few months, our fortunes improved. People had no money to pay, but they traded food for remedies, and that helped us a great deal. My mother also made love charms for the young girls. She said they were just a bit of whimsy, but the girls believed that a love charm could help them win the heart of the one they loved."

Brendan held Rowan close and kissed her temple. He could guess what was coming, but Rowan needed to speak of it in order for the memories to loosen their hold over her.

"There was one girl in particular. Her name was Ellie, and she often came by our cottage, eager to learn anything that my mother had to teach her. She was lively and anxious to learn, so my mother showed her the different flowers and roots, and taught her how to mix them together to ward off fevers and prevent festering of a wound. I used to help out, too. I'd grind things in a mortar or chop up roots and boil leaves for tea. Those were happy times. We'd sit around the table and my mother would tell Ellie and I stories about knights and ladies, and the great astronomers like John Dee, who Queen Bess used to consult before making any important decisions. My mother thought John Dee was a wizard and could probably turn brass into gold."

"What happened then?" Brendan asked carefully, sensing that Rowan was becoming more agitated as she spoke.

"Ellie had her heart set on a boy from the village. Edgar, his name was, and he was apprenticed to the blacksmith. She dreamed of marrying him and asked my mother about what happened in a marriage bed, since her own mother wouldn't tell her. My mother laughed at her and teased her, but I think she told her in the end. That made Ellie want him even more. She thought that if she got him to kiss her, he'd ask her to marry him. Edgar did kiss her, and possibly did more than that, but it was Daisy he made an offer of marriage to. Daisy's family owned the smithy, so Edgar would inherit the lot once Daisy's father died. Ellie's family was barely scraping by, like us."

Rowan turned on her side and pressed her back against Brendan's chest. She couldn't bear to look at him as she told the rest of the story, so he just held her close and let her talk.

"Ellie was heartbroken when Daisy and Edgar announced their betrothal. She was sure that Edgar loved her and only wanted Daisy for the smithy, but there was naught to be done. The banns were read, and the date of the wedding set. A week before the wedding, Daisy was found dead with a piece of seedcake still in her hand. She'd been poisoned. My mother was the only person in the village who knew about remedies and poisons, so suspicion instantly fell on her, even though she had nothing at all to gain by killing Daisy. Daisy's mother called my mother a witch, and stood in the village green screaming her accusations of murder and calling on the people of the village to punish the witch.

People who were our friends and neighbors — people whom my mother had helped and cured — turned into a vicious mob within an hour. The war was raging all around us. People were losing their menfolk, starving and doing without, so it didn't take much to ignite the dry kindling. My mother and I were blissfully unaware of what was coming. We were at home, baking bread and making a rabbit stew.

The mob dragged my mother from the house and accused her of murder. She begged and pleaded with them, swearing she had nothing to do with Daisy's death, but they weren't inclined to listen. The reverend proclaimed that witches should be burned, so they tied by mother to a stake in the village square and piled firewood and branches all around her. She was still proclaiming her innocence when they set the wood alight at her feet. I couldn't bear to watch, but Daisy's father and Edgar held me fast and forced me to watch, telling me to see for myself what happens to those who practice witchcraft. The last thing I saw before I passed out was my mother calling to me to save myself before she was engulfed in flames."

Rowan was crying openly now, the salty tears running into her mouth as she tried to speak. "When I awoke it was dawn. I was alone in the village square, shivering in the cold, my clothes damp from dew. The pyre had burned out, and the air was filled with the acrid smell of damp ashes and roasted flesh. I dared not look closer for fear of seeing what was left of my mother. I forced myself to get to my feet and trudged back to our house, but it had been burned to the ground, smoke curling from the charred beams. I just sat on the ground and cried until Ellie found me. She leaned over me and whispered into my ear, "You'd better leave before they burn you too, Rowan. You know what they do to witches around here." And then she giggled and smiled at me. "Edgar will marry me now," she said before scampering away.

Rowan angrily wiped the tears from her damp cheeks. There, she'd finally said it out loud. Telling Brendan had been difficult, but at least now, he could help her carry the terrible burden of the past. He wasn't there to help her then, but he was here now, and he would keep her safe from people whose friendship and trust could turn into a murderous rage on the turn of a coin.

Brendan didn't say anything. He just held Rowan and let her cry, years of pent-up agony silently sliding down her face and onto his hand. What could anyone say to minimize the tragedy that befell her? It was shattering enough to lose both parents within the space of a year, but to be forced to watch your mother burn for a crime she didn't commit was more than anyone could bear. The Church preached forgiveness and tolerance, but what they practiced was quite different. The reverend could have saved Rowan's mother, but he slyly brought up burning, an act that would unite the villagers against a common enemy, and bring them closer to the Church in their self-righteous war against Satan and his disciples. How cruel human beings could be, especially the ones who pretended to love us. Brendan hoped Ellie had gotten her just desserts, but he doubted it. Even now, she probably lived happily with her Edgar, rewarded by God for the death of two innocent women.

The Present

Chapter 48

I snuggled closer to Aidan, listening to the rhythmic beating of his heart. Our hands were intertwined as were our legs, and it actually felt as if we were a part of one whole rather than two separate human beings. I'd made no mention of the future for fear that Aidan would think me clingy or pushy, but he spoke as though we were now an established couple, which made me inwardly jump for joy. Several times he'd referred to us as 'we' and I loved the sound of that.

I suppose I was used to American guys who always wanted to keep their options open and play the field for as long as possible, but Aidan showed no fear or reluctance to commit and see where the relationship would take us, which in turn made me curious about what happened with his fiancée. I suppose we were at that part in our blossoming romance when people shared their pasts, but I didn't want to interrogate Aidan. He had to tell me in his own time. He hadn't asked anything about my past relationships, not that there was much to tell. A few short-lived romances that meant the world at the time, but seemed awfully trivial now, in the face of what I was feeling for Aidan.

Aidan seemed to be reading my mind, because he disentangled his hand from mine and rolled onto his side, supporting his head on his elbow, his lips stretching into a slow smile.

"What are you grinning at?" I asked, happy to see him so relaxed.

"I'm just happy," he said simply, as if it was self-evident. "I hadn't realized how long it's been since I felt this way. It's overwhelming."

I realized that was the opening I'd been looking for. He was clearly telling me that he'd been unhappy for a long time, so it wasn't wrong to ask why. Was it?

"Aidan, what happened with your fiancée?" I asked carefully, watching his face for any indication that he was angry at the question, but I saw no resentment, just a sadness that briefly clouded his eyes. "Why were you so unhappy?"

"After Noelle and I split up, I sort of just retreated. At first, I needed time to heal, but then a few months turned into a year, and I realized that I'd been avoiding involvement or making any major decisions. I'd been drifting, waiting for something to shake me out of my complacency, and then this gorgeous American girl showed up and I didn't stand a chance." He was trying to charm me in order to distract me, but I wasn't having it. I wanted to know.

"Dot intimated that you broke it off because you got cold feet," I said, curious as to the real reason Aidan had been so hurt by the breakup.

"It's sort of what I let people believe. You know how gossip travels around here, and I didn't want anyone to know the truth, especially Noelle's parents, since she never told them. I was so numb that I didn't really care what people thought as long as they left me alone to deal with it in my own way. Noelle left shortly after I called off the wedding, so that just fueled speculation."

"Why *did* you call it off?"

"I called it off because I felt betrayed. I loved Noelle and trusted her implicitly, but I discovered that she didn't feel the same about me. Her love was a lot more calculated."

I laid my hand over his wrist, but kept silent, giving him a chance to speak.

"We met in our second year at Uni. She was reading Finance and I was studying Architecture, so our paths crossed in math tutorial. She wasn't particularly interested in me at first, but Scots are known for being pesky buggers, so eventually I got her to go out with me. I'd had a few other girlfriends before, but it was never anything serious. But Noelle was it; she was the one. Being with her made me feel complete, and I knew that I wanted her to be not just my present, but my future. I thought she wanted the same thing."

Aidan took a deep breath, as if bracing himself for the next part of the story. "After graduation, Noelle wanted to come back here to be close to her family, so I came with her and rented a flat while she moved back in with her parents. We saw each other every day anyway at my place. It was our little love nest. She'd gotten a job with an investment firm in Lincoln, and I worked to get my business off the ground. We were busy, but happy. I proposed on her twenty-third birthday and she accepted. I would have been happy to get married in a Registry Office, but Noelle wanted a long engagement and a church wedding, so I agreed. I wanted her to have the wedding of her dreams. We were engaged and planning our life together; another year wouldn't have made that much of a difference."

Aidan grew quiet for a moment, clearly reliving the past. "What happened then?" I asked, feeling an overwhelming need to know.

"I thought that a one-year engagement was long enough, but Noelle wanted to wait. She was working long hours and moving up in her company, so planning a wedding had to take a back seat. Before I knew it, another two years had gone by. I kept pressing her to set a date, and she finally agreed. She was busy at work, so her mother made most of the arrangements. It's almost as if Noelle didn't care; she simply wanted to show up and get it over with. I should have seen the signs, but I was too eager to start our life together. I booked our wedding trip — two weeks in Paris, which Noelle felt was too long to be away from her job, but I held firm. How often do you go on a honeymoon?"

Aidan took a labored breath, but I didn't interrupt him this time. He needed to tell the story at his own pace. I could tell that it was difficult for him since he clearly hadn't spoken to anyone of what happened, possibly not even his own parents. Funny how women needed support, pints of ice cream or endless glasses of wine and dinners with girlfriends to work through a split, but men just go on with it.

"I often brought up starting a family. I wanted to have children while we were still young, not one of those couples who put their lives on hold until they established their careers. I didn't want to have my first child at forty, and I certainly wanted to have more than one. Noelle said that she wanted that too, but it would have to be the right time, since she didn't want to lose everything she'd worked for. She promised that we would have a baby within the first few years of marriage. I would have been happy to get her pregnant on our wedding trip, and she said that it wouldn't be such a bad idea."

Aidan rolled back onto his back and stared at the ceiling as he recounted the rest. "It was the night of Noelle's hen party a week before the wedding. She went to take a bath and asked me to tell her friend Tracy, in case she called, that she'd be ready in an hour. I never bothered to look at the caller ID when her mobile rang. I assumed it was Tracy, but it wasn't. It was a nurse from a clinic in Lincoln, calling to check how Noelle was feeling after the procedure, and confirming that her prescription for birth control pills had been called into the chemist, as requested."

"She had an abortion?" I gasped.

"Yes, she had; just the day before. My first thought was that she'd been unfaithful to me and terminated the baby because it wasn't mine. I confronted her when she came out of the bath, but she denied having an affair. I'm not sure what I expected; remorse or a plea for understanding, but the worst part was that she wasn't even sorry. She said she'd accepted a new job, one with more responsibility and longer hours, and didn't want to waste her youth on changing nappies and cleaning up spit; these weren't the 1950s. She wasn't ready for saggy breasts, stretch marks, and afternoons at the park pushing a swing. She wanted to be successful in her field and make a name for herself among the traders. Having a family wasn't a priority, and might never be."

"So, you broke off your engagement?" I asked, feeling a surge of pity for Aidan. He'd so clearly wanted a family with this woman.

"I did. I'm not even sure why she agreed to marry me, since she clearly didn't want the same things. I suppose she thought I'd come around in the end, or maybe we would start a family when she was good and ready, but in the meantime, she'd take her tablets on the sly and let me believe that we were trying. She lied to me, terminated my baby without even consulting me, and had been interviewing for a new job when all along we'd been talking about her scaling down her hours so that we could start a family."

"Were you ever sorry to have broken if off in the heat of the moment?" I asked, hoping that his feelings weren't still engaged with someone who clearly didn't love him.

"No. Had she discussed it with me and told me her reasons, I might have understood, if not been happy about it, but she made the decision without a thought for how I would feel. That's not a person I want to spend my life with." Aidan sighed and turned to face me. "In my mind, I knew all the reasons why it had to end, but it took my heart a very long time to catch up. I'd truly loved Noelle and felt as if the rug was pulled out from under my feet. Sometimes I still do."

"I'm sorry, Aidan. That must have been very painful."

"Our baby would have been about eight-months-old now. I can't help wondering if it had been a boy or a girl, and who it might have looked like. What particularly struck me as I spoke to Noelle was that the decision had been a foregone conclusion. She never even considered keeping the child. She never felt any remorse or regret. It was just an inconvenience to be gotten rid of."

"I'm sorry," I said, and meant it. I hated that he'd been so hurt.

"Don't be. I believe that everything that happens makes us the people we are meant to be, and when the right thing comes along, we are ready and able to make the most of it." He kissed the tip of my nose and smiled in a way that made me think that he was referring to me when he spoke of the 'right thing', and that made my heart smile.

Chapter 49

I was still grinning from ear to ear as I closed the door behind Aidan on Sunday night. He'd been with me for nearly twenty-four hours and had to go home and feed his cat, Leomhann. When I asked Aidan what the name meant, he informed me that it translated into 'big cat' from Gaelic.

"Very imaginative you are," I said laughing. "So, if you get a dog, will it be called 'big dog'?"

"Neh. Dogs are easier since they show more of their personality. Cats are an enigma, and I wouldn't want to give the wrong name. Leomhann is the perfect name for that self-absorbed, lazy brute. He's probably going to give me the cold shoulder when I get home for not being there last night. He's very territorial and views me as his property."

"Well, you'd better get him something yummy to make up for your desertion. Can't wait to meet him." I actually wasn't a fan of cats, but this one sounded like quite a character.

I was actually in very good spirits as I climbed back up the stairs. The past weekend had been unexpectedly wonderful and I knew I would sleep soundly tonight, knowing that it was only a few more hours until I would see Aidan again. He said that the work would continue as planned, and he might have to hire an additional man to take Colin's place. I didn't want to talk or think about Colin. I'd give my cooperation to the police, but I couldn't care less what happened to the man after that.

I glanced out the window at the gathering clouds. It looked as if it might rain again, so I went around closing the windows to keep the rain from drenching the floor. The air in the rooms was flat and heavy, as if all the oxygen had been sucked out by the coming storm. I supposed it was the calm before the storm that people talked about, when everything was strangely tranquil, as if the world was holding its breath.

I walked into the room where Aidan had spent Friday night. He'd taken his sleeping bag, but the window was still open, the ashtray on the sill. I shut the window and turned to leave when I noticed the box. There was a torn sheet of paper tucked into the flap. It read:

Lexi,

This is the box of albums you'd asked about. I brought it down from the attic while you were sleeping.

Cheers,

Dot

I was grateful to Dot for remembering about my interest, but honestly, I wasn't sure that I wanted to look at the pictures. I realized that subconsciously, I'd been putting it off, afraid of what I might find. I didn't really want to see the faces of the Hughes women, but I needed to put my mind to rest. Were people really seeing something that wasn't there because they wanted to find a connection, or was there really some resemblance between myself and Kelly?

The box was just sitting there in the corner where Dot had left it. There was nothing to sit on, so I sat cross-legged on the floor and pulled it toward me. There were several albums and a few framed photographs that someone had carelessly thrown on top as they packed away the photos. I picked up the uppermost album and turned back the heavy brown cover to find black-and-white snaps dating back to the war. There was a man in uniform, a young woman in a polka dot dress with her hair in a Victory roll so popular during the war, and pictures of an older couple who might have been either of those people's parents. I flipped the pages until the pictures became more current. There were lots of shots of

258

two little girls, who I assumed were Kelly and Myra, and an attractive woman who must have been their mother.

I felt a wave of melancholy as I looked at the old snaps. At one time, these people were happy, blissfully ignorant of the future that was to come. They were laughing and posing playfully, the girls now in their teens, sitting on the couch with their arms around each other. I pulled out the photograph and held it up to the light as a shiver of apprehension raced down my spine. I didn't have to ask which one was Kelly and which one was Myra. Myra was dark-haired and a little chubby, her dark eyes smiling into the camera as she rested her head on her sister's shoulder. Kelly was a redhead, her eyes either blue or green, and a sprinkling of freckles across her pert nose. She had a wide mouth that gave just a hint of a smile as she looked into the lens.

My hair was darker, more auburn than red, and my eyes hazel, but the girl in the picture could have been my sister. It wasn't just her features, but the expression on her face. There was many a picture from my teenage years when I looked just like that, as if I were hiding some great secret and I could barely contain the enigmatic smile that resulted in that playful look. How was it possible for us to look so alike when there was no connection between us whatsoever?

I turned the page and looked at some more photos. Toward the back of the album, there were pictures of Kelly with a man who was probably her husband, her belly round and her face filled out with the glow of pregnancy. The man looked at Kelly with a look of such devotion and love that it was hard to believe what I'd heard only a few days ago. What had gone wrong between these two young people who looked so content?

I got to the end of the album and two loose pieces of paper fell out into my lap. I picked them up and felt a chill that had nothing to do with the summer evening. I was suddenly sick to my stomach, my hand shaking violently. What I was looking at were the drawings of a child. The first one depicted a mom, dad, and a little girl between them with the house in the background. It was almost identical to the picture I had given my dad years ago. The

259

signature at the bottom was written in a childish hand, the N drawn backward, and the letters crooked and slanted. It said, "Sandy," with a little flower drawn underneath.

The second drawing was even more disturbing. It showed the ruin and a man kneeling beneath a tree. He was just a stick figure with long hair, but what it meant was unmistakable. Sandy had seen him, and maybe her mother had as well. Despite my reservations, I pulled out the second album. This one was full of baby pictures, the baby growing older with every page. I kept looking at pictures of a blissful Kelly, her daughter in her arms as Neil looked on contentedly. My eyes slid to the little girl. I hadn't focused on her at first, eager to see Kelly with her husband, but as I looked at the child's face, I felt the hairs stand at the back of my neck, cold fingers of dread closing around my heart. I'd seen that little girl many times before in the pictures all around my parents' house. There was a portrait of her by my mother's bed, only the child was slightly older. I was looking at a picture of myself, my face alight with happiness as I posed with my parents.

I took out the picture and slammed the album shut before carefully placing it back in the box, but the damage had been done. Memories came rushing back like an incoming tide, fragments of the past that I had somehow suppressed all these years. I squeezed my eyes shut and put my hands to my pounding temples, but I couldn't stop the onslaught. The images came in a flood, flashing before my eyes with alarming frequency. They weren't in any chronological order, but rather like colored pieces in a kaleidoscope, shifting and rearranging themselves into something different every few seconds. I had glimpses of being put to bed by my mother — my real mother. My father reading me a bedtime story, and my grandmother handing me a cookie that was still warm from the oven as I gobbled it up and licked my fingers. I was playing in the yard, chasing a ball, then putting my doll to sleep in her dollhouse.

I rested my head on my knees and wrapped my arms around them to keep myself together, but nothing I could do would make any difference now. I was standing in front of the ruin by myself, a doll hanging from my chubby, childish hand as I stared at the man in front of me, his face twisted in anguish and tears running down his lean cheeks. I was crying too, but I wasn't sure why because I wasn't afraid of him. Perhaps I simply felt sorry for him. I wiped my tears with the back of my hand and offered him my dolly, but he didn't seem to notice me; didn't accept my heartfelt offer.

And then the image melted away and was replaced by another. My parents screaming at each other in the front room as I played with my dollhouse in the corner; my mother's voice shrill and taunting as my father's face crumpled and fell, before being replaced with a look of such rage that I hid behind the sofa in terror.

"Are you so blind that you can't even see that she's not yours?!" my mother screamed. And then I heard her cry out and crash to the floor, and all was quiet for a moment as I crept from behind the sofa, thinking the argument was over. My mother was lying on the floor, a pool of blood spreading beneath her head as it trickled from the gash at her temple. I could see my three-year-old self throwing myself at my mother, crying and begging for her to wake up; my beautiful mother who was staring at the ceiling with sightless eyes as my father fell to his knees, his head buried in his hands as he cried like a child.

I could hear the anguished scream of my grandmother as she came running into the room and wrenched me from my mother's body, her own slight frame shaking violently as she carried me up the stairs and locked me in my room to keep me from returning downstairs and seeing what was left of my mom.

The pretty colors of the police lights were now flashing before my eyes, reflecting in the pane of glass as I pressed my nose to its soothing coolness in an effort to understand what was going on. There were people coming and going, and I saw my father being led to a police car, his hands behind his back as a stern man put a hand on his head to prevent him from hitting his head as he got into the back of the car.

Later on, all was quiet, except for my grandmother's weeping as she held me against her and rocked me to sleep, repeating over and over that everything would be all right somehow. And then everything went blank.

I grabbed the photograph and the drawings and ran from the room. I couldn't bear to be in that house any longer. The ghosts were all around me, not outside as I suspected. They were in every room, suddenly clearly visible to me now that the veil had been lifted. I grabbed my purse and ran outside without even locking the door. I had to get away; had to flee to a place of safety where I could come to terms with what I'd just discovered.

I ran down the dark lane, the wind whistling in my ears as the first fat drops began to fall. The sky was overcast, the stars and moon hidden behind a thick cloud cover, and I stumbled and almost fell several times as my foot landed in an unseen hollow. I wouldn't have been able to see them even if it had been light outside. I was blinded by tears; could taste their saltiness as they rolled into my mouth and down my throat. My chest was burning, so I eventually slowed down to catch my breath, but no amount of gulping in air could seem to fill my lungs. I was suddenly an entity unknown to myself. I didn't feel right in my body, and I didn't recognize my mind or my soul. My whole life had been a lie perpetuated by others, and now I had no idea who I was.

October 1650

England

Chapter 50

The dining room of the tavern was unusually quiet for early evening, the fire glowing in the hearth and the serving wench eyeing Sexby with a practiced eye, wondering how much she could take him for if he invited her up to his room. He looked like a man who had money and would pay generously for her services. Sexby gave the girl an appreciative smile and turned back to his mutton and boiled potatoes. The girl would wait; she wasn't going anywhere, and at the moment, neither was he. Will drained his tankard of ale and motioned the girl for a refill as he tucked into his food. Sexby never failed to marvel at how much Will could drink without showing any traces of intoxication. Sexby, himself, preferred to stop after one tankard in order to keep a clear head and quick reflexes. One never knew when either would come in handy.

"I think he's long gone, Edward," Will said through a mouthful of mutton. "We've been asking for days and no one has seen him. Maybe we should return to Scotland."

Sexby speared a piece of meat on his knife and looked at it for a moment before putting it in his mouth. This was the best meal he'd had in weeks, and he meant to enjoy it. "I disagree, Will. The men Carr killed were found almost five miles away from Lakeview, and we know that Carr didn't go back home. He's a fairly good swordsman, but I refuse to believe that he got away from that skirmish unscathed. One against three is not good odds in a fight. He must have been wounded, so he couldn't have gotten very far. According to Jasper Carr, his brother never showed up at

263

the uncle's house, but suppose the uncle was lying? Brendan Carr might have deduced that this wasn't a random robbery. If he thought his brother might be behind the attack, he'd make sure his whereabouts weren't made public, especially to his brother's man. No, Will; I think Brendan Carr is wounded and in the vicinity of Caleb Neville's house. And that's where we go next."

Will smiled, revealing slightly crooked teeth. "Sometimes, I wish I had your brains, Edward," he said without any bitterness. "I see what's in front of me, but you look three steps ahead."

"That's what's kept me alive all these years." Sexby pushed away his plate and rose to his feet, signaling for Will to remain in the dining room and finish his meal. Will grinned in understanding, turning his attention back to the tender meat. Maybe he'd have a turn after Edward was finished. He watched as Sexby whispered something in the girl's ear that made her smile before following her up the stairs. She was a pretty little thing, with big tits and a plump ass. That's just the way Edward liked them. He was surprisingly gentlemanly when it came to women, whether dealing with a lady or a whore. Will finished his ale and shook his head with confusion. Edward was a very complex man, which made him extremely dangerous if you got on the wrong side of him.

Chapter 51

Reverend Pole looked from Brendan to Rowan's glowing face and back again. He really must be getting on in years if he missed a courtship right beneath his nose, or in this case, above. Granted, he hadn't really been upstairs much while the two were together, but he never thought that a chaperone might be warranted for a critically injured man and a mute woman. But, the Lord had always worked in mysterious ways, and he would continue to do so. Reverend Pole had to admit, rather guiltily, that like most people in the village, he didn't pay much mind to Rowan. She was a beautiful young girl, but her lack of speech and desire to always remain on the fringes of village life rendered her a shadow, but clearly not to everyone.

"So, will you, Reverend?" Brendan asked, his patience running out.

"Will I what?"

"Will you marry us?" Reverend Pole could see Rowan getting anxious, her eyes full of worry that he would refuse. He couldn't help noticing the way she moved closer to Brendan, his hand reaching for hers in a gesture of reassurance. He'd better marry them, and soon. Judging by the intimacy of their behavior a child could already be on the way, and it was his moral duty to prevent that child from being born a bastard. Reverend Pole supposed that it was too late to ask Brendan if he'd thought this through, so the only thing he could do was marry the young people and wish them well. They'd be away from here in less than two weeks, so their fate would no longer be his responsibility. He would pray for their safety, however, and hope that Brendan was able to win back his inheritance and prove his innocence in the murder of his attackers.

Normally, the banns would be called a month before the wedding, but in this case, the marriage had to be kept secret, especially from poor Stephen Aldridge, who would be in for a surprise. Reverend Pole had been of a mind that Aldridge only wanted to marry Rowan to provide his children with a mother, but now he had his doubts. Maybe the man truly was in love with her, as Brendan clearly was. Reverend Pole sighed and sat down heavily on the wooden bench by the table. One day, very long ago, he had been in love. He was sixteen then and life was full of promise and possibilities, until he told his father that he wanted to ask Delwyn Jones to be his wife. He thought his father might object to her Welsh background, on account of thinking them backward and wild, but his father barely even registered the name of the girl. It didn't matter who she was, for Hugo Pole was meant for the church, and to the seminary he would go despite his wishes. Reverend Pole momentarily wished that he had been stronger and stood up to his father. How different his life would have been. He might have known happiness, and possibly even joy; instead, all he knew was the cold comfort of a benevolent God who never saw fit to grant a heartbroken boy's dream. And now, Brendan and Rowan were taking matters into their own hands and making their own future, and he would help them. Oh, yes, he would help them.

"I suppose there's no time like the present, is there?" Reverend Pole asked, smiling at the light in Rowan's eyes. "I will perform the ceremony, but I will not enter the marriage in the parish records book until a week after you've gone."

"Yes, that would be best, Reverend. No need to alert anyone to the fact that I was here."

Reverend Pole nodded at the wisdom of this thinking and turned to Rowan. "And what of your aunt and uncle, young lady? What am I to tell them? They've had the care of you these past years; they don't deserve this ingratitude from you. Will you at least let them know you're leaving with Brendan?" Reverend Pole tried to look stern, but he couldn't help grinning at Rowan. She was so clearly anxious to be married; she was bouncing up and down on the balls of her feet, her eyes pleading with him to dispense with the questioning and get on with the wedding. He'd explain the situation to Caleb and Joan if it called for it, but he hoped she would at least say goodbye.

"All right, then. Let's begin."

***

Brendan locked the door behind Reverend Pole and turned to his bride. Rowan just stood in the middle of the room where Reverend Pole married them a few minutes ago, looking as if she was afraid to move or the illusion would shatter. She raised her eyes to Brendan, a slow smile spreading across her face as Brendan walked over to her and took her in his arms. There was so much he wanted to say, but somehow couldn't find the words to express exactly how he felt at that very moment until their eyes met.

After years of silence, nature compensated by making Rowan's face a map of her soul. Brendan could read the myriad emotions shifting in her eyes as clearly as if they were written on a page. Rowan was feeling as he was: shy, expectant, apprehensive, impatient, but most of all happy and amazed that such joy could come from such savagery. Brendan pulled her to him and kissed her, slowly and deeply. They had a few hours till Reverend Pole returned, and he planned to make the most of them. This was the closest to a wedding night they were likely to have, so the old reverend's bed would have to do.

Brendan was no stranger to women, but all his experiences had been a transaction; pleasure given and pleasure received after money changed hands. He'd never made love to a woman he had any feelings for, nor had he ever been with a maid. The women had been coarse and cheap, skilled in the art of love the way he'd become skilled in the art of war. He suddenly felt nervous; an unfamiliar fluttering in his belly making him wish he'd had some mead before consummating the marriage. How he acquitted himself now would have a lifetime effect on Rowan. He'd met many men who, when in their cups, complained that their wives wanted nothing to do with them, and lay there with a pained expression on their faces in the hope that their husbands would finish their business quickly and leave them in peace. They had no objection to their husbands slaking their lust on whores, as long as they didn't saddle them with another child.

Brendan didn't want that type of marriage. He wanted his wife to be his lover, strange as it would seem to some. No matter how much he wanted Rowan right now, this moment was about her, and he would put his needs aside and devote the afternoon to her, initiating her into the art of love with all the gentleness and skill he could muster.

***

Rowan purred like a kitten and snuggled closer to Brendan, her body aquiver with feelings she had no idea she could experience. She'd been a little nervous, but her fears were unfounded. From the moment Brendan kissed her after the wedding, she knew that this would be different. They'd kissed before, and he'd held and caressed her through the fabric of her dress, but this kiss was different. This kiss wasn't just a kiss, a moment unto itself, but a beginning of something wonderful. Brendan's lips weren't soft and tender as before, but firm and demanding, letting her know that she was his at last and he meant to possess her, body and soul, and he meant to give himself to her completely. Rowan melted into his arms, allowing him to take control and show her what it meant to be his wife. She'd expected it to be quick and painful, a deed done, but Brendan had other ideas. She felt as if she were falling, freewheeling through the air with no fear of crashing to the ground as Brendan kissed nearly every inch of her as he marked his territory. By the time he slid his fingers inside her, she was quivering with desire, ready to receive him and satisfy his lust, but he wasn't quite done with her yet. He wanted her to yearn for something she couldn't name, her body aching for fulfillment that could only come from him.

The sharp pain that tore through her womb was short-lived and quickly forgotten as he filled her body and carried her with him to a place she never knew existed. It wasn't at all what she had prepared herself for, and she sighed with pleasure, her full mouth spreading into a smile of joy as her husband buried his face inside her neck, his forehead damp with effort and his heart hammering against her breast. Rowan wrapped her arms around him, wishing that she could hold him forever, and reminded herself that she could. They were now man and wife, and this was just the beginning of their life together. She felt as if she would burst with joy at the thought of the future, traveling away from this place and all the painful memories, and setting on a journey that would carry them to the New World and be the start of a wondrous life. She'd forgotten what it was like to be happy and hopeful, and was overcome with the intensity of her feelings.

Brendan raised himself on one arm and looked into her face, his eyes asking a question that needed no answer. It had been beautiful. Rowan would have said "sacred" if that didn't border on blasphemy. She just smiled into his eyes, and he knew that he'd served her well.

The Present

Chapter 52

Aidan stopped to stretch in front of his house before going inside and stripping the sweat-stained clothes from his morning run. The day was overcast with a light mist falling, but he didn't mind. His run was a part of his morning routine that began after Noelle left. He'd been so consumed with grief and hurt that he needed a physical outlet for his pain. He hadn't meant to start running, but one day he just came outside and took off, his legs pumping and his chest burning with the unfamiliar sensation. He'd run until he couldn't run anymore and then he collapsed on the grass beside the lane and cried like a baby, his heart no longer able to hold on to the pain he was so desperately trying to keep at bay.

Surprisingly, he felt much better once he finally got hold of himself and sheepishly looked around to see if anyone had seen his breakdown, but he was blessedly alone and marginally cleansed. And so he began running every day. There were no more tearful outbursts, but the physical exercise helped purge the ache in his heart, and day by day he began to regain some control over his inner life. It still hurt to think about that time, but the pain was now a dull ache, not the razor-sharp agony of those first few weeks.

He'd lost himself in work and began making plans to return to Skye, but the jobs kept coming, and he kept putting his departure off, until suddenly he wasn't thinking about it anymore. Noelle might be gone, but he had no wish to return home with his tail between his legs. He'd made a life for himself here, and here he would stay until he was ready to start again with someone else, someone who would hopefully value his heart a little more. He smiled as he thought of Lexi. The time with her seemed to heal him more effectively than any amount of boozing, running, working, or avoidance. He couldn't wait to see her in a few hours and reassure her that he meant to stay and hoped she wanted him to.

Aidan came out of the shower, his hair dripping with moisture and a thick towel wrapped around his waist. He always liked this part of the morning, when he dressed for the day and had his breakfast. Every day was a new beginning, and every day was full of promise, especially now.

Aidan was just pouring himself a cup of coffee when his mobile rang, the number of the pub appearing on the screen. Aidan swallowed a gulp of hot coffee and answered the phone. Likely, Abe just needed something mended in a hurry. They were old friends, and Aidan often did minor repairs at *The Queen's Head* in exchange for a pint and a plate of fish and chips.

But the voice on the line wasn't Abe's; it was Lexi's. She sounded strangely flat, as if all emotion had been drained out of her voice as she inquired if this was a bad time.

"No, not at all. Lexi, what's wrong?" he asked, sensing that whatever happened after he'd gone had left Lexi in tatters. "What are you doing at the pub?"

"I got a room here last night," she answered quietly. "Aidan, would you mind coming over? I really need you right now."

"Sure, I'll be there in a few minutes. Are you all right?" The question seemed awfully banal, but he wasn't sure what to say until he knew more of what happened, and rather than spend time on the phone he was better off talking to her in person. Aidan pulled on his trainers, stuffed his mobile into his pocket and raced out the door.

***

Aidan found Lexi sitting at a corner table on the back patio of the pub. The patio was deserted so early in the morning, the

271

benches and tables covered with a slick film of dew that would evaporate as the sun warmed up. Lexi was staring out over the garden, a cup of something in her hands. She turned at the sound of his footsteps and put the cup down before hurling herself into his arms, her heart hammering like a drum. Aidan lowered himself to the bench and pulled Lexi onto his lap, holding her like a child who'd had a fright. She buried her face in his chest as if she were hiding from the world, and he just held her until she was ready to tell him what had happened to upset her so.

Abe appeared in the doorway and offered Aidan a cup of tea, but Aidan waved him away.

"Lexi?" Aidan finally murmured. "What is it, love?"

Lexi reached into her bag and extracted some papers which she passed to him silently. Aidan gazed at the photograph in his hands and the realization of what happened last night began to dawn. The picture was dated and slightly faded, but there was no mistaking who he was looking at, or the resemblance between the woman in the picture and the one sitting across from him. He also looked at the photo of Kelly with her daughter. The little girl was smiling up at the camera, her pigtails tied with pink ribbons and her hazel eyes full of mischief. It wasn't difficult to add twenty years to that girl and see how much she would resemble the woman sitting in his lap, crying silently. Aidan glanced at the drawings and felt his heart turn over. They were so sweet, so innocent, and yet so full of meaning. No wonder Lexi fled the house.

Aidan wasn't sure what to say. He'd been dead wrong on all counts. People in the village weren't just looking for random connections, they actually saw one, and Lexi had been seeing the man in the ruins since she was a child. Aidan had never been one to believe in fate; people chose their own path and paid for their mistakes, but what he was looking at was inexplicable when using that particular bit of logic. Something had lured Lexi back to this place, that house. A force stronger than logic, a pull stronger than mere desire was at play. She'd been brought here for a reason, and that reason was now clear — she was meant to learn about her past.

"My whole life has been a lie, Aidan," she finally whispered, "an elaborate lie. I've seen pictures of my mother when she was pregnant with me. There were baby pictures and even a sonogram. I never questioned why my mother never showed me my birth certificate, even when I applied for a passport as a teenager. She'd come with me and filled out all the paperwork. That story about giving birth to me in England while on a business trip was all a lie. I was probably born in Lincoln as she said, only not to her and my father." Lexi took a shuddering sigh, and her eyes met Aidan's for the first time. "But why did they give me away? I still had a grandmother and an aunt. Why was I sent to a couple in America? Was I too much of a reminder of what happened?"

Lexi angrily wiped a tear from her cheek, her hand steadier than Aidan would have expected. Her eyes were blazing and her body was suddenly tense, her face full of resolve. "I intend to get to the bottom of this. Will you help me?"

"Like you even have to ask? Lexi, I'm honored that you would share this with me, and I will do anything I can to help, but don't you think you should talk to your adoptive mother first? She can probably answer all your questions. There must be an explanation as to why they chose to keep your past a secret."

Aidan felt Lexi shake her head against his shoulder as she pulled away and looked into his eyes. "I no longer trust anything my mother has to say. I am going to do this my own way, and I can begin right now if you're willing to drive me to Lincoln."

"All right. What's in Lincoln?" Aidan had a fairly good idea. Lexi probably wanted to visit the hospitals and locate a record of her birth, but what she replied wasn't at all what he expected.

"Neil Gregson — my biological father."

273

Chapter 53

I couldn't help but smile as we pulled up outside of HM Lincoln Prison. The red-brick building with truncated towers, graceful arched windows, and a massive tower gate that at one time probably came with an equally massive portcullis was like something out of a picture book about knights and princesses, and nothing like I would expect a prison to look. Only in England could a prison look like a castle and not a high-security, cinderblock monstrosity surrounded by chain-link fences crowned with barbed wire and guard towers. The inmates probably had a chef and tennis courts, and practiced gardening as part of their rehabilitation.

"Would you like me to come in with you?" Aidan asked, already opening the driver's door, but I put my hand on his arm and shook my head. I needed to do this alone, and I needed to do it now, before my nerve failed me. It was all well and good to want to confront the man who killed your mother and was biologically your father, but my stomach was doing somersaults and backflips, and the tea that I'd drunk that morning was rising up my esophagus like mercury in a thermometer.

I tried to keep calm as I signed in, went through a mandatory search, just in case I was trying to sneak in weapons, drugs, or a cell phone, and was led to a utilitarian room with a barred window set high in the wall and a scarred plastic table flanked by two chairs. I expected to talk to Neil Gregson through a partition, using a telephone as I had seen people do in movies, but the realization that I would be sitting so close to him nearly drove me to change my mind. I wasn't afraid for my safety, but the partition provided a mental separation as well as a physical one, whereas now we would be sitting here like father and daughter, facing each other across the narrow table for the first time in over two decades.

My legs shook under the table as a guard led my father in. He was wearing a prison jumpsuit and his hands were cuffed, but I still leaned back into my chair as far as I could. I was tempted to look away, but I'd have to face him sooner or later, so I braced myself and looked up. The man in front of me was no longer the lean, young man of the pictures. He was still handsome in his own way, but he'd gained weight, and his hair, which was once worn carelessly long, was buzzed and almost all gray. The dark eyes were round with shock behind rimless glasses that reflected the fluorescent light fixture from the low ceiling.

I wasn't sure what I expected, but it wasn't tears. Neil Gregson slumped heavily into a chair as his shoulders heaved and his face contorted with grief. He raised his cuffed hands to cover his face from me and buried his head in them, blowing his nose loudly when the guard silently offered him a tissue and patted him on the shoulder. It took Neil a few moments to finally compose himself before he could meet my shocked gaze. His eyes were glistening with tears behind his glasses and his skin was ashen, as he absentmindedly tore the tissue to shreds with nervous fingers. I was speechless. I opened my mouth several times to say something, but no sound came out. I seemed to have lost my voice.

"Sandy," he whispered. "Oh, Sandy. I'm so sorry, so very sorry. They never let me see you after what happened, never let me try to explain or even say goodbye. I didn't think I'd ever lay eyes on you again." He wiped the tears from his eyes and the guard, who stepped from foot to foot in obvious embarrassment, handed him another tissue just in case. He wiped his nose and eyes and gave me a watery smile. "You're so like her," he said hoarsely, "so like your mother."

"Why?" I asked. I'd finally found my voice, but that was the only question I could think to ask. "Why did you do it?"

"It was an accident, a terrible accident. I never meant to hurt her. I loved her since I was a boy." His eyes were pleading for understanding, but I couldn't understand; not my mother's death, and not my father's subsequent refusal to fight for his own life. If he'd agreed to legal representation the charge could have been reduced to manslaughter, if it had truly been an accident.

"Why did you refuse an attorney?" I asked, not sure I wanted to hear the answer.

"Because I'd killed the love of my life; I'd robbed you of a mother, and I'd taken a daughter from a woman who treated me like a son. I didn't care how long I got. I could never lead a normal life again. It just didn't seem to matter at the time."

"Why did you hit her?" I whispered.

Neil shook his head as if trying to ward off the memories. It took him a long time to answer, but I waited patiently, needing to know what led to the moment that left me motherless. "We had a terrible row that night. We'd been fighting more and more, and I had no idea how to get through to Kelly. It just seemed as if she couldn't find peace; something was gnawing at her. She was like a caged tiger, pacing back and forth, growling, clawing at the bars, but unable to escape. I'd brought up the notion of having another child, thinking it might make her happy.

She'd been serene when she was pregnant with you and for a time after you were born, but the idea seemed to infuriate her. I couldn't understand why she was so angry. She loved being your mum, so her fury took me completely by surprise. It's as if something came unhinged at the thought, and she turned on me, furious. That's when she finally told me that you weren't mine. She said she'd never known what love was until she met your father, and that I was just a stand-in for the man she loved. I was second best." He sighed and looked away. "I never meant to hit her. It was just a knee-jerk reaction of someone who was coming undone. She broke my heart that night."

I just stared at him. I was reeling. I thought that what I'd remembered last night was just a child's interpretation of the quarrel, but it seemed that I had it right. According to Kelly, he wasn't my father. But maybe she'd just said that in anger. Maybe she'd been taunting him because she wanted to hurt him.

"Are you certain you're not my father?" I asked, not sure anymore what I wanted to hear.

Neil nodded miserably, his eyes on his folded hands. "I requested a paternity test after I was arrested. I had to know. Had you been my daughter, I would have fought for my life, would have fought for you, but the test came back negative. You were never mine."

"I'm sorry; I really am," I said and meant it. This man was so broken that no prison sentence could come close to the suffering he was inflicting on himself. I just wanted to flee from that room, but there was one more thing I needed to know.

"Mr. Gregson, why did they give me away? Why didn't my grandmother and Myra raise me?"

Neil Gregson looked up at me, his eyes clouded with the recollections of the past. He shrugged, as if everything that happened had been completely out of his hands, which I suppose it had. "Myra was living in New York when it happened, and your grandmother suffered a breakdown after Kelly's death. She didn't object when Myra took you away. I'd assumed she was going to raise you, but it seems she decided to put you up for adoption. Myra never really cared for children; she wanted a career."

"Thank you, and I wish you well. I doubt we'll meet again," I said as I rose to leave.

"I loved you, Sandy, and I still do. It doesn't matter if you were mine or not, I would have loved you till the day I died," he said to my back. His words choked me up and I wanted to say something comforting to him, but nothing came to mind. Intentionally or not, this man was responsible for everything that happened to me, and although I wanted to pity him, I couldn't ignore the resentment that was blooming in my belly — so I just left.

Chapter 54

The rain pelted the countryside, rivulets of water coursing down the windshield as I sat in the passenger seat and stared at the road ahead. The sky appeared low and menacing, the gray clouds pressing down on the hills like shreds of a dirty blanket with its stuffing hanging out. The landscape was deserted except for several fluffy balls that on closer inspection appeared to be sheep. They bleated miserably, drops of rainwater sliding down their noses as they shook their heads in an effort to get the rain out of their eyes.

I could barely make out the road, so I leaned back against the seat and closed my eyes. It took me a moment to realize I was crying, the tears silently sliding down my face and into my mouth: hot, salty, and bitter. So many things now made sense, and I felt a bubbling rage at the people who'd let me down, not the least of them my adoptive parents.

As a child, I suffered terribly from separation anxiety, screaming in terror if my mother so much as walked out of the room. My eyes were always following her, terrified of being left behind and forgotten. She told me I was a silly girl as she gave me a hug and a kiss and promised that she would never leave, but the fear never left. As I got older, I had difficulty forming lasting friendships, my fear of abandonment turning me into either a clingy mess or later, an emotionally distant, guarded woman. Several men had given up on me, tired of trying to break through the wall of self-doubt and mistrust that I had built around myself to protect my fragile heart.

Now it all made sense. I'd watched my mother die before my eyes, and in the space of a few weeks lost the man I believed to be my father, my loving grandmother, and then my aunt. I was torn away from the only home I'd ever known, given to strangers who did little to help me overcome the emotional trauma I'd suffered as a child. And now I was back where it all began, led here by some unseen force of destiny, my psyche subconsciously begging for some resolution and peace of mind. What was I to do? My adoptive father was gone, but my mother was still very much alive. Was I to hold her accountable for her mistakes? Had she even known what happened to me, or was she simply handed a three-year-old girl with no notion of her past? Could I blame her for failing to help me or was I just looking for someone to vent my anger on, someone to blame?

They'd known I came from England. Their reaction to my drawings and dreams showed by the pained looks on their faces, the pursing of the lips and the desperate attempts to change the subject. How much had they known when they took me on? How much had they cared? They'd even changed my name, taking away the only thing left to me by my mother. I went from being Sandy, short for Alexandra, to Lexi, still short for Alexandra, but completely different — a different name for a different girl.

And my mother... It hurt to think of her, especially after my conversation with Neil Gregson. He hadn't painted her in a very favorable light, despite his love for her. Had she been selfish and manipulative, or simply a frightened girl of nineteen who got in over her head and had no idea what to do? Maybe she truly believed that I had been Neil's until she saw something of my real father in me, something that gave her pause. Had she loved me, or was I just a mistake she should have taken care of when she'd had the chance? And who was my real father? Did he even know of my existence? Had he known I was given up for adoption or had he gone on with his life, completely unaware that somewhere out there a little girl's life had been torn apart by one act of violence?

I was sobbing hard now, the sound of my anguish lost in the howling wind and rumble of thunder that now echoed over the distant hills. And I'd have felt completely alone in the world had Aidan not pulled over and held me in his arms, whispering softly in my ear that everything would be all right somehow, just as my grandmother did the night my life fell apart.

Chapter 55

The rain finally let up, and Aidan pulled away from the shoulder, his anxious eyes seeking reassurance that I was all right. He never asked where to take me, but drove straight to his house in Upper Whitford, and I didn't object. I barely noticed the tidy kitchen or the living room that was so masculine in its lack of ornament and frills. I just needed to lie down. My head was pounding, and my eyes were closing of their own accord, my mind desperate to find oblivion after the events of the past twenty-four hours.

I barely noticed as Aidan drew a blanket over my shoulders and closed the blinds to keep the dreary afternoon light at bay so that I could sleep. I fell asleep before my head hit the pillow, dreaming of things that had nothing to do with the events that were crowding my mind. I suppose the mind has a way of protecting itself and distancing itself from things that are too much to bear, so I was able to sleep peacefully and find some solace in my dreams.

By the time I woke up it was fully dark, and I could smell the appetizing aroma of roasting chicken and potatoes wafting from the kitchen. I smiled at Aidan as he came into the room and gathered me into his arms. "Are you feeling any better?" he asked, his voice full of concern. I did, and I lifted my face to his, my mouth finding his lips as I ran my tongue over them in invitation. My hands went to the buttons of his shirt, opening them one by one as the kiss deepened, and I felt a jolt of desire coursing through my body. At this moment, Aidan was the only person who could make me feel better and take me away from my turbulent thoughts, if only for a little while, because tomorrow I would have to re-evaluate the facts and proceed to step two.

Chapter 56

Aidan was surprised when I asked him to drive me home after dinner, but I needed time to think, time to process everything that had occurred in the past twenty-four hours. My life had imploded, but I still didn't have all the answers, and the only person at this point who could answer my questions was the woman who'd taken me to New York and given me away all those years ago.

Deep in my gut I felt a burning resentment toward Myra, but it wasn't fair to judge her without hearing her side of the story. She was only a few years older than Kelly, so maybe she simply couldn't take me on, especially since she didn't have a family of her own, and would have had to completely change her lifestyle to accommodate a three-year-old.

I needed to speak to Myra, but I had no idea how she would react to hearing from me after all these years. I suppose I could have found her phone number, but what I wanted to do was ambush her and talk to her face to face. It's too easy to fob someone off over the phone, but it's considerably harder to maintain an emotional distance when looking into someone's eyes. I could think of one person who probably knew where to find Myra, but I would have to approach her in such a way that she didn't suspect anything, or she just might withhold the information and blame it on some confidentiality clause.

I walked over to the window and gazed over the dark stretch of lawn, the creek invisible, but the rushing of the water still audible over the sound of the falling rain. I watched the pinprick of light that was my ghost's candle as he read, resting his back against the wall, his legs pulled up on the narrow cot. Tonight I knew just how he felt, for tonight I was a ghost myself, a person whose life had been turned upside down and whose soul couldn't find peace until some kind of resolution presented itself.

***

Last night's rain had tapered off by morning, leaving a thin fog in its wake that swirled above the ground and softened all the edges until the trees and houses seemed to float directly out of the mist. It was cool for July so I pulled my denim jacket closer around me as I walked up the nearly deserted street. It was just before 10 a.m. and most places of business were still closed, their windows looking forlorn and slick with moisture as they floated out of the fog to meet me.

I slowed my gait in the hope that Paula would be in the office by the time I got there. Thankfully, the light was already on in the estate office, Paula's face clearly visible through the window as she typed something, her fingers flying over her computer keyboard. I took a deep breath and entered, hoping that this would be easy rather than hard. At the moment, Paula was about the last person I really wanted to see.

Despite her smile of welcome, there was a noticeable frostiness to Paula's demeanor as she offered me a seat. Neither one of us made any allusion to Colin, who was awaiting a hearing, but what happened between us was like a two-thousand pound elephant in the room, ready to charge us at the slightest provocation. I could see wariness in Paula's eyes as she waited for me to state my business. I was proving to be a nuisance, her gaze said, but she was a consummate businesswoman and would kill me with courtesy and kindness. I could see that Paula's façade of civility was fragile at best, so I plunged in.

"Paula, I wonder if you might help me out," I began.

"Is this about the ruin again?" she asked with a false smile as she took a sip of her coffee. "I swear to you, I don't know any more than I did a few days ago."

"No, it's not. Actually, I came for a completely different reason. You see, I've cleared out the house, but there are some family pictures and personal papers that I just don't feel comfortable throwing away. I'd like to mail them to Myra Hughes

282

and let her decide what she wants to do with them. Would you happen to know of a way I can get her address?" I asked innocently. Technically, the house had been sold by Roger Hughes, but it wasn't him I was interested in. However, if that's all I could get, I might approach him next.

Paula was about to refuse, but seemed to waver for a moment, fully conscious of the harm her brother had tried to inflict on me. It wasn't her fault, but I could see guilt lurking in her nervous gaze as she made up her mind to give me this little bit of assistance to appease her conscience. "I think I have it in the file somewhere. Myra lives in London now. I shouldn't be giving it to you," she said as she handed me the address written on a post-it, "but I would hate for someone to throw away a part of my history. She probably thought that Roger cleared out the house, but Roger is not one for sentimental clap-trap, never has been."

"Thank you. I'm sure she'll be happy to have the albums returned to her." I rose to leave, but Paula called out to me.

"Have you given up on your ghost then?" she quipped as I turned around to face her, just in time to see the color drain from her face in alarm. I'd never said anything about a ghost; that I was sure of.

"You do know something, don't you?" I said, staring Paula down over the top of her computer monitor and nailing her with my relentless gaze. A telltale flush spread across Paula's cheeks as she quickly averted her eyes and began to scan the contents of the file in front of her.

"I've heard it said that old Mrs. Hughes was always ranting and raving about the man in the ruins, especially after Kelly died, but she'd had a breakdown. Dot Martin is not one for being discreet, so word got around that Mrs. Hughes was mad as a hatter. Personally, I thought she'd lost the plot long before that, but it's not nice to speak ill of the dead." Paula finally looked up, her cheeks flushed with shame.

"No, it isn't," I replied and walked out of the office. It was encouraging to know that I hadn't been the only one to see the ghost. Mad or not, my grandmother had seen him too, and it was quite possible that so had Myra.

October 1650

England

Chapter 57

Stephen Aldrich took off his hat and gazed up at the sun. It was wonderfully mild for late October, the sun riding high and the wispy clouds floating lazily across the startlingly blue sky. Ordinarily, he would be content and happy to be alive on a day such as this, but he'd felt unsettled since the night before, his sleep interrupted by disturbing dreams and frightening images of crows and dark forests. He was tired and in a foul mood, but there was work to be done, and in his opinion, that was usually the best remedy for whatever ailed a man.

Stephen waved to Lizzie as she carefully walked across the field, bringing his midday meal. At ten, she was so like her mother in looks, but more like Stephen in temperament. Stephen loved watching her with Rowan as they sat side by side, Rowan showing Lizzie how to make the even, neat stitches in her sewing. Rowan was wonderful with five-year-old Tim, too. She managed to win over his children without saying a word, making them feel at ease and cared for in her presence. He was sure she'd make a wonderful mother to them, but something had shifted, and he couldn't make out what.

Rowan had been in church on Sunday as usual, but as soon as the service was over, she hurried home, and Caleb apologetically informed Stephen that Rowan seemed unwell and wouldn't walk out with him after dinner. Stephen decided to use the opportunity to go visit his brother. Eugene Aldrich was a few years younger, but they'd always been close, especially since Stephen's wife died. Eugene's wife Amy had helped with the children whenever she could and Lizzie and Tim loved spending time with their cousins, playing in the yard while the grown-ups sat over their meal and enjoyed a second mug of ale as they discussed the political situation in the country and the happenings in their own village. Stephen had always firmly remained on the side of the monarchy, but Eugene loved to play Devil's Advocate, bringing up various opposing points just to get Stephen going. Eventually, Eugene would concede that Stephen had the right of it, and pour them both more ale as he winked at his wife. Secretly, Eugene sided with the politics of Cromwell, but he never told Stephen outright, for that would be the end of their relationship. Stephen could accept many things, but he was a man who believed in God, King, and country, in that order, and would entertain no other notion of government. Things were the way they were for a reason, and so they should remain, in Stephen's opinion. He firmly believed that a monarch would be restored to the throne in due time, and all they had to do as Englishmen was do their duty and wait patiently until such a time came.

Stephen missed the wink, but he saw the smile on Amy's face as she gazed at her husband and put her arms around him, resting her chin on top of his curly head. Stephen jokingly said that he envied Eugene his marriage, since he'd never had the kind of bond with his wife that Amy and Eugene seemed to share. Their affection was obvious to anyone who cared to look, and there was a comforting sense of peace in their home that came from two people who were always working toward the same goal and were eager to be kind and helpful to each other. Stephen had never had that with Betty, but he'd hoped to have that kind of union with Rowan. He was beginning to have his doubts though, more so after the visit to his brother. Rowan seemed to be pulling away from him over the past few weeks, her attention clearly occupied by something or someone else. She seemed eager to part company, running off as if she had a pressing engagement somewhere else. What would a girl like her have to rush to?

Stephen cast his mind over the young men of their village. There were a few eligible bachelors, but as far as he knew, none of them had ever shown the slightest interest in Rowan. She was truly beautiful, but the men were put off by her silence. Life was hard enough without having a wife you couldn't talk to, one who couldn't comfort you in your hour of need, or nurture and discipline the children. Stephen had never felt that he had to compete for Rowan's affections, but then again, maybe she never felt any affection for him at all. Had she agreed to marry him for lack of a better prospect? He'd hate to think so since he genuinely believed that Rowan cared for him, but now all these doubts were gnawing at his insides, making him question everything he knew to be true.

***

Stephen gratefully accepted the still-warm pot from Lizzie and sat down in a shady spot to enjoy his meal. Lizzie sat down next to him, her golden head on his shoulder, her eyes fixed on the clouds floating overhead. She was a dreamer, his Lizzie, and he didn't like to discourage that in her. Life would take care of that soon enough, but for now, he just wanted her to be happy.

"That one looks like a pony. Don't you think so, Da?" she asked as she shielded her eyes from the sun to get a better look at the strangely-shaped cloud floating by.

"Hmm, I'd have to say it looks more like a turnip, but maybe that's because I'm hungry," Stephen replied, smiling at his daughter. Whatever his inner feelings, he was happy to spend a few moments in her company. Her feelings and emotions were so pure that he often felt guilty for having uncharitable thoughts, especially about someone as guileless as Rowan.

"Da! It doesn't look like a turnip," she squealed, enjoying the game. They played it often, her finding lovely images in the sky and Stephen comparing them to household items to make her laugh. Everything was either a pot, a broom, or a vegetable in his eyes, but to Lizzie it was all fancy carriages, candied apples, and castles. How wonderful it was to be young and full of confidence that life held nothing but beauty. Even her mother's death did nothing to quell her spirit.

"Da, will we see Rowan on Sunday?" Lizzie asked as she finally scrambled to her feet, ready to return to her chores and her little brother. She'd left him sleeping in his cot, but he'd be up soon, hungry and eager for Lizzie to play with him before she started on supper.

"Yes, I'm sure we will. Why don't you go over before supper and see if she's feeling better? I wager she'll be happy to see you," Stephen suggested. Rowan always lit up at the sight of Lizzie, and having Lizzie check up on Rowan for him wouldn't hurt.

"I've already been," Lizzie said matter-of-factly as she took the empty pot and spoon from her father. "Mistress Joan said that Rowan went off to Reverend Pole's cottage. She must be feeling much improved." Lizzie gave her father a brilliant smile as she set off for home. "See you later, Da," she called over her shoulder, but Stephen barely heard her.

Rowan seemed to be spending an awful lot of time at Reverend Pole's lately. Stephen suddenly had a strange thought. What if Rowan had become interested in religious life? There were no monasteries left in England since the dissolution initiated by Henry VIII, but there were Anglican religious communities, where men and women took vows of chastity, poverty, and obedience, and dedicated their lives to prayer and hard work. Stephen had to concede that that kind of life would probably suit Rowan very well, but he'd be damned if he allowed her to just leave him for God. Stephen cast his eyes at the sky for a moment, a guilty smile passing over his face. So, he was in competition with the good Lord now, was he? Suddenly, he wished it was another man. At least he'd know how to wage that battle.

Stephen picked up his tools and headed back to the fence he'd been mending, but stopped dead in his tracks after a few steps. He'd never be able to rest until he found out what was really going on with Rowan, and there was no time like the present. Stephen carefully gathered up his tools and slung the leather satchel over his shoulder. It was a long walk to Reverend Pole's house, but he didn't mind. His decision made him feel better, and he felt renewed optimism that he was simply imagining things and was about to be disabused of his notion that Rowan was anything but a little under the weather. Stephen began to whistle a merry tune as he walked briskly toward the reverend's cottage.

As Stephen approached the cottage, he suddenly felt foolish. What would he say to Rowan once he got there? That he didn't believe her, didn't trust her? That he suddenly had an urgent desire to see her and assure himself that she was well? He stopped for a moment and looked around. Once he stepped from behind the cover of the trees, he'd be out in the open and Rowan might see him from the window of the cottage. She might be frightened, or worse, angry with him for spying on her. If she were doing household work, as Caleb intimated, then she'd have to come out sooner or later, and he might watch her unobserved from his vantage point. Stephen set down his bag of tools and crouched beneath a tree, his eyes glued to the cottage. Smoke curled from the chimney and immediately dispersed among the clouds, but that was the only sign of any life in the house. Reverend Pole preferred to spend his time at the church where he was closer to his parishioners, so Rowan would be alone, going about her chores with no inkling that she was being stalked. Stephen felt ashamed of even allowing stalking to come to mind. He wasn't hunting her, just putting his mind at rest that all was well and he was imagining things that weren't there.

The sun began its descent toward the horizon, lengthening shadows casting the scrim of trees into near darkness and hiding Stephen from sight. He leaned against the trunk of a tree, his eyes never leaving the cottage. What was she doing in there? He was tired of sitting there, and soon he'd have to return home. Lizzie would be worried if he didn't come home in time for supper, and he had no desire to alarm the children. He was just being a silly fool, he admonished himself — an old fool in love.

Stephen nearly jumped out of his skin as the door of the cottage finally opened and Rowan stepped over the threshold. The glowing rays of the setting sun illuminated her face, and Stephen's breath caught in his throat as he saw the blissful expression that stole over her features. He couldn't see the man clearly until he stepped into the doorway, but then the fading sunlight painted him in stark relief. He was tall, lean, and dark-haired; his linen shirt untucked, and his feet bare as he leaned in for a final kiss before Rowan spun around and raced for home. Stephen felt the sting of tears in his eyes as he angrily wiped them away. He hadn't been a fool after all, and Rowan was secretly meeting her lover at the reverend's cottage. Did Reverend Pole know and sanction this scandalous behavior? Stephen grabbed his satchel off the ground and made for home, making sure to give Rowan a healthy lead. He didn't want her to see him, partly because he felt foolish and betrayed, and partly because he couldn't be responsible for his actions. He'd never felt such thirst for vengeance as he did at this moment, against both Rowan and her lover.

Chapter 58

Meg continued to sit by her mother's bedside long after she closed her mother's eyes for the last time. Strange that she should finally give up the fight against her illness on the day of Jasper's wedding. It's as if she couldn't bear the thought of Mary coming to live in the house and treating Meg as her unpaid servant. Meg thought she'd be heartbroken when her mother finally breathed her last, but she felt strangely calm, grateful to the good Lord for finally releasing her mother from her pain. But he'd also released Meg in a way. Her mother was the last tether to the family they once had, the family that was like a steady ship surrounded by the roiling waters of turmoil that swept England years ago. Meg thought then that nothing would change, that they would weather the storm and come out stronger, but she couldn't have been more wrong. Her parents were dead, as was her husband. And Brendan was in mortal danger, not from fighting on a battlefield, but from his own brother, who wanted him dead and gone.

Meg finally rose to her feet and made her way downstairs, wary of the silent house around her. Everyone was at church for the ceremony, but she stayed back, knowing that her mother had hours left to live. The wedding feast would take place at Mary's parents' house, which was just as well, since this was no time for celebration. Meg wanted to prepare her mother for her final journey herself. There were women in the village who normally did that, but she wanted to do it, to feel that last connection to the woman who'd loved her so. Meg filled a basin with water and took a clean towel and a hair brush before treading back upstairs. She set the basin on a low stool, but couldn't bring herself to begin just yet.

Meg gingerly opened the heavy trunk at the foot of the bed and reached for the folded length of fabric carefully placed at the very top. It was her mother's shroud. As a girl, Meg always fled the room when her mother worked on the garment, but her mother simply smiled and told Meg not to be frightened. Death was a part of life, and she wanted to go to her Maker wrapped in a fine shroud, one she spent hours making and embroidering with flowers and vines. It was a fine garment for her final journey, and she intended to put love and care into the sewing of it. Now that Meg held the fabric in her hands, she was glad her mother had taken the time to make it beautiful. She deserved to be wrapped in something fine and precious, something made with love. Meg sighed as she laid it aside to be used after her mother had been washed, groomed, and ready to be laid in her coffin. The day after the funeral she would begin working on her own shroud. It was time.

Meg was startled by the banging of the door and Jasper's voice booming through the house. "Meg, come congratulate me. I'm a married man." He looked well pleased with himself, his face ruddy with the cool wind of an October morning and his hair escaping the leather thong holding it together.

"What are you doing here?" Meg asked, her voice flat.

"I got a little present for Mary, but forgot to take it to the church. I'll be on my way now," he said as he slid something into his pocket. Meg strongly suspected that by "got" he meant took from his mother's box of valuables. She had very few, but they were all from their father, given with love and gratitude. That made Meg angry.

"Mother has passed," she said, pleased to see Jasper's look of shock. "Not a good omen for a wedding day, is it?" Meg felt momentary shame for being spiteful, but she couldn't help herself. Jasper had treated their mother shabbily in the past year, and he deserved to be reminded of it, even if it was his wedding day.

Jasper just shook his head and sank into a chair. He'd been their mother's favorite; her darling, born after several miscarriages and stillborn babes. She adored him, and expected the rest of the family to do the same, which they had. And now this "baby" couldn't even be bothered to shed a tear for the woman who loved him, as he jumped to his feet and turned to Meg before leaving the house. "Why don't you come along, Meg? There's nothing left to keep you here. Your boys are there already, and you could use a bit of gaiety."

Had Meg been a man, she'd have decked Jasper in the face and watched him go down like a tree, but she was a woman, and her only weapon was her tongue.

"No, Jasper. I think I'll stay here and keep watch over our mother. May you and Mary have much joy of each other, and may she love you at least half as much as she loved Brendan." Meg nearly laughed out loud at the expression on Jasper's face. She'd hit him where it hurt, and she felt strangely gratified. Jasper was always insecure where his older brother was concerned, and if he felt he was competing with Brendan in his marriage bed, then so much the better. Meg smiled and cocked her head as she looked at Jasper. "Well, why are you still here? Your bride is waiting."

"You'll pay for that," Jasper hissed before he flung the door open and disappeared into the misty morning. Meg was sure she would, or perhaps she was paying for it already.

Chapter 59

The house was cold as a tomb, the silence loud with reproach and judgment as Jasper sat staring into the cold hearth. The acrid smell of ashes filled his nostrils and the frosty air nipped at his bare feet, but he didn't care. He couldn't go up to seek the warmth and comfort of his own bed. The ironic thing was that he was really happy that morning, happier than he'd been in years. Everything he'd planned for was finally coming together and falling into place. His father was rotting in his grave, Brendan was out of the way, soon to be permanently, and Mary was his wife at last. He'd meant every word when he made his vows in church that morning, but Meg had found his Achilles' heel, and used it to disquiet his mind. He might not have gotten so angry with Mary had Meg not planted the seed that morning, forcing him to question Mary's love for him.

Jasper barely made it through the wedding celebration, so eager was he to take Mary home and consummate their union. She looked so fetching in her indigo gown, which so exactly matched the shade of her eyes and made her auburn hair seem even brighter. She was flushed with happiness, dancing with any man who'd asked and not even bothering to stop for food or drink. Jasper wanted to claim every dance, but the men wanted to drink with him and wish him well, knowing that they'd better stay on the good side of the new master. Jasper had eaten his fill and drunk twice as much, but he was clearheaded when he came to bed, his blood singing with lust at the sight of his darling.

Mary was already in bed, her beautiful hair tumbling around her shoulders and over the white linen of her high-necked nightdress. She looked so demure and virginal that Jasper nearly unmanned himself right there and then, but this was their wedding night, and he would make sure it was memorable for them both. The quick tumbles to satisfy his lust would come later, once Mary was used to him and as aroused as he was. Jasper recited psalms in his head to keep his desire at bay and devoted himself to pleasuring Mary. He didn't notice at first that she seemed strangely unsurprised by the things he did, just gave herself up to him in a submissive way that he found most pleasing. Submission in bed was a wonderful quality in a wife, he'd thought.

It was only when he finally penetrated her that he realized that his cock slid in without any resistance or obstacle. It was a smooth ride, not something one would expect of a maiden. And that's when it hit him. Mary wasn't a maid; she'd lain with other men, most likely Brendan, and then the rage took over, painting everything in front of Jasper in blood-red hues, his fist striking Mary before he even knew what he was doing. He didn't hit her again, but her pitiful whimpering kept echoing in his ears as he stumbled from the room and ran downstairs to hide in the darkness with only the corpse of his mother to keep him company as she rested on the kitchen table with a candle at her head and feet.

Jasper suddenly wanted to cry and ask for her advice, but it was too late. His mother, his staunchest supporter, was gone. Brendan, who'd loved him and guided him was most likely already dead, betrayed by the brother he trusted. And his sister lay alone in her widow's bed, cursing Jasper to a life of misery, which in truth, he deserved. Jasper slid out of the chair and onto his knees, ignoring the cold, hard floor as he clasped his hands in front of his chest and bent his head in supplication. "Dear Lord, forgive me my trespasses and grant me absolution for my sins, which are many. Amen." Jasper remained on his knees, waiting for some kind of sign from God that his contrition was to be rewarded, but all he heard in the silence was the muffled sound of his wife's weeping.

The Present

Chapter 60

I walked down the street slowly, peering at the house numbers and somehow hoping that number ninety-seven wouldn't be there and I could just go home, having told myself that I tried, but there it was. The house was just like all the others, white and two-storied, with a black door and a wrought-iron gate that led to the short path. I could have sworn I saw a curtain flutter as I unlatched the gate and trudged up the path, my heart pounding in my chest. I was nervous to see this woman who was my aunt, and who had made the choice to give me away and tear me apart from everything I had ever known.

I rang the bell and waited. The door opened and a small, dark-haired woman appeared on the top step, wiping her hands on her flowery apron as she glanced up to see who was calling. She tried to smile, but faltered, her face crumpling as she saw the resemblance to her sister and the realization of who I was hit her like a freight train. *At least I still had the power to make people cry*, I thought vengefully as I watched Myra's futile attempt at composure.

"Myra Hughes?" I asked, more for the need to say something rather than to confirm that it was really her. I'd seen her in pictures with my mother and grandmother. She was no longer the smiling young woman of the photos, but other than some gentle aging, she hadn't changed all that much. She would be a few years younger than my adoptive mom, but the gray, if she had any, was skillfully covered with hair color, and the few wrinkles actually gave her face character rather than making it look old. Myra's make-up was artfully applied, bringing out her large dark eyes and arched brows and downplaying her full lips with earth-tone lipstick. A colorful scarf was wrapped around her neck, picking up the blue-gray of her sweater set. She looked elegant and well-groomed, no longer the girl in bell-bottom jeans and tie-dye shirt.

"Yes," she choked out, holding the door open wide for me. "Please come in."

I followed her into the sunlit front room. Myra stood in the middle of the room, her face a mask of confusion as she tried to figure out how to begin this conversation. Finally, she seemed to come out of her trance and offered me a seat on the tan leather sofa. Her house was much like the woman herself: elegant, uncluttered, and full of light.

"I'll just make some tea, shall I?" I didn't really want tea, but I realized that although I'd been somewhat prepared for this meeting, I had taken her completely by surprise, and she needed a few minutes alone to compose herself. I owed her that much, so I set down my bag and took a seat.

"That would be great," I said, granting her the time she needed. I could use a few minutes to calm my thundering heart as well. The idea that I might be on the threshold of learning the truth left my mouth dry and my hands shaking. Aidan had offered to come with me, but this was something I needed to do on my own, and he respected my wishes, extracting a promise that I would call him as soon as I was finished with Myra.

My aunt finally returned to the room with a tea tray laden with a pot, cups, and a plate of carefully arranged cookies. The china rattled softly as Myra tried to steady her shaking hands. She poured a cup for me and then one for herself before setting the pretty teapot down and turning her gaze on me.

"What must you think of me?" she asked, probably hoping that I wouldn't answer. "Not a day has gone by that I haven't thought of you, Sandy, or of Kelly. It's as if someone made a hole in my heart the day she died and no matter how I've tried to fill it, I haven't been able to. We'd been so close and then she was just…

gone." I'd never had a sister, but I could imagine what it would feel like to suddenly lose someone, someone who'd been like your other half. But she still had me. She could have done the right thing by her sister and taken care of her daughter.

"Why?" I asked, cutting straight to the chase. "Why, Myra?"

"I had no choice." She set down her cup and looked at me, her eyes searching my face. "He never told you, did he?"

"Who should have told me what?" I didn't really like the sound of that, but it was too late to back out now. I'd come to find out the truth, and the truth would set me free — or so I hoped.

"I worked for your father, Jack Maxwell. That's how Kelly met him. She came by the office to pick me up after work one day. She'd come to visit me in New York, you see," Myra said wistfully. "I'd never seen him like that. Mr. Maxwell was usually cool and businesslike, but he was all smiles, asking Kelly about England and flirting with her as if she were a grown woman and not a teenage girl. He suddenly offered to take us out to dinner. I felt awkward; he was my boss, but Kelly was eighteen, and she just wanted to eat out at a nice restaurant in New York. This was the type of place we could never have afforded. I tried to show Kelly the city, but I was a secretary living on a tight budget. Five-star restaurants were quite out of my league."

I set my cup on the table with a clatter, my stomach twisting and churning as I saw where this was going. Myra gave me a look of pity as she stopped, giving me a moment to compose myself.

"Was he…?" I whispered.

"Yes, Jack was your father. Kelly was supposed to leave after a few weeks, but she stayed on, hoping that Jack would offer her a future. She'd fallen in love for the first time, you see, and she wouldn't listen to reason. He talked of leaving his wife, but of course he never did. She finally went back home — heartbroken and pregnant. She married Neil within a month. She liked him and might have been happy with him had she never met Jack, but now she'd known real love, and nothing less would do for her. She only married Neil for your sake. She didn't want you to be branded a bastard. I know that sounds old-fashioned, but in some places such stigma can still carry a lot of weight."

"Did my father know?" I asked, desperately hoping that he hadn't.

"Oh, yes. She telephoned him when she found out. He and his wife had been trying to adopt for years, so Kelly thought that a baby of his own might tip the scale in her favor, but he just wished her luck and sent her some money. That was their last contact."

Myra silently handed me a tissue, her hand brushing mine in a gesture of comfort. "I'm sorry, Sandy. I'm sure you didn't expect to hear this about your father, but it's the truth, and that's what you came here for, isn't it?" I just nodded, my mouth dry and sour, my vision blurred by tears.

"What happened when she died?"

"I couldn't keep it from him, and he demanded that I bring you back to New York after the funeral. He was the natural father, as a DNA test would prove, so I didn't have a legal leg to stand on. My mother was inconsolable over Kelly's death, and having you ripped from her just sent her over the edge. She was never the same after that. I should have come back home to be with her, but I was so torn by guilt, I just couldn't bear to see her pain. So, I ran away, like the coward that I was."

"And left me?"

"Jack Maxwell and his wife legally adopted you. Corinne was over the moon. She'd wanted a baby so desperately, and she thought that something positive had come out of this terrible tragedy. She had no idea you were really her husband's daughter."

"Did you know they'd changed my name?" I asked through tears.

"Yes. I thought it was very callous of him, but what could I do? Your father paid me off to leave. He didn't want anyone around who could betray his secret to his wife. I took the money and went to London. I couldn't stay in New York, not if I couldn't be a part of your life, and going home was too painful. I've been here ever since."

"So, my mother never knew?" At least my poor mother couldn't be blamed. She was an innocent victim in all of this, completely unaware of what her husband had done.

"No. She just thought she was getting a poor orphaned little girl. She'd despaired of ever getting a baby, and there you were, vulnerable and in need of a good home and someone to love you. It was a private adoption, and it happened very quickly. They took you home after a week and I never saw you again. I'm so sorry, Sandy. I wish I would have fought for you, but I felt powerless."

"Why did you never try to contact me?" I already knew the answer, but I had to hear it anyway, just to be sure.

"I have, but I never heard back. Jack must have destroyed the letters. Besides, I didn't want to spring all this on you without warning. They were your parents now, and I knew they'd do everything in their power to make you happy. Jack had his faults, but I was sure he loved you. I saw the way he looked at you when I brought you to the lawyer's office, and I knew he'd lay down his life for you if need be. Was he a good father to you?"

"Yes, he was, but I also thought he was a good husband. I believed my parents had a happy marriage."

Myra just shrugged, smiling ruefully. "Maybe he'd changed."

"Were there others, besides Kelly?" I probably shouldn't have asked, but I needed to know. I wanted to believe that my father had fallen in love with my birth mother and that she had been the only one, his secret vice that he'd taken to his grave, but Myra shook her head.

"Yes, there were others. I was his secretary for several years, so all their calls went through me. He never gave them his personal number for fear of your mother finding out. He did love her, you know, but he wasn't content with just one woman. Some people aren't cut out for monogamy."

Myra refreshed my tea, watching me with those dark eyes. I could see she wanted to ask me something, but was looking for the right moment. She took a sip of tea, staring down into her lap before her head snapped up, decision made. "May I call you in New York?" she asked. "I know I have no right to ask anything of you, but you are the only person left of my family. Is there any chance we can be friends?"

I looked away for a moment, my glance falling on a framed picture of Myra and Kelly, two young girls sitting on the top step of the house, their arms around each other, dark hair mixing with red as they smiled into the camera, completely unaware that in a few short years, one of them would be dead and the other would face exile from the home she couldn't face.

"I think my mother would have liked that," I said, smiling at Myra as she breathed a sigh of relief. "Myra, I don't hold you responsible for what happened. You did the right thing, and I've had a good life and a happy childhood. My father loved me, despite his failings, and he probably believed that he was doing what's right for me. I'm very sorry that I never knew your mother or had a relationship with you, but it's not too late. We can start again, and you can tell me all about my mother, and Grandma Hughes. You might even want to visit me in Upper Whitford, see your old home. I now own it."

Myra's face went slack with shock. "You bought the house?"

"Didn't you know?"

"No. Roger took care of all that. He just sent me my share. I had no idea. What an odd coincidence, or was it? Did you already know the truth when you bought the house?"

"No. I didn't put two and two together until I saw a picture of Kelly."

"What a miracle that you of all people bought it." Myra's face suddenly grew serious as she thought of something, her mouth opening and then closing again as she searched for the right words.

"Sandy, or should I call you Lexi now, have you experienced anything odd?" she asked, carefully watching me, her head cocked to the side. I could see the tension around her mouth, the air of expectation as she waited for me to answer her question.

"Like what?"

She shrugged noncommittally, assuming I didn't know what she was referring to. "Never mind," she smiled, "it's nothing."

"You mean him, don't you, the man in the ruin?" I was gratified to see the change that came over Myra's face. That's exactly what she'd meant, curious if I had seen what she knew to be there. So, I wasn't the only one.

"Myra, tell me about him."

"His name was Brendan Carr. All I know is that some terrible tragedy took place at that house many years ago. The thing is that only certain people can see him. Kelly, my mother, and her mother saw him too, but not my father or his sister who'd lived with us after her husband died and before she remarried and moved to Manchester. My grandmother tried to find out what happened to him, but it was a conspiracy of silence. No one would talk about it; no one remembered."

"But you don't believe them?" I asked. Myra was echoing my own misgivings.

"People in small villages have a long memory, and many of the families can trace their roots to the Saxons who settled the region centuries ago. I don't believe that no one remembers what happened to Brendan Carr or why his spirit has been unable to find peace, kneeling under that tree day after day. Maybe that's where he died."

"There must be a way to find out what happened," I mused, even more curious than I'd been before. "Someone must know."

"Well, if they do, they're not telling. I'm glad you can see him though. Kelly was obsessed with him, glued to the window every day, waiting for him to appear."

"Did you know that his tomb is in the cellar?" I asked, watching Myra's face for any reaction. Her mouth hung open in shock.

"His tomb is in the cellar?!"

"Yes, we found it when the electrician was there doing some work."

"I had no idea. How extraordinary." Myra just gaped at me. Her reaction was genuine, but it was hard to believe that no one had known the room was even there.

October 1650

England

Chapter 61

Brendan kissed Rowan goodbye and watched wistfully as she slipped out the door and into the gathering darkness of the October evening. The past week had been the most bittersweet of his life, filled with the wonder of a new marriage and the gnawing worry about the future. Rowan seemed to be blissfully unaware of the danger they were in, choosing to focus on trivial domestic matters and clouding his mind with her unwavering devotion. He knew he needed to think clearly and anticipate every eventuality, but every conversation with his wife ended up in hours of lovemaking that left him pleasantly weak and stupidly happy. Brendan ran his hand through his hair and climbed up the ladder to his loft where he promptly began pacing. Pacing always focused his mind, and his healing body sorely lacked exercise and training. His fighting skills were rusty and his reflexes slow, but he had no one to practice with, unless Reverend Pole decided to take up the sword. The old reverend was more likely to fight with a quill, using his words to score a victory and not his steel.

Brendan clasped his hands behind his back and continued his walk. Now that he'd be traveling with Rowan, clerical robes would be pointless. A reverend traveling with a young woman was more likely to arouse suspicion. The magistrate's men were on the lookout for a single man fitting his description, but no one was looking for a couple, though traveling with Rowan was certainly no protection against being recognized. Rowan mentioned that she'd seen several broadsheets by the tavern and church offering a reward for his capture. They'd even drawn a likeness of him, but

Rowan assured him that it looked more like some maniacal wild man than the handsome, aristocratic man she married. Brendan chuckled without mirth and sat down on the cot, tired of pacing. His original intention was to borrow a horse from Uncle Caleb, but a couple traveling on horseback on All Hallows' Eve would attract too much attention, and not mistaken for village people out to celebrate the holiday. So, they would have to walk and buy horses later.

Brendan had a purse full of coin and the money would buy them horses, provisions, and eventually, passage to America, but only if he could infringe on someone's hospitality for the winter months. After that, they'd be on their own, and he'd have to find a way to provide for them in their new country. But, he was getting ahead of himself. First, they had to get to London.

Brendan stretched out on the cot and folded his hands behind his head. He couldn't wait to be out of this miserable little village. He could already see the streets of London, teeming with wagons and fine carriages making their way along narrow streets crowded with passersby. The lowliest servants mixed with finely-dressed ladies and gentlemen, who navigated the streets and jumped out of the way as wheels splashed them with muck, or someone upturned a chamber pot from a second-story window without so much as a warning. The nobles dashed through the streets, their pomanders held to their delicate noses to make the passage more bearable.

London smelled of garbage, soot, and decay, but Brendan loved its stately mansions, grandiose palaces, and the general feeling of life flowing and pulsating all around him, like blood through the heart. He'd enjoyed walking by the river, its briny smell carried on the breeze, and dozens of packet boats, merchant vessels and barges bobbing gently on the murky water, sometimes completely invisible in the soupy yellow fog that enveloped London in its shroud, blurring the edges of buildings and swallowing people whole as they disappeared into its folds. He looked forward to showing Rowan the markets and the theaters, and maybe taking her to see some mummers or acrobats. She'd like that. Rowan had never been further than this village; she would be amazed by the overwhelming tide of life she was soon to encounter. She might be frightened at first, but she would learn to appreciate the city as he did.

Chapter 62

Stephen tucked in the children and kissed them goodnight before descending the ladder from the loft and taking his seat by the low-burning fire. The house seemed to settle around him, creaking and sighing like a human being who's tired after a day's work. Normally, Stephen stayed up for an hour or two after the children had gone to bed, cleaning his tools, reading a few passages from the Bible, or simply dozing by the fire, but tonight he couldn't settle to anything and suddenly missed Betty. They used to sit up and talk over the day's events after the children had gone to sleep, and make plans for the morrow. Betty had been a tough, no-nonsense woman, but Stephen always knew that he could rely on her to be loyal, hardworking, and fair. What would she have thought of Rowan, he wondered, and chuckled to himself? He could almost hear Betty's voice, "She's an insipid, damaged little thing, you fool, and she'll do nothing but bring you grief in the end. Find a strong, healthy girl who'll take care of you and the children, and not the other way 'round."

Stephen shook his head to dislodge Betty from his mind. As usual, she had a point, even in death, but Stephen couldn't help the longing in his heart. Rowan made him feel things that he'd never felt for Betty. Betty never needed coddling or protecting; she could take care of herself, but Rowan was like a wounded little bird that needed a bit of tender care before it could fly again. He knew he was being a sentimental fool, but that's how he felt, and he wasn't ashamed of it, which brought him right back to the problem at hand. He'd followed Rowan twice more, and although he hadn't actually seen the man again, he knew she wasn't alone in the house. Stephen had seen the light of a candle dispel the darkness of the loft behind the shutters after she left. Reverend Pole wasn't there, so someone was. Rowan seemed unusually giddy after she left the reverend's house, humming to herself as she walked home, her basket swinging on her arm in tune to the music in her head. Once, he even thought he heard her singing, but that was impossible. His mind was likely playing tricks on him.

Stephen scratched his stubbled jaw and gazed miserably into the dying flames. What was he to do? His initial reaction was to confront Rowan in the lane and ask her what she'd been up to and with whom, but that would only make her angry and defensive. He had to tread carefully with her and not make any accusations until he was sure that something was indeed going on.

The second option was to go to the house and confront the man, but he might not even come to the door, or if he did, not acknowledge that he had any relationship with Rowan. Perhaps he was a guest of Reverend Pole's or some distant relation. But, if that were the case, why did no one see him in the village or at church? Why did he choose to remain hidden? Stephen briefly thought of asking the reverend, but then chided himself for his foolishness. He had no right to question Reverend Pole about anything. What he did in his house, and whom he chose to give hospitality to was none of Stephen's business. Reverend Pole was one of the kindest, purest souls he'd ever met, and he'd rather die than cause him any affront. Hence, he was back to square one.

"When in doubt — do nothing," Betty said in his head, her voice almost as clear as if she were right next to him. "Bide your time and the answer will come to you. In the meantime, pray. God answers every prayer, even one as foolhardy as yours."

"Good night, Betty," Stephen said out loud, "and thank you. Maybe I underappreciated you while you were alive." Stephen could almost hear Betty's harrumph of triumph.

Chapter 63

Edward Sexby reined in his horse and took in his surroundings. Another typical English village, with a cluster of houses around the green, and an old Norman church made of gray stone and boasting one central, truncated tower that cast a permanent shadow over the stone arch crowning the wooden door. Dozens of lichen-covered gravestones dotted the grounds; an unwritten history of its inhabitants catalogued only in dates of birth and death, as if nothing in between actually mattered. For these people, it probably hadn't, since most of them lived lives of little or no account. They were born, they spent their days in monotonous drudgery, and then they died.

"The usual, sir?" Will asked. He was already licking his lips in anticipation of a meal and a tankard of ale.

Sexby just nodded. The only place to get any information in a village like this was the tavern, and this time, they had to tread carefully. This was the home of Caleb Frain, uncle to Brendan and Jasper Carr, and any questions about Brendan would arouse instant suspicion.

"You keep quiet, Will, and leave the talking to me," Sexby instructed, although he didn't have to say a word. Will was happy enough to let Sexby do the talking as long as he got to participate in anything that required the use of fists or arms, but since none of the people they'd come across seemed to know anything, Will's talents were unnecessary and he was becoming visibly restless, itching for someone to truss up. He'd get his chance soon enough. Sexby trusted his instincts, and his gut told him that this was the place where they'd finally learn something of Carr's whereabouts.

The tavern wasn't hard to spot as it was the only building that displayed a creaky sign out front depicting a crowned woman with a severed head. The sign swayed slowly in the gentle wind making the head look as if it were nodding. Edward gave her a wink and a nod. *The Queen's Head* it is then.

The interior of the pub was pleasantly dim after the brightness of the afternoon and almost empty. A few old men sat around nursing their drinks, but otherwise, the dining room was unoccupied. A merry fire blazed in the grate and cast shifting shadows onto the whitewashed walls and dark wooden beams. The publican didn't seem to be about, so the men took a seat at a corner table and set aside their weapons and hats. They were in no rush, and had no desire to start off on the wrong foot with the proprietor. A few minutes passed before a plump, middle-aged woman came waddling out of the kitchen and made straight for them.

"I'm ever so sorry, sirs. I didn't know there was anyone waiting. What can I get you? We have some lovely pigeon pie, just out of the oven and piping hot. Shall I fetch you both a slice? Or there's some cold ham left over from yesterday. Goes ever so well with some fresh bread and a bit of mustard and pickle." She seemed out of breath as she blathered on, unnerved by Sexby's gaze. He liked to make people nervous. It got them talking.

"That sounds divine, mistress. Pigeon pie for me and my companion, and a slice of that ham wouldn't go amiss, and some ale, of course." The woman dipped down in an imitation of a curtsy and looked like she was about to sprawl on the floor, but she righted herself in time and scurried back to the kitchen.

"I think she fancies you," Will said with a chuckle. "The poor cow nearly pissed herself just looking into those eyes of yours." He made Sexby laugh by batting his eyelashes and looking soulfully into his eyes. Sexby never considered himself a handsome man, but a few women had commented on his deep brown eyes, saying that they could get lost in them had he ever given them the chance. Edward gazed into his eyes in the cracked mirror above his bed, but saw nothing extraordinary about his brown eyes. They were just eyes, fringed with thick lashes and slightly slanted, like those of a cat contemplating a mouse just before it became its next meal. But, if the ladies admired his eyes, he'd use them to his advantage and gaze at them as if enraptured to get whatever it is he wanted or needed at the moment, and what he needed right now was some hot food and a bit of information.

"You're a joker, Will, but we must all use the talents the good Lord blessed us with," he replied with a look of mock seriousness making Will guffaw. Will was about to make some rude comment when the woman came bustling out of the kitchen with two plates in one hand and two tankards in the other. She executed this balancing act more gracefully than the curtsey and set the food and the drinks on the table, her eyes darting to Sexby's face. "I do hope you like it, sir."

"Oh, I'm sure we will. The pie smells wonderful. Did you make it yourself?" Sexby asked with a warm smile.

"Oh, yes. I do all the cooking. If you enjoy it, you can get some for the road," she suggested slyly, already counting the money she was about to earn on this slow afternoon.

"I think we just might, but we're not leaving just yet. We're supposed to meet a friend of ours here, a Brendan Carr. Has he been by?" Sexby took a deep pull of his ale and a bite of pie, which made him roll his eyes in ecstasy. The woman blushed with pleasure and made a pretense of thinking hard.

"Why, I don't rightly know. The name sounds familiar, but I can't recall from where. We get so many travelers passing through."

"He's got some kin here, a Caleb Frain," Sexby offered helpfully.

"Oh, of course, young Brendan. I remember him now, but I haven't clapped eyes on him since Maisie's wedding. That'd be five years ago now, or thereabouts. Heard he went off to fight, he did." She was about to say something else when she realized that she had no idea whose side these men were on, so she opted for another curtsey. "I'll be off to the kitchen now. Call if you need anything."

"Well, that went well," Will observed with a mouth full of pie. "She's not much of a cook either."

Sexby took another bite of pie and chewed thoughtfully. "Not a total waste. She's a talkative one, make no mistake, so if she'd seen him, she'd have said something, or at least showed a reluctance to speak. Her answer was genuine. What we need to do is come back when there are more men in here, drinking. We might get more information then. They might not tell us the truth, but at least we'll be able to see if they're hiding something."

"What shall we do till then?" Will was hoping Sexby would want to get some sleep. He was tired and saddle-sore, and not averse to some rest. It'd be nice to find a willing girl, but this didn't look like the type of place where those kinds of pleasures could be found.

"Let's get a room. I'm tired and in sore need of a bath. A man who's clean and well-dressed always makes a better impression than one who stinks of sweat and horses. These peasants tend to be impressed by gentlemen, so let's act like it, or at least try." Sexby laughed at Will's face. He was as much of a gentleman as the publican's wife was a lady, but it never hurt to try.

Chapter 64

Lizzie was just clearing away the supper dishes when a knock on the door distracted her and made Tim look up from his wooden horse, which he was moving back and forth in front of the hearth in simulation of a gallop. They had few visitors, and even fewer in the evening. Stephen opened the shutter and glanced out the window before unlatching the door to his brother, who came in bringing a gust of cool wind scented with decaying leaves and the smell of impending rain. Eugene was carrying something wrapped tightly in a piece of muslin; something that was seeping juices and instantly filled the house with an appetizing smell.

"Good evening to all," Eugene called out cheerfully as he kissed the top of the children's heads and handed the package to Lizzie. "Amy made some blood sausage today. Thought you might like some." Eugene took a seat on the bench and gave his brother an expectant look. He clearly wanted to talk, so Stephen sent the kids off to bed, promising to do the washing up, and poured Eugene a cup of beer before taking a seat opposite him.

"Thank you for the sausage, Gene, and thank Amy for me. She's been so good to us since Betty died." Amy was always sending over a little of this and a bit of that; anything she could spare from her own family, and Stephen was most grateful, especially since he didn't have any notion of how to make these things himself and Lizzie was too young to do it on her own.

"Think nothing of it," Eugene replied, taking a sip of beer and casting his eyes upstairs to make sure the children couldn't hear him before speaking in a low voice. "I stopped at the tavern this evening for a quick drink," he began, smiling guiltily. Amy didn't like it when Eugene went to the pub, especially during the week. She thought it was an awful waste of money when Eugene could have the same ale or beer at home, but that wasn't quite the point of the visit, as Amy well knew. Eugene simply wanted an hour to himself, away from the never-ending chores and the demands of the family. He wanted to talk to other men, exchange news and bits of gossip, and play the occasional game of dice. Who could blame a man for that?

"Was Amy upset with you then?" She must have been very cross if Eugene felt the need to escape the house for a bit.

"No, no more than usual, but I overheard something that I thought was strange." Eugene was warming up to the subject now, his beer forgotten. "There were two men there, gentlemen by the look of them, drinking. Seems they're here to meet a friend by the name of Brendan Carr, Caleb's nephew."

"Is that the one who's been accused of killing those three men?" Stephen asked. "Why would he be here?"

"I don't know, but I got the impression that they are less friends and more enemies, if you know what I mean. They didn't look too friendly."

Stephen shrugged his shoulders. What did he care about Brendan Carr? He'd met his family years ago at Maisie's wedding, but the Carrs never came back again after that. Stephen glanced at Eugene, who was still looking over-excited. "Why do you think this is significant?"

"Well, think about it, Stephen. Three men are murdered in cold blood, and the murderer just happens to be the nephew of one of our neighbors. Clearly, he wouldn't go home, as that would be the first place anyone would look for him, so maybe he came to hide with his kin. We might have a murderer among us." Eugene leaned across the table and whispered in a conspiratorial manner. "I think those are the magistrate's men, and they mean to see him hang."

"You always were fanciful, even as a child," Stephen remarked as he rose from the bench. "I think we are safe, at least for tonight. Now go home to your wife and thank her for the sausage."

Eugene drained the last of the beer and got to his feet, grinning at his brother. "All right, just thought I'd tell you, since you happen to be betrothed to the niece of a man who might be hiding a killer." Eugene clapped his brother on the shoulder and disappeared into the night.

Stephen bolted the door and turned his attention to the dirty dishes. He didn't mind doing the washing up from time to time to give poor Lizzie a break. No ten-year-old girl should work as hard as she did, little lamb. Stephen went to work, but his mind kept returning to the conversation with Eugene. Maybe what Eugene was suggesting wasn't as unreasonable as he first thought. He'd heard of the murder about a month ago, and it was just around that time that Rowan seemed to start spending more time at Reverend Pole's. Before, she used to go over about twice a week to cook and wash for the reverend, but the past few weeks she seemed to be stopping by nearly every day. And then there was the man he'd seen at the cottage.

Stephen dropped a plate into the basin and sat down heavily on the bench. Of course! Brendan Carr was said to have been wounded by the men. Somehow, he managed to get to Caleb without being seen, and Caleb had hidden him with the reverend, knowing that no one would ever suspect Reverend Pole of harboring a criminal. Rowan, who had some knowledge of herbs and remedies, would be the most likely person to care for Carr since no one would think anything of her going to Reverend Pole's house. No wonder she'd been so distracted of late. Had she developed feelings for Carr?

Stephen turned the empty cup in his hands over and over, his mind on the situation at hand. What Carr did was none of his business, but Rowan was. What if he'd hurt her or threatened her in some way? What if he'd violated her? The man was a murderer and a fugitive, and his poor, sweet Rowan was sent to care for him, left alone with him for hours on end, hours when anything could have happened.

Ordinarily, Stephen would mind his own business and leave justice for others to carry out, but this was different. His

315

future was at risk, as was the woman he loved dearly. If the men were from the magistrate, then would it be wrong to inform them of the whereabouts of a murderer? After all, if Carr had a good reason for killing those men, he could defend himself at the trial and prove his innocence. It wasn't Stephen Aldridge's responsibility to protect him from the law. And if the men removed him from the village and took him to Lincoln to be tried, all the better for Stephen, who could comfort and support Rowan until she forgot all about the scoundrel and turned her thoughts once more to their life together.

Stephen rose to his feet, pulled on his coat and jammed his hat onto his head. He was just about to head out into the night when a cry from the loft stopped him in his tracks.

"Da, I'm scared." Tim's little face was peering down at Stephen, his nightshirt flapping around thin, white shins. "Da, where are you going?" he wailed.

"Nowhere, son. I'll be right up. You just go back to bed and I'll come up to tell you a story."

"All right," Tim replied, but remained exactly where he was, waiting for Stephen to take off his coat and hat and bolt the door for the night.

Chapter 65

Rowan hung her cloak on a nail by the door and rubbed her hands in front of the fire to warm them up. It was a chilly afternoon, a breath of approaching winter in the air. Over the past few weeks the leaves had begun to change, going from the vibrant green of summer to the crimson and gold of fall, and setting the village and forest ablaze with glorious color until they began to fall, twirling to the ground in an annual cycle of death and rebirth.

Aunt Joan was sitting at the table, defeathering two fat pheasants, their skin pallid and wrinkled in the spots that had already been cleaned. Rowan wondered briefly where they came from, as Uncle Caleb didn't do much hunting, but it didn't matter. It'd be nice to have something different for a change. Rowan smiled at Aunt Joan and patted her on the shoulder in a gesture of affection before going up to her room at the top of the stairs.

She felt a funny fluttering sensation in her stomach at the thought of tomorrow night. It was All Hallows' Eve, and the night of the escape. Brendan had told her not to take too much, but she couldn't just leave with the clothes on her back. She'd need a change of clothes, her winter boots, the comb and hand mirror set that Aunt Joan and Uncle Caleb gave her for her sixteenth birthday, and a nightdress. It didn't seem like much, but it made a sizeable bundle nonetheless. Rowan stuffed the bundle under the bed and sat down, her hands folded in her lap. She had no reservations about leaving with Brendan, but the thought of leaving her aunt and uncle made her sad. They'd been the closest thing she'd had to parents since her mother's death, and to leave without a word was a sure sign of ingratitude and betrayal; something she never wanted them to feel.

Brendan never actually said that she couldn't tell her aunt and uncle they were leaving, so she decided to say goodbye tomorrow and thank them for everything they'd done for her.

They would be shocked and maybe disapproving, but in time they'd come to accept her decision. Stephen, on the other hand, was a different matter. She owed him an explanation and an apology, but she couldn't tell him the truth. He would have to hear of her desertion from Uncle Caleb, and Stephen would no doubt feel angry and betrayed, as would his children whom she'd grown to love. She never intimated that she loved Stephen, but she did accept his proposal and had been planning a life with him until Brendan arrived. Rowan hoped that Stephen would forgive her in time, and not think too badly of her. He was a handsome man with much to offer to any woman, and she knew that, in time, he would forget her and find himself a suitable wife; one who would appreciate him and love him in a way he deserved to be loved. He was still a relatively young man and could have a long and happy life with someone. Rowan knew that she was thinking these thoughts to make herself feel better and assuage some of her guilt, but there was nothing to be done. She'd made her choice, and now all she could do was hope for forgiveness from those she wronged.

Rowan sighed and got to her feet. She'd go downstairs and help Aunt Joan with supper. The pheasants were already cleaned and gutted, a small basin at the end of the table containing what was once their lifeblood, but now just a disgusting mess of innards and gore. Aunt Joan was arranging the birds in a clay pot, and stuffing chopped chestnuts, slices of apples, and pieces of old bread into the cavity between their legs. The bread would absorb the fat and juices of the birds, and cooked together with the apples and chestnuts would make a nice stuffing to enjoy with the meat. Rowan had never heard of anyone stuffing meat with apples, but her Aunt Joan liked to try new things, and they usually came out quite good once you got past the notion that you were eating things that wouldn't be normally eaten together.

"Lovely, plump birds," Joan announced as she patted the breast of one of the pheasants. "Pip Wilkinson brought them by this morning. I think he might have poached them, but by the time anyone suspects anything, they'll be long gone." Aunt Joan grinned at Rowan in a conspiratorial fashion. "I do love pheasant."

Rowan just nodded and smiled as she checked on the loaves of bread in the oven at the side of the hearth. The coarse brown bread would go well with the gravy. Rowan was just about to take the bread out of the oven to make room for Joan's pheasants when Uncle Caleb came bursting through the door, bringing a gust of cold air and the pungent smell of rotting leaves.

"Caleb, what is it, man?" Joan asked, alarmed by the look on his face. "Is anything amiss?"

"Two men arrived in the village yesterday and have been asking after Brendan at the tavern. Pip just told me that they've asked for directions to Reverend Pole's house. I must warn Brendan."

"Nooooo!!!!!" The scream was more like a roar that tore from Rowan's chest as she dropped the loaves of bread and flew out the door. Joan watched Rowan hitch up her skirts and run, her expression one of stunned disbelief. She'd forgotten the sound of her voice, but what she heard was not a girl's soft voice, but a cry of anguish so deep that it tore at her soul. Joan knew Rowan had grown fond of Brendan, but this was something else, something primal and raw. This was love.

"We must go after her," Joan said, snatching the loaves from the floor and covering the pot of pheasants with a cloth. Supper would have to wait. Caleb nodded. "Let me get my blunderbuss."

Joan just gaped at her husband. "Caleb, you can't shoot the magistrate's men, if that's who they are. They'd hang you, even if you missed. Leave the gun. All we can do is warn Brendan. The rest is up to him." Caleb nodded. Joan was right. This wasn't his fight. He did, however, grab his dagger and slide it into his boot. It didn't do to be completely unarmed.

***

Rowan ran through the woods as if the devil himself were in pursuit. She'd avoided the lane and sprinted through the forest in the hope that she would get to Reverend Pole's before the men.

319

Branches tore at her clothing, and she tripped and nearly lost her balance a few times, but she hardly noticed. Her cap had fallen off, and her hair fell down her back free of its pins. It blew into her face as she ran and nearly blinded her, but she just brushed it out of her eyes without breaking stride. Rowan was panting by the time she burst into the cottage, shocking Reverend Pole and alarming Brendan, who was sitting at the table drinking a cup of ale with the reverend.

"Brendan, go now. There're men coming for you. Go!" she screamed. Reverend Pole just stared at her, but Rowan had no time to explain anything. "There's a thicket about half a mile southeast. Go hide there until I come and get you, you hear?" She was beating her hands against his chest, tears streaming down her face.

"I can't just leave you," he replied, gazing into her eyes as if he had all the time in the world.

"They're not interested in me; it's you they want. Go! I'll come for you." Brendan thought of climbing to the loft to get his sword, but there was no time. He had his dagger on him; that would have to suffice. He kissed Rowan as he ran from the house, headed in the direction she specified and vanished into the woods just as two horsemen came into view at the top of the lane. The men seemed to be in no hurry as they cantered toward the house, talking quietly between themselves. Thankfully, they hadn't seen Brendan, so he had a chance of escape. Rowan let out a long sigh of relief as she smoothed down her apron and tried to tidy her hair. She reached for the pot warming over the fire and carefully stirred the contents. Let them think she was preparing supper for the old man. Reverend Pole gave her a reassuring smile. "It will all come out all right, my child," he said just as the door flew open, nearly coming off its hinges.

"Good afternoon, Reverend," a man said as he stepped into the small room. He was the shorter and older of the two, but clearly the one in charge. His companion filled the doorway with his large frame, but didn't step inside, effectively preventing any attempt at escape.

"Good afternoon, my son," Reverend Pole answered quietly. "How may I be of assistance?"

"My name is Edward Sexby, and I'm looking for one Brendan Carr. We have some business, he and I, so if you would kindly tell him we're here." He glanced upward toward the loft, but then turned to face the reverend, his expression one of expectation.

"There's no one by that name here, Mr. Sexby. It's just Rowan and I." Sexby's gaze settled on Rowan, making her feel as if she were suddenly naked before these men. His eyes roamed over her in a most insolent fashion, making her blush nervously as she fixated her gaze on the pot to avoid looking at the men.

"Rowan, is it? What a pretty name. And do you know Brendan Carr, Rowan?" Rowan just shook her head violently, hoping her face wouldn't betray her. She felt weak in the knees and just wanted to sink down on the bench, but she remained standing by the hearth, a long spoon in her hand as she pretended to mind the stew.

"The child doesn't speak," Reverend Pole said, stepping in front of Rowan. Sexby cocked his head to the side and gave Rowan a winning smile before turning back to the reverend.

"I'll just look around, shall I?" Sexby didn't wait for an answer as he climbed the ladder into the loft. Rowan could hear heavy footsteps as he walked around, stopping once or twice to look at something. Brendan hadn't had any time to hide any of his belongings, so the man was sure to find something of interest. The other man stood silently by the door, his face tense as he waited for his master's orders. He flexed his muscles in a way that Rowan found intensely threatening and gave her a slow smile as he caught her eye. Rowan whipped her head away, terrified by what she saw in the man's eyes. She sank down on the bench next to Reverend Pole, praying fervently that they would just leave.

Finally, Sexby came back down carrying Brendan's sword. "Where is he?" he hissed.

The reverend didn't answer, but returned Sexby's gaze without fear, resigned to whatever Sexby planned to do. Sexby looked at the old man and then allowed his eyes to travel to the girl. There was no proof that the sword belonged to Carr, but the expression on the girl's face told him that he wasn't wrong. Her eyes opened wider in fear as Sexby said Carr's name, and she quickly averted them to stare at the floor. These two knew where he was, and after spending weeks in pursuit, Sexby wasn't about to just accept defeat. He glanced at Will and gave him a brief nod, which Will intercepted and acknowledged with a small bow. He left the house, letting the door swing shut behind him.

Rowan continued to stare at the floor, terrified to meet the man's gaze. The other one probably went to check the outbuildings, but he wouldn't find Brendan, and sooner or later they would be satisfied that he wasn't there and leave them in peace. Rowan willed herself to breathe slowly to calm her racing heart. It would be all right. Brendan had enough time to get away.

She started as the man spoke again, his voice low and silky, but full of menace. "Reverend, I know that you know where he is, so I will ask you one last time. If you decline to answer, you leave me no choice but to force the information from you. I would really rather not. I find it distasteful to harm clerics and young girls."

Reverend Pole stared the man down, his resolve unshaken. "Mr. Sexby, I do not know where Brendan Carr is, and neither does Rowan. She's just a simple girl who comes to help me with some domestic chores. Soft in the head, you might say," he added for good measure. "She knows nothing."

"We shall see." Sexby suddenly grabbed the reverend by the arm and forced him outside, with Rowan following on their heels. She wanted to protest that the reverend didn't know, but it would be pointless. The men suspected the truth and wouldn't just leave them alone. Rowan stifled a scream as she saw two nooses hanging off the oak in front of the house. The other man had not been checking the outbuildings, but making a gibbet. He now leaned against the stout trunk of the oak, his face alight with expectation. *This wasn't distasteful to him; this was what he lived for,* Rowan thought as she met his eyes which were fixed on her.

"Reverend, do you have anything to tell me?" Sexby asked as he stopped just short of the tree with the noose swaying above Reverend Pole's head.

"God has a plan for us all, my son, and if this is His plan for me, then I will accept His will." He crossed himself and began to pray under his breath, infuriating Sexby.

"And does he have a plan for your simple girl? Are you willing to let her hang as punishment for your stubbornness?" Sexby hissed, amazed by the old man's resolve. Was he really willing to die to protect Carr? And the girl? He didn't want to hurt her, but the old man was making things difficult.

"She knows nothing. She understands nothing. Please, let her go. She's naught by a simpleton," the reverend begged, but Sexby wasn't so sure. The girl's eyes told him everything he needed to know. She understood perfectly well, and she knew what he wanted to know. He hoped that threatening the reverend would scare her into revealing what she knew, but she just stood rooted to the ground, her eyes on the tree and her mouth open in horror.

"This is your last chance, old man," Sexby said, willing the reverend to speak. Why did these people have to make things so difficult? All they had to do was give up Carr, and he'd leave them in peace, but the Reverend gazed at him defiantly, daring him to do his worst.

"Any last words?" The old man shook his head as Will detached himself from the tree and came forward. He seized the old man and dragged him toward the tree. Rowan stuffed her fist into her mouth in terror as Will tossed the rope over Reverend Pole's thin neck. Sexby was watching her intently.

"Where is he?" he asked again, his eyes never leaving Rowan. A small scream tore from her chest as she wrapped her arms around herself in a futile attempt at protection. She fixed her eyes on the ground, staring at his boots as if she could see God in them. Sexby exhaled loudly, hating the position he was in.

"Go on, Will," he said and turned away from the tree. He didn't wish to see this. Will pulled the rope with both hands, lifting the reverend off the ground as his body swung wildly, his legs kicking at the empty air. He could hear horrible choking sounds, and watched Rowan's face as she shook violently in front of him. She was rocking back and forth on the balls of her feet, tears streaming down her pale face as the noises grew quieter, and the air stilled around them with the sound of death. Will secured the rope to the trunk and turned his attention back to Sexby, waiting for orders.

Sexby took hold of Rowan's face and forced her to look at him. "You don't have to say anything if you can't. Just point. Which way did he go? You don't need to protect him. He's not here to protect you, is he?" he asked, turning her face forcibly toward the tree and the slowly rotating form of Reverend Pole.

Rowan began to shake with terror as her gaze fell on the reverend. His light eyes were bulging out of his head, staring unseeing at the world he would never behold again. His tongue protruded from his mouth, and his skin was ashen against the brilliant foliage of the tree, made even whiter by his black attire. She knew she was next, but she couldn't betray Brendan. These men were not here to take him into custody to face trial. They would surely kill him just as they killed the poor reverend, and would kill her if she failed to tell them what they wanted to know. She wanted to point in the wrong direction, but she knew Sexby would know she was lying. Years of not speaking had made her face too expressive and she couldn't fool a man like that.

"Which way?" Sexby roared, but Rowan just stared at him as hot urine ran down her legs.

The Present

Chapter 66

I stared at the phone, picking it up again after putting it down half a dozen times. I had to call my mother, had to tell her what I'd learned, but I couldn't trust myself not to lash out, not to accuse, not to cry. She'd raised me and loved me as much as any mother could, and it was just a strange twist of fate that alerted me to the fact that she hadn't given birth to me. Had she panicked when I took off for England, or had she known nothing at all about where I'd come from, where my heart led me?

I took a deep breath, finally dialing the number. She'd left three messages, so I had to call her back before she showed up on my doorstep, demanding to know what had happened. We spoke every day, sometimes for hours, going over every detail of our day, sharing gossip and reminiscing about Dad. And now the conversation was going to change — forever.

"Hello," my mother's voice was cheerful and full of expectation. "Lexi, where have you been? I was getting worried. I left several messages," she informed me, her voice full of righteous indignation. I took a deep breath and plunged in.

My mother didn't interrupt as I blurted out everything that had been on my mind for the past week. I heard a sharp intake of breath as I described my visit to the prison, and a shaky sigh as I spoke of my meeting with Myra. I finally came to the end, waiting for her to tell me that she hadn't known, hadn't suspected, would have told me the truth had she had any inkling of what I left behind in England, but she didn't say any of those things. She just remained quiet, the only indication that she was still on the line the barely audible intake of breath and something that sounded like a sniffle.

"Mom? Are you still there?" I demanded, needing some kind of response.

"Yes," she breathed out. "Oh, Lexi, how I hoped you'd never find out."

"So, you knew? You knew it all?" I felt my heart crack just a little bit more, as I realized that the woman I had trusted above and beyond anyone else had lied to me and betrayed my trust, but I owed it to her to hear her out, even if my knees buckled under and I slid into a chair, unable to stand. My hand shook as I held the phone to my ear, pressing hard as if that would somehow make learning the truth more bearable. Was it going to be the truth, or would my mother spin some tale in the hope that I would accept it and move on? Had my parents had some kind of a contingency plan in case I stumbled onto the truth?

"Lexi, I know you're angry and hurt, but please, let me tell you my side of the story and explain why we kept the truth from you, and for that, I need to start at the very beginning." My mother sounded breathless, and I could hear her blowing her nose as she took a moment to compose herself.

"Go on," I breathed. At this point, nothing would surprise me, but I hoped beyond hope that something my mother said would justify the lie. I wanted to believe that it had been out of love for me, and not out of selfishness or cowardice.

"Lexi, when I was a young woman, many women still wanted to be homemakers. It wasn't as shameful to want to devote yourself to your family as it is today. Nowadays, women are embarrassed to admit that they'd rather have a baby than a successful career, but honestly, that's all I'd ever dreamed of. My friends talked of climbing the corporate ladder, but all I wanted was to pick out a layette and decorate a nursery. When your father and I got married, I hoped to get pregnant on our honeymoon, but it hadn't happened; not then, and not for the next ten years. I was devastated. The field of fertility was not as advanced then, so I was simply pronounced barren and sent home. There was nothing they could offer me. I wanted to die. I tried to talk your father into adopting, but although he wanted a child, he wasn't convinced that he wanted someone else's child. He had his company, and that fulfilled much of his dreams."

I could hear that my mother was trying not to cry, but I had no words of comfort. I was numb.

"I finally convinced your father to register with an adoption agency, but his requirements were so specific, I knew we'd never get a baby. He would only consider a Caucasian newborn, one that could pass for our own child in front of friends and family. I became more miserable, and he became more distant. I suspected there were other women, but I was so wrapped up in my heartbreak I couldn't be bothered to try and win him back. We weren't even making love anymore. It seemed pointless to me since I knew there was no chance of getting pregnant. At any rate, it was nearly fifteen years into our marriage when you suddenly came along. Jack came home one day and showed me your picture. He said that it would be a private adoption and would happen very quickly. We wouldn't have to wait or meet with anyone's approval. I couldn't believe my ears. Here was this beautiful little girl and within a few weeks, she would be mine. I think it was probably the happiest day of my life in nearly fifteen years."

I wiped away a tear, but allowed my mother to go on. I needed to hear all of it.

"And so you came. You were shy and frightened, but I didn't care. I devoted myself to you, and within a few months you began to come out of your shell. The first time you called me 'mom' I cried and cried. I thought I'd never live to hear that word." I could almost hear my mother smiling through the tears as she recalled that moment.

"I have to be honest; I hadn't asked too many questions about where you came from. I was afraid of the answers. I was just too happy to have my baby. It was your father's idea to fake a few photographs and get a copy of someone's sonogram picture so you wouldn't ask too many questions. You eventually seemed to forget your old life, and it seemed cruel to remind you of it."

My mother paused for breath, giving me a chance to say something, but I remained silent, needing to hear the rest of it.

"It wasn't until you got a little older that I began to notice little things: the way your ears stuck out just like Jack's, the way you were allergic to strawberries like him; the way you cocked your head to the side and squinted when you were really concentrating on something, or the way you walked. I rejected the idea for a long time, but eventually I knew. I knew you weren't some random child of his secretary's sister. You were his." My mother drew in a shuddering breath, the memory of her discovery as painful and fresh as it had been all those years ago.

"Lexi, I just couldn't bear to tell you that not only were you not mine, but that your father had cheated on me and betrayed me, and fathered a child I would have sold my soul for with another woman. So, I pretended you were my own and hoped that you'd never find out. I suppose I was just deluding myself, but I'd prayed that you would always be my little Lexi, even if your father was no longer my Jack. Can you forgive me?"

"Yes, Mom; I can," I said, and meant it. I could hear her anguish through the long-distance line, and I knew that no matter what wrong she'd done me, she'd done it out of love for me and to protect her own damaged heart. She'd suffered, too. And now I finally understood what she'd meant all those years ago. Be careful what you wish for. Now I knew. She'd wished for a baby so desperately, she just never thought that her dearest wish would come true through her husband's infidelity and my birth mother's untimely death. Life had fulfilled her wish in the cruelest way possible.

"I'm sorry, Mom. I really am. You must have suffered so much."

"Lexi, believe it or not, it'd been worth it. I got you, and I wouldn't change a thing. You are the daughter of my heart, even if you didn't come from my womb. No mother has ever loved a child more. And I'd eventually forgiven your father. I made his life hell for fifteen years," my mom added with a shaky giggle.

"Mom, will you come to England? I want to show you the house and have you help me decorate. And most of all, there's someone I want you to meet. I think you'll like him."

"I will book a flight tonight — a one-way flight," she added, and I heard her smile through the phone.

I hung up feeling lighter than I had in the past week. No matter what happened, I still had my mother, and that was worth more than anything. And now that the question of my paternity had been solved, I had one more mystery to unravel, but I would wait for Aidan to start reading the manuscript. It would be fun to do it together, and truthfully, I wasn't ready to face the story of Brendan alone.

October 1650
England

Chapter 67

The blazing orb of the sun was just skimming the treetops when Brendan stepped from the thicket. It had been at least an hour since he ran, and Rowan still hadn't come for him. He wasn't a superstitious man, but the gnawing feeling in his stomach that something was terribly wrong couldn't be ignored. He didn't know who the men were, but although they should have no interest in the old reverend and a young girl, he couldn't shake the feeling that he'd made a horrible mistake in leaving them alone. He had to go back; had to make sure that Rowan was safe. If only he'd taken his sword.

Brendan turned toward the cottage. He hadn't realized it, but he was running, his weakened body protesting and making him pant with exertion. He didn't care if he were seen. He just needed to get back and make sure Rowan was safe. He erupted into the clearing just as the sun began to dip behind the horizon, casting long shadows and turning the trees and the house into dark outlines. The sky above the tree line was crimson, as if blood had been spilled in some celestial battle and was now running and pooling in the mortal world. Brendan saw the outline of the bodies before he could make out their faces, but he knew. There was no doubt. He fell to his knees in the mud before the tree, his vision blurred with tears. He'd run away to save himself, and now Rowan and Reverend Pole were dead, their bodies still warm, but their hearts stilled. It was all his fault, and they'd paid with their lives to keep him safe. Brendan couldn't bring himself to look up at Rowan; to see her face in death. If only it had been a peaceful death, but she died in agony, frightened and alone. All because of him.

Brendan wrapped his arms around himself in an effort to keep from falling to pieces, but it was no use. For the first time in his life, he felt no desire to carry on, no desire for a future. His chest felt so tight, he could barely breathe, and his mind tormented him with cruel images of Rowan fighting for breath before it all went dark, and her last thought that he had failed her. He was oblivious to the two men who stepped out of the trees, the shorter one putting a restraining arm on his companion. They were in no rush.

Brendan unsheathed his dagger and looked at it dispassionately for a moment before turning his eyes up to Rowan's distorted face. "I'm so sorry, Rowan," he whispered, "you were the best part of me, and now we'll never meet again, not even in the afterlife." Brendan slid the dagger between his ribs directly into the heart, relishing the exquisite pain that left him breathless with its intensity. He fell sideways, his sightless eyes fixed on Rowan.

Chapter 68

Caleb whipped the horses, desperate to get to Reverend Pole's cottage. The sunset had brought out all their neighbors, eager to begin their All Hallows' Eve procession. The lane was congested with young people, carrying pitchforks and boxes of tinder. He shouldn't have taken the cart, but Joan wasn't good on horseback, and she insisted on coming. Besides, he thought he might need it. Caleb finally managed to get out of the village and raced toward the reverend's cottage.

"It must be a good hour since Rowan took off," Joan moaned. "Oh, what if we're too late?" She was wringing her hands in her lap, straining to see past the scrim of trees that blocked the view of the cottage. Two strangers on horseback cantered past them, but Caleb scarcely noticed them as he tried to maneuver the wagon around them in the narrow lane. He was startled by Joan's scream as her hand flew to her mouth. He glanced up and felt the blood drain from his face. Two bodies could be seen swinging from the lower limb of the stout oak in front of the house. One of them was clearly a woman, her skirts billowing like a sail in the evening breeze, the crimson sky painting a bloody backdrop, the bodies clearly visible in stark relief. Caleb whipped the horses again, and they reared and took off, galloping toward the gruesome scene. It was only as they got closer that they saw a shape on the ground, one arm outstretched, the other still on the handle of the dagger.

"Dear God, please don't let that be Brendan," Joan wailed, but Caleb was already jumping off the bench of the wagon and running toward the tree. He stopped momentarily to check Brendan's wrist for a pulse before grabbing Rowan's hand.

"Joan, she's still alive," he screamed. "Quick, bring the wagon closer." Caleb jumped onto the wagon in order to reach the rope behind Rowan's neck and sawed at it furiously with his knife until Rowan's body collapsed into his waiting arms. He laid her on the wagon bed and pulled frantically at the rope, trying to loosen its hold. Rowan didn't move, but Caleb could see a faint rising and falling of her chest as air began to penetrate her swollen throat.

"Breathe into her mouth, quick as you can," he shouted to Joan as he managed to get two fingers between Rowan's neck and the rope. The rope left a livid, puckered scar on Rowan's neck, but thankfully, the neck wasn't broken. Joan could feel the faint heartbeat beneath her hand as she leaned over Rowan and tried to breathe life into her limp body. Rowan's lips were blue, and her tongue protruded from her mouth, but the heartbeat grew a little stronger.

"Keep blowing into her mouth," Caleb instructed as he continued to loosen the rope until it hung loosely around Rowan's neck.

Joan nearly fell over as Rowan began to convulse and cough violently. She desperately tore at her neck as she gasped for breath, her body arching and her legs twitching uncontrollably as she tried to draw air into her lungs. Rowan's eyes flew open as she sat bolt upright before vomiting over the side of the wagon. Her hand flew to her chest as she continued to heave, gasping and choking until the air finally started flowing into her lungs, bringing some relief.

Joan just threw her arms around Rowan, sobbing soundlessly as the girl sagged into her arms, too exhausted by her ordeal to even remain seated. Caleb drew both women to himself in a bear hug, blocking Rowan's view of Brendan's body. They sat like that for some minutes until Rowan finally regained her breath and stopped shaking.

"Brendan…" she croaked. It was a ragged whisper, hardly more than air passing between her lips as she wildly looked around. Caleb pushed her down in the wagon so she couldn't see Brendan on the ground.

"Shh," he said. "Don't worry about Brendan now. All will be well." Caleb met Joan's gaze over Rowan's head, his mouth pressed into a stern line.

"Joan, take Rowan home and see to her," he commanded. "I will see to Reverend Pole. Go, woman."

Joan smoothed back Rowan's hair as she closed her eyes and covered her with her own cloak. Better if Rowan didn't see anything. She moved to the bench and yanked on the reins, the wagon slowly rolling away from the scene of the massacre.

***

It was past midnight when Caleb finally crawled into bed next to Joan, who was wide awake. She was dead tired, but unable to get the events of the night out of her mind. She got up every few minutes to check on Rowan, who seemed to be in a state of semi-consciousness. Joan just reached for Caleb's hand, and they remained that way for some time before Joan finally spoke.

"Caleb, what did you do with them?"

"I cut down Reverend Pole and laid him out in the house. They will have to send a new reverend down to perform the funeral. I'll have some of the village women go over tomorrow and see to him." Caleb sighed and grew quiet.

"And Brendan?"

"I buried him, Joan."

"What? Why? Doesn't he deserve a Christian burial as well?" she hissed.

"Joanie, Brendan took his own life, so the Church would not allow him to be buried in hallowed ground. They'd bury him at the crossroads as a suicide, and I didn't want that for him. I laid him to rest beneath the tree, and I will carve his name into the tree to honor him. There's nothing more we could have done."

Caleb held Joan as she cried quietly into his shoulder. This was an All Hallows' Eve they'd never forget.

Christmas Day

December 1650

Chapter 69

The room was chilly, the window lightly frosted with snow as the cold rays of winter sunshine tried in vain to dispel the gloom created by the partially closed shutters. It had snowed the night before, and the trees outside were covered in a fine layer of snow that was merrily sparkling in the weak winter sunshine. Squeals of happy children could be heard from outside as they threw snowballs at each other and tried to make a snowman. The brightness hurt Rowan's eyes, so she turned away from the window and pulled the coverlet up to her ears, desperate to get away from the sounds of gaiety. She'd barely gotten out of bed the past seven weeks, her desire to live extinguished the minute she found out about Brendan's death.

Aunt Joan forced her to wash and take some broth and milk, since that's all she could manage to swallow, but Rowan only went through the motions, oblivious to the life around her. Not a day went by that she didn't wish that Uncle Caleb and Aunt Joan hadn't come in time and let her just die as she was meant to. Had it not rained a few days before, the hemp in the rope might not have been damp, and choked the life out of her before they had a chance to cut her down. The scar around Rowan's throat was ropey and angry-looking, and she was scarecrow-thin, but she no longer cared. She hadn't looked in the mirror since that day — the day that was to be the true beginning of their life together.

Stephen came to see her a few times, but Rowan had refused to see him, unable to bear his kindness. She only wanted to be left alone in the hope that she would just float away quietly without making any fuss. Even the notion of meeting Brendan in Heaven had been snatched from her. He'd killed himself when he saw her hanging there, damning his soul to eternal torment and ensuring that they would never meet again. At least if he had been killed by Sexby his soul would not be damned for eternity.

Rowan closed her eyes in the hope that Aunt Joan would think her asleep, but the older woman wasn't fooled. She came in and set down the bowl of beef tea next to Rowan's bed, smoothing away a stray lock of hair and smiling kindly at her niece.

"Come now, my girl. Sit up and take some broth. I won't leave until you do, so it's no use pretending you're asleep." Rowan put her hand over Joan's in a silent thank you for all her care, and forced herself to sit up and swallow a spoonful of hot broth. It soothed her raw throat and warmed her from the inside, although physical comforts no longer mattered. She'd tried to speak once she was sufficiently recovered, but all that came out was a hiss, or a whisper at best, so she reverted back to silence. What was there to say anyway?

"Rowan…" Joan began hesitantly, "there's something I must ask you." She averted her eyes for a moment and focused on spooning more broth into Rowan's mouth, clearly thinking of how to phrase her question best. "Have you, eh, lain with Brendan?" she asked at last.

Rowan pointed to the ring finger of her left hand. She'd tried to make them understand that they'd been married, but no one seemed interested. So, she just nodded.

Joan sighed and set the plate down before finally making eye contact again. "Rowan, I can't help noticing that you haven't bled since early October. Are you with child?"

Rowan just stared at her aunt. The thought never even occurred to her, but then again, she hadn't been paying any attention to anything other than her grief, wallowing in self-pity and wishing for death. Could she really be pregnant? Rowan gingerly put her hands over her stomach, caressing the warm skin.

337

She'd lost a lot of weight, but her belly was slightly rounded and firm to the touch, and her breasts had been a little tender. She hadn't had her courses since early October as Aunt Joan mentioned.

"Rowan, if you are with child, there's no time to lose. You must be married."

Rowan stared at her aunt. She was already married. She pointed to her finger again.

"I believe you when you say you married Brendan, but Brendan is gone, and so is Reverend Pole. He never entered the marriage in the parish register, so there's no way to prove that it ever took place. Rowan, you must think of your child. If you are indeed pregnant, it will be born a bastard and have to live with that stigma for the rest of its life. Is that what you want?"

Rowan shook her head, tears beginning to slide down her cheeks. She wanted her child to be born to happy, loving parents, who were eagerly awaiting its arrival, not to a heartbroken mother and a father whose soul was rattling around in Hell. What did Joan expect her to do and who was she supposed to marry?

"You must marry Stephen as soon as possible. We can say that the baby came early. Stephen has been to see you nearly every day. He loves you and wants to help."

"No," Rowan whispered, horrified by the thought. How could she marry Stephen if she were carrying Brendan's baby? What would he think if he ever found out the truth?

"Rowan, no one must ever know what happened. People think that you and Reverend Pole were attacked by ruffians. No one knows that Brendan was there or that you two were married. You must marry Stephen for the sake of your baby, and you must do it very soon. The banns need to be read, so you won't be able to marry for a month after, but you must seduce him and lie with him, so he thinks the child is his."

The thought of lying with Stephen left Rowan sick inside. How could she do with him what she'd done with Brendan? She'd given herself to him in love, and now she'd have to play the whore in order to cheat an honest and decent man. Rowan wiped her runny nose with the back of her hand and hung her head in misery. The whole scheme was abhorrent to her, but if she could protect Brendan's baby, if she could keep it safe and give it a legitimate future, it had to be done.

"Listen to me, girl. You need to get washed up, brush your hair, get some color into those cheeks and go visit Stephen under the pretense of wishing him a happy Christmas. Kiss him, lean against him, touch him. He'll take care of the rest. Just let him know that you're willing. Can you do that?"

She'd have to, wouldn't she, and she'd have to do it today.

February 1651

England

Chapter 70

Meg smoothed back Mary's hair and kissed her on the forehead in a sisterly gesture before scooping up the bloody rags and tossing them into the red-tinged water in the basin. She averted her eyes from the bloody lump that rested at the bottom of the basin; a lump that would have been her niece or nephew come summer. Mary was crying quietly. Her face was swollen from the latest beating, and there were angry bruises just above her breasts and on her arms. Meg knew there were more just like it on her belly and thighs. Jasper had beaten her savagely, causing her to lose her baby. And now he was drunk as usual, sleeping it off in the barn.

A few months ago, she'd felt a burning hatred toward her brother, especially after the two men had come back, bearing the news that Brendan was dead. They'd hanged a reverend and an innocent young girl just to draw him out, and they laughed loudly when they recounted how they didn't even have to bother killing him since he'd done the job himself. It seemed Oliver Cromwell had wanted Brendan brought back for trial, but this outcome was just as satisfying. The men drank with Jasper and spent the night, before setting out on their way back to rejoin Cromwell's forces. Meg thought her heart would break when she heard the news, but Jasper forbade her to speak of Brendan or even mourn him. Well, he couldn't do that. She prayed for Brendan's soul every single day, hoping against hope that he wasn't in Hell. At least had the men killed him, his soul would have gone to Heaven, and he would have gotten a proper burial, instead God only knew where his remains were; likely, his bones were picked over by beasts in the forest.

Meg disposed of the sad remains and washed her hands before making her way to the barn. Jasper was laid out like a king on a bed of straw; snoring loudly, his chest rumbling like thunder. His breeches bore a wet stain since he'd obviously pissed himself. Meg wrinkled her nose in disgust as she led the two horses and the donkey out of the barn to graze before returning. Meg just stood still for a moment, looking at her brother. Whatever love she'd ever felt for him was replaced by a hatred so deep, it shook her to the core.

She hadn't liked Mary or wanted Mary to be Jasper's wife, but no woman deserved what that poor girl had suffered since their wedding. And Meg was partially to blame. Well, she would undo the wrong she'd done to Mary and her unborn child. She would avenge Brendan and their father, and she would set herself free to seek her own future and make her own life. Meg took the tinder box and flint from the pocket of her apron, and set about starting a fire close to the doors. A tiny flame leapt into life and Meg blew on it cautiously until the straw caught, and the fire began to spread and crackle as it devoured the straw and began to lick the beams of the barn.

Meg calmly walked out of the barn and barred the doors behind her before walking some distance to the tree by the paddock. She wrapped her shawl tighter around her body, shivering with cold, but her eyes never left the barn. It took about a quarter of an hour for the little fire to turn into a conflagration as the barn went up in flames, the dry wood crackling and shooting sparks into the colorless February sky. Meg heard a great roar, but she wasn't sure if it was the fire or Jasper, nor did she care. She continued to watch, transfixed as the fire devoured the barn with Jasper inside it.

Two hours later, there wasn't much left but a few blackened beams and a column of smoke rising from the ashes. Meg finally detached herself from the tree and walked back to the house. She never looked at the charred remains of her brother as she passed, nor did she bother to say a prayer for his soul. She had no right. Soon enough she would join Brendan in Hell, for now she was a murderer.

July 1651

England

Chapter 71

Stephen Aldrich tried to arrange his face into an expression of joy as he gingerly entered the room, his eyes glued to Rowan's blissful expression. What he wouldn't give to have her look at him like that, if only just once, but this was the first time since she'd come to him last Christmas that he saw anything even resembling happiness. Rowan ignored him as she continued to devour the baby in her arms with a look of such naked love that Stephen nearly choked on the bile that rose in his throat.

Over the past seven months, he'd hoped and wished that Rowan would lose the baby, or have a stillborn. He wasn't proud of himself for such unworthy thoughts and never voiced them out loud, but he secretly prayed that he would be spared raising another man's bastard. He supposed this was his penance for the role he played in the events of All Hallows' Eve that were still on everyone's lips. No one knew for certain what had happened or why, since Reverend Pole was gone, Rowan refused to speak of it, and the Frains kept their counsel as well. The men who'd been looking for Brendan Carr vanished that night, possibly ashamed of how far they'd gone to capture a man who managed to elude them.

Till this day, Stephen had no idea what happened to Carr, but he suspected he was dead. Why else would Rowan give herself to Stephen in an act of such heart-wrenching desperation that it nearly broke his heart? Of course, he'd known what she was about when she came to him that night, just as he'd known that although it wasn't him she wanted, he had to play along to give her peace of mind. He'd been solely responsible for what happened to

Rowan that night, and he would love her and care for her till the day he died, not only because he wanted to, but because he felt it was his duty to her.

Stephen sat on the side of the bed and accepted the small bundle that stared back at him with complete indifference. The little face was red and wrinkled, the dark fuzz plastered to the skull, and one fist poking out of the wrappings as if wagging at him and promising vengeance for the death of its father. Stephen forced himself to smile as he looked at Rowan, who was watching him expectantly.

"Anne, I think, after my mother," Stephen said. Calling the girl after his mother would no more make her his than giving her his own name, but he felt he had to make some claim to her, if only for Rowan's sake. He would make a show of loving this child and cherishing her as if she were his own, but what he felt deep inside was a different matter altogether.

Stephen handed the baby back to Rowan. "I'll call the children, shall I? They're desperate to meet their new sister, especially Lizzie. Tim would have liked a brother, but there's time," he added. "There's time."

Chapter 72

Rowan watched as Stephen stepped from the room. There were days when she was sure he knew the truth, but she couldn't afford to dwell on her suspicions. She'd made her bed, literally, and now she had to lie in it, and lie in it with Stephen. Not a day went by that she didn't mourn Brendan, her heart contracting painfully every time she remembered his face as he looked at her those last couple of days when they were on the threshold of their life together. The pregnancy had been a double-edged sword, soothing her aching heart with the knowledge that something of Brendan was left behind, and simultaneously breaking it with the certainty that Brendan would never see his child and its paternity would have to be kept a secret.

Despite Uncle Caleb's warnings, Rowan made a weekly pilgrimage to Reverend Pole's house. The new reverend had chosen to live in the village, closer to his church and parishioners, so the house stood empty, its windows staring blindly at the scene of the murder. Rowan laid a small bouquet of flowers beneath the tree every week, partially for the memory of Reverend Pole, but mostly for Brendan. She didn't believe that his soul was in Hell, nor did she believe that he was gone forever. She couldn't see him or speak to him, but she could feel him in the babe moving in her womb, and in the acute pain she felt every time she thought of him. He would always be with her, and she would always guard his resting place, albeit it was known to only three people.

From the day she discovered she was pregnant, she'd made it her purpose in life to protect the tiny life growing inside her, and she would do everything in her power to give her daughter a happy, safe life. Stephen was a good man who cared for her deeply despite her own lukewarm feelings toward him, but she would try to make him happy and be a good wife to him, if only for the sake of her baby daughter.

Rowan gently caressed the chubby cheek with her finger and bent her face close to the baby. "In my heart, you will always be Brenda, after your father," she whispered, and kissed the baby's forehead in benediction. This was the first day of a new life.

The Present

Chapter 73

The opportunity didn't present itself until a few days later. Aidan and I finally took out the manuscript and he began to read, since I had a hard time making out some of the old-fashioned phrases. It began with Anne Hughes's introduction, which might have been added later, but the narrative was actually written by her mother, Rowan Aldridge, recounting the events that led up to her beloved Brendan's death. Both Aidan and I teared up as we read about their tender love story and the hanging which led to Brendan's suicide, but it was the later chapters that left us stunned. Rowan stoically described her life with Stephen, a life that she accepted for the sake of her daughter and never complained about. She'd learned to live without Brendan, but it was him she'd always loved. By all accounts, Stephen had been a good man who loved and cherished her, but it wasn't until the day he died that Rowan found out the truth.

Aidan's voice shook slightly as he read of Stephen's deathbed confession to Rowan that he had been the one to tip off Cromwell's men as to Brendan Carr's whereabouts, and therefore responsible for the death of both Reverend Pole and Brendan. It was thanks to him that Rowan nearly died and was left widowed only a few weeks after her marriage. It seemed that Stephen knew all along that Anne wasn't his, but he raised her as his own as penance for his guilt. Rowan spent thirty years married to a man who destroyed her happiness and nearly caused the death of her and her child, and she never forgave him.

"Does it say anything about the tomb?" I asked Aidan, peering over his shoulder.

"Yes, there are a few pages written by Anne in 1726." Aidan held up the pages and began to read.

"The year of our Lord, January 1726.

I will always be grateful to my mother for making the ultimate sacrifice and marrying a man she didn't love to give me a better life, and so I made a vow to her before her death that I would give her the thing she wanted most. Luckily, my own marriage was based on a deep and lasting love, and my husband built this house for me on this site because I asked him to. He knew what it meant to me to live in a place where my parents fell in love. Bartholomew bought this land from the Church for a much inflated price in order to make sure that my father's resting place would never be disturbed, but I always worried that future generations would clear away the ruin and cut down the tree. I had my husband order a stone coffin in Lincoln and had my father's remains exhumed and put to rest in the cellar of this house. It would be my dearest wish to have him buried next to my mother in the cemetery, but that was not to be, so I interred him here with us. How can he be in Hell when he's so loved?

Since I'm now an old woman and will likely not live to see another summer, I write these things down to be cloistered underneath my father's tomb, so that my mother's words of love can keep him safe and soothe his wounded soul. My children will keep vigil over their grandfather long after I'm gone, but I pray that their children and their children's children will not forget him, and let him live in death longer than he lived in life."

I was sobbing by the time Aidan finished reading, overcome by grief for two people who were long dead, but whose love managed to live on for generations. No wonder Brendan couldn't rest. He felt responsible for the death of his wife, and she, in turn, felt responsible for his suicide. It was like a real-life Romeo and Juliet.

"So, Brendan and Rowan Carr were your ancestors," said Aidan as he set aside the fragile pages. "And now you can carry on their legacy as you were meant to. Funny how things work out, isn't it?"

Funny is not a word I'd use, but I knew what he meant. I'd never been someone who believed in Fate, Destiny, or God's plan, but there was no other way to describe what had happened to me. An unseen celestial hand had guided me step by step toward this moment, toward this end, and for the first time in my life, I felt as if I were truly home. This is where I belonged, and this was the man who belonged here with me.

I walked over to the window. The sky above the tree line was streaked with bands of pink; the clouds lit up as if from beneath with a rosy glow that gave them a magical aura. It was still light outside, but the lavender sky would quickly give way to a deeper shade of purple as the first stars began to twinkle in the dusk, and the last glimmer of light would be leached from the day. I had about ten minutes.

"Where are you going?" Aidan called after me as I sprinted from the room.

"To the ruin," I called over my shoulder.

He made to follow me, but I called out for him to stay back. I needed to do this alone, and I needed to do this now — finally. I ran across the meadow and over the stone bridge, hoping I wouldn't be too late, but no, there he was, emerging from the ruin as he did every night at this time. My heart nearly jumped out of my chest as I drew closer and closer until I could see his face clearly.

Brendan Carr was younger than I'd expected him to be — my age to be exact. I'd never seen him up close before and I was surprised by the wide hazel eyes and the generous mouth that was probably beautiful when it smiled. His lean face was covered with day-old stubble, and his dark brown hair fell to his shoulders in waves, but looked surprisingly masculine all the same. I watched as he sank to his knees below the tree and went through his routine, only now I knew exactly what he was seeing. He saw the bodies of Reverend Pole and his beloved wife swaying in the evening breeze, their necks scratched and bloody from tearing at the rope that was preventing them from taking that breath that would make the difference between life and death. Now I understood the anguish and the guilt, and the soul's refusal to seek peace in the face of such loss.

Brendan finally got up, and as he did, I approached him slowly, calling his name. I don't know what I expected, but he seemed to hear me. Our eyes met. I held up my hand, and he brought his palm to rest against mine. It didn't feel solid or warm, but I could feel something that was more than just vapor. I felt contact.

"Brendan, she didn't die," I whispered. "She lived, and so had your daughter."

His hazel eyes gazed into mine, and a slight smile appeared on his lips, and for that one moment, we were both at peace.

Epilogue

I glanced gleefully at my bookings, excited as ever to have a full house for the next few months. We'd opened our doors only last summer, but except for a few slow weeks after the New Year, business had been brisk. I still couldn't believe that the rundown house I'd found two years ago was now this elegant establishment that gave my guests a glimpse of what it was like to live in a grand manor house of centuries past.

No one knew of the secret room in the basement where the remains of my great-great-great-grandfather rested, but I'd made the story of Brendan and Rowan public, feeling that they deserved to be remembered by this village that had been responsible for their fate. Strangely, it'd been Paula who approached me first after the news of the manuscript spread like wildfire, thanks to Dot. She'd barely spoken to me since Colin was sent away to prison for attempted rape, but now she came to the house, asking to speak to me.

I suppose it came as no surprise that Paula already knew the story, or at least part of it. She was a direct descendant of Timothy Aldrich, who had been a staunch monarchist and was deeply embarrassed by the role his father had played in the death of the reverend and Brendan Carr, more so because it was at the hands of Cromwell's men. Paula squirmed as she confessed this to me, almost asking for forgiveness. I found it strange that she still carried this shame all these years later, but I suppose some family secrets never truly die.

It had actually been Paula's idea that I speak to the vicar and see if Brendan might be buried in consecrated ground at last. Vicar Sumner heard me out, a look of astonishment on her face as her eyebrows nearly disappeared underneath her fringe and her eyes twinkled with excitement, but she promised to see what she could do. After an extensive campaign on her part, she was finally given permission by the bishop to bury Brendan Carr in the cemetery despite his status as a suicide. I suppose the bishop figured the poor man had suffered long enough. Strangely enough the letter came a week before Halloween, so the service was scheduled for All Hallows' Eve to mark the anniversary of Brendan's death.

Nearly the whole village turned out for the memorial held at the church, and then everyone trooped out into the churchyard to see Brendan laid to rest. There was no room to bury him next to Rowan, since the older part of the cemetery was full to the bursting with graves which were so close to each other that one could barely walk between them, the lichen-covered stones barely legible after centuries of harsh English weather, but it was agreed that under the circumstances it would only be right to bury them together. Brendan was laid to rest in Rowan's grave, and they were together at last after nearly four centuries of being apart.

I had to admit that I felt somewhat apprehensive as the sun began to set that October evening. I stood at the window, hand to my mouth as I watched the ruin begin to fade into the twilight, its edges blurred and the empty windows just black rectangles until the sun touched the tree line and arrows of crimson burst through the gaps, filling the place with light for just a few moments before night descended. I hadn't realized I'd been holding my breath, but the sun finally sank below the horizon, the old oak just a dark shape against the lighter shade of the sky, but no grieving man beneath it. Brendan was gone. Tears of relief coursed down my cheeks as I leaned against Aidan, his arms encircling me as his lips brushed my cheek. He didn't have to say anything. He knew how I felt, because he felt it too. This wasn't exactly a happy ending, but it was the best outcome we could have hoped for, and we were content.

***

I left my office and walked past the kitchen where Dot was busy preparing breakfast for the early risers, dressed as a maid from the 1700s. I gave her a brief wave and walked out into the glorious August morning, eager for my walk with Aidan. He was

352

already waiting for me by the gate, his gaze rooted to the stone walk as he doubtlessly spotted a crack or something that needed fixing, but he forgot all about it as he saw me coming toward him and held out his hand.

I could walk perfectly well on my own, but he felt protective of me now that I was in my third trimester and my balance was sometimes less than perfect. I secretly enjoyed his fussing. We'd been married on Skye over Christmas, and I still shivered with pleasure every time someone referred to me as Mrs. Mackay.

I placed my hand in Aidan's, but turned to face the house before walking down the lane, as I did every morning. There it was, grand and proud, the windows glinting in the morning sun and the gray stone looking as impregnable as it doubtless did centuries ago. I smiled at the discreet sign above the entrance. *The Rowan Tree Inn.* Somehow the name seemed appropriate to me.

The End

Please turn the page after the Notes for an excerpt from

The Hands of Time.

Notes

I hope you enjoyed *Haunted Ground*. The idea for this book came to me when my husband and I were on vacation in Ireland and stayed in a manor house hotel such as the one I described in this book. The place was absolutely beautiful and steeped in history, but what really affected me was the ruin visible just beyond the stream that crossed the lawn behind the property. I'd seen many ruins in my life, but this one had an aura of sadness I just couldn't shake. Every time I looked at it I felt a desire to cry, and it made me wonder why I should have such a reaction to a pile of stones. Of course, my imagination chimed in to tell me that something tragic must have happened there to make me feel so melancholy. None of the hotel staff seemed to know anything about the ruin, which made it even more mysterious, and the idea was born.

Although the place was in Ireland, I chose to set the book in England, since I love British history and wanted to write something about the English Civil War. Oliver Cromwell was a fascinating man and although I don't give him much to do in this book, I felt it was important for him to make an appearance. Another interesting character was Edward Sexby, who was in Scotland with Cromwell in 1650 and had fought as a mercenary before that. Not too much is known about him, especially his early life. Some say that he was a distant relation of Cromwell's, but there's little proof of that.

Sexby was a Leveller and an ardent supporter of Cromwell and the Commonwealth, until he became disillusioned and began to think of Cromwell as a tyrant. He plotted Cromwell's assassination with several other conspirators in 1656, but the attempt failed and Sexby fled to Flanders. Sexby returned to England in 1657 with a view to starting another conspiracy, but was captured and imprisoned in the Tower of London after a forced confession. He subsequently became ill, went insane, and died in 1658. I'd actually never heard of him until I saw him portrayed in a movie and thought he would make a nice addition to my cast of characters. He had just the right amount of bloodlust and cunning that made him a great villain.

If you enjoyed this book, I would ask you to take a moment and leave a review on Amazon, but of course, you are not obligated to do so. I hope you will check out some of my other books, particularly The Hands of Time Series, which is my personal favorite.

I love hearing from you. Please visit me at: www.irinashapiroauthor.com and http://www.facebook.com/pages/Irina-Shapiro/307374895948375

Printed in Great Britain
by Amazon

25105677R00202